CHAOS

A YOUNG DECAY NOVEL

JACK WHITNEY

FOR NICOLE
*Who knew one coffee chat could inspire such a
badass, plant-loving, neurospicy woman?!
I didn't know how much I needed to write her,
and in doing so, I started my own journey.
Thank you for the inspo.*

AND FOR ALL MY NEUROSPICY BABES...
*May you find someone who not only fucks like a god, but also makes
sure you have your safe foods and favorite music.
No matter the occasion.*

WARNINGS

CHAOS is an adult, rockstar dark romance.
It is therefore **not** intended for persons under the legal age
of 18.

**The following are the triggers to be made aware of in this
book:**

Graphic depictions of sexual assault, mental abuse, death,
self-harm, suicidal thoughts, and gun violence. Mentions of
family death, organ trafficking, and kidnapping.

Explicit sex scenes including voyeurism, breath play,
bondage, rage sex, pegging, and more.

No sexual acts within this book are in any way meant to be
a guide to exploring sexual fantasies or give suggestion.
If you are curious about any acts, please do your own
research, be safe, and remember aftercare.

This is a work of fiction.
Your mental health comes first.

Suicide and Crisis Lifeline
Call or text: 988
988lifeline.org

National Suicide Prevention Lifeline
1-800-273-TALK

PLAYLIST

ACCESS FULL PLAYLIST HERE:

TAKE ME BACK TO EDEN
SLEEP TOKEN

THE DEATH OF PEACE OF MIND
BAD OMENS

COME HELL OR HIGH WATER
IMMINENCE

DROWN
BRING ME THE HORIZON

HELENA
MY CHEMICAL ROMANCE

A PLACE FOR MY HEAD
LINKIN PARK

FOLLOW YOU
BRING ME THE HORIZON

SYMPATHY
TOO CLOSE TO TOUCH

THE END OF HEARTACHE
KILLSWITCH ENGAGE

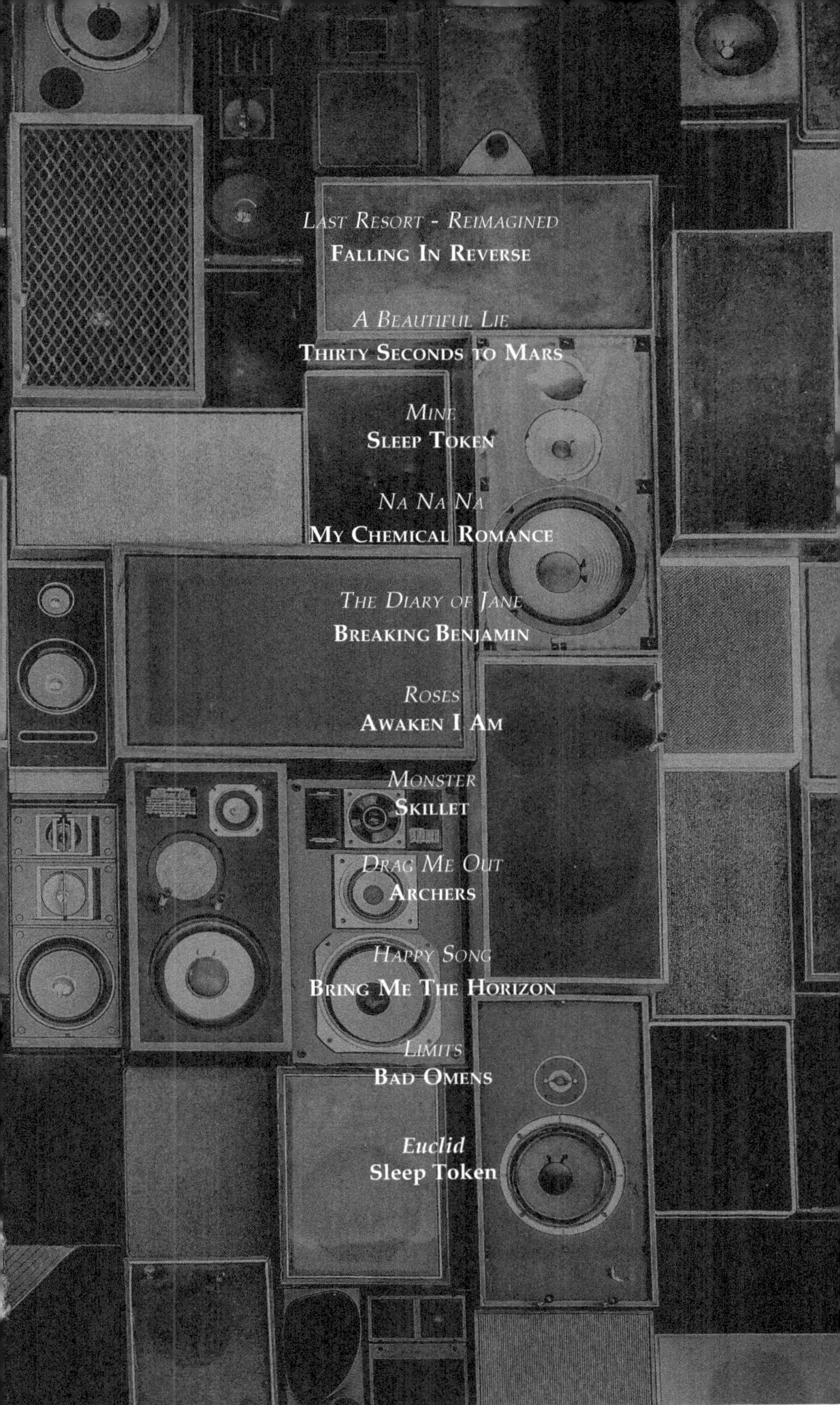

LAST RESORT - REIMAGINED
FALLING IN REVERSE
A BEAUTIFUL LIE
THIRTY SECONDS TO MARS
MINE
SLEEP TOKEN
NA NA NA
MY CHEMICAL ROMANCE
THE DIARY OF JANE
BREAKING BENJAMIN
ROSES
AWAKEN I AM
MONSTER
SKILLET
DRAG ME OUT
ARCHERS
HAPPY SONG
BRING ME THE HORIZON
LIMITS
BAD OMENS
Euclid
Sleep Token

SWEAT BEADS down the side of my face, puddling in my collar before sinking into the ripped tank barely covering my tattooed chest. I'm acutely aware of the next traveling salty drop threatening to fall from the shag of hair wanting to mat to my heated forehead. The surrounding stage lights are an incubator growing me into the person I only know on this stage, a creature feeding on the energy of the crowd and clinging to it as their life source.

God, I fucking love this.

I signal with my fist in the air to my bandmates for a short break after the end of this song. There's a double-tap response from our drummer, Bonnie, that also lets Mads and Zeb know just in case they didn't see me.

Lights dim with the final note, and as I take a circle in the middle of the stage, I feel the fatigue catching up with me. Throat aching, breaths short, I kneel in the center and close my eyes, my mic pressing to my forehead as I sink my head.

Screams surround us. Lights dance behind my closed eyes, and I'm not entirely sure it's just from the strobes. I can feel the vibration of the crowd's enthusiasm in the stage floor—

Water.

Shit, I need water.

Our new tour manager, Stella, is standing in the wings. I stand and sign 'water' to her, and she quickly grabs two bottles, then tosses them onstage and into my open hands. I gulp back one, crinkle it in my fists when it's empty, and throw it into the crowd. Fevered chills run up my spine as the water quenches my decaying muscles. It awakens my skin and fuels the adrenaline writhing through my veins.

The second spills over my hands when I crack it open, but it's not for drinking. Lights cascade over us from the sides as I pour this water over my face and the back of my neck, causing the audience to go wild when I shake my hair out and send that water spraying over those closest to the left side of the stage where I am.

I can do better.

We have a walk that goes out into the crowd for this tour. It was a shit attempt at trying to keep me on the stage instead of jumping into the crowd. Honestly, it's only made the pit more accessible. When they told me I needed to dial back my energy as far as jumping into the crowd, I told them to kiss my ass.

This stage is my altar.

I am music's conduit.

If I want to join the masses and satiate their need for the touch of music's salvation, I'll fucking do it.

Stepping out onto the walk, I pour water into my mouth, and at the very edge, I fling the remainder into the crowd and spray my mouthful into the air.

There's a girl at the edge just in front of me that sticks her tongue extended like she means to catch my spit, and I point my finger at her.

"Someone's a good girl," I say into the microphone.

The audience loses their shit. I skip back to the main stage with a Joker-esque grin. I don't need to see our bassist, Mads's, mouth to know he's laughing beneath the skull neck gaiter mask. Bonnie taps the bass drum twice, her and Zeb grinning. Zeb, our guitarist, steps up onto the platform at the edge of the stage and throws a few guitar picks out into the hands of jumping fans. I circle back around and jump on the platform at his side.

"Hey, Rock, let me get some lights so I can see all these beautiful faces," I say to our lighting guy.

More than half of the audience throws their arms in the air as the stage lights illuminate their faces enough that I can see the sea of people in the concert hall. I pause not only for effect, but to catch my breath.

"How we holding up, Vegas?" I ask the crowd.

They roar back at me, and I balk as if the cheer wasn't good enough. Mads strums two unimpressed notes behind me, followed by Zeb raising his arms in the air to egg the fans on. I laugh into the mic.

Toying with them is one of my favorite parts of this gig.

"I thought this was Vegas," I say, turning back to the audience. "Let's go again—on the count of three, I want everyone to scream as loud as you can. I don't want you to be able to hear the voices in your head. We're going to banish them the rest of the night. Alright?"

Bonnie begins a drum roll.

"One. Two—"

The side lights cascade over the stage with the third count, and the crowd erupts. Bonnie's symbol strike rings behind me. The noise of the ongoing jeer threads newfound energy into my core. A cool breeze brushes over my sweating skin, and I know it isn't just the whisper of air that causes the hair on my neck to raise.

I fucking love my job.

"That's what I'm talking about," I say to the horde. "This is our first time playing in Vegas that isn't at a festival, and honestly, I think we were pretty nervous—" I glance between Mads and Zeb, who both nod.

"But you guys… *fuck*, you've been amazing," I go on. "Thank you for welcoming us into your circus and making us feel at home."

Bonnie gives a short celebratory solo behind me, causing the crowd to cheer loudly again. I jump down from the platform, grab the mic stand from beside one of the speakers, and drag it to the middle of the stage.

"Do any of you know a little song called 'Pieces?'" I ask.

The audience shouts again, causing me to smile up toward the balcony area. Pride swells within me at the sight of the elated people watching, each one ready to sing every fucking lyric on our record.

Mads strums the bass line.

"Well, fuck, I'm glad *you* know it," I tell the audience. "I might need your help on this one. Do you think you can do that?"

They cheer as I click the mic into the stand. I swallow the dryness in my throat and wipe my sweating face with the bottom of my cropped shirt.

"Let's fucking go," I say, and Zeb starts us off.

I don't have to sing more than the first line because the audience recites the words back to us in a deafening roar. I glance over at Mads, point at him—knowing how much this song means—and grin as I begin a steady bounce on my toes, ready to sing the next lines.

This is my favorite part.

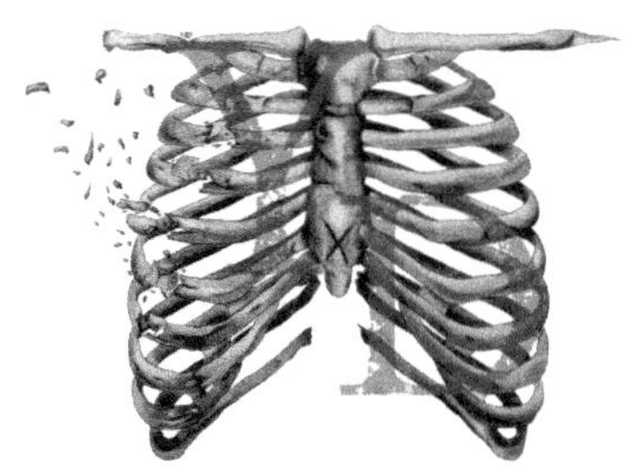

Even when the concert is over, I can't stop moving. I have too much energy. Too much adrenaline. My muscles—no matter how hard I try to push that restlessness out of my body and into my singing, feeling every note and verse with every fiber of my soul—continue to tingle. I can't stretch my fingers wide enough, can't jump high enough, can't run fast enough. It takes over my mind to the point that I don't know how to stop.

After running down the hall and high-fiving a few crew members, I circle back around to the dressing room where my bandmates have gathered. Bonnie throws her arms up, shouting a "Wooo" to me that fills the room. I laugh and catch her when she launches herself into my arms, energy drink shaking and spraying everywhere. Between the sweat beading off of us and the spray, we're both soaked within seconds.

I can always count on her to match, and sometimes exceed, my after-hours energy.

"Jesus, fuck, I don't know how you two have this after every show," Zeb says, shaking his head and grinning at us.

"Superpowers," I say as Bonnie hits the ground again.

She slaps my hand and pulls me into a hug. "Fucking insane show, dude," she exclaims. "That was wild! I didn't think they were going to let you out of the pit."

"Yeah, I thought I was going to have to get in there," Mads says from a few feet away, his dislike apparent in his tone.

"What? No," I brush them off. "I was fine."

Zeb reaches out and tugs on one of the few threads that my ripped shirt is hanging onto. "I think this is all James had in his hand when you toppled over."

I recall the moment when I lost my balance on the barrier and almost face-planted into the crowd. Luckily, though, a few fans caught me and helped me back up so that I could continue singing.

"You scared the shit out of me," Mads says.

"Yeah, I heard you miss that note," Bonnie replies to him. "I was like 'oh, fuck. Mad Mads is about to show up!'"

I laugh, and Mads shakes his head at her, grinning crookedly. "Fuck off, Bon," he jokes. "Hey—" Mads slaps my stomach. "Are you still heading out to that party?"

He's shed his mask now that we're backstage, letting it dangle around his neck beneath his beard. He swipes his forehead with a white face towel, black shirt drenched in sweat.

The party is on the outside of town at model Anne Tober's mansion. It won't be the first time I've attended a party there. Within the last year or so of our popularity skyrocketing, we've received invite after invite to parties like this one, though only Bonnie and I attended the last one.

"Yeah," I answer. "You still being a little bitch about going with?"

Mads grins. "You know that's not my scene," he says.

"Come on," I nearly beg. "Bon and Zeb are going. We'll make it a family affair."

A soft chuckle sounds from Mads, and he glances past me

to Bonnie who is already shedding her clothes to jump in the shower before we sign autographs.

She always calls first dibs on the shower if we're attending a party after.

Mads takes a sip of the coconut water waiting for him at his seat. "You really want me to go?"

"Yeah," I say. "It'd be fun. Don't have to stay the entire time."

He considers it for another beat, pushing his mustache back as he takes another drink. "Ah, fuck it," he finally says. "If only to keep you out of fucking trouble."

"Yes!" I punch the air and high-five Zeb.

"Let's go sign some shit first," Mads says, pushing off the counter. "This was a good crowd. Give them a few extra minutes while Bon gets ready."

"Hang on." I grab my favorite black jacket—lots of pockets and belts, the bottom hem sitting at my ribs—and push it on over the ripped t-shirt, then fluff my hair in the mirror.

I really need to fucking shower.

"You look pretty already," Mads teases, clapping my shoulder twice. "They all know we're sweaty as shit."

"Yeah, they like it, too," Zeb grins, hands in his pockets as he leans on the door. "Let's go."

CHAPTER TWO
REED

"I CAN'T BELIEVE you talked me into this," Mads says as we stand on the balcony of Anne's mansion an hour later.

"I don't think it took much convincing," I reply. "Besides, we're late as hell."

"Thank fuck for that," Mads says, and the smirk on his lips lets me know he's only winding me up. I shove him sideways just as Bonnie comes up behind us and drapes her arms around ours, having to extend her limbs wide just to reach our shoulders. She's only wearing a black suit blazer over her slim chest, a long necklace dangling on her sternum, and when she toys with her lip ring, I hear her let out a satisfied groan.

"Look at all the candy, boys," she leers. "What time is our plane tomorrow?"

"Not until two," Zeb says, hands in the pockets of his leather jacket when he pauses on my other side.

"So much time for activities," Bonnie says. She nudges my side. "Want to share something later?"

I chuckle. "We'll see," I tell her. "Let's go get a drink."

"Matthews!" someone from below shouts. "Tourning!"

I know the voice. It's Foster, the drummer from a metal

band called New Dawn that we opened for in our early days. We've remained friends with them ever since.

I throw my hands in the air, mirroring him, but Bonnie pushes in front of me.

"The fuck, Fos? What, am I chopped liver or something?" she shouts.

Foster grins and points her way. "There's my girl! Come on. I'll make you a special drink."

And I know he means he'll make her the same mocktail he's drinking since he's going on a year sober now, Bonnie going strong on year four.

A few other musicians and friends we've formed over the years greet us as we make our way down the stairs and into the throng. The music is a numbing blur of notes and lines. One thing I've always disliked about Anne's place is how stark white and blinding her interior seems to be. Even with the lights slightly dimmed, it feels like a museum.

I try to ignore it as I move through the crowd.

I lose count of the number of people I chat with, the leering smiles I give a few models, and the hugs I greet friends with. It's a blur of beautiful bodies and faces. And after an hour or so, I feel my adrenaline beginning to wane.

Zeb hands Mads and I energy drinks and shots of vodka, and together we cheer's it back.

I slam my glass onto the bar top and double over slightly, gagging on the bit of the liquid that goes down the wrong pipe, and as I choke, I back into the person behind me.

"Shit—Ah, fuck, I'm sorry," I ramble, turning around. "Sorry, I'm fucking clumsy—"

My entire body tenses when I face the person I've bumped.

Because I haven't just run into any someone.

I've run into *her*.

Wren Kelly—actress, plus-size model, resting-bitch-face-extraordinaire, and thinks-I'm-an-emo-poser-boy.

I still think about the interview she gave to a magazine before DeathFest a year or so ago. It breaks my confidence some days, makes me think twice about who I am. It might be a little thing to some people, but for someone who it took a long while to figure out who they were, to be okay with it, and tell the rest of the world to fuck off, her words stuck. She told the interviewer that I looked like the 'emo member of a boy band,' and since, every time we see each other, she looks at me like I'm trash, even speaks to me like I'm an idiot.

The worst part?

Fucking hell.

The worst part is that she's the prettiest fucking creature on this entire goddamn planet.

She's one of those beings who you find yourself staring at as if they're some sort of alien creature, who it almost hurts to look at, who any smart guy would take one glance at and know she's out of their league.

I'm not smart.

And she hates me.

My palms immediately begin sweating, heart dropping for some fuck-all reason that seems to happen every single time I see her in public.

Her bold emerald eyes narrow in like daggers upon meeting mine. It's barely a second, and yet in that fraction of time, I see the waves of her ginger hair pooling over her pale shoulder, the freckles on her cheeks flushed and bright beneath these incandescent lights. Her long-sleeve, short, black bodycon dress falls off her arms, the pillows of her breasts spilling tastefully over as her hair sweeps her skin.

The way this dress hugs her generous curves has my mouth drying.

I fucking loathe what she does to me. I don't know why she's singled me out, even if Mads likes to assure me that she doesn't like many people to begin with.

"Sasquatch."

Her voice drips with disdain, and almost every drop of attraction I have for her seems to bury itself away as I blink back into reality.

Almost.

"Does your stature make it hard to maneuver in tight spaces like this?" she goes on.

God fucking dammit.

"I'm sorry," I drawl. "I didn't realize I had run into the Wicked Witch of the West."

She gives a sarcastic, tight-lipped smile. "And I thought beasts like you were supposed to be elusive, not standing in front of every camera in the room."

Bonnie snorts.

I grit my teeth. "Kelly."

"Matthews," she bites out. "Aren't you going to ask me to smile next? Tell me how much prettier I'd be if I would just 'loosen up' or 'let go?'"

I scoff, forcing a smirk on my lips to ease the tension in my shoulders, and I slap my drink back on the bar top before rounding over her. "I wouldn't dream of asking you to do either of those." Our chests bump, and I lean closer. "I'd rather ask you to get on your knees. I'll fix your fucking attitude myself."

Zeb whistles.

Wren's gaze drags over me, a sneer forming on her lips. "You wouldn't know what to do with me on my knees," she retorts. "I've seen you perform. You're like a dog chasing a squirrel. You wouldn't know what to do with it if you ever caught it."

"Oh, I know *exactly* what to do with you," I say.

"Okay," Mads says. He wraps his arm over my shoulders, hand slapping my chest in a not-so delicate manner. "Always nice to see you, Kelly," he says tiredly to her.

"Tourning," she acknowledges, and I notice her gaze move past my shoulder, see her shift on her feet slightly before turning her eyes back to mine. It causes my own eyes to narrow, and I wonder what she's seen that's spooked her.

She takes her drink from the bar and pushes off of it. "No worries, Tourning. I'll leave the poor little beast alone. With any luck, he'll return to the woods where he belongs," she adds with a sarcastic smile.

I can't even form a retaliation, and it's all I can do to stare at her, the pit in my stomach hollowing out. I feel like a part of me is breaking away when she walks off, her back turning toward me, ass swaying with the determined swagger of her modeling days.

Fuck.

Sasquatch.

Mads slaps my chest twice as she leaves us, and Zeb lets out another whistle.

"Bad luck, brother," Mads says.

"She's so *mean*," Zeb drawls, rocking on his toes. "Why do I like it?" he adds with a crooked grin.

Bonnie pokes at me. "I think our little Reed likes it, too."

I shove her off, though I don't look away from Wren, who's now far enough away from us that she's nearly lost in the crowd.

"All that tension gave me chills," Bonnie adds.

Mads's phone buzzes in his hand, breaking my attention away from Wren as I nosily peer over to see who's calling him, even if I already know it's my sister.

"Late for a chat, isn't it?" I ask. "For her, I mean."

Mads chuckles. "Fiancée, man. She just got home from her gig," he says as he puts an earbud in and answers the video call. His entire face lights up as the video comes on, and he says, "Hey, beautiful."

It's a look that only she brings out, and every time I see the way he loves her, envy swells in my bones.

I don't know what my sister says in response to his greeting, but I squeeze around to Mads's side, and he hands me the other earbud to hear her.

Andi, my sister, is sitting in the living room of her and Mads's apartment wearing a fuzzy hoodie. The light of what looks like the television lights up her beaming face and now pomegranate-pink hair. Her move into Mads's place is new, and luckily only about a two hour drive from Heartless and Death Tower Records. They've assigned her to a few underground bars around the area to photograph indie rock bands out of since.

When the pair began dating last year, I think what hurt me the most wasn't that Mads broke his promise never to date her. No, what fucking hurt was that he never told me he was in love with her. We've known each other since we were in primary school—over twenty years of friendship. I always knew he had a crush on her, but I thought that was as far as it went.

I constantly wonder how I might have reacted had he told me when we were younger that he loved her, that half the reason he went on living despite the shittiness of his childhood and the bullshit stories made up about him over the years, was the hope that one day, he might have a chance with her.

I felt like such a dick the night he went to jail for beating the life out of her ex-boyfriend after the asshole tried to kidnap her. Mads didn't care that I'd lost my shit. All he cared about was that she was safe, and that I forgave him.

I've never questioned whether he would look after her or not. Never thought I needed to tell him if he breaks her heart, I'll break him.

There's no one like Mads. There's no one who could treat

her as well as he does. No one who protects or loves harder than him.

And I've never been more fucking jealous in my life.

"—are you?" she's asking.

I grin, blocking out the sudden emptiness in my gut. "Hey, sis," I say.

"Oh, that explains it," she teases me. "The rockstar needed to attend the model's party. Tell me, Reed, have you found one to take home yet?"

I glance around us. "Nah, not—"

"He found a feral cat to tame instead," Mads says, and I shove him sideways.

Andi laughs. "Wait, what?"

"Your fiancée is an ass," I say.

"That actress model girl is here," Mads explains. "The one that didn't know who he was. Called him a poser."

"Ohh… Oh, no. Poor Reed," Andi says with a pout. "You're talking about Wren Kelly right?"

"Yeah," Mads says. "She was pretty mean to him. Called him Sasquatch."

Andi snorts. "Oh, god," she laughs. "I think I like her already. Will you be bringing her home for Thanksgiving this year?"

"Shut up," I grunt, eyes flickering across the room.

I don't know why I'm looking for her.

Maybe I'm a sucker for pain.

"You were always the best with the feral cats growing up," Andi adds. "Maybe that will work in your favor with this one."

My gaze meets hers, and I flip her off, but Andi just grins wider.

"Love you, bro," she taunts.

I roll my eyes. "Yeah, yeah. Love you, too," I mumble,

looking up. I meet a set of green eyes across the room, and I hate the way my body responds to Wren's stare.

Fuck, I wish I knew why she hates me so much.

"Hey, I'm going to take this outside," Mads says, nodding toward the back doors. "See you in a few?"

I take the earbud out and hand it back to him. "Yeah, I'm nearly ready to head back. One more drink."

Mads claps me on the arm. "Okay, man—" He turns his full attention to Andi. "So, how did the gig go tonight?"

His voice trails as he makes his way outside, and I'm left staring longingly after him.

I want that.

It wasn't until the pair became a couple that I began to notice the feeling of loneliness that I'd buried beneath every meaningless night with groupies, two-week relationships that I fell too hard and too fast for before they began to fade, shallow conversations with strangers, and pushing myself to the very edge of my own limits.

I'm constantly riding a wave of newness, spontaneity, and adrenaline that's destined to fucking crash, and as we draw closer and closer to the end of this tour, I feel it slowing.

I think it might be the first time in years that I'm actually looking forward to a tour break.

I spot Zeb not far away chatting with a woman I don't recognize, Bonnie across the room chatting up a model with her own brand of charms.

Sasquatch.

Why can't I get her out of my head?

I take another swallow of my energy drink and eye a blonde woman approaching nearby. She's cute, and I think I've seen her in a few ads around the country, though I can't for the life of me remember her name.

I give her a little smile as she draws closer, ready to flirt a little in the hopes it'll get my mind off of Wren fucking Kelly.

"Hey! Reed Matthews!"

Shit.

Walker… Fuck, I don't even know his last name.

I really need to learn names better.

He's the singer for an alt band that we've performed at a few festivals alongside. I barely know the prick, but I've seen him at enough of these parties that it shouldn't come to any surprise that he's here.

Especially when he's dating the host's best friend.

"Walker," I say, snagging my attention from the blonde I was hoping to make out with and possibly finger-fuck in the coat closet.

I'll find her after I tell this guy where to take himself.

"Hey, man!" Walker exclaims. "I thought that was you squaring up with the hot tamale," he adds, grinning at me.

I can smell the alcohol on his heated breath.

I scoff. "The hot tamale?" I ask.

"Yeah, that fiery redhead—what's her fucking name… ah…" He snaps his fingers, and it's all I can do to peer the creep over and wait for him to stumble upon Wren's name.

As if it's any of his business.

"Kelly," I finally answer, getting tired of his stammer.

"Shit, yeah—Kelly. Her name is some fucking pigeon name, right? Jay… Robin…"

"Wren," I say through my teeth.

The blonde that I've been eyeing snickers at me as if she can see me trying to hold myself together. Fuck, I just want to tell this ass clown to hit the road.

I'm too nice.

"Wren! Yeah, Wren Kelly. What's the beef there?" Walker asks, leaning on the bar. "I mean, other than her being a tight ass—Oh, man, I have to tell you. A friend of mine asked her out once. Bitch told him to get in line, can you believe that?"

"One of your friends? Yeah, I can," I say, barely paying

attention as I nudge my chin in the blonde's direction, hoping she gets the message that I want her to wait on me. She points toward the foyer and wraps her lips around her straw, long lashes hitting her lids when she smirks my way.

Hell yes.

I knock back the last few drops of my energy drink.

Walker's laughter is like nails on a chalkboard. He claps my shoulder so hard that I choke on the liquid, spilling it on my shirt.

The fucker doesn't even notice.

"Yeah, you're right," Walker says. "Girl was a walking *cunt* about it, too—"

"Whoa," I interject, hand up.

My attention is suddenly fixated on him. Forget the blonde. *The hell did he just call her?*

I don't know why his words make me balk, cause my insides to squirm in a protective, threatening way—especially when he's talking about Wren Kelly.

Yet, they do.

"Don't call her fucking names, dude," I snap. "Just because she's not smiling at all the guys here or getting on her knees to suck every dick in Hollywood doesn't make her a target."

Walker raises his hands and backs up. "Easy, man. I was just going off your vibes—"

"It's about fucking respect," I argue.

"Chill, bro. It was a joke," he says. "What—are you sleeping with her or something? All this hate a little act because she's sucking *you* off at night?"

I straighten over him, nostrils flaring. I hate fuckboys who think all women should smile and bow at their fucking feet. Like they only exist for them to toy with.

I wonder if talking shit about her somehow makes him feel empowered.

No wonder Mads hates this guy.

—*Speaking* of Mads.

I see my best friend moving my way through the crowd, his hood up over his head. It's written in his eyes that he knows something's up, and he's preparing himself for whatever shitstorm he's about to walk up on.

If there's one thing I know I can count on, it's him.

Every fucking time. Without question.

One eye on me at all times. Whether it's onstage, at a party, or on the street, it doesn't matter.

Always.

Mads whistles a warning noise as he approaches on Walker's right, directly at his shoulder. Walker looks around, then flinches when he comes face-to-face with Mads's poignant stare.

"Take a walk," Mads says.

Without question.

Walker huffs, still wearing that drunk grin that I'd love to punch away. "Calling your dog on me, Matthews?" Walker asks.

I smirk confidently. "He bites, too," I say, and Walker's smile drops.

He looks between us as if he's just realizing that we're serious, and as his eyes land on Mads again, Mads jerks forward and snaps his teeth, making the idiot flinch.

Mads still hasn't taken his hands out of his pockets. Still has his hood up and appears entirely in control of himself, though I know he's only keeping his hands there to stop himself from punching this guy.

Because if his hands come out, it's over.

Walker brings his arms up at his sides and takes a step back. "Easy," he says defensively. "No worries, Tourning. Didn't know Matthews had forgotten how to take a joke."

"Fuck off, Walker," Mads says.

Walker peers between us once more, picks up his drink, then leaves us alone.

The blonde has completely disappeared.

"The hell was that about?" Mads asks when Walker is out of earshot.

"Just being a dick as usual," I sigh. "He asked what the beef was with me and Wren, then called her a tight ass bitch."

"Fucking hell," Mads mutters as he drops his head into his hand. "The girl insults you, and suddenly you're defending her?"

I know he's teasing me, and I flip him off, much to his amusement.

"Kiss my ass, man," I say.

Mads snickers. "I'm just saying—"

"What?" I ask, hands slapping when they hit my waist. "What do you want me to do? Go ask her what her problem is?"

"That'd be a start," Mads says.

"I thought you were ready to leave?" I ask.

"This is more entertaining," he replies.

My eyes stagger on him for a beat, and I realize he isn't joking.

"Yeah. Fuck it. Fine."

CHAPTER THREE

WREN

GOD, this dress is the fucking worst.

I don't know why I chose to wear this absolute sensory overload to one of Anne's parties where I'm expected to stay more than just an hour.

—Per my publicist, Shannon.

I get it. I know she's trying to get me into more public spaces with my latest movie wrapping up filming. It's a leading role. I need my name out there more, need my persona to read more than the bitchy model from 'that one movie.'

Fuck my life.

I need to pull this dress up *and* down. It's simultaneously riding up my hips and down my tits. I make a mental reminder to throttle my assistant, Larry, for telling me the strapless would be worth it for how hot it looks. He wasn't wrong. I would fuck myself in this dress, and probably will later, but shit, I wish it had straps so I at least wouldn't have to worry about flashing some rando my boobs.

I have no idea what the two guys I'm talking to are saying. Between the dress making me want to rip my skin off and the eyes I know are searching for me on the other side of the room, I can barely think straight.

The guys laugh, and I force a small smile as I wrap my lips around the straw in my drink. The smile feels awkward as hell, but I hear Shannon's voice in the back of my head.

Try to smile and tolerate them, even if they're all idiots.

I don't think she expected me to be followed here, though.

At least these guys are tall enough to keep me hidden for a few more minutes. It shouldn't be this hard to stay out of sight, not in a room full of people as tall or taller than me.

Yet somehow, it is.

The hair on the back of my neck stands, ears heating.

I think I need to move. Staying stagnant at this party is a bad idea.

I excuse myself and start back through the crowd, even going as far as to saunter through the sea of dancing couples in the hopes of getting lost amongst them. I take my phone out and text my security, Tara, to let her know that I'm ready to leave. Maybe I can sneak out of here without Erik finding a way to corner me.

I know why he's here.

I've shown my face at too many parties this month.

Talked to too many people that they don't recognize as 'safe.'

I know because of the texts I get at three a.m. with pictures of me chatting up any person I spend more than ten seconds with.

Damn my brother for getting me into this fucking mess, for introducing me to the creeps who are now constantly on my ass.

—A hand grabs my wrist at the edge of the dance floor.

My heart jumps. I flinch, rounding on the person with a scream on the tip of my tongue.

Blue eyes stare at me from inches above, and as much as I hate seeing him, it's almost a relief.

"Oh my god—*you, again?*" I force out, attempting to keep myself stable.

Though I'm sure my darting eyes are giveaway enough that I'm distracted.

Reed Matthews is holding onto my wrist like it's his lifeline. And the way he's staring at me… God, it's like he can see into my nonexistent soul.

"What do you want?" I manage. "Didn't you get enough already?"

He leans closer to my ear so that we're not yelling over the music. "Is there somewhere we can go to talk?" he asks.

I scoff. "What makes you think I want to—" My mouth stops moving as I see Erik past Reed's shoulder. I blink, quickly debating my next move.

Walk.

Just fucking walk.

I pull out of Reed's grasp, glaring up at him. "Can't you leave me alone?" I ask, turning on my heel.

Please follow me.

"No," he replies at my back.

I shove through a few people toward the back doors. Maybe I can lose Erik outside. He wouldn't be stupid enough to approach with Reed Matthews on my ass…

Would he?

—That is, if he even knows who Reed is, though it'd be hard not to. His stupidly sexy face is plastered on magazines everywhere, the band's stardom rising so quickly this last year that they broke records, their tour selling out in minutes.

I know because my assistant is obsessed with them.

I can feel Reed close behind, and when we hit the back deck where people are chatting around fire pits and standing tables, I finally stop at an empty one.

"What do you want, Matthews?" I ask tiredly, though I'm glancing past him inside to see if Erik is lingering. I don't immediately see him, so I try to turn my attention fully on Reed.

"Who do you keep looking for?" he asks, turning around.

Shit.

"No one. Are you investigating me now?" I snap.

"You look scared," he says.

"Nothing scares me," I retort. "What's this about? What do you want?"

He finally focuses in on me and sets his drink down. "I just wanted to talk. Like… *normal* people do when something is wrong."

"I don't believe either of us are 'normal' people," I say. "But here we are. You got your wish. We're talking. Are you happy?"

His jaw sets. "Can you cut out your rage for two fucking minutes?"

"Nope," I reply. "If you can't handle it, there are plenty of other people around here who I'm sure are desperate to hang onto your every word, so why don't you go bother them?"

"Because—" His tongue darts out over his lips, and as a few people walk past us, he looks like he's trying to appear entirely calm, like he's pushing away the frustration I've caused and wants to appear like his usual happy self.

I almost laugh.

He forces a smile and gives an upward nod to the familiar faces walking by, and when another model passes, he doesn't hide the way his gaze follows.

My arms cross over my chest. "Are you done flirting?" I ask, low enough that only he can hear.

His eyes move back to me, and I stiffen when they rake over my figure. "Why? Does it bother you?"

"Everything about you bothers me, Matthews."

My phone buzzes, and I look down to see a message from

an 'unknown' caller, the words making my stomach twist to the point that bile rises in my throat.

UNKNOWN

You can't run from us.

I swallow, close my phone, and stuff it into my purse.

I really hope Tara is close.

"Something you need to take care of?" Reed asks.

My lashes lift, teeth grinding when I meet the concern in his eyes. *Why does he think it's any of his business? Why is he being polite about this? Why isn't he being like every other asshole here?*

Even as the questions race through my mind, I know the answers to all of them, and it kills me.

Reed Matthews is dangerous.

He's a threat to everything that I've worked for, to every wall I've ever built—

And he doesn't even know it.

I have to get away from him.

Drive in the knife.

"You know what?" I snap. "That was your two minute chance to get off your chest whatever you needed to say, and you squandered it by flirting with anything that fucking walks. So, you can stew in your disappointment until the next time we see each other when I'm sure we'll do this same little dance again, and then you can tell me what's on your mind—if you can keep your dick from doing the talking." I grab my drink again and nod politely. "Have a nice night," I coo, voice dripping with contempt.

I start into the crowd, and I hear him launch after me.

God, why does he have no quit?

"Wren, wait—"

"I don't believe we're on a first name basis," I throw over my shoulder. I hit the steps and start to go through the open door, but freeze upon seeing Erik on the other side, hands in the pockets of his suit and staring at me like he means to ambush me the moment I cross the threshold.

Mother fucker.

Reed bumps into my back. I hear him curse, and the second the word leaves him, drink spills onto my left shoulder, into my hair, and down my dress.

I gasp dramatically at the cold ice hitting my bare skin. A few people nearby stop talking.

"Shit," Reed says as I pivot.

It isn't even that big of a deal, yet it's a better distraction than I could have ever thought of myself.

Maybe he's useful after all.

I whirl on Reed with daggers in my eyes, ready to yell, but he's white as a ghost—as if he knows exactly how much he's just fucked up.

And yet, his fear washes away the moment our eyes meet.

"Are you fucking kidding me?" I hiss, shaking out my hand where the liquid is now dribbling down my arm.

This is perfect.

"You—*ugh*—do you have *any* spacial awareness?" I go on. "Is the air around your fat head too thin up there? Or is your ego so fucking big that you can't see the rest of the world beneath you?"

His gaze turns to ice, shoulders rounding as he hovers over me. I see his chest rising and falling evenly as if he's taking deep breaths to keep himself from losing his shit in front of all these people.

That's new.

I don't think I've ever made someone so angry that they had to check themselves.

A couple others around us offer their handkerchiefs to help me clean up, but Reed finally snaps out of his gaze enough to smile politely at them. "I have it," he tells them. "Just me being clumsy," he adds before looking at me once again. "I'm *so* sorry, Wren," he forces through his teeth. "Here, let me help you clean that up."

In my peripherals, I notice the man I'm avoiding watching me more intensely than he was before. I wonder if he knows I'm trying to hide myself within this distraction, or if he's too stupid to realize I'm doing everything I can to avoid having to face him.

To any outsider, one might think he's just some stalker.

Honestly, I wish he was. That would be simple enough to explain.

However, this man is anything but.

I lock eyes with Reed, jaw setting as the wind brushes over the sticky liquid already drying on my skin. "Fine," I say.

With one last glance at him, I turn on my heel and push through the crowd toward the bathroom at the front of the house where I know no one is hanging around. I've been to Anne's house enough times over the years that I know the hideaways in case I need a few minutes to myself.

"Oh, my god, *Wren!*"

The party host, Anne Tober, is coming toward us, her mouth dropped as she looks at my wet hair and dress.

"Oh, no—what happened?" Anne says, leaning forward to greet me with a faux kiss on my cheek.

"Just a mishap," I say.

"My fault," Reed says behind me.

Anne's eyes light up upon seeing him. "Reed Matthews," she says, his name rolling off of her tongue in a seductive way.

I wonder how many times he's fucked her silly.

"Hi, Anne," he replies, leaning down to kiss her cheek.

I'm going to vomit at the leer in his tone.

Anne squints between us. "This combo seems dangerous. Please don't break anything fighting in my bathroom—" She looks directly at me. "You can always use my shower and grab a dress out of my closet. We're the same size. I actually got a new line from a local designer. So comfortable and absolutely snatched at the waist. If you look in the front of my closet, it's the—"

"I think I would get lost in your closet, Anne," I say.

She laughs, beaming and touching Reed's arm when she does. "Fair enough," she says. "Make sure you clean her up well, Matthews. She's been dirty for too long," she adds with a wink.

My lips flatten into a thin line. "That's not what—"

"Oh, look at that—I have to go—" Anne leans closer to me. "Try to keep the screaming to a minimum. I know it's hard when he's going down on you like a god, but—"

I slide out of Anne's grasp and give her a dull smile. "Go fuck yourself, Anne," I say.

Anne chuckles under her breath. "Please, *get* fucked, Wren," she replies before batting her lashes at me. She squeezes Reed's arm and turns her attention on him. "Feel free to stay as long as you like," she tells him.

The funny thing is, I really like Anne. She's one of the few people I've become, at least, better than acquaintances within our circles, though something about the way she's assuming right now makes me want to throw hands.

The knowing look in her gaze when she smirks at Reed has my insides churning for some unholy reason, and it makes me loathe him even more.

"We'll see," he replies.

Anne smiles and leaves us then, and I glower at the pleased look on Reed's face.

"You're such a smug little prick," I say.

"I can't help that people like me," he says.

I turn to head toward the bathroom again, pushing through anyone in my way. "You *could* help it, you just choose to kiss people's ass instead," I say.

"I don't—is that what you think being a likable person is? Constantly kissing people's ass?" he asks.

We're finally out of reach from the rest of the crowd, the music fading behind us as we near the bathroom beneath her stairs.

"Literally, in your case," I mumble as I twist the knob.

"Hey—" Reed launches for my arm and draws me into him, practically throwing us into the bathroom. The abruptness sends me off-kilter, rage boiling over its edge when he slams the door behind us.

"Get your hands off of me," I hiss, twisting out of his grasp and nearly losing my footing.

Thank fuck this bathroom isn't a tight space.

"Why do you hate me?" he asks.

I regain my balance, move to the sink, and turn on the water to wash the stickiness off my arm.

"I don't hate you. You're just annoying," I argue.

"Why? What the hell have I ever done to you? If anyone has reason to be pissed, it's me."

I meet his gaze in the mirror and turn the water even hotter. "Then why aren't you?" I ask.

"I am," he says. "I want to know what I ever did to make you say those things about me. I want to know why you look at me like I'm no better than dirt under your fucking nails. Why do you glare and roll your eyes at me any time we see each other?"

"What are you talking about?" I turn off the water and face him. "You act as if I'm singling you out. I look at everyone like that."

"Not like you look at me."

My teeth grind against one another. He appears pained, and I don't understand why this bothers him so much.

Why can't he just let us be what we will always be?

Absolutely nothing.

"It must be weird for someone not to fall at your fucking feet when you smile, isn't it?" I ask, voice low. "For someone to actually resist your charms and not think you're a god among men?" I slide my arms across my chest, hoping to hell this hurts him enough that he finally leaves me alone.

"I have news for you, Matthews. Some of us actually have dignity. Every model or actor you meet hasn't sucked dick on their way to the top. You're just another rockstar-wanna-be poser trying to worm your way through the ranks to the top so you can prove to the awkward teenager you once were that even *you* can be the popular kid."

His nostrils flare, jaw setting. He's completely rigid—so rigid I barely see him breathing.

"What makes you so much better than me?" he asks in a hoarse voice.

"I'm not," I reply. "I'm just not afraid that I won't make it into the Cool Kids Club like you are."

Reed stares at me for a few moments longer than I'm used to anyone looking at me. It makes me want to shift my feet. And when he finally moves, I can't discern the look on his face.

He doesn't lose my gaze as he deliberately shrugs his jacket off, and when he tries to hand it to me, I balk away from him.

"Take it," he says.

"What's this for?" I ask.

"Because I ruined your dress," he says in a solemn voice. "You can't walk around the rest of the night with a stain like that and photographers on the prowl."

I stare at him. "I don't need you to be nice to me."

He huffs out a breath. "Go fuck yourself, bird," he says, and as he turns to head out of the bathroom, I fume.

Ex-fucking—

"*Bird?*" I repeat, nearly dry heaving at the word. "Fucking, *bird?* That is not my—"

Reed rounds on me. I barely have a chance to react. I'm

trapped between him and the counter, his hips pushing so harshly on mine that the counter lip digs into my ass. I squirm and fight, but the look in his eyes rattles me to the marrow of my bones before I can think of a single word to say.

"I'll call you whatever the fuck I want," he seethes in a dangerous voice, his face inches from mine. "Your name is a *poison* on my tongue. It sticks to the roof of my mouth and swells my throat. You're a disease, Kelly. Every time I see you, I want to crawl out of my own skin. You absolutely *wreck* my nerves and my sanity. To put myself anywhere near you feels like I'm cutting my own wrists."

He's much too close.

"Your being bothered by my comments is a 'you' problem," I hiss. "That's not my issue. And if I annoy you so much, why did you come back for more?" I ask. "Why not leave our conversation where it was? Why couldn't you let us go on hating each other from afar?"

I can feel his breath on my cheek.

"Because I can't get you out of my fucking head," he growls. "And I need to know why."

I gape at him, unwilling to look away before he does. Every breath is a challenge to draw in. I haven't blinked in so long that my eyes are drying out.

"Why don't you go find one of those therapists out there to help your fucking issues? Better yet, find a model to suck the tension out of your dick."

"I'd rather you did that," he rasps.

I strike him across his face before I even realize my hand is moving.

The slap rings in the still air. His shaggy hair splays over his reddening cheek, and for a second, he doesn't move. It's only when I see the lick of a smirk daring to tug at his lips that a hollow pit forms in my stomach. Somehow, that little smirk is more deadly than my slap, and I feel my every muscle tense.

He grabs me by the thighs and hauls me onto the sink. I push back, but he wraps his hand around my wrist and my throat, and my head slams into the mirror. I reject my wince at his jerk. The faucet jams into my ass. I grab his arm with my free hand, glaring through my wild hair as he stills over me.

I'm trapped against him, jaw trembling, and yet, as I feel his quaking grasp, as I see the glare of pure hatred in his icy eyes, a sick satisfaction worms its way into my bones.

I wonder if anyone else has ever had him in a twist like this.

If anyone has ever pushed him to this limit, or if the adrenaline that feeds him onstage is seeping into the stiff muscles around me, pushing him to react in a way that he usually suppresses.

Silence encompasses us. All I can hear is our steadying breaths. I can't figure out what he might do next. I wait patiently, refusing to show any uncomfortableness as he visibly weighs his next move. His gaze darts toward my lips, his hand tightening around my throat to the point that I have to stifle my fluttering eyes and the chills that prick the back of my neck. And just when I think he might strangle me in that very room, his grip loosens, and he releases me, taking a step back.

My nostrils flare as I finally let loose a staggering breath.

"If you ever—"

He reaches around me, stifling my voice and making me look twice at his stern face as I immediately think he's coming back to finish the job. However, I realize that he's grabbing his jacket from between the wall and me. I slide off the sink as he fluffs it open, and when he holds it there as if he's waiting to push it around my shoulders, I stiffen.

"Give me your arms," he says and gestures with his chin toward the arms of his jacket.

The air is too thick to think.

He opens the jacket around my shoulders, his long arms

having little trouble getting around me. I don't know how he's making me feel small or why I suddenly can't inhale a single drop of air without thinking it's somehow going to impede his own space.

"You're going to make things even worse for us if the photographers figure out this is your coat I'm wearing," I manage.

"Just shut the fuck up before I regret this," he says when I push both arms through it.

He straightens out the collar and meets my eyes one more time.

"I don't want it back," he says, stepping away from me.

Cold air sweeps between us.

"Because I'm a *disease*?" I ask through trembling teeth as he reaches for the door knob.

A muscle in his jaw feathers, and he glances back over his shoulder. "Because you do things to me that I don't understand, and now that jacket is tainted with everything about you that I need to forget." He starts to twist the knob. "Goodbye, bird."

Three knocks pound on the door before he can open it.

Reality slaps me like cold water to the face. My heart drops. Oh, *fuck*—

CHAPTER FOUR

I LAUNCH from the sink and throw myself against the door before Reed can open it.

"The hell—"

"*Just shut up*," I hiss, making him balk.

Three more knocks.

He glances between me and the door, his voice lowered this time when he whispers, "What's going on?"

"Wren?" someone says on the other side.

I know the voice, and it immediately turns my stomach. I lift my finger to my lips as I look at Reed, and he steps back.

"Wren, I know you're in there," Erik says on the other side.

I know the tone of his voice.

"You know better than to hide from me," he goes on. "We need to chat. I can wait as long as I need to."

Go away.

Go away.

A hand touches my waist.

Mother fuck, I'd nearly forgotten Reed was standing beside me.

He has his phone out, and when I look at him, he jerks his head toward the shower. "Get in," he mouths.

My brows furrow in confusion.

He holds up his hands like he means to make peace. "Trust me," he mouths.

I don't know what he's planning, but nothing can be any worse than what's waiting for me outside this door.

I quietly move into the shower and sink into the corner. Reed pushes his phone into his back pocket and drags a hand through his hair just as Erik pounds on the door again.

"I saw you come in here, Kelly. Don't make me take down this door."

Reed reaches for the toilet handle and flushes. Two more knocks rattle the door, and before I can stop him, Reed throws it open.

"The fuck do you want, man?" he snaps.

Silence encompasses the other side of the door like Erik is stunned.

"Jesus, a guy can't take a shit without some creep trying to get in anymore?" Reed goes on. "I mean, I know I'm pretty, but you're really not my type," Reed says, pushing Erik back.

Erik gives him an annoyed, flat stare. "I'm looking for a girl," Erik says. "I saw her come in here."

Reed chuckles under his breath. "If there was someone else in here, they'd have a mouth full of my dick by now. And I definitely wouldn't be answering the door for you."

"I know I saw her come in here—Don't think your little friend can hide you, Wren," Erik calls out.

"Wren? Like Wren Kelly?" Reed laughs. "Yeah, go fuck yourself, man. Wren Kelly wouldn't come near me with a ten-foot-pole. If you read a gossip mag once in a while, you might know that. Wait—can you read?"

There's a beat of silence, and I wish I could see the look on Erik's face.

"Sorry, didn't mean to offend," Reed goes on. "It's a serious issue in this country. I get it. Personally, I enjoy audiobooks.

The letters get all mixed up on the page when I read print. I get distracted, jump paragraphs, spoil shit for myself… It can be a fucking mess. Don't really have time to sit down anymore, too—"

"Wren, get out here before your friend finds himself without teeth," Erik says. "That'd mess up your pretty boy look, wouldn't it?"

"I mean, it would definitely hinder it, except Wren isn't in here so I'm not sure why you think putting your hands on me is a good idea." Reed's gaze moves past Erik, and he jerks his chin toward someone. "What's up, James?" he says, and I know it's the name of his bodyguard.

That must have been who he was texting.

"This guy bothering you, Reed?" I hear James ask.

I see Erik's shadow shift under the door, hear his annoyed voice. "I'm not—*get your fucking hands off of me*—"

"Says he's looking for a girl," Reed answers. "Pretty creepy the way he was pounding on this door. If I was the girl, I'd be hiding from him, too."

"Ah, looks like you snuck past security," James says, apparently not seeing one of the gold bands Anne was giving out at the door on Erik. "Don't worry, bud. We'll help you find your way out."

"I was invited by a friend," Erik argues.

"Yeah, that's not going to fly here," James says. "Let's go."

Erik continues to argue as James drags him away. I hear his voice getting fainter and fainter. Reed finally closes the door, and with the click of the lock, he peers my way.

"One day, you're going to have to tell me what the fuck that was about," he says. He pushes his palms off the wood and proceeds to hold out his hand to help me up.

"Ex?" he asks.

I swat away his helping hand and rise to my feet on my own. "Not hardly," I mutter.

"Stalker?" he asks.

"Why did you help me?" I snap instead of answering him.

His gaze darkens as he watches me straighten my dress. "Because you looked terrified," he says. "And while I might be an ass, I'm not a monster."

"Well, as long as we're both in agreement that you're an ass," I grunt.

Reed looks like he might smile, and I hate that I amused him.

My teeth clench together as I glance toward the sink and gather my bag. I realize I should push my pride to the side and thank him for helping, but fuck, I don't want to. It irks me to the point that my cheeks heat.

Shit.

"Ah… can you please not tell anyone about this?" I ask him instead.

His brows narrow. "Do you think I'm that kind of person?"

"I don't know what kind of person you are," I reply.

"Well, I'm not the kind of person who would mouth off to the tabloids about this when clearly that wasn't just any normal person looking for you." His gaze washes over me again. "Are you in some kind of trouble?"

"It's really not—"

Knocks sound on the door once again, and I feel my blood drain as I look toward it.

"Just me," we hear James say on the other side.

Relief sweeps over me. Reed opens the door, revealing James looking utterly annoyed on the other side.

"We're leaving," he says. "That goes for you, too, Miss Kelly."

I balk. "What? I'm not—"

But my phone rings. And when I see the name on the screen, I answer in relief.

"Tara," I say to my own security.

"Get in the car with the Young Decay boy," she says.

"Hello to you, too," I mutter. "Wait—what?"

"The singer from Young Decay," she repeats. "You're with him right now, aren't you?"

I glance between Reed and James, who are talking a few feet away. "Yes…"

"Someone just sent me a *fun* little message, along with a photo of the two of you," Tara goes on. "So, for your own good, get in the car with him. I'll meet you at your condo."

"What was the message?" I ask.

"I don't want you to worry about it," she says. "Just do this for me. No arguments. Please, Wren."

I can't swallow.

Tara knows everything about my past. Everything I've been running from. If someone is sending her pictures, sending her threatening messages… and with the way Erik just reacted to being thrown out?

Fuck.

"Let's go, Miss Kelly," Reed's bodyguard says to me.

Reed's eyes meet mine, and I let out a heavy breath as I hang up the phone. "I'd almost rather risk the mob," I say under my breath.

He leads us out to the foyer, the noise of the music still muffled behind us. I always forget how damn large this place is. Maybe that's because I only ever bought a luxury condo while the other models and actresses I came up with were buying mansions for the sole purpose to host parties like this one in.

"Neither of you move from here," James says as we start to follow him out the door. "Valet is already bringing the car around, but I want to make sure it's in the front before you two go out."

"What's with the Secret Service exit?" Reed asks.

James glances at me, and I want to crawl into a fucking hole.

"I'll text when we're ready," James says, leaving Reed and I alone in the foyer. A few people are walking by, most of them drunk, though they pay us no mind, not even when Reed circles in front of me.

"The fuck is happening with you? Do you have a rogue stalker?" he asks.

"No," I answer. "It's not your business."

"Considering my bodyguard just got himself involved, I'd say it is," he replies.

I wait a beat for him to tell me that I owe him an explanation after his helping me in the bathroom.

Yet, the demand never comes.

I shift on my feet when he continues to watch me.

"What? Why are you looking at me like that?" he asks.

"Aren't you going to ask for payment for helping me in the bathroom?" I ask, tilting my head.

His gaze narrows. "No. No, why… why would I do that?"

"Because you helped me," I say. "Don't I *owe* you something now? Don't you think I owe you an explanation for what's going on?"

He releases his hands from his hips in an almost faltering manner. "I helped you because you were scared, not because I wanted anything in return."

I gawk, repeating his words back in my head.

He has to want something.

No one helps someone who treats them like shit for nothing.

His phone buzzes before I can reply, and as he glances down at the text, his tongue swipes over his lips. He leans closer to the door, hand on the knob. His nose is nearly pressed to the glass as he searches the seemingly innocent people standing outside. Just when I think he's going to open the door for us to go out and get in the black SUV now waiting, he pauses.

"Take my hand," he says.

"Oh, fuck you," I snap.

Reed turns into me and leans closer. "You know as well as I do that some of the people working this party are itching to get a glimpse of anyone leaving together in various states of inebriety or otherwise. Not to fucking mention whatever the hell just happened outside that bathroom. I don't know if someone is trying to kidnap you, kill you, or just fucking scare you, but the best way for none of those things to happen is for you to walk with me. So, what's going to happen right now is you're going to get over whatever pride you're hanging onto and take my fucking hand."

And this time, when he goes to interlace his fingers with mine, I don't resist.

James beeps the horn, and Reed and I exit the mansion hand-in-hand.

The clammy sweat on my palms mingles against his own. I force my eyes down and follow behind, knowing that if I look up, I'll get caught by either a cell phone camera or one of…

God, I don't want to think about it.

Bile rises in my throat.

Reed opens the door to the black SUV and waits for me to enter first, then climbs into the back after. I throw myself as far away from him on the bench seat as I can manage and pull his coat tighter around my shoulders.

A shiver rolls down my spine when I look out of the window.

Erik is standing on the opposite side of the lawn, his hands in his pockets, and despite how dark these windows are, I swear he's looking directly at me.

"Ready?" James asks.

"Yeah, let's go," Reed answers.

Reed and I don't speak as James pulls off the curb. I slump in my seat, almost banging my head against the window when I feel emotion burning behind my nose. All I can hear is the noise of those knocks, of Erik's threatening voice.

This is so embarrassing.

Darkness swarms around us when we head down the community drive. I'm grateful that no one can see the tears rising in the corners of my eyes.

"Do you need to talk about it?" Reed asks after a few minutes.

I sigh and stare at the border trees that we're passing. "I do not," I manage.

And it's the only thing we say to each other the remainder of the ride.

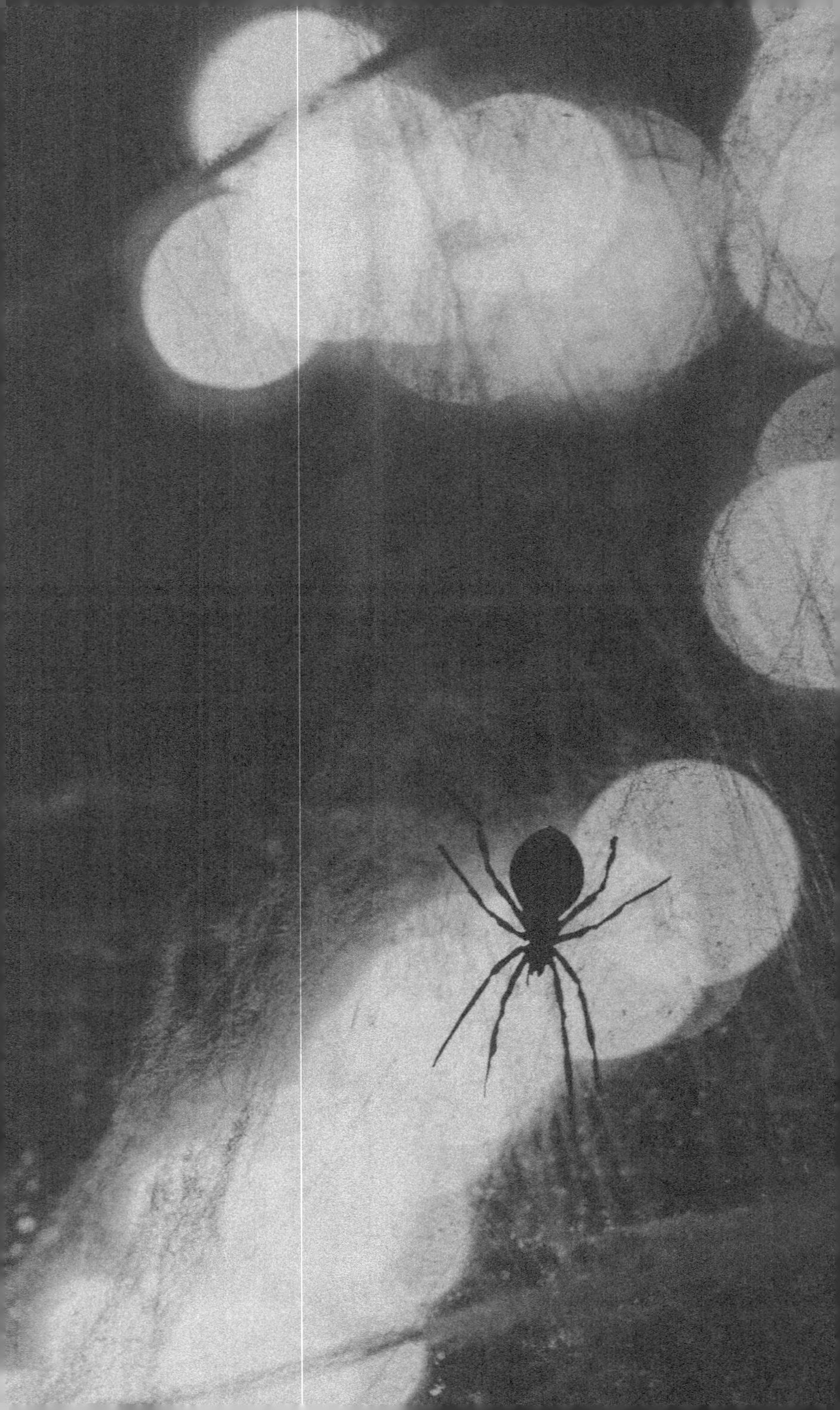

"WHAT CAN WE DO?" *I ask Tara.*

"I don't know that there's anything you can do," Tara replies. "I'll stick with you from now on. Damien is relentless. He's not going to let up, nor is he going to let any of his minions leave you alone, including Erik. But I won't let anything happen to you, Wren. You know that."

I sigh and lean my head against the back of the couch.

"Call me if you spot him and I'm not here," Tara goes on. "If any of his minions are following you or he texts. I want it all recorded."

"Why?" I ask, frowning.

"Amuse me," she says, and I don't argue.

I stare at the ceiling fan going round and round above my bed two weeks later, still replaying the conversation I'd had after the party with Tara. Since, my phone has been silent. I'm not sure why, maybe because I've practically hidden myself away for the last couple of weeks, telling my agent and assistant that I'm not feeling well enough to mingle.

Thankfully, they respect me enough that they don't question when I need a few days to regroup.

However, the current, *insistent*, knocks on my door make my teeth grind.

I haven't bothered answering my phone this morning. There are five missed calls and ten texts, all from my assistant, Larry. I groan when the person knocks again. It's more than likely Larry. But I haven't showered in two days, haven't taken the trash out in three or cleaned in seven, and my mind is so heavy that I've been looking at the mess and walking away.

I know they say 'out of sight, out of mind,' but somehow, I can ignore things clearly in my sightline. I know it would take me two seconds to clear, yet finding the effort makes it seem like it'll take ages.

I roll over and groan into the pillow when Larry knocks again, hearing him call my name in a sing-song, chipper voice on the other side.

Goddamn it.

My dog, Anita, jumps onto the bed and eagerly wags her tail, her long nose sniffing into my hair and making me smile. She's a blue merle Australian Shepherd, still with her tail, and she's the only light in my life. I hug her close, playing with her for a moment and only breaking when my phone rings.

I know it's Larry again.

Dragging myself out of bed, I make my way down the hall and to the door, my bare feet and Anita's tip-tapping nails sounding on the cold hardwood floor.

At this point, Larry is knocking to the beat of a Young Decay song, and I know he's doing it out of spite.

I throw open the door as he's strumming up to the chorus of their most popular jam, and Larry's hand falls over the threshold, rocking him off balance.

"Well, good morning," he says in his overly chipper voice. "And good morning to you, too, gorgeous," he says to Anita.

I give him a flat look, trying not to focus on the box of donuts, the paper bag with what appears to be champagne and a few other things, the purple narwhal plush, or the balloon that says 'sunshine.'

However, the balloon is too obnoxious to ignore.

Larry grins.

"Really fucking funny," I mutter, leaving the door open for him to come inside.

"I thought you would like it," he says, following me in. He pulls a plush out of the bag and tosses it over to the couch for Anita, who eagerly grabs it and begins to play.

"What's the occasion?" I ask as I start my espresso machine.

I hear the elevator ding down the hall as he's come inside without closing the door, and Larry smirks. I frown at the secretive smile on his lips.

Am I being ambushed right now?

"The fuck is this?" I ask, looking between him and the open door.

Heels clack on the floor, the shadow of the newcomer silhouettes on the wood, and when they reach the threshold, I almost balk.

It's my agent, Amanda.

My stomach instantly drops. Amanda rarely comes to my condo, and when she does, it's because there's something going on that couldn't wait. And if she's here with Larry…

"What's happened?" I ask, peering between them.

"Merry Christmas," she says in delight, the smile on her face making me wary.

"Okay, one: it's fucking July," I say. "And two… You know I don't celebrate anymore."

Because why would I celebrate when I'm completely on my own?

Amanda beams at me as she sits her own bags on the counter. "I know, I know," she says, dragging out what looks to be plates of food. "But I thought, what the hell?"

My espresso machine clicks, letting me know it's done, and I bring the steaming hot liquid to my lips as I peer between their secretive expressions.

"Okay, what the hell is happening? What have I missed?" I ask.

Amanda bites her lip, exchanging one more look with Larry before finally reaching for her iPad. She taps the screen a few times, then slides it across the island to me.

"This is what's going on," she says, raising her brows. "Have you seen it?"

I don't want to see it.

I don't know what it is but something tells me I'm going to hate it.

Larry slides the narwhal plush toward me, and I take it into my arms like it's some kind of security blanket. And when I look down at the page she has pulled up on her tablet, I cringe.

"Oh, god fucking dammit," I grunt.

It's a photo of Reed and I leaving the party hand-in-hand… Just like I knew would happen.

It's better than the alternative, I remind myself.

The headline questions whether we've put aside our previous squabble and started dating.

"You two look rather cute together," Amanda teases.

I flip her off, taking a sip of my coffee as I do. Larry slides a mimosa my way, and I kick it back like it's a shot. The champagne forces a chill over my arms, and the dry taste makes me remember why I dislike it.

I make a disgusted face his way. "Right on the alcohol, but not that one," I say.

Larry beams and pulls out the rest of what he has in the paper bag—ingredients for a Bloody Mary.

"Spicy?" he asks.

"Please. I don't want to feel any part of my face after I'm done drinking it," I reply before turning my attention back to Amanda. "Big whoop. We were at the same party. Why do you look like you've found a million dollars on the sidewalk?"

"Because he's it," she says.

"What? Annoying? Bane of my existence? Dangerous to be near—"

"Your next boyfriend," Amanda cuts me off.

I hear Larry snort, yet I can't move.

She has to be joking.

"Ex-fucking-scuse me?" I finally manage.

Amanda takes her tablet back and files through a few pages, going back to her emails. "In the two weeks since being seen with him, you've gotten three scripts and two phone calls specifically asking for you to come on their show to promo the upcoming movie, *not* Chris," she says about my co-star. "So, unless something else happened at that party that I don't know about, I'm going to pin this on your hanging out with the beloved musician that you once belittled in an interview."

"Oh my god—I didn't belittle him. It was a joke. I didn't know who he was at the time," I say.

"Amber called this morning," Amanda says, and I gulp at the dryness in my mouth.

"Amber… Amber Weisen?" I ask.

"Mhm," Amanda says with a nod. "She wants to know if you're attending the charity concert next month here in LA."

I blink. "What?"

Larry spins around with a drink in his hand. "It's a new event. They've gathered around twenty musicians and bands from Death Tower Records to perform and raise money for… Shit. I don't actually remember which charity it is. But Young Decay is on the list of bands attending. Of course. Death Tower wouldn't be crazy enough to have an event like that without them." He raises a suggestive brow at me. "Think about it. Good press. Hot guy on your arm…"

I take the Bloody Mary from him and sip it, immediately regretting telling him to make it so strong. I almost choke on the spice. Even so, the pain of it releases an addicting amount of dopamine that relaxes my tight shoulders at an instant. I gather my breath and blow out audibly, nodding at Larry's concerned face.

"Just what I wanted, thank you," I manage. I take another sip, blinking back the tears that it's bringing to my eyes, and glance across the bar at Amanda.

"Why would Amber Weisen want to know if I'm attending?" I ask.

"She's only one of the executives of the production company and best friends with Death Tower's CEO," Amanda says, and I sigh.

"I'm not dating Reed Matthews," I say. "He'd see right through it. He'd know I was only being nice to use him."

"I didn't say it had to be real," Amanda says, and my brow raises.

"You want me to fake date him?" I ask deliberately. "And bring him in on the plan?"

"Well, you said he's smart. He'd figure it out on his own," Amanda says. "You can tell him."

"What exactly am I offering him out of this?" I ask.

Because he's going to be risking his life without knowing it.

"He's a nice guy," Larry says. "He'd probably do it just to help you—"

"You're supposed to be on my side," I say to him.

"Um. Have you seen him? Fake date or not, he's hot," Larry says. "You could have worse options."

"You *don't* think he's hot?" Amanda asks me. She pulls a copy of Rolling Stone magazine out of the paper bag and slaps it onto the counter. Young Decay is on the cover, and I drag the magazine across to look at it more closely.

I clench my teeth and stare at the image, at Reed's annoying smirk as he tries to appear as if he isn't sex on a stick.

"Of course, he's hot. Look at him," I grunt, picking up the magazine and thumbing through to their article. It's praising their explosion after the bassist's bout with the law, though most of the bold quotes seem to be from Reed instead of Mads.

This is the worst idea anyone has ever had in the history of humans.

"I still don't get why we're discussing this," I say, setting down the magazine. "Why is this something I need to do?"

The sound of bubble-like beeps chimes from Amanda's tablet. I glance at the screen, and as Amanda hits the green answer button, I feel my already annoyed expression somehow tighten.

Shannon, my publicist, is beaming at me when her face pops up.

"What the fucking hell," I say in a deadpan voice.

"Morning, Wren—hey, Mandi, have you told her?" Shannon asks, looking for Amanda.

"Oh, god. *You too?!*" I ask.

Amanda shifts so that her face is in the camera by me. "Just told her," she replies. "Does her face not tell you her reaction?"

"I told you she wouldn't like it," Larry chimes in.

"Shan, can you tell them this is crazy?" I ask.

"It was her idea," Amanda argues.

My gaze moves back to Shannon, jaw set. "Traitor," I accuse.

"Oh, come on, Wren. I told you: we have to get your likability numbers up for this movie release. As of right now, people either love you or hate you for what you said about him, and I'd like to get more people on the 'love you' side, so can you at least entertain it?" Shannon asks.

"How the hell does one interview have so much power?" I ask.

"Because it's *him*," Shannon says. "Everyone loves him. Everyone wants to either be best friends with him, fuck him, or *be* him. He's hot, charming, nice... Looks like a bad boy that will lick you until you faint—"

"Yes, he does," Larry mutters.

"—And from what we hear, he's a great guy," Amanda says. "What's the issue?"

I hug the narwhal tighter in my arms. "The issue is, I didn't get into acting to become the Prom Queen or Miss Congeniality," I say. "I'm good at my job. Why isn't that enough?"

Shannon sighs. "I know, Wren. I get it. I know this is frustrating, but social media is a bitch, and right now, the more media presence you have, the more likely people will pay attention to your shit. People are on so many streaming services, you can't just shove a movie down their throats anymore with movie trailers or morning show publicity. You need to breathe a new presence online, and Reed—"

"Mother fucker," I grunt.

"Amanda, help," Shannon says.

"He's one of the hottest stars right now," Amanda says. "People who don't even know his music love him."

I chew on my tongue for a beat, my heart falling with every word they're saying.

"So, you want me to pretend to be someone I'm not," I ask. "To put on just another mask and blend in with all the others?"

"No," Amanda says. "We want you to be you, but we also need you to open up a little more, relax a little in front of the press. And having a very popular, very lovable significant other is one way to get more people paying attention to you."

I realize the plush I'm holding turns inside out. I frown down at it and flip it, finding an angry narwhal face hidden on the other side. It almost makes me smile, but the current predicament drags my lips back down.

"Why would he ever help me?" I ask deliberately, though as the words leave my lips, I remember the night at the party and how he helped me without question.

"I vote for not telling him," Shannon says.

"I'm not doing that to him," I say. "I might be cold hearted, but I'm not totally dead inside yet."

"Then try apologizing to him first," Amanda suggests. "Tell him you're sorry for saying those things about him in that interview, and then plead your case. Maybe he'll have enough of a heart to agree to helping you without anything in return. It's only one or two events per month for the next few months. He'll be out of your hair by the end of the year."

"Five months seems like a lifetime," I mutter.

"Maybe you'll grow to like him," she says, and I feel my brow elevate, causing her to smirk.

"You're an actress, Wren," Shannon says. "You can do this. And when it's done, when the movie grosses some insane amount of money and the studio is happy, you'll never have to see him again."

I huff an annoyed breath.

I can't believe I'm about to agree to this. This is insane.

Not to mention how my *'friends'* are going to react to this.

Even still, my career comes before them. I might live every day scared as hell that I'm going to make the wrong move, but if it's for my career, they usually let it lie.

Shit, I need to call Tara ASAP.

"And with any luck, he'll have a huge—"

"I am *not* sleeping with him," I snap at Larry, making all three of them laugh.

"Suit yourself," Amanda says.

I'M STILL STARING at my phone in shock of the conversation I had yesterday. Still wracking my brain over the party four weeks ago. It's nearly been a fucking month, and it's taken everything in me not to ask James what the hell happened that night.

I've tried to push it out of my head with every concert, with every strange fuck, yet I can't.

I was right.

Wren Kelly is a disease.

I tap my phone twice just to read the texts back one more time.

UNKNOWN

I need to talk to you.

Wrong number.

I had no fucking clue who it was.

Fuck off, Reed. I'm serious.

... and who tf is this?

Wren.

What do you want?

I just said I need to talk to you. Can't you
read?

Funny. The last time I said that to you, you
told me to go fuck myself.

Are you going to be in LA any time soon?

Nope. East coast leg.

For how long?

I'm not sure. I mean, we'll be in town for the
charity concert next week, but that's it.

Oh. Okay.

Why?

I just said I need to talk to you.

Do you want me to call you?

God, no.

So, come to the festival tomorrow.

What?

If you need to talk to me so badly, come to my
concert tomorrow. We're in New York at the
music festival. You know what those are,
don't you?

I've been to a few.

> Try not to give any interviews this time, or if
> you do, keep my name out of your mouth.

She sends back the middle finger emoji, and that's it.

It's the second most cryptic conversation I've ever been a part of—the first one being the conversation I had with her 'stalker' at the party.

Though, if the radio host from yesterday and my sister's texts are any indication of what's to come… if they're right… Maybe it wasn't so strange.

I wonder if she'll come.

Just the thought of it has me in more knots than five minutes earlier. It's been a long time since someone has come to a concert for me, not that Wren coming is a happy occasion.

Maybe that's why I suddenly want to vomit.

"—You going to join the conversation or stare at your phone all morning?" Mads asks, drawing me out of my daze.

We're in New York at the music festival already, sitting in the grass behind the stages and sharing a couple of pizzas. Zeb and Bonnie have press in a half hour, and I'm thankful as fuck I don't have to talk to the press today. My throat has an itch, and I hope to hell it doesn't hurt my singing tonight.

"Sorry, man," I say, turning my phone over on the grass.

"Reed—"

Stella is coming toward us with a tall, insulated cup in her hand. I take it eagerly and thank her, then bring the warm drink to my nose.

The smell of peppermint tea wafts my way.

"Throat still itching?" Bonnie asks.

"A little," I say, sipping my drink. "Nothing this tea can't fix," I add as I wave her off.

"Hey—" Bonnie kicks Mads. "Remember that designer we met last month in the city? When we went shopping?"

"Yeah, why?" Mads asks.

"I got in touch with him—check out the suit he's making me for your wedding." She leans over with her phone in hand, showing off a sketch that makes all of us whistle.

"That's fucking sick," Zeb says.

"Damn. Can he make me something?" I ask in envy.

Mads slaps my chest. "My girl is making yours," he says. "You don't get to deviate."

"But reception outfit," I say.

"But '*not your wedding*,'" Mads says, and I laugh.

"You sound like my sister," I say.

"That was definitely the point," he grins.

"Tell me again why you two aren't getting married on Halloween?" Bonnie asks Mads. "You two love Halloween."

"Because we want to be able to do something special—just us—on our anniversary," he answers. "And also throw a fucking wild Halloween party."

"Yeah, Bon. Don't you know it's bad manners to get married on the same day that you murdered your wife's ex?" I say.

Zeb snorts water through his nose, kicking up from his lounging position as the liquid spews onto his lap and the grass.

Mads shoves me sideways, Bonnie's laughter rings through the space, and I grin at my best friend.

"I'm glad we can all laugh about this now," Mads says sarcastically.

"No one misses that prick," I say.

"He was by far the biggest tool I've ever met," Zeb agrees. "I still have a question about the wedding date, too, though."

"What's up?" Mads asks.

"Why aren't you waiting until after the tour is over to get married?" Zeb asks. "We have a gig three days after."

"Andi wants the gothic fall wedding," Mads says.

"Yeah, she has a black dress and everything," I say absentmindedly.

It's only when I feel three sets of eyes on me that I realize I fucked up.

"*Dude,*" Zeb drawls.

Bonnie's eyes bulge. "The fuck, Reed!"

"Shit," I mutter, scratching my head. "I wasn't supposed to say that, was I?"

But Mads's mouth is slightly open, and he's staring at me in apparent awe. "She has a black dress?"

My sister is going to kill me.

The look on his face, though… yeah. Maybe that makes my fuck up worth it.

Because he looks like he's about to cry.

"Yeah," I answer. "Yeah. It's stunning, man. Lace. Tulle—"

"*Reed!*" Bonnie hisses, and I shut my mouth before I can say anymore.

Mads groans and sinks his face into his hands as if the thought of Andi in a black wedding dress is what will finally keel him over. "Fuck, I'm a goner," he mutters.

I chuckle softly and clap him on the back, patting him in a mocking way. I'm so fucking happy for them. Seeing my best friend this happy? That's better than anything else.

Even if every time I see his elation, it reminds me of my own stagnant loneliness.

Bonnie continues to shake her head at me. I mouth, "What?" to her, and she throws a drumstick at my head.

"I can't wait to tell your sister you told him," she says.

Fuck.

"Oh, come on, Bon," I plead. "You don't have to do all that —he'll still be surprised!"

Bonnie already has her phone out, fingers tapping on the screen.

"What happened to band confidentiality?" I ask her.

"That doesn't apply to this," she answers as she pushes her

phone in her back pocket. She grins smugly at me. "You're going to be in so much trouble."

And my phone rings as if on cue.

"Fuck me," I grunt. I grab my phone and look at the name calling, groaning when I see that it's Andi—on video chat.

"Answer it," Bonnie says.

"We're no longer friends," I tell her, rising from my ass and hitting the green button to answer. I put on my best grin for her, ignoring the fact that she looks as if she can kill me through the phone with only her stare.

"Hey, sis," I say.

"Do not 'hey, sis' me, *bro*," Andi drawls. "Step away from my fiancée," she orders.

"Come on—it was just a slip—"

"Move away from him so I can yell at you," she says.

"Why can't you yell at me here? Look—" I turn the phone so that she can see Mads, and I hear her start to argue.

"No—do not use him as your shield—*Reed!*"

However, the moment Mads smiles at her, I hear her curse.

"Goddammit, Reed," she mutters.

"Hey," is all Mads can manage, and I know he's picturing her in that black wedding dress.

"Hey," Andi sighs. "He wasn't supposed to tell you," she goes on.

"Kind of glad that he did," Mads says. "I was already going to be a fucking mess watching you come down that aisle. If I hadn't known…" His voice trails as he wipes his face in a restless way. "Fuck," he mumbles under his breath.

I sneak around into the screen to see Andi's face, noting the glisten in her eyes as well.

"See? I'm helpful," I say.

Andi's look of awe flattens with her glare. "You're still in trouble—Maddox, give him back the phone," she says.

"Oh—look at that!" I clap my hands together upon seeing

our manager, Avie, coming toward us. "Avie's here. Yeah. Sorry. Got to go, sis."

"Reed, do not hang up this phone—"

"—We love you, too. Have to go!"

"REED—"

I hit the red button and take the phone from Mads's hand before she can start yelling again.

Mads snorts. "She's going to fucking kill you, man."

"Probably," I agree as Avie reaches us. "What's happening, Av?" I ask him.

"Remind me never to tell you any secrets," Avie says, apparently having heard the conversation. "You two—" He points to Zeb and Bonnie. "You have press in ten. You two—" he looks at Mads and I. "I don't care what you do as long as you—" he peers at me "—aren't using your voice. If you're walking around to watch the other bands, put on your masks, whatever you need. I want you sipping every tea that Stella brings you. No talking, backstage singing, nothing. Save it for your warm-ups."

"Good fucking luck with that," Mads mutters.

"I'm supposed to go on with Global Break," I say, talking about a band we've toured with before that wanted me to join them for a song.

Avie presses his forehead to his fingers. "That's before our set?"

I nod. "It's just a few lines."

"Fuck," he grunts. "Fine. That's it. Nothing else. Don't go running onstage with anyone else." He looks at Mads. "I'm counting on you."

"To keep him in line?" Mads laughs. "Yeah. Okay. I'll do my best."

"Reassuring, Maddox," Avie grunts. "Let's go."

We all split up, and I put on a checkerboard five-panel hat, white neck gaiter mask, and long sleeve, knowing it's for nothing. Anyone who knows my tattoos will know who I am. I'd put on a hoodie, but it's the beginning of August, and honestly, I'd rather walk around fucking naked in this heat.

"Hey, you have your knife?" I ask Mads.

"Yeah, why—oh, we're cutting this?" he asks about the bottom of my shirt.

"Yeah, just so I don't need to change before going onstage," I reply.

Mads swiftly cuts a notch into my shirt, then rips half of it off, turning it into a crop. The white fabric is discarded into the bin, and Mads looks at me expectantly.

"Feel better?" he asks.

"Yeah. Let's find some trouble," I say.

Mads chuckles. "Hell yeah."

Mads and I head out into the festival, taking time to greet friends along the way. I know I'm not supposed to be talking. I try to be good, though it's hard as hell with this much energy pinned inside. I finish my tea and switch out to a gallon of water with a text to Stella, who ends up chasing us around the festival to bring shit to me.

A few fans recognize us, and Mads has to explain why I'm being quiet—which all of them happily understand. We take pictures and sign shirts, arms, and even a few tits, stopping to chance the mosh pit to listen to some friends' bands along the way.

When it's time for us to head backstage so I can jump on with Global Break, we stop to climb onto one of the high VIP platforms, where Mads helps me run notes to warm up my vocals.

He isn't the greatest singer, but it's the thought that counts.

"Whoa, I thought I heard your voice from a few blocks over," Bonnie says as she climbs up the ladder to join us. "Mads, you're sounding a little better. Those lessons paying off?"

Mads flips her off, making Bonnie grin.

"How was press?" he asks her.

"Ah, same as always. Asked about new music. I told them we were taking off next year to work on the new shit…"

I barely hear her as she goes on. I'm too busy staring at the stage and the audience, hands on my hips as I try to gauge how long it might take to cross the gap between them.

Though, in the back of my mind, I'm wondering if Wren is somewhere in this crowd.

Fuck that.

I can't keep thinking about her.

"Hey—" I interrupt them, jerking my chin toward the stage. "Think I can crowd surf from the sound stage to the main during the first song?"

Mads balks slightly as he turns to me, then laughs. "Ah… and give me a goddamn heart attack in the process, but yeah. I'm sure if anyone can do it, it's you."

"Hell fucking yeah," Bonnie encourages. "That would be epic."

My eyes dart between the stages, trying to figure out exactly how long of a walk that would be. "I'm going to talk to James."

"You have to be onstage in twenty," Mads reminds me. "We need to circle around that way."

"James is taking a quick break anyway," Zeb says as he reaches the top rung of the ladder and joins us. He takes a draw from his vape and lifts his chin when he pauses beside me. "You're going to surf this entire thing, aren't you?"

"Tell him he's crazy," Mads says.

"Definitely crazy," Zeb agrees. "Stella will lose her shit."

"Limits are made to be pushed," I say. I glance between my friends and grin. "Let's fucking go."

They all laugh and shake their heads.

"Yeah, let's fucking go. We're going to be late," Mads says.

CHAPTER SEVEN

THIS IS FINE.

It isn't a big deal.

I'll just talk to him. Like a normal human.

Except, neither of us are normal, regular people.

And something tells me this is about to blow up in my face.

Young Decay walked offstage about an hour earlier, and since, I've been hyping myself up to talk to Reed. I've seen the band play four times now, and every time, I'm in awe of watching them. Reed's presence, as much as I hate to admit it, is magnetic. He's a whirlwind of energy, stamina, and passion on that stage. It's never the same show, even if their setlist is. Reed somehow makes it different every time.

This time?

This time it was crowd surfing from the sound stage to the main stage during the first song.

I don't know how his bodyguard or tour manager hasn't put a leash on him yet.

I leave Larry at the VIP tent—much to his chagrin—once I've talked myself in and out of this at least ten times. I have to talk to Reed alone. I don't need anyone else hearing whatever we might say to each other if this is going to work—

If Reed even agrees to it.

I pause to snap a photo of the view from the side of the stage per instruction from my publicist, and I post it on my socials with only the horns hand emoji as the caption before stepping into the blocked-off backstage area of the festival.

The music from the band currently playing onstage becomes a muffle on this side, the noise of laughter and chatting musicians and friends replacing it. I flip off some familiar faces in jest, nodding at a few more who actually catch my attention as I'm so focused on looking for Reed that I barely notice them trying to talk to me.

One would think he'd be easy to spot. Yet, as I look around, the sea of dark shirts, tattoos, and flannel seems to meld together into one hot melting pot of alt, grunge, metal, and goth beautifulness.

I am so entirely intimidated by all the gorgeous people around me that I can't focus. Dangerous smiles and darting dark eyes cast over me as I try to look for him. My heart rate is rising. I try to blink and squint. However, with everything so glaring around me, it's nearly impossible.

I spot a walkway that leads up to a backstage platform and dart toward the staircase in the hopes that I can use the platform to search the grassy area for him.

It's nearly as useless as walking through the sea was.

"Wren Kelly," someone calls out.

I stagger and swivel in the direction of the voice, finding Young Decay bassist, Mads, leaning against a lighting rig and glancing through his phone. He pushes off the rig and moves toward me as I pause to speak.

"Tourning," I reply. "Nice show."

And it feels like an insult to call what I just witnessed only 'nice.'

"Thanks," he replies, smirking at me. "What are you doing here? Backstage, I mean."

"I was just looking for your other half."

"I have two of those," he replies. "You'll have to be more specific."

I know he's messing with me. "Obviously, I don't know your fiancée, so I'm going to take a wild stab here and say she's not who I'm looking for," I answer, much to his apparent amusement. "I'm looking for your retriever. Where is he?"

Mads snickers softly and pulls a tin from his pocket. "James took him on an outing, I think. He likes to keep Reed on a tight leash. You have to walk out his energy, otherwise he starts ripping things apart when you leave him on his own."

I stare at him flatly. "Mads," I drawl.

Mads grins as he takes a gummy from the inside of the tin. "Why are you looking for Reed?" he asks.

"Why do you need to know?" I ask.

"Because it's my business when someone who supposedly hates my best friend travels across the fucking country and her only explanation for why she's there is that she's *looking* for him," he says, his voice a little less amused than before. "Did you come to insult him to his face this time?"

I tense immediately.

He's not exactly who I want to piss off.

A smile slips up in his eyes as if he's pleased that I look scared.

"I'm fucking with you, Wren," he says, relaxing. "But I am genuinely curious. Why are you looking for my best friend?" he repeats.

"I need to talk to him about something," I say. "Something personal."

Mads's eyes downcast when he considers me. "I honestly don't know that I ever thought I'd hear you say you need to see him for something personal."

"It's new for all parties involved," I mutter. "Can you tell me where he is?"

"I don't know if I want to," he says. "Kind of fun watching you beg to talk to him. He'll get a kick out of it when I tell him later."

My jaw tenses, and I chew on the inside of my mouth for a beat, watching amusement cloud his sage eyes.

"You're kind of an asshole," I say.

"And you're a lot of a bitch, yet somehow, I still like you," he says, grinning again.

"Does this mean you're going to point me in Reed's direction, or should I just wander around aimlessly a little longer?"

"Really tempting," he says. "It's been pretty amusing to watch you angrily search for him through this crowd."

The glare I meet him with only makes his smirk widen.

"You know, I actually like you, too, Tourning," I say tiredly. "So, why don't we keep it that way, and you just tell me where he is—*Please*," I add.

Mads beams at me. His phone vibrates then, and judging by the look on his face when he glances down at it, I'm assuming it's his fiancée on the other line. He taps the green button and jerks his chin toward a dark corridor that wraps behind the dressing rooms.

"That way," he tells me. "Hey, beautiful," I hear him answer as he walks away.

I stare after him for a moment, listening to his conversation and finding myself jealous of the enthralled smile on his face as he speaks to his soon-to-be wife.

I've seen the tabloid stories about them—the one of the Halloween show that made the band even more famous than before. I've seen the mugshot, the picture of the guy Mads beat to death, even the videos fans took that night of Reed and Mads fighting after. It's weird seeing Mads in a normal setting, smiling happily, or even playing onstage, when you know he could easily—and without a doubt—ruin anyone that comes near his loved ones.

I think I fear him more than I do their bodyguard.

He seems like such a sweet guy, too.

Pushing the thought from mind, I make my way toward the area where he'd pointed. Nerves thread through me again, my palms beginning to sweat. If my conversation with Mads is any indication of how the rest of today is about to go, I might vomit.

God, I don't want to do this.

I begin repeating what I want to say to Reed in my head, hoping to fuck I remember all of it when I reach him. I open and close my right fist over and over as I walk, something about the motion helping to regulate my anxious emotions.

This is fine.

It's fine.

Just remember what—

I halt abruptly at the corner of the corridor as I hear someone moaning out a *"Fuck."* It's a sound that works its way into my gut, causing my neck to heat, and I flatten myself against the adjacent wall so they can't see me.

Is someone really getting off in this hallway?

Slowly, I glance around the corner, too curious for my own good. However, the way this guy is groaning and cursing has me itching to find out who it is.

There's a man on his knees in front of another. The one leaning against the wall has his chin gutted up toward the ceiling, shadows from the rafters above cascading over his face. He thrusts deliberately into the other's mouth, and I feel my eyes widen at the size of his dick when the first draws his lips back.

"Fuck, that's it," the second hisses.

I know that voice.

Oh, *goddamn* it—

The one against the wall looks down at the first, and as the light catches his features, my mouth nearly drops.

I'm going to murder Tourning for sending me this way.

Reed is getting sucked off.

Reed is the one making the insatiable noises that caught my attention.

I recognize the man on his knees as the sexy blonde guitarist from a punk band, and I swallow.

I can't look away.

Reed is holding his shirt at his sternum with one hand, showcasing the tattoos that seem to melt into his skin. He wraps his other arm over his face, nose into his bent elbow as he sucks air through his teeth. His hips roll forward, dick thrusting into the guitarist's mouth.

Fuck, why is this so hot?

Why am I still watching?

I shouldn't be watching.

I need to look away.

I need to get myself far away from here and never look back.

A smirk splits Reed's lips on the right side, the corner tugging up high enough that it looks as though someone is purposefully pulling it by a string. It's the only thing I see beneath his elbow as the darkness hovers over the rest of him, shadows clinging to his creases as if he's wielding them himself.

He releases his shirt and threads his long fingers through the man's hair. His own dark, shaggy strands fall over his eyes as he removes his arm from over his face, and when Reed dips his chin to watch and control the guitarist's motions, my mouth goes entirely dry.

The man gags as he takes Reed's length, his lips still a few inches away from the base.

Jesus.

He wraps his hand around Reed's dick as Reed tugs him by

his hair. I can hardly tell what magic this man is doing to have Reed cursing at the sky as he is.

"That's it," Reed says. "That's—*shit*," he mutters as he slumps slightly. His breath is catching with the guitarist's increasing motions. Reed shudders, his jaw visibly trembling as he starts to squirm, as his hips press forward eagerly. He hiccups a whine and slams his fist behind him, rattling the makeshift wall, and as he curses to whatever god he prays to, his body jerks, his neck strains, and he releases with a groan that even I feel.

Holy shit.

Reed's eyes are closed as he tries to catch his breath, as he spills and spills over the edge. After a couple of seconds, the guitarist pulls his lips back, throat bobbing when he swallows, and yet, I still see the milky white substance lingering in his mouth when he looks up at Reed.

Reed licks his lips and stares down at him. "Come here," he instructs, his voice hoarse.

The guitarist stands, his tongue stuck out and coated with Reed's cum, and Reed grins as he takes the man's cheek in his spread hand.

"Mm…" He licks the corner of the guitarist's lips. "What a good little cum slut."

Their tongues meet, and as the kiss deepens, I swallow once more.

I hate what watching this is doing to me.

My entire body is on fire. I have to shift and squeeze my thighs together just to get enough friction in order to breathe. I can see Reed's cum dripping from the guitarist's tongue as they kiss in a sloppy, deliberate way. As if they're alone together and not exposed down a dark corridor—outdoors at a music festival, at that.

I don't think I've ever been kissed like that.

It's slow and messy and sensual and—

Oh my god, he's looking at me.

My heart drops.

Our eyes lock. I'm rooted to the spot, paralyzed by his icy orbs. The guitarist releases Reed's open mouth and moves to kiss down his cheek and jaw. The corner of Reed's lips twitch upward, his eyes somehow darkening, and he tugs the guitarist back to his open mouth for a greedy, consuming kiss.

Yet, his open eyes stay fastened upon mine.

Why am I still standing here?

Dizziness spills over me. I realize I haven't taken a breath the entire time our gazes have been on one another. I blink and gulp at the dryness on my throat, quickly turning away as I feel warmth travel from my chest up to my face. My feet are moving. My head is down.

Why did I just stand there? Why did I watch him—

"Bird," he calls out.

Shit.

I freeze, though I don't know why. I hate that fucking name. I hate that he's already decided I need some ridiculous nickname.

He thinks he's cute.

My chin hits my shoulder, and for whatever stupid reason, I can't move.

I don't want to do this.

I push my bag up further on my arm and shut my eyes tight.

I don't want to do this.

You have to do this, I tell myself.

Or I could just let people hate me.

And never get the chance to truly choose a role.

Fuck.

"Hey, bird!" Reed calls out again.

I open my eyes. Toward the stage, I see Mads leaned

against the same lighting rig on the phone, staring in my direction, and I flip him off—making him smirk.

Damn him.

Footsteps pound the makeshift floor, growing louder and louder.

Finally, I turn around.

CHAPTER EIGHT

WREN

REED IS ONLY a few feet away from me, his hair askew, belt still unbuckled from his rendezvous with the guitarist. I give him a tight-lipped glare as he squints my way.

"What…" His tongue darts out over his lips, hands pressing to his hips when he stops. "What are you doing here?" he asks.

"Matthews," I acknowledge him shortly. "I came to talk to you. Though, I didn't realize you would be so *occupied*," I say, and a grin splits his lips. I cross my arms over my chest. "You're still exposed, by the way."

He scoffs and reaches for his pants to finish buttoning them, then fastens his belt. "Did you enjoy the show?" he asks, and as he does, he pushes past me, making sure to bump my arm.

"It was—"

Oh shit, he's walking.

I dart forward to keep up.

"It was certainly entertaining," I answer.

It was fucking amazing.

Reed peers over his shoulder at me. "I didn't mean our set," he says.

His long strides eat up the walkway. I'm struggling to stay within speaking distance.

"Can you slow your Sasquatch-pace?" I almost beg.

"Nope," he replies.

He heads down the stairs and toward an awaiting golf cart where his bodyguard is tapping his heel in the front. Reed slides into the back seat and leaves room enough for me, and I pause.

"I need to talk to you," I say.

"I heard you the first time. Get in," he replies.

I glance at James in the front seat, yet he doesn't say anything.

Reed adjusts himself. "I don't bite, bird," he says. "Unless that's what you're into." He jerks his chin toward the empty seat at his side. "Get in."

"I think we can talk just fine from—"

"Either get in the fucking cart or get the hell out of my face," Reed says tiredly. "I don't have time or energy for your games."

I hesitate for another beat before sliding onto the bench at his side. Reed claps the back of the front seat twice, and James accelerates without so much as a glance back.

I grab onto the handle beside me out of surprise as the cart jerks forward. I don't know where we're going, and maybe it was a stupid idea to get in this with him. What's even more stupid, however, is what my agent and publicist feel is best for my career.

"You know," Reed begins after a few moments, his voice low. "There's something to be said for a person who doesn't bother looking away when they find another in the midst of passion—"

"Is that what you call what just happened?" I laugh sarcastically. "From where I was standing, you just fucked some poor musician's face off. Nothing passionate about it. That was clear-cut use."

"Yeah? And what would you know about passion?" he asks.

We hit a bump in the path as our eyes meet, and I press my mouth into a thin line, chin rising. "Wipe the cum from your lip," I snap.

"Why? Don't you want to lick it off instead?" he taunts.

"Not in a million years," I seethe.

James drives through a few more dips in the uneven terrain, and I have to brace my hand against the front seat to stay balanced.

"Have you spoken with Heartless?" I ask Reed.

"I was in Chicago last night," he says, shaking his hair out of his face. "Thrown on a red-eye flight to New York right after. I woke up in a hotel around ten today. Ate a salad and a half a pizza with the fam. Ran around this festival in masks with Mads for a couple of hours while Bon and Zeb did press. Then we went onstage. So, no. I haven't. Why don't you tell me whatever it is you're being cryptic about instead of having me guess."

I clear my throat, neck heating.

Just spit it out.

"I have a proposition for you," I say.

"No," he says bluntly.

Dick.

"Trust, this isn't ideal for me either," I go on.

"What could you possibly need me for?" he asks, his voice sounding defensive.

"My publicist thinks it would be a good idea to be seen with you more," I blurt out. "That it will improve my 'likability.'"

His gaze narrows on me. "What?" he asks.

"Apparently, after seeing us together the other night, the numbers for my next movie went up. Searches. Hashtags. Everything," I say, recalling all the statistics Shannon had taken the time to send over in the hopes of convincing me further. I hug my bag tighter. "And they think it was because of you."

For a few seconds, he doesn't respond. I chew the inside of my mouth as I wait for him to say something—*anything*—back.

And then, he begins to chuckle.

It catches me off guard, making me glare sideways at him.

"What exactly is so funny?" I ask.

"Oh, bird," he sighs. "I told you. People like me," he adds with a shrug.

"For reasons I have yet to figure out," I mumble. "Nevertheless, they seem to think it'll help."

"Help what?" he asks.

"Publicity," I answer.

"So, what does that mean? You want us to pretend to be friendly? Get photographed together so that the masses don't see through your resting bitch face?"

"Resting bitch face isn't going anywhere," I say. "It's my face."

"The people think differently."

"The *people* can kiss my ass," I snap. "I didn't get into acting to please them. I got into acting because I love it. Not because I wanted to be famous."

"And yet, compromising photos of you sell for thousands," he drawls, and I squint over at him.

"How would you know that?"

"My sister is a photographer for Heartless. She hears things."

Something about the sentence makes me shift. His gaze meets mine, and I see it. I see the knowing look in his eyes. I see why he was grinning at me when I found him in the hall getting sucked off—not because of the situation I'd found him in.

But out of triumph that I'd actually come to him.

Smug fucking bastard.

"*You* already knew," I realize.

"What? That rumors of us secretly dating were already swirling because the press loves drama?" He slouches in his seat, appearing entirely calm despite the situation. "Bon and I did a phone interview with the radio station sponsoring the festival yesterday. He asked if you and I had 'made up' after the interview of you slamming me, and if there was anything between us."

Shit.

"What did you say?"

"I told him to mind his fucking business," he says. He taps James on the shoulder. "We'll get out here," he tells him.

The golf cart comes to a halt, jerking us both forward. I grab onto the back of the seat again as he does the same. Our pinky fingers brush, and I flinch away.

Reed shakes his head. "Do you react to every touch like it's fire?" he asks as he gets out of the cart.

Why does he have to walk so fucking fast?

I grab my bag and dart out of the cart after him, almost sprinting. A few people pass by us, and Reed greets all of them by name, most of which he gives a hand slap, high five, or fist bump. I recognize a few of the musicians, though I barely speak more than a 'hello' because I don't know what to say. Some look me up and down and glance between us, smirks on all their good-looking faces.

If I wasn't so annoyed with Reed, I might have taken a few extra moments to inhale a steady breath and flirt a little. However, he's catching the grass like he's walking on stilts, and we're almost at the back of one of the smaller stages.

Catcalls echo from a few of his friends as we approach, and I practically run into him when he abruptly stops.

"Jesus, Matthews—"

"Walk in front of me," he says, eyes glancing toward the throngs of people.

I gawk at him. I don't know where we're going. Why would I walk in front of him?

"What?"

"I don't want to lose you behind me in the crowd, and something tells me you're not going to let me hold your hand again to make sure of it," he says, and I can hear the restraint in his voice. "Walk in front of me."

"I don't even know where we're going," I argue.

"We're going to the green room," he says.

"That tells me nothing," I argue.

Someone calls his name. He glances over, smiles, and jerks his chin in their direction, then holds up a finger signaling to the guy that he's coming.

"What do you need from me, bird?" he asks, his voice low enough that no one else can hear, eyes narrowing in on me.

I twist my fingers together. I can feel his impatience. "I need… fuck, this is stupid."

"Do you need me to say we're not fighting anymore or—"

"No, I need you to pretend like we're dating," I finally admit.

Reed's brows raise. "Dating?"

"I'm not repeating it."

"Friendly isn't enough?"

"According to my publicist, no," I say impatiently.

"So, the press was right yesterday? Did your people already put it out there?" he asks.

"Of course not," I say. "Press loves gossip. You know that."

A muscle feathers in his jaw when he braces his hands on

his hips. He glances around us again like contemplating his surroundings will help him make up his mind.

I hate the amount of power he has in his hands.

I swallow nervously, gaze darting toward the people watching us. I can feel their eyes all over me. It pricks the back of my neck, tingles running over my skin as the sun bakes on us.

Come on.

Decide.

Tell me to go to hell already.

"If we're going to do this, I need to know something," he finally says.

My chest has a crushing knot in it. "What?" I ask, folding my arms across my body.

"The very first question anyone is going to ask is if I've forgiven you for the comment you made about me at DeathFest."

"Oh, grow the fuck up, Matthews," I snap. "I didn't know who you were. Some interviewer showed me a picture of Young Decay and asked me if I was excited to watch you guys. They wanted me to comment on the rising band that they thought was likely to hit the same popularity levels as the headliners. I'd never heard of you, your music, nothing. I'm sorry if that hurt you, but it was a joke—I got *death threats* after that festival, you know."

"I heard," he replies. "What do you think those people are going to say if I announce we're dating?"

"Are you saying I'll have to win over your fans as well?"

"I'm saying you'll have to do more than pose with me to sell it. Our fans are fucking smart. They know when they're being duped. I can't say I'm excited about lying to them."

"Why do they need to know?" I ask.

A smile crooks his lips, and his shaggy hair falls into his

eyes when he steps closer. I force my legs rigid, my fingers paling against my folded arms.

"If you expect them to believe this, then you'll have to let me past your wall," he says, voice dark as he hovers over me. He bends slightly, his shoulders rounding when his nose brushes my hair. "You can't be scared of me."

I feel his breath on my temple, and I know he's messing with me to see my reaction.

"You don't scare me," I say, my eyes lifting to his.

He holds my gaze, smile fading, and he pulls back only enough that my chin can lift without our faces touching.

"I should," he says.

I resist rolling my eyes. "Why's that?"

His tongue darts out over his lips. I hear the noise of people shouting nearby, of his friends calling his name, yet it's muffled. An echo in the warm air.

"Walk two steps ahead," he says in a low voice.

There isn't enough air between us. I try to suck in an even breath, though it's useless. "Why are you so close to me?" I manage.

"Because you're going to walk two steps ahead of me, and then I'm going to pull you back and kiss you," he says, face just inches from mine.

"You kiss me, and I'll slap you," I say through clenched teeth.

"There are a dozen cameras watching us right now," he says. "Do you want to give them us walking together and leave them speculating, or do you want to give them the show they're waiting for?" He presses his knuckle beneath my chin, and I feel my nostrils flare when he tips my head back and our eyes meet.

"This starts *right now*," he hisses.

"Why would you do this for me?" I force out. "You could easily tell me to go fuck myself."

Reed's lips twitch at the corner. Even so, I know it's only for appearances. It's the same crooked, charming smirk I saw on his lips five minutes ago when he was getting sucked off.

"Revenge? Boredom? What do you want to hear?" he replies.

"The truth," I say.

"You sure about that?"

"Positive."

He leans closer, and I want to flee when his nose brushes against mine. "I'm doing this because you're the fucking worst," he says. "And I can't wait to see how far I can bend you before you break."

"That's never going to happen," I hiss.

"Hm," he mutters, appearing wholly triumphant and pleased with himself. "Walk away from me."

I want to tell him no. I want to slap him and leave him stinging with my handprint as the crowd nearby 'ooo's over his pain. I want to tell him to kiss my ass, that I don't need him, his smart mouth, his smug smile, or his ridiculous charm.

I don't need *him*.

And yet, something within me wants to prove him wrong.

More than wanting to run away from this, I want to show him that he's mistaken.

He'll *never* break me.

I let my breath slowly release, and as my chest brushes against his, I lift a brow.

"You'd better make this kiss worth the chaos you're about to cause," I say to him.

The corners of his lips deliberately rise as if someone is pulling them up by marionette strings.

"Oh, bird," he chuckles. "Chaos is my middle name," he says in a voice that sends the hair on my neck rising.

Someone calls his name again. I turn like we're heading that way.

This is just a role.

An acting job.

Easy.

Reed grasps my wrist, the weight of his fingers nearly bruising me. I glance back, but he's already tugging me into him. I hardly have a second to prepare myself, to hang onto some last-second boundary—

His lips land hungrily upon mine, and the moment the hesitation passes, the moment I open up to him, he wraps one arm around my waist, the other at my neck, and Reed unleashes.

Oh. My. *God.*

I've been kissed by a number of people throughout my acting career. However, no one—*no one*—kisses like Reed Matthews.

He kisses as if he's starving. As if he hasn't seen the sun in years, and I'm its warmth. I want to pull away and slap him for causing the blank space in my head that's suddenly growing out of control.

Nevertheless, I hear the click of a camera, and my insides knot in response.

I reach up and thread my fingers into his hair, drawing him closer and hoping to hell that these photographers are getting the photo they need to get this lie going.

Reed squeezes my hip as he goes all in, and as his fingers drift a little further down my backside than I'd like, I open my eyes, only to meet his.

"Get your hand off my ass," I say against his teeth. He kisses me again, this time in a chaste manner, almost sealing our deal, then grips my ass like he's claiming it.

"I knew you'd enjoy tasting my cum," he says.

I want to *throttle* him.

"I hate you," I hiss through my teeth.

Our noses brush when we part, and I have to hold myself back from punching him in the gut.

"Don't ever kiss me like that again," I say with a tug on the end of his hair.

Reed leans forward and bites my bottom lip, his thumb pressing into the soft space beneath my chin, and the darkness in his gaze seems to waft out over the rest of his features.

"Just follow my fucking lead," he practically growls.

MOTHER, goddammit, fucking *fuck*.

Five minutes ago, I was single and getting sucked off by a sexy guitarist. And now… god, now I'm in a relationship?

I'm too fucking nice.

Or I like sabotaging myself too much.

Fuck my challenging nature and need to prove others wrong.

Fuck.

Fuck. Fuck. Fuck.

I'm screaming inwardly, not only out of frustration, but out of sheer fucking panic. The hopeless romantic in me wants to savor the heat of her hand against mine, the passion in her returning kiss, the gaze we held as I was kissing that guitarist, and the way she seemed to peer through my soul.

And yet, the sad realist in me is tugging at the back of my mind reminding me that she thinks I'm vermin, and no matter how she might respond to any kiss, how she might smile in front of a camera, I'll never be good enough for her.

I'm so fucking fucked.

Even as frustrated as I am right now, I can't let it hinder me. I have friends waiting ahead, colleagues eyeing us as we approach. They're expecting *me*. Reed fucking Matthews. I have to find a way to push past this rage of having her at my side and act like my usual self.

I thread my fingers into hers and feel her push back like she doesn't want to hold my hand; however, at the shout of a photographer narrowing in on us, I see her visibly slip into the role that she's now playing:

Reed Matthews's girlfriend.

A deep breath fills my lungs. It's clear and concise and filters out the racing thoughts enough that by the time I reach Zeb and the drummer from the band that performed before us, I have a smile on my lips.

Zeb's brow raises as he stares at me over his shoulder, chewing on a paper straw. Alex, the drummer, whistles at us, beaming at Wren.

God fucking help me.

"The fuck is this?" Zeb asks, his voice only loud enough for me to hear him over the muffled sound of the nearby stage.

Alex is already zeroing in on Wren. "Hey, Kelly," he says, grinning as if he shares some history with her. "Long time since I've seen you at a festival. I didn't think you liked them."

I slide my arm over her shoulders and turn my attention to him. "Helps when you have a little candy to cheer on," I say with a wink.

"Oh, shit," Alex drawls. "You two?" His gaze moves to Zeb. "You didn't tell me about this."

"It's still new," Zeb says, not missing a beat as he plays along. "I didn't know you were coming, Kelly," he says to Wren.

"Someone was insistent," she says with a look to me.

"Never known Wren Kelly to bow to anyone," Alex mutters.

She zeros in on him, gaze growing cold. "No, you've never

known me to bow to your shit-for-friends," she says. "Where are they, anyway?"

"Why? Interested in adding to your party?" Alex asks leeringly.

"No, I wanted to tell them how much bigger Reed's dick is than all of theirs added together," she quips.

Zeb snorts.

A grin licks my lips that I can't help.

Maybe this won't be so bad—at least, in front of everyone.

Alex's smile fades, and he scoffs, eyeing her sideways. "Always good to see you, Kelly." He reaches out to give Zeb a casual handshake, then does the same to me.

"Zeb. Reed… Have fun," he says suggestively.

"Always," I reply, and Alex walks off toward the green room.

Zeb chuckles, shakes his head at the ground, then turns into me. "I'm actually going to grab a ride with James before he takes off." He presses his hand into mine and brings me in for a short hug.

"I don't know that I want to know what's happening here," Zeb says in my ear.

"Tell you on the bus," I reply when we part.

Zeb claps my shoulder twice—the motion seeming as if I've just told him someone died and that's his way of consoling me. "Catch you later, man. I think Bon is hiding around here somewhere."

"Yeah, I'm sure I'll see her," I reply.

Zeb makes his way over to the golf cart where James is chilling on his phone, and I drag my focus back to Wren, who's staring out at the sea of people. I force a smile and turn into her, taking her by the waist and leaning my forehead against hers like I can't keep my hands away.

"I realize this attitude is your default, but you can't insult all of my friends," I say through my smile.

"I didn't insult Zeb. And Alex is an asshole, as is the entire band he's a part of," she says.

"You're not wrong, but—"

"I'm not pretending to like people who know I hate them," she says.

"You're pretending to like me," I say.

"Something I'm quickly regretting," she replies.

A familiar whistle sounds nearby, and it draws my attention.

Mads stands five feet away, hands in his pockets as he stares between us, and I can't tell if he's amused or concerned.

"You know what? Fuck it. I don't want to know right now," he says with a shrug. He jerks his head toward the next stage. "Horizon is about to play on the big stage. I promised Andi I'd get a video of them. You two in?"

I straighten up and hug my arm around Wren's shoulder, stifling a wince when she pinches my side. "Absolutely. Bird was just telling me how much she wants to get in the pit."

Wren presses her hand to my stomach, batting her lashes tauntingly in Mads's direction. "Getting trampled by sweaty, drunk men shoving one another and screaming *is* on my bucket list," she says dryly.

A smirk curls on Mads's lips, and he chuckles under his breath. "Whatever the hell this is is going to be fun as fuck to watch."

"You think you're funny," Wren says, though I'm not sure why she sounds so accusatory.

Mads shrugs. "I expected to see you running away faster, not waiting it out watching."

"Wait—" I look between them, and as it dawns on me that he's the reason she actually found me in the particular situation I was in, I laugh. "You fucking ass," I say between my bellows. I hold up my hand, and Mads slaps it, still grinning widely at Wren.

"I wondered how the hell she knew to find me there," I say.

"If I'd known it was going to end in whatever this is, I might have sent her in the opposite direction," he replies. "Come on. You two can explain once we're away from everyone."

"Why? Don't believe that maybe we're just into each other, Tourning?" Wren asks.

Mads snorts. "Him? Maybe. You? Fuck no." He stuffs his hands back in his pockets and starts by us. "It's cute that you think so, though."

Wren chews on the inside of her mouth and glances up at me. "I thought he was the less annoying of you two."

"Family trait," I reply. "We were heading to the green room first."

Mads scoffs. "Snacks?"

"Fuck yeah, I want snacks," I reply. "Wren's going to feed them to me," I grin.

"I'll shove them right up your ass," she says through a clenched smile.

As much as I want to lose my smile, I won't let her turn me into someone I'm not.

I lean down and kiss her nose—much to her chagrin—before threading our fingers together once more and looking at Mads. "It's adorable, right?"

"She's going to fucking kill you," Mads laughs. "Kelly, just make sure you leave the body behind somewhere safe. His mom wouldn't know what to do with herself if something happened to her precious boy, and she didn't have a body to bury."

"Shit, can you imagine?" I ask as we start walking.

"Remind me never to meet your mother," Wren says.

"My mom would eat you alive with kindness," I reply.

"Slower pace," Mads mutters beside me. "You look like you're running from each other."

The fucker doesn't even know what's going on, and he already has a better mind for it than me.

We reach the green room within another few minutes, and I pause at the entrance to take her waist.

"I trust you can handle yourself for a few minutes?" I ask.

"Yes, I don't need to follow you around like a dog, Matthews," she says. "I'm not changing who I am for this, and I wouldn't expect you to either."

"Thank fuck for that," I mutter. I kiss her lips, feeling her stiffen and hesitate against me, and when we part, I whisper in her ear, "We're going to have to work on your response to me."

"Maybe you should work on your need for public affections instead," she retorts.

"Considering it's you who needs me, we're going with my idea." I squeeze the top of her ass before pulling away, and when I see the glare in her eyes, I flick her chin with my knuckle.

"Fix your face," I tell her.

"You fix your face," she snaps, and it makes me snicker.

"Be back in a few," I say. "Don't miss me too much."

The forced smile on her lips when she shakes her head is amusing, but I try not to think too much more about it as I leave her to dart around the space from person to person, greeting a few friends and hugging others. I barely last in conversation more than a minute before another friend comes up to chat. I love the community we have, the friends we've made. A lot of these bands welcomed us in without missing a beat, and we've felt at home at these festivals ever since.

I'm so used to not having someone on my arm that I almost forget about Wren, especially when Mads approaches the group I'm talking to a few minutes later. He claps my shoulder and jerks his head toward the opposite corner of the covered area where Wren's perched herself on the edge of one of the many couches, drink in her hand, and chatting with a few people that I don't immediately recognize.

"God, I'm fucking starving," I say offhandedly.

"I feel like you're always starving," Asha, the guitarist from the band I joined onstage earlier, says.

"I am," I say.

"If I ran around like you do onstage and off, I'd be fucking starving, too," their drummer says.

"All the food is good," someone says. "Careful on the fucking queso, though. It's spicy as shit."

Asha joins in the talk about the food, yet my ears perk when I hear my friend, Marty, asking his bassist about a hot model.

"Hey—" I hear Marty say, smacking his bassist on the arm. "Is that that hot model chick?"

The bassist stretches his neck to get a look. "The Kelly girl, right? She's into acting now, dude. Damn. She's pretty. Hey, Matthews—" He grins when he peers my way, and I pretend like I've just dragged my attention his way.

"Make sure you're looking more like an actual rockstar today, not a poser," he jokes.

"Yeah? Why's that?" I ask, waiting for it.

"That hot redhead is here," he replies. "The one that talked shit about you a couple years ago to Tony's mag."

"Ah, Wren Kelly. Yeah, I know she's here," I say.

The guy beside me chuckles. "Actively avoiding her?"

"Nah, man," I say. "She's here with me."

One look around at their surprised faces makes my ego grow.

"No shit," Asha says. "How'd that work out?"

I shrug and glance back at her, pretending to beam at the woman who is already driving me to my limit. I'm not sure what the hell kind of story Wren has cooked up for us, but maybe I won't destroy it with this conversation.

"We've kept it quiet a little while," I answer. "Wanted to make sure it was actually something before going public."

"Aw. That's kinda cute," Asha coos.

The bassist nods toward Mads. "Hell of a secret there," he says jokingly.

"You're telling me," Mads agrees, smirking at me.

"You should bring her over," Asha goes on. "Introduce her to everyone."

I run my hand through my hair. "Hate to scare her away on the first public appearance, Ash. I'm trying to keep this one," I say to her, and Asha laughs.

"That's definitely fair," she agrees. "Will she be at the charity concert? Maybe we can all meet her there."

"Ah… yeah," I agree. "I think so." I take a step back and squeeze Mads's shoulder, trying to back out of this conversation before they ask me anymore that I don't know the answer to. "I'll catch you guys later—" I look at Mads. "I'll grab her and some food, then we can head out to watch."

"Yeah, man," Mads says, mildly shaking his head at me for leaving him after that announcement.

People normally stare at me, but this time, it's for entirely different reasons.

When I reach Wren, I hear her talking about her upcoming movie. I don't want to interrupt, especially if she's networking, so I gently slide onto the arm of the couch beside her. She stiffens slightly, and the people she's talking to's eyes narrow in on me like they think I've lost my mind.

Which, if I'm being honest, I think I have.

"—work with Chris," she's saying. "He's easy enough to be around."

I take her drink from her and wrap my lips around the straw, sipping on the… sparkling lime water with cherries?

Interesting.

The pair she's chatting with are saying something to each other, and I realize Wren is staring at me as if she wants to throttle me for taking her drink, yet knows she has to appear halfway nice.

"Enjoying my drink?" she asks in a quiet, annoyed tone.

"I expected vodka," I reply.

"If I drink vodka, I'll forget what we're doing here," she mutters with a fake smirk.

My lips curl. I lean over and kiss her jaw, pausing at her ear to whisper in a low tone, "And what a shame that would be." I squeeze her thigh when I pull back from her, meeting the blaze of her green eyes.

"Are you ready to get your face rocked off?" I ask.

"Why the hell not," she says, lips pressed together in what looks like a fake smile.

I smirk, then turn to acknowledge the guy she's chatting with, Dave. "What's up, man?" I say to him, and he fist bumps me. We've met a few times at festivals like this one. "Hate we missed you guys yesterday."

"No big," he says. "It was fun. We had Devroux come in and jam for a song."

"Oh shit. That's huge," I reply.

"Not nearly as huge as whatever this is." He points between us. "How the hell did this happen?"

"Persistence," Wren says, brow raised in my direction.

I stifle the way I want to dig my fingers into the sides of her knee, and instead smile at her. "Sometimes there's a fine line between love and hate," I say.

Wren looks like she wants to punch me in the face, and it only makes me grin wider.

Dave chuckles. "Sounds explosive," he replies.

I flick my knuckle beneath her chin just to piss her off even more.

"I like to call it passionate," I say,

"What band are you checking out?" Dave asks us, and I know Wren is grateful for the shift in conversation.

"Horizon is onstage in a few," I answer, turning my attention back to him and sipping Wren's drink. "This one hasn't seen them before."

"I have a bet that their lead puts on a better show than Reed does," Wren taunts me.

It's a stab right to my ego.

The pair 'ooo' at us, chuckling softly, and I feel my jaw clench.

"That's cold," Dave laughs.

"Frigid," I bite out. I wrap my fingers into hers and bring her knuckles to my lips, watching her every expression as I do. "Luckily, I enjoy breaking ice," I say as my lips meet her soft fingers.

It's barely a second that our eyes stay upon one another, yet somehow long enough that the woman clears her throat. I turn back to them and stand, fist bumping Dave and his partner, as Wren stands up beside me.

We exchange goodbyes, and I take Wren's hand to meet Mads outside—though not before walking by the catering table and quietly grabbing a whole tray of food without missing a step.

"What are you—"

"Just keep walking," I tell her.

Mads is waiting for us, and he jerks his head in the direction of the main stage for us to follow.

I DON'T LOSE Wren's hand as we follow behind Mads. Especially not when some friends pass. Most of them make surprised comments, some spectators even grab photos. I slow up a little and gaze down at Wren, smiling for effect, remembering what Mads said about us looking like we were running from each other.

I'd love to know what she's thinking, what's going on behind those gleaming daggers. I wrap my arm around her shoulders and lean closer to her ear.

"Are you having fun yet?" I ask her.

"Having you touch me this much? Yes. Loads of fun," she grunts. "If it wasn't apparent, you should know I hate this."

I smirk at her, removing my arm from her shoulders and taking hold of her hand again instead. "Look at us getting to know each other already," I say. "When we get to the platform, I think we need to set ground rules."

"So many fucking ground rules," she says breathlessly.

Stella has one of the cushier VIP platforms cordoned off for us, the extra security she's ordered for the tour standing by. I pause at the bottom of the steps and gesture to Wren, letting her climb up ahead of me. Screams and shouts follow us as we ascend. I wave to a few surrounding fans, seeing their phones out and snapping more photos, and it makes my stomach knot.

Am I really fucking doing this?

Even with the question running through my mind, it still doesn't quite hit me when I reach the top of the steps, or when Wren waves at a few people who call her name below. Mads waves the rock-on horns hand gesture to a few guys shouting at him before grabbing a seat on one of the couches opposite Wren—who already has her phone out.

I toss Mads the tray of food and dart to the rails where I climb up the corner, throw my hands in the air, and scream.

Fans meet my energy with their own shouts, obviously eager for Horizon to hit the stage, and I soak it in for a minute before jumping back down.

Fuck, I needed that.

Mads laughs quietly and picks up a hot wing from the tray. "Feel better?" he asks.

"Yeah," I say as I flop in the seat beside Wren. I nosily peer over to her phone, seeing that she's posting a photo of me standing on the rails from where she's sitting.

"Is that our 'it's official' picture?" I taunt her.

"My assistant just texted to say that photos of us were already circulating," she mutters, focused on her phone. "Thought I should perpetuate it a little."

"I think we can do better than that," I say.

A muscle twitches in her jaw when she eyes me sideways. "If you kiss me again—"

"How about you respond to me like an actual girlfriend and not in a way that makes me feel like I'm forcing myself on you considering this was your idea," I argue.

Mads chokes on his water.

A chime comes through on her phone, and she turns back to it before she can reply. The pink on her cheeks seems to whiten as she reads the message, her chest stilling like she's forgotten how to breathe.

"Everything okay?" I ask, and I wonder if the lapse has to do with the guys from the party.

Wren's eyes lift to a blank space by the stairs, and she closes her phone quickly. "Why wouldn't it be?" she asks as she leans forward to take a bottle of water off the table.

I exchange a quick glance with Mads, who appears just as confused as me.

Wren gulps down half the bottle, letting some of the liquid drip from the sides of her mouth, then practically tosses it back onto the table. "So, how exactly do you think we can do better than the picture I just posted—*without* you kissing me?" she asks.

I would love to know what the hell is going on with her.

Though something tells me no matter how this goes, I'll never find out.

I take my phone out, slide the front-facing camera on, and scoot close enough to her that I can pull her thigh onto my lap. "Do you know what a smile is, bird?" I ask.

"Unfortunately," she replies.

"Good. I'm going to do something, and you're going to pretend to enjoy it."

"Oh, fuck—*Reed!*"

The moment I start tickling her, she balks. She twists. She shoves. And yet, through every motion, she seems to fall into the role, somehow appearing entirely gorgeous with what I assume is a fake smile and high-pitch laugh.

I snap a few photos through it, making sure to keep my face visible, my nose skimming her cheek. She pulls my hair, my shirt, and when I finally stop, she's out of breath.

"Rule number one," she hisses as our eyes meet. "Don't ever fucking tickle me again."

I chuckle and kiss her tauntingly, then sit back in the seat, releasing her from my clutches. Wren runs her hand through her ginger waves and wipes the tears from her flushed cheeks. Her shirt is askew but she straightens it out and shoves my knee away from her.

"Careful," Mads mutters from his chair, and Wren slides closer to me again.

The photos are fantastic. I slump against the couch, grinning like a child, and select a few to post to my page, mildly letting it sink in what I'm about to do.

Any regret I might have is a tomorrow problem.

"Wait—let me see it before you post," Wren says, mirroring me.

I show her the photo, and she wrinkles her nose at it.

"What's wrong with it?" I ask.

"It's adorable, and I hate it," she replies dryly. "But my publicist will do a fucking victory dance when she sees. As will my assistant who is on his way over here now."

Here goes fucking nothing.

The picture has barely been posted for more than thirty seconds when my phone dings with a message from the band's publicist.

I'll get back to her later.

"How cute," Mads mocks as he shakes his phone at us. "You actually look like you like each other."

I glance over to Wren, who has her phone out and staring at the notifications already, scrolling through the comments. I don't know what people are saying, but the look on her face is enough to tell me that it might not all be positive.

Fucking social media.

I reach out and take her phone from her hand, then place it on the table face-down. She doesn't need to read those comments. I know how fucking crazy and bold people can be online, and it's never easy to swallow.

Standing, I hold my hands out to her and gesture for her to stand with me. "Watch the show and talk to me," I say, nodding toward the railing.

Wren takes the offer.

At the edge, I stand up on the bottom barrier and cup my hands around my mouth, shouting and clapping with the rest of the fans eagerly awaiting the show. Wren grips the railing, and as the intro graphics and opening music begins, I lean my elbows onto the cold bar, then glance her way.

"What's rule number two?" I ask Wren.

A soft sigh leaves her as she stares at the stage. "Don't expect me to smile, kiss your ass, or act like some lovedrunk teenager over you," she says plainly.

"We're grown adults. I would never expect that," I say. "Three?"

"Public affections are for show only." She closes her eyes and inhales sharply for a beat as if she's trying to carefully choose her words. "And even though I know it's part of the deal, I need you to *slow down*," she says exasperatedly. "I realize it's just what couples 'do,' especially new couples, but the last hour has been *suffocating*. That was way too fast."

I swallow at the admission. "I didn't know—"

"No, because how could you?" she says, her voice hoarse. She scoffs and shakes her head, now looking out at the concert again. "Rule four: No dramatic gestures, showboating, or surprises. While the public affection is something that I'll grow to tolerate, dramatics and forcing surprise is something that I'm not willing to compromise on. I don't handle any of those things well, so while I would never ask you to change who you are, just know that if you do them, I'm not going to give you the 'show' you're expecting."

Every rule gives me a little more insight into her fortress.

"And the last rule?" I ask.

She finally looks at me, and I can't for the life of me figure out why she looks so damn sad.

"Don't *ever* expect this to be real," she says.

I don't know why the rule stings. There's an itch that worms into my hands, making me straighten over her so that I can clench the rail as tightly as she is.

"The thought never crossed my mind," I reply.

Our gazes stagger, and the music seems to melt into the distance. I swallow beneath that momentary lapse, not knowing what the hell I'm supposed to say next. I'm drowning in her darkened gaze, suddenly anxious to figure out how to help her, wondering who made her feel less than—

"Wren!" someone shouts from the ground. "Wren! Tell them I'm with you! I'm her assistant—"

Thank fucking *fuck* for the distraction.

Wren lets loose a stolen breath when her focus switches to her assistant, though it takes more than his voice to drag my stare away from her. She's so guarded, so secretive… It makes me feel like she's living another life—or perhaps just found herself free of one.

"—my assistant, Larry," she's saying. "Can you tell your—"

"Oh, right, yeah. Hey, let him up!" I force myself to shout to the guards.

Her assistant comes bounding up the stairs, all grins, and beams when he stops beside me.

I still haven't fully recovered from watching her.

"Oh my gosh, I'm such a huge fan of Young Decay," Larry exclaims, and I try to shove the thought of her solemn stare to the very back of my mind.

"I've been following you since your college days—I was actually at the concert when Bonnie became your drummer," Larry goes on.

"No shit," Mads drawls in surprise. "Damn, that was a long ass time ago."

"Yeah. You still had long hair," I say to him.

Mads runs his hand through his strands. "How do you think Andi would like it if I grew it out again?"

I almost laugh. "She'd love it. You would not."

"Yeah, you're right—" He leans over and extends a hand to Larry. "Looks like we'll be seeing more of you around," he adds, smirking at me.

"So much of me," Larry grins. "But first, *you* have a plane to catch," he says to Wren.

"Oh, shit. What time is it?" she almost panics.

"After eight," Larry replies. "Flight is at eleven."

"You're going back to California tonight?" I ask her, and I don't know why I thought she might stay longer.

Wren's brows furrow when she looks up at me. "What, did you think I was spending the night with you?" she asks.

"Thought you might stay for a little longer," I say.

Wren's gaze moves over me. "Not today."

She starts to head down the steps. I launch for her hand to stop her. The moment my fingers land upon her wrist, I see her flinch like she's going to rip her arm away, but thinks twice upon remembering her role.

My tongue swipes over my lips, and I give her a coy smirk, hiding everything I'd been feeling deep inside. "You're leaving me without a goodbye kiss?" I ask.

Her jaw sets. "How could I forget?" she says with a forced, tight-lip smile. She allows me to pull her into me again, and her lips land upon mine—soft enough that it stills me.

I'm so not fucking smart.

I clear my throat when we part. "When… When do you need me again?" I ask, barely recovered.

"Ah… Larry? When do I see him again?" she asks, the question entirely professional.

"Charity concert," Larry answers.

"Charity concert," Wren repeats. "I'll text you."

She releases me with nothing more than a squeeze on my elbow, and I almost fall forward at how abrupt her exit is.

Within seconds, she's down the steps and disappearing into the backstage area, the darkening space swallowing her.

And as she walks away, it finally hits me.

I agreed to date Wren Kelly.

I kissed Wren Kelly multiple times today.

She's my…

She's my fucking girlfriend?!

I'm dating a woman who, twenty-four hours ago, absolutely hated me. And now… fuck, now I have to find a way to date her without us killing each other?

I think I need to vomit.

I barely realize I've sunk my forearms onto the railing when I feel Mads clap my shoulder in a comforting way. Nausea twists my stomach, my hands clammy.

"You're so fucking fucked," he says.

I press my forehead against my thumbs for another heavy sigh, then straighten. "What's the worst that could happen?" I ask.

Mads lifts a brow, mouth twisted, and I can see exactly what he's thinking behind his eyes.

"Fuck off," I mumble. "Aren't you the one that told her where to find me?"

"Well, yeah, but I was just looking to make her jealous," he replies.

"How did you think that would happen?" I ask.

"I was honestly hoping you'd convince her to join in," Mads says with a shrug. "Instead you roped yourself into dating her."

My mind goes back to how she found me, the look in her gaze as our eyes locked while I kissed… oh fuck, *what was his name?*

What kind of person am I if I can't even remember the guy I face-fucked three times now—the last time less than an hour ago, at that.

"When this ends poorly, just remember: you told me to be nice to her," I say.

Mads grins. "Blame it on me all you want. You would have said 'yes' regardless."

"Yeah, but why though?" I ask exasperatedly. "Why have I done this to myself?"

"Because you're a nice guy," Mads says.

I toy with my fingers for a moment. "What if it's for revenge?" I ask.

Mads scoffs. "We can go with that if it makes you feel better."

A text comes through on my phone, and as I look down at it, I groan inwardly.

ANDI ANDI BO-BANDI

What the fuck have you done?

It's Andi, and no sooner than I've read the words, a photo message comes in. It's a picture of Wren and I kissing here on this platform just minutes earlier.

Relax. It isn't real. I'll call you later.

That's the most hilarious thing you've ever said to me.

Good fucking luck. You're going to need it to stay above water.

I don't know what that means.

You know exactly what I mean.

Be careful.

I curse under my breath and stuff my phone back in my pocket.

Because as much as I don't want to admit it, I know she's right.

THE RAP of the double bass in the heavy metal music I'm listening to thuds my bones.

It blares loud enough that it drowns out my thoughts while the amber fairy lights illuminate the plants they're threaded through, lights bouncing off the dark walls and black brick.

I like my music heavy and numbing. I always have. And for the last few years, louder has always equaled better. I want to drown beneath the strum of the bass, the pound of the drums, the guitar's riff, and the lyrics that I don't always understand. I want it all to choke me until I'm struggling for air, then hold me at the absolute edge within its grasp, letting me drift in and out of consciousness.

I want to see whatever fucking god people say waits for us on the other side just so I can spit in their face.

A few years ago, I had to pay for more soundproofing for my walls because the neighbors complained. Larry told me I should send gift baskets to apologize for the noise and construction, so I did.

—Gift baskets with noise cancelling headphones, a candy I found called 'cum drops,' and heart-shaped cookies that said 'go fuck yourself' on them.

Needless to say, we don't exchange Christmas gifts.

The memory makes me smile at the ceiling. I've just finished my morning yoga, and I haven't bothered getting up from the floor yet.

I just need a few minutes.

Anita is staring at me from the couch, her nose between her white paws. She's so cute that I want to squeeze her. At least she is a welcome distraction from all that's going on around me.

Every time I close my eyes, all I see are the pictures of Reed and I that have posted the last few weeks, hear the speculating remarks, and the comments from Reed's adoring fans—not to mention the messages I've gotten.

They're relentless.

I can't blame them. We were quick to jump into this with little planning. Of course, the festival was a disaster. It *felt* like a disaster.

Even so, my publicist doesn't seem to care. She says I'm trending up and tells me to continue posting.

Don't read the comments.

Don't reply to the DMs.

Keep your chin up and let Reed work his charismatic magic.

Lean on him to help you rise.

It's all so fucking annoying.

My phone vibrates against the floor a few feet away from me, the notification chime stark against the noise of my music. It's a curse, I think, always being able to hear the sound of a phone despite my best efforts at drowning it out with music. What's worse is others playing videos on their phones around me.

It's like nails on a chalkboard, I swear.

Don't these people have their own headphones?

I turn my head and stare at the black rectangle, unsure if I want to attempt to find the energy to answer it or not.

However, when it goes off again, I force myself to roll over and grab it.

UNKNOWN

Adorable.

Bile instantly rises in my throat.

The sight of the message from the unsaved number launches me to my knees. My heart sinks. I swipe up, enter my passcode, turn the volume down a little so I can resume thinking, and quickly tap on my texts with already shaking fingers.

Another photo of Reed and I from the music festival pops up. My stomach hollows out, breakfast that I forced myself to eat this morning churning its way back up.

It's the third text over the last two weeks, and with each message, I hear Damien's mocking voice in the back of my head.

I explained to you that it's nothing. It's for my job.

The swiftness that the asshole texts back is unreal.

UNKNOWN

I hope so.

Rockstar might sell for triple the usual.

My gaze flickers in the direction of my bedroom, thoughts going to the locked top drawer of my dresser, and I swallow.

Leave him alone.

Why? Do you have a soft spot for him?

I don't like him, but that doesn't mean I want him dead.

Pity.

> You swore you would never interfere with my
> work.

> This is work.

> Stop interfering.

> That means you don't follow him or me. You
> don't need to send any of your goons to
> check in on me. You leave me alone.

It's a shame you have to go to the lengths of
sucking some idiotic boy's dick and smiling in
front of the cameras with him just to get a few
scripts.

I guess the cringeworthy performances that
you call your 'talent' isn't enough.

I hate the way he mocks me.

> I'm not sucking anyone's dick.

> Nor am I smiling.

A picture of Reed and I when he was tickling me comes through, and I feel my teeth clench.

What were you lying?

An angry groan escapes me, and when I type this time, my thumbs hit the screen so hard that I hear the taps.

> This conversation is over. Leave Reed alone.

> You have nothing to worry about.

Cross your heart and hope to die?

I blow out a quaking breath and force myself to reply.

Stick a needle in my eye.

The words prompt that very image into my mind, and I throw my phone across the room without waiting on his reply.

I fucking *hate* this.

My face is wet with tears I didn't realize I was shedding. I quickly swipe them away and try to focus on the music surrounding me on every side, but it's too much. The anxiety is too overwhelming. I can't breathe.

I knew getting involved with Reed was a bad idea.

I'll drag him into my mess.

He doesn't deserve whatever being attached to me might bring.

You destroy everything you touch.

I fall face down onto my yoga mat and scream until my throat is raw.

A hard, beating knock sounds on my door, and I nearly jump out of my skin at the sound of it. Yet, even as I prepare myself for one of Damien's men on the other side, the knob turns. I grab the closest thing—a yoga block—and hold it as if it's any sort of weapon—

Larry strides in half a second later without waiting on me to answer.

"Hello! I'm here—if you can hear me over this music. I've been knocking for damn ages. And I have—oh my gosh, *are you still curled up in your paralyzed position?* Wren! I texted you an hour ago," he exclaims.

I let my head drop for a beat before reaching for the remote to turn my music down enough for normal conversation.

However, one glance at the weeping plant on my fireplace mantle sends me into a deeper panic.

"Shit. What's today?" I ask as I stand.

"Friday," Larry answers. "Why—do you not know what today is?"

"Should I?" I ask as I step up to the fridge to see which color plant flag I'm supposed to water.

I've looked at the same chart for over a year—have it committed to memory—but for whatever fucking reason, I double-check it every day to make sure I water the correct ones.

Plants keep me from losing track of time.

"Today is the charity concert event," Larry says as he hangs a very large garment bag on one of the hooks by my door.

Oh.

"Oh, fuck," I manage.

Anita finally jumps off the couch, and Larry greets her with wide arms, making her tail wag so hard that her butt wiggles with it. I chuckle softly upon seeing her excitement as I fill up my water and grab a spray bottle.

Larry makes himself comfortable when I begin my plant watering ritual.

"Tell me what I need to know," I say, pushing thoughts of Damien's messages to the back of my mind.

"Okay, hair and makeup will be here in… an hour—"

"*One hour?*" I repeat, panicking slightly. "What—you give me one hour to… can they hold off a little bit? Thirty minutes even?"

Larry stares poignantly at me. "I did text you," he says. "*Very* early."

I stroke the black velvet leaf of the plant I'm watering, memorizing its pale veins for a beat before glancing Larry's way.

"I'll make it work," I concede, though the thought of forcing this timeframe on myself makes me want to curl up into another ball. "What else?"

"Young Decay is playing at… seven. You're watching them

from the upstairs VIP balcony. They'll join after for a little mingling and press. It isn't an all night event. I've been told that they need to get on the road by midnight."

I nod as I squeeze the spray bottle. "Anything else?"

"Ah… Well…"

"Oh god, spit it out," I grunt. "How bad could it be?"

"You'll be hanging out in the VIP area with Mads's fiancée," Larry says quickly.

I drop the water bottle on my foot, yet the pain barely registers as I gawk at him. Anxiety grips my insides—worse than the messages.

So much for feeling zen after yoga this morning.

"You've got to be kidding me," I say. "That's Reed's sister."

"Hang on—"

"That means I have to be *nice*."

I can feel the spiral beginning.

Larry tosses me a stress ball from the bowl on my counter as my hands begin to stretch in and out, anxious movement taking over my previously stable state.

"What if she doesn't know it's fake?" I begin. "What if she tries to get to know me? Or worse, what if she *does* know it's fake?" I ask out loud.

"Or—or, and it's just a thought, what if we *don't* panic about this," Larry suggests.

I give him a flat stare. "Great. I'll just go kill myself then. Because that's the only way I'm *not panicking*."

Larry smirks at me. "I hear she's a really nice person," he goes on. "Probably nicer than any of the others you tolerate on a daily basis."

I sigh and toss the ball back and forth, images and words already running through my head of what she might look like or what she might ask. My brain is trying to form witty answers to questions no one has ever thought of.

Except me.

"I think I need to go shower," I finally say, pressing my fingers to my temple. "Can you… can you water my plants? — Only the orange plant tabs. And they say on them how much."

Larry gives me an apologetic smile. "Lovey, I watered your plants for two months while you were on location. I think I'm fine. Anita and I are going to go on a walk after."

I swallow the dryness in my throat and nod, ears beginning to numb.

The moment I step into the shower, I turn my music back up and blast the water hotter than I can stand it.

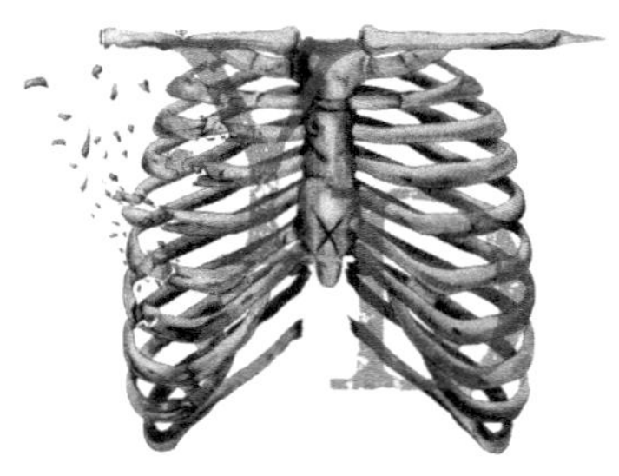

POSER BOY

Are you coming tonight?

I'll be there.

I'm already on my way to the venue, nerves continuing to plague me.

POSER BOY

Rule number six. If you're at my concert, you
meet me backstage after.

                                                        Why?

So I can kiss you.

                                    What is it with you and kissing?

I enjoy kissing, and I also enjoy pissing you
off. It's a win-win.

                        Why would you want to kiss me when you
                        come offstage? Aren't you tired? Don't you
                        want to shower?

I have a lot of energy after. Trust me. You'll
enjoy it.

                                                I doubt that.

Come backstage, and I'll prove you wrong.

I hate that he already knows challenge is my weakness.

Tara is accompanying me to the concert, along with Larry. I
asked that he come with so he could remind me of people's
names and who they are since the party after will be filled with
press, execs, and more.

I didn't even know Larry had been shopping for me, but I
trust him completely. He knows my style, my body, my curves.
He normally does a great job at taking some of my issues with
clothing into consideration—Unless it looks really hot. Then he
basically tells me to suck it up, buttercup, and nine times out of
ten, I make the sacrifice.

Tonight's dress, though…

I toy with the fabric of my black sheer dress, the asymmetrical hem reminding me to sit properly if I take any sort of bend tonight. The fabric bunches up as it hugs my dips and curves, and I'm grateful that this one allows for a lacy bodysuit beneath it. It's comfortable enough that I won't be tugging at it over and over like the last dress Larry forced me into.

Tara checks her phone again as we pull up to the back of the venue. I sent her screenshots of the messages from Damien earlier, putting her on extra alert tonight. I know she has people inside the concert hall already and that she's done her diligence pouring over the VIP guest list so that she knows exactly who will be there and who might not be supposed to be there.

She's thorough, that's for sure.

"Everything okay?" I ask when we park.

Tara sighs and closes her phone. "Looks good. I'll be around tonight even when you don't see me. One text, Wren. Even one letter. I'll be there."

I nod, anxiety pushing up into my throat. "Okay."

The roar of people talking fills my ears when we step inside. The lights are dim. Tara ushers us toward a set of stairs —but not before I hear loud, celebratory claps and a familiar voice shouting down the hall. I glance over my shoulder in time to see Young Decay exiting the dressing room. Reed jumps onto Mads's back, and the bassist spins them around and around like children.

"Wren? You coming?" Larry asks.

"Yeah," I reply. "Yeah, I'm…"

I draw my attention away from the display and hurriedly climb the stairs behind him. When we reach the lounge, Tara leads us over to a table near the balcony edge where a woman with neon-pink hair is already hanging out. She has a short drink hugged to her chest, a flannel shirt tied around her waist, covering the black shorts and fishnet tights she's wearing.

Tattoos cover her body, and I don't need an introduction to know exactly who she is.

She glances over her shoulder as we approach, and her eyes brighten upon seeing me.

"Shut the fuck up," she drawls, the smirk on her face looking entirely too Reed-like. "Wren goddamn Kelly. He said you might come, though I honestly didn't believe him." She sets her drink on the table and holds out her fist. "Andi," she tells me.

"Hey," I say as I bump her fist. "Reed's sister, right?"

As if I haven't been stalking her social media for the last few hours and learning everything I can about her.

"If that's the title we're going with," she says.

"Do you prefer sad bassist boy's fiancée, instead?" I ask.

Andi's grin widens. "Sad bassist boy's fiancée is my favorite title," she replies as a waitress comes over. "Drink?"

"Last Word," I answer as I place my bag down in the chair.

Andi lifts a brow. "I didn't peg you as a gin girl," she says.

"I always feel better torturing myself when I'm in unfamiliar surroundings," I reply.

The crowd down below begins to chant Young Decay's name. I press my hands to the banister and lean over slightly.

"That explains it," Andi jokes.

"Why wouldn't you believe that I was coming?" I ask, the sentence continuing to vex me.

Andi considers me for a moment, a soft smile growing on her lips. "I love my brother, but Reed can be a lot sometimes. I thought after the last concert, you might have decided it was too much to handle a charade with him."

So, she does know.

The waitress returns with my drink, and I sip it as I lock eyes with Andi.

"Is that an insult to me or him?" I ask, tensing.

"Neither," Andi says. She sets down her drink again and turns into me. "I don't entirely understand why you need him specifically when you could barely stand to be in the same room as him before, but I'm here to be the stereotypical older sister… Fuck with my brother's heart, and no one will find yours."

"Wow," I balk. "Guess I'll just go ahead and jump off this balcony, then. Save you the trouble. If they ask you for my last words, tell them I said something witty and mean. I'm sure you won't have a problem coming up with that."

"No problem at all," Andi replies. "I'll tell everyone to go fuck themselves in the eulogy, too."

I don't know that I've ever beamed before, but I fucking beam at her so hard that I don't recognize myself.

"I think we just became friends," Andi says.

"Is that what just fucking happened?" I reply, twirling the straw in my cup.

Andi snickers, grinning.

The house lights go down then, prompting a roar from the crowd and dragging our attentions to the stage. I take another sip of my drink when the intro begins.

"I have no intentions of hurting your brother," I tell her. "It's just for publicity, nothing else. We'll be done in a few months. All they want is for me to 'trend' enough that more execs notice me. They seem to think he'll help with that."

I don't know why I'm sharing this with her. Maybe its the two sips of my drink warming me up or the fact that we've just bonded over her threatening me.

"That's annoying," she says.

I scoff. "It's fucking ridiculous," I mutter. "You work your ass off just to get where you are and then they tell you it isn't enough. It's like being back in high school and needing to kiss people's ass so you can be crowned Homecoming Queen."

Andi gags. "If it makes you feel any better, he was never Homecoming King," she says. "Hard to believe, I know," she adds. "I'm sorry you have to deal with him that long."

I huff because I know she's joking. "As annoying as he is, at least he's not a scumbag," I say, thinking of the way he helped me at the party. "I can think of much worse people to have to fake date."

"Yeah? Like who?"

"Like my costar from the movie coming out in November," I reply.

Andi cups her hands around her mouth and shouts as the drummer takes the stage on her platform, and I join her in with my own clapping. Larry is having his own little celebration on my other side, jumping up and down, shouting their names.

"Juicy celeb gossip," Andi says. "I love it. I need you to spill the details after the concert—Yeah, Bon!" she shouts when Bonnie sits down.

Smoke rolls over the floor, sending the crowd into a frenzy.

Mads walks onto the stage then, and the grin on Andi's face is something I don't think I've ever seen on anyone. It's written in her eyes, in the way she responds to him simply being nearby.

And when Mads looks up to where we are, his eyes soften above the mask, and he holds up three fingers—signing 'I love you,' to her.

Andi signs it back without hesitation.

"You two make me want to vomit," I say when I catch her eye.

Andi laughs. "We make me want to vomit as well," she replies.

The room goes black, and from the back of the stage, Reed's voice fills the room.

I curse the chills that rise on my arms.

It's hard to hate him when he's performing.

Reed's gaze moves to the left balcony as he reaches the edge of the stage, and he grins widely. I know the grin isn't for me, because as his eyes land upon mine, his tongue swipes over his lips, and he points my way, leading into the first verse.

Larry could not be more excited watching Young Decay from this area. Everyone around us is singing along, jumping up and down every time Reed tells them to.

I find myself drowning under the bass line. I feel it in my toes, in the hair standing on my neck. Reed's voice is beautiful and haunting all at once. It's easy to see why his fans love him, why they're so protective over him.

By the time they wrap up the thirty minute set, Reed is drenched in sweat from running around. They take their bows, and as he talks about the charity, thanks everyone for their donations, and tells people to stick around for the next band, I feel the knots begin to weave in my stomach.

This was the easy part.

Rule number six.

Come backstage so I can kiss you.

My ears are ringing. I see Andi put her glass down on the table, and she jerks her head in the direction of the stairs.

"Let's go," she says to me.

"Where are we going?" I ask, my face beginning to heat.

"You're Reed's girlfriend," she says. "And Reed's girlfriend meets him when he gets off stage to tell him how hot he was. Come on. Larry will keep the table—won't you, Larry?"

"Got it covered," Larry replies.

Andi drags me to the stairs and down them, and I note the two photographers that get pictures of us together. Andi barely has to do more than smile at the security waiting to keep random people from entering backstage.

I hear Reed before I see him.

Hitting the bottom of the steps, we find him jumping

midair and chest bumping one of their equipment guys. His ankle rolls when he lands, but he plays it off with the biggest grin on his face. I've never seen him directly after a show. He's manic and full of adrenaline and…

When he spots his sister, his arms open wide, and he grabs her up before she can reply to his shouting her name.

Maybe I can sneak out of here and pretend I'm sick.

He sets her down after a spin and places a smacking kiss on her forehead, and when he looks my way, he does a double take.

"Hi," he says, his gaze raking over me like he's forgotten how to focus. His tongue darts over his lips, smirk spreading when he finally meets my eyes. "You came backstage."

"More like dragged down here, actually. Your sister was insistent," I reply, crossing my arms over my chest. I shift on my feet, hating the way he's watching me. "The set was great," I add.

"Sorry, what was that?" he asks, stepping closer.

I want to slap the smirk off his lips.

"I said the set was great," I repeat quickly.

"Hm… That was a compliment," he beams.

"It was not a compliment. I was being polite. That's what you want me to say, isn't it?" I ask.

"That's not what I want you to say," he says, cornering me in. "I want you to tell me why you came down here."

"Your sister told me Reed Matthew's girlfriends meet him backstage to tell him how hot he was," I say as my back hits the wall.

"Nothing to do with my text?"

"Nothing at all," I reply.

"Wait—you thought I was hot?" he asks.

"I thought you were mildly entertaining," I reply.

"Somehow I don't believe that Wren Kelly gets hot and bothered for 'mildly entertaining.'"

His chest brushes against mine. I glare up at him, setting my teeth.

"What makes you think I'm hot and bothered?"

"Because you're not pushing me away," he says.

Damn him.

"Rule number three. No cameras, no kissing," I manage as his fingers curl around my neck.

"I'll get a fucking camera on us," he breathes.

The words have no sooner left his lips before his mouth lands on mine.

Every ounce of the energy I'd seen him exude onstage seems to also exude in this kiss. It's just as numbing as the kiss on the field had been—just as passionate and relentless. I struggle to keep up, to contain my focus and not give in so much that I lose my mind.

I pull his hair when his hands move too close to my ass, though all it does is make him smile against my lips. And when he bends his knees and grasps me around my thighs, picking one of my legs off the floor, I can't help the way I clench around his narrow waist. My back slams into the wall again, the jolt reminding me of who exactly I'm kissing like this, and I softly squeeze his shoulder.

A camera flashes when he pulls back, his eyes so dark that barely a sliver of blue remains. The way he stares is haunting, as if he can see secrets even I don't know I'm holding onto.

He swallows, his chest heaving with mine, and he whispers, "Promise is a promise," against my lips. He kisses me one more time, releases my legs, and my feet hit the floor once again.

"Reed Matthews!" someone says down the hall.

Reed doesn't look away from me immediately. "Showtime," he mutters before letting a natural smile grace his lips. He takes my hand and throws his other up in the air in a welcoming manner, acknowledging the person coming up to us.

"Tony!" Reed exclaims.

I still haven't recovered from his kiss, yet as I look up to see who the new person is, my stomach sinks.

It's the magazine interviewer from DeathFest.

This should be fun.

CHAPTER TWELVE

REED GREETS Tony with a casual handshake. "Long time, no see, man," Reed says.

"Took a little break from the festival circuit to spend some time at home," Tony replies. "Hate I missed you guys. You've been on a fucking spree. Congrats."

"Ah, thanks. It's been insane, honestly. The trajectory went straight up this last year," Reed says.

"I hear you're taking some time off next year to work on new material," Tony says.

Reed smirks crookedly. "Here I thought this was a casual, off-the-record convo with a friend," he teases.

"You know what I'm digging for, man," Tony grins.

"Yeah, you're a fucking shark. Always with the first exclusive, right?" Reed asks.

Tony laughs. "Says the guy who just chummed the waters. You thought I was going to go back upstairs without asking for a quote after that little display? Not a fucking chance." He jerks his chin in my direction and grins knowingly. "Hey, Kelly," he says, looking me up and down. "Funny seeing you on this side of the Young Decay stage."

"I was invited," I reply as Reed sinks his arm over my

shoulders. "How's it going, Tony? I heard your wife divorced you for cheating on her with some intern," I say smugly.

Reed snorts.

Tony's mouth twists, but he chuckles softly after a beat. "Yeah, she did." He holds up his left hand and wiggles his ring finger. "Luckily, the intern was worth it," he says.

"Wow. Fast. Is that why you had to take a break from the festivals? Recovering from the whiplash you got jumping from one cunt to the other?" I ask.

Tony blinks, though the amusement doesn't leave his face. He looks at Reed and jerks his chin my way. "Is she this mean to you, too?" Tony asks.

"Worse," Reed replies with a smile.

"So, how exactly… How did this happen?" Tony asks, pointing between us. "The last anyone knew about the two of you was that your fans were basically threatening to end her career over comments she made about you—"

"Comments you so dutifully posted," I say with a sarcastic smile. "How much of a bonus did you get for that interview, by the way? It trended for a while."

Tony scoffs. "Enough to afford the lawyer for my divorce," he says.

"Glad creating animosity between us paid off for you," I say.

"Clearly, all it did was put him on your radar, thus making way for whatever this is," Tony says.

"Are you taking credit for us dating?" I ask.

"So, you *are* dating," he grins.

I bite my tongue to keep myself from mouthing off more than what I'm already doing.

Fucking with him is one thing, if I go on record saying too much or going too far, Shannon will kill me.

"Yeah," Reed recovers for me. "Mean girl meets the lovable rockstar. Tale as old as time, right?"

I resist rolling my eyes, creating a mental note to make a rule about cheesy, romantic lines in interviews.

Tony chuckles and jots down a note. "This interview might pay for the pool the little lady wants," he says with a glance at me. "When did this start?"

Reed's chest moves with his deep chuckle. "Well—"

"Keep it classy, Matthews," I say, my nails grazing Reed's sweaty stomach.

Reed smiles and looks down at me. "Do you want to tell him?"

I sigh. I think I've thought of ten different scenarios for a meet cute for us, and each one of them makes me want to vomit.

"Let's just say, he's very persistent," I reply. "We run in similar circles on occasion."

"Like the Anne Tober party," Tony says. "I heard you two had it out on the dance floor and then ended up leaving together. What, ah… what happened between those two events?"

Memory of the party almost makes me forget what we're doing here.

"I spilled a drink on her favorite dress," Reed says. "I think anyone would get upset about that."

He smiles. "And after?"

"Couple of dates and texts later…" Reed pushes my hair back and grazes his thumb beneath my chin, staring at me as if he actually likes me. "What can I say? I had to have her."

Tony chuckles. "Wore you down, huh?" he says to me.

"You have no idea," I say when I look at the journalist again.

"So, Kelly. Now that you clearly know who Young Decay is, what's it like watching him perform in front of thousands?"

Amazing.

Earth shattering.

Life changing.

"It's insane. The entire show, watching them perform. They're amazing, really. I don't know where the hell he gets the energy from," I say instead.

"Okay. So, Reed, you guys had the single release of 'Pieces' just a couple of months ago. It's getting wild radio play, especially because people are speculating it was written for Mads's fiancée—who also happens to be your sister. Is that weird?"

"Music is music," Reed says. "Pieces means a lot to all of us, not just Mads."

"And its sound—you guys included more dramatics in it. Is that a clue for what we can expect with the new album?" Tony asks.

"Dramatic shit? Hell yeah. When are we not doing things over-the-top?"

Tony laughs again, his attention turning to me. "Does he scare you as much as he scares the rest of us when he's stage diving and climbing rafters?"

"Definitely. He's absolutely chaotic," I say.

Tony grins at his notes. "That *is* what we call him," he mutters. "Surprised you haven't convinced him to simmer it down."

The question strikes something within me. "What does that mean?"

"Just… I know a lot of these guys on the road. The moment they get serious with someone, you see them start to dial things back. On stage and off," Tony replies. He shrugs. "It just happens."

My teeth grit, the playful nature of the interview suddenly coming to a halt. "If you're asking if I would ever try to stifle or contain him, rest assured that will never happen," I practically snap, stepping forward. "Reed is a rock god. If I want to put a leash on him, it'll be in the bedroom, not on the stage."

Zeb whistles as he walks by.

The moment the words leave me, I hear them echo in my ears.

Flashes of Shannon reading this and wanting to kill me while running around doing damage control runs through my mind.

Oh, mother fuck.

Why the hell did I just fucking say that?!

Tony stares at me, a smirk playing on his lips. "Thank you, Wren fucking Kelly," he drawls happily, his pen going.

Shit.

Shannon's going to murder me.

Backtrack it.

Tell him not to publish that.

Fucking fuck. Fuck!

I'm screaming inwardly. Stiff in Reed's grasp.

"Hey—" Reed nudges his chin toward Tony as he writes the quote down. "No," he says about the quote. "You don't need to quote that."

"She said it," Tony says with a laugh.

"You pissed her off, man. Come on. We both know that's bullshit," Reed argues. "I thought you were a rock mag, not a gossip columnist."

Tony shifts on his feet, staring at Reed. "What are you going to give me instead?" he asks, and I suddenly feel worse about it.

I need to crawl into a hole.

Reed chews on his mouth a little. "Exclusive in-studio interview. First listen to the new album," he offers.

Tony considers it, then glances at me. "Done," he says, holding out his hand to Reed. "You're lucky I need to be on the good side of your boyfriend. That was gold, Kelly."

Reed fucking Matthews to the rescue.

I don't respond.

I can't. If I open my mouth, who the hell knows what might fall out of it.

"All good?" Reed asks, holding out his fist for Tony.

"Yeah. All good." Tony bumps Reed's fist, smiling as he starts away from us. "Catch you two next time."

And as he walks off, I pull out of Reed's grasp, expecting him to glare at me or tell me off for being a bitch to the guy. Or worse, for having to cover for me.

But Reed is beaming at me.

"What?" I ask.

"You're fucking punk," he declares.

I wrinkle my face in confusion, heart pounding. "You didn't have to do that," I finally say.

"Yeah, I know," he says. "Figured it'd be less hassle on both our asses if I did, though. Tony's a reasonable guy. He'd have gotten the album exclusive anyway." Reed's gaze rakes over me, hands on his hips. "We have to work on your tact."

"Tell me something I don't know," I grunt, head in my hand.

God, I hate myself for this.

I hate myself even more for the next word that comes out of my mouth.

"Thanks," I say defeatedly, the word feeling disgusting on my tongue.

Reed grins. "That sounded *terrible*—"

"Oh, shut up."

Nevertheless, his laughter wanes after a few seconds, and I don't like the way he's staring at me. "You're welcome," he says.

Cold sweat beads on the back of my neck during the beat of silence that follows. I don't know what else to say, what I *should* say...

"Don't you need to shower?" I finally ask.

"Do you know how fucking sexy you look tonight?" he asks, and my face furls.

"You don't get to compliment me," I say.

"No? Is that another rule I should know about?" he asks.

"It is now," I say.

He lets out a huff of amusement. "It's just a compliment," he says. "It's not a declaration."

"Maybe I don't like the way it makes me feel," I argue.

His playfulness fades before my eyes as if he's truly taking my words in. "Okay," he says solemnly. "Ah… I'm going to go shower then. Maybe by the time I get out, you'll feel differently."

"I won't," I reply, and he takes a step back, still holding the tips of my fingers.

"One can hope," he says. "What are you drinking tonight?"

"Gin and vodka," I reply.

His brow arches. "Looking to forget what we're doing here, bird?" he teases.

"I'll see you upstairs," I say as I turn around.

I hear him slap the brick wall in a rhythmic way, almost celebratory in nature, though I don't turn around to see him leave.

Back upstairs, I make my way over to Larry, who's sitting down watching the backstage crew switch sets. There are two more bands left to play, and I know some of the people down below have been here all day.

"Do you know what's great about social media?" Larry asks as I reach him.

I give him a deadpan stare and pick up my drink to suck down the last sip. "What's that?"

He turns his phone around. "I don't even have to follow you to get updates," he says as he shows me a post of Reed and I just seconds earlier from Tony's platform with the quote,

"*I had to have her,*" followed by a small paragraph about the charity event tonight.

"Jesus fucking hell," I mutter. "Why are people obsessed?"

"Sounds adorable," he teases me. "Tell me about the first date."

"Shut up," I grunt.

The next band comes on as we're waiting. I see Bonnie and Zeb, though they're both consumed enough in conversations with others that a nod and small wave of acknowledgment is all I get from them. Not that I'm complaining. I needed a minute after using so much energy during that interview.

Mads and Andi make their way upstairs after a while, and Mads greets me with a smirk and hug that I don't expect.

"You should know, I'm not a hugger," I say when he releases me.

"And you should know, if you're dating my best friend— pretend or real—you're now part of our fucked up little family, and I'm going to hug you." He claps my shoulder. "As will Bonnie. And, god fucking help, if you ever meet the rest of his family, they will too."

My gaze moves to Andi, who has her lips wrapped around her straw, grinning slyly.

"Why would you welcome me into your group this easily?" I ask, wary of their intentions.

"Because we love him," Mads answers. "And if this is going to pass any radars, people will be looking at how we treat you, too."

I glance between him and Andi again before sipping my own drink.

"I see. Wow. I should have picked some poor, lonely bastard with nothing to lose," I say.

Mads grins. "Yeah, that might have been smarter."

We hear shouting coming from the area by the stairs, and all of us turn to find Reed yelling as he hits the top and sees familiar faces. I shake my head and turn back to the concert with Andi. Mads kisses her cheek and leaves her to join Reed.

After a few minutes, I forget why I'm there. The heavy music consumes my ears, and I find myself nodding along, whispering familiar lyrics under my breath. It isn't until I feel an arm slide around my shoulders, lips press to my temple, and a hand reach for my drink that I blink out of my daze.

Reed takes a sip and sits it on the table behind us before cupping his hands around his mouth and shouting something at the band. The lead singer's head jerks in our direction, and he points to Reed with a huge grin on his face.

"Animals," I taunt him.

Reed smiles my way. "You seem more relaxed today," he says.

I blow out a sarcastic huff. "Yeah? Must be the gin."

"Is that what it takes?" he asks, leaning his forearms on the railing. "To work out your nerves?"

"I don't have nerves," I argue.

A quiet chuckle leaves him. "Well, thank fuck for that. I'm all fucking nerves. The only time I'm not a drowning mess is on the stage."

I hate how much I want to give in and talk to him. It worms beneath my skin, nearly causing me to unwind. I shift on my feet and grip the rail tighter, hair falling over my face as I close my eyes and force words out.

"Reed, can we agree to not do this?" I ask, interrupting him.

I can see his frown from the corner of my eye. "Do what?" he asks as he straightens.

"Be… *friendly*," I say, turning into him. "We can't… I can't do this."

"You're going to have to do a better job of being mean to me, then," he says.

I feel my gaze soften. "That's going to be an issue when we're in public."

"I expect you to step up your game when we're not, then," he says, coming closer. He slips his hand around my waist and rests his forehead against mine. My breath shallows at the proximity, at the ease of the entire night.

"Do your fucking worst, bird," he tells me. "Make me go home weeping. I don't care. As long as we're doing this, I'll keep chiseling at your walls. I told you you would bend, and the fact that you're already saying we can't be friendly tells me I'm *winning*."

My teeth set. "You're wrong," I say.

He steals a swift kiss and toys with the sheer fabric of my dress.

"I think we should amend part of rule three," he says.

"Why?"

"Because this is supposed to be a new relationship that needs selling. So I'm going to be *me*, and while I know this isn't real, that won't stop me from pretending that it is. And that means I'm going to kiss you when I think I should. I'm going to hold your hand and your waist. When some prick dares to even look at you in this goddamn dress, I'm going to pretend that it doesn't bother me because I know you're coming home with me—or at least, that's what I'll tell anyone who asks."

He braces his palm against my neck and tips my head back with his thumb, and I fight how tense I've become against him.

"You want to use me for some stupid fucking PR stunt, bird? Then fucking *use me*," he hisses. "Don't think for one second that you'll get in my head."

I gawk at him, syllables unable to form on my tongue. He saves me with another kiss, and this time, I play along, opening up to him and pressing my own hand against his face, my nails digging into his jaw.

"When I say jump, you fucking jump, got it?" he says in my ear.

"Not hardly," I grit out.

"Hm…" There's a delight in his eyes that makes me want to shift. I'm not sure if it's for show, or if he's purely delighted in my attitude. "Keep it up, bird."

I scoff. "Or what?" I dare.

His gaze darts to my lips, yet he doesn't reply directly to the comment. "Are you ready to make the rounds?" he asks me.

I glance around us. "Yeah," I say. "Let's get it over with."

"Such enthusiasm," he teases. "It's like you know it's my birthday."

"Is it your birthday?" I ask.

He chuckles, and I know he's smiling like he is because a friend is approaching. "I wouldn't tell you if it was. You'd find some way to ruin it—hey, Tim."

Reed casually shakes his friend's hand, then presses his arm behind me, hand gripping the rail at the top of my ass. "Have you met my girlfriend, Wren?"

Tim—who I recognize as the drummer from a band who played the stage before Young Decay, smiles at me. "Never met, but I've seen a few modeling ads with her. Hi, Wren."

A breath leaves me when I take his hand. "I'm afraid to ask which ads," I reply.

"Let me rephrase," Tim says. "I've seen you on the posters on my younger brother's bedroom ceiling."

Reed laughs and drags me closer to him.

"Well, at least he's enjoying them," I reply.

HOLLYWOOD

CHAPTER THIRTEEN

AFTER THE TENSE night at the concert gala, I've texted Wren more than I should have—if only to get her to open up to me a little more. She barely replies with more than a few words. I know she's trying to protect herself, but fuck, it's frustrating.

And something tells me she isn't just pushing everyone away because she *wants* to be alone.

It's been a couple of weeks. I took a flight out on our day off just to attend this party with her tonight. Luckily, it's only a short flight from where our show is tomorrow in San Diego. Mads seized the opportunity to fly with me to see Andi and go with her to a dog rescue adoption interview.

The party Wren and I are heading to now is in the valley. It's an exclusive showing of an independent film whose director has expressed interest in Wren for a role in his next flick.

I'm here as a buffer.

I can tell this party is getting to her more than the concert did, though I'm not sure why. This event is more with her acting circle of friends, not musicians. I thought she would be more at ease, not fidgeting in the bench seat beside me like she is now.

She's as jumpy as I always am, constantly moving. Most people think my insistent tapping on my knee as if it's a piano is just from being a musician.

Wren is rocking back and forth—it's barely noticeable, and I only see it because I know it's there. However, the way she's tapping her ring finger on the window controls makes me chuckle.

She glares sideways at me upon hearing it. "What's amusing?"

"I thought you didn't have nerves," I tease her.

"I don't," she says.

"So, you just tap the window for no reason?"

"There is music playing," she says.

"Yeah, okay."

Her teeth set, gaze moving away from me. She sits up straight and brings her hands in front of her, then begins picking at the skin on her nails as if it's less noticeable.

"If you tell me I should stop fidgeting for any reason at all, I'm kicking you out of this car," she mutters.

"My car. My driver," I say. "Maybe I'll kick you out instead."

She doesn't say anything as she glances out of the window again, still toying with her fingers.

"Do people tell you you shouldn't do that?" I ask after a moment.

"No, they've always thought it was adorable," she says, her voice dripping in sarcasm.

I don't speak, and she peers my way, hair falling over her shoulder as she glances down at her bare feet.

She still hasn't put her shoes on.

"Yes," she admits softly. "My publicist tells me to hide my

anxiety like a duck's feet underwater. Better to be seen as a steady river than the choppy rapids."

"People who want to stifle you are afraid of being pulled under," I say, and her eyes narrow when she looks at me.

"I told you not to be nice to me," she says sternly.

I huff, feeling a smile tug on my lips. "It's kind of fun being nice to you," I say. "You don't know what to do with yourself."

She crosses her arms around her chest, and as she does, her foot begins to tap instead. I can see her chewing on the inside of her mouth, and I smirk.

"Oh, fuck," she bites out, glaring. "Now you have me aware of it."

"What do you do to get rid of them?" I ask.

She unwraps her arms and presses the heels of her hands tightly together. "Music. Yoga. Though I think I've become immune to both. Normally, by the time we reach the event, I've talked myself out of attending a few times and then told myself to suck it up and figure it out. Put the mask on and get out there."

"Great pep talk," I mutter.

"What do you suggest then?" she asks, turning into me. "Is there some magic trick you know about that I don't?"

I raise a suggestive brow her way, and her lips press into a flat line.

"Besides that," she grunts. "What do you do? Before a show. You said you were all nerves the other week."

"I thought we weren't supposed to be friendly," I taunt her.

Her jaw tightens. "Amuse me."

I run a hand through my hair. "Ah… I actually meditate for an hour before a show," I answer.

She gawks at me as if I've grown another set of eyes. "You… meditate?"

"Is that so hard to believe?"

"Yes," she says wholeheartedly. "Yes, that is very hard to

believe. How do you get your brain to turn off enough to meditate?"

"How do you get yours to turn off to do yoga?" I ask.

"Heavy metal music," she declares, and I fight laughter.

"Heavy metal? Yoga?"

"Yes. And I don't mean the metalcore you guys play," she goes on. "I mean… *heavy* metal. Death metal. The kind where you can't understand what the fuck they're saying."

"No shit," I chuckle. "I didn't peg you as a death metal girl."

"Honestly, it's only when I need to not feel anything for a few hours."

"What do you listen to otherwise?"

"Less aggressive sounds," she answers.

I grin slyly. "So you do listen to our music."

Wren glares, but doesn't answer directly. "Blasting death metal and yoga are the most numbing things I know to do without taking some kind of drug. And I'm *not* doing that," she adds as she sinks her face into her hands.

I squint at the solemn look on her face when she drops her arms onto her knees once more. "Is there a particular reason for that?" I ask.

Her throat bobs with her swallow. "We're not talking about it," she replies, shifting in her seat and straightening.

"What would you like to talk about instead?" I ask.

For a few moments, she doesn't speak. She stares ahead at the road, her mind obviously working overtime with something heavy. "I don't know," she finally says as she grabs her shoes.

"Give," I say, curling my fingers.

"Give what?"

"Give me your feet," I say.

"Why?"

"Amuse me," I reply.

She hesitantly picks her feet up into the seat and hands me her shoes, and I bring her foot into my lap before she can muster a protest.

"Tell me what about the director is so important," I say as I start massaging her insole.

Wren slumps her head onto the headrest. "He's a genius. His movies have won multiple indie awards. My agent wants me to do more mainstream movies, but I just want to act. I want to be considered for a role without it being a popularity contest. This guy... he's seen me since the beginning. We've always talked about working together, but haven't found the right role—okay, what are you doing to my feet and why is it making me talk this much?" she asks abruptly.

I huff amusedly. "Superpowers," I say. "Why did you want me to come with you to this?"

"My costar from the last movie I did will be there," she says. "I thought it would be easier to avoid him with you. Especially since he hates your music—"

"I love going to parties where people hate me," I say. "It's my favorite."

She gives me a flat stare like she knows I'm fucking with her. "This is my attempt at using you to your fullest," she adds.

"That hurts, bird," I say.

"You're the one that told me to take advantage of you," she says. "This is me. Taking advantage."

"Thorough advantage, Miss Kelly," I say, quirking a brow at her. "I don't know that I should let you get away with it."

She looks like she might find me mildly amusing. However, as my finger runs deliberately down the middle of her foot, she jerks it away from me and sits straight up.

"If you tickle me again—"

I chuckle softly and gesture for her other foot, which she hesitantly provides.

"So, what do you need from me tonight?" I ask as I start massaging her again.

She sighs and lays her head back on the headrest. "Just… support me like a real boyfriend would, I guess—a good one, though. Not some shit asshole looking to get his own name out there," she adds quickly.

"Is that from experience?" I ask.

"Something similar," she says.

"That's low."

"That's most men," she says with a sigh.

I scoff. "You're not wrong," I mutter.

"Is that your experience with men?" she asks.

I begin to massage her calf without thinking. "My experience with men is all one-night stands," I admit. "As is a lot of my experience with women, actually. Had a lot of relationships at the beginning of my career, all through college, whatever. But not everyone trusts the lead singer of a rock band for more than a few weeks."

"Do you think that's due to the stereotype or to the fact that you're a slut?" she asks.

I beam at her, a chuckle leaving me, and even James laughs in the front seat.

"Shut up, James," I say, grinning.

"She got you there," James says.

"Okay, so I don't have the best reputation—"

"When's the last time you were tested, by the way?" she continues to jab.

"Valid question." I pause, trying to remember what month it is. "Two… Two months ago. I think. That's a Stella question. She takes care of that."

"You don't keep up with your own testing?"

"I barely keep up with what day of the week it is," I answer. "We're in two or three different cities a week sometimes. You can thank James for getting me here. Stella keeps on top of anything like that that we might need. She has me and Bon tested often. Our band manager, Avie, had Mads tested when he and Andi started officially dating."

"And Zeb?"

I huff, barely realizing I've moved closer and I'm massaging behind her knee. "Zeb is… selective. He doesn't really do random hookups," I answer.

"No? Is that for a particular reason?" Wren asks.

I eye her. "Are you actually interested?"

"Not entirely, but it's keeping my mind off of what's coming, and you're a willing participant. So, keep talking, poser boy."

A quiet laugh leaves me. "Using me," I mutter.

"You're easy to use," she says. "Tell me about Zeb."

"Zeb likes… more than a random blowjob from any strange groupie," I say.

"I don't know what that means," she says. "Like he wants a relationship?"

"More like he wants to take them into the woods and chase them," I say, and Wren's eyes widen.

"He has a primal kink?" she asks. "How… how does that work with being on the road?"

"It doesn't. I think the last time he hooked up with someone was when we had a break over Halloween last year. He went back home where some of his friends were planning a Purge hunt."

"That sounds absolutely terrifying," she says.

I laugh. "That's what Mads and I thought, too. Terrifying, but fuck it might be fun to get that scared of what isn't real."

James slows at a gate to chat with the guard outside, and Wren has to roll down her window so the guard can verify it's her. Her legs fall out of my lap when she moves, I lean forward a little so I can see the mansion we're pulling up to.

"Holy shit," is all I can manage upon seeing the massive home.

"Yeah," Wren says as she flutters through her purse for lipstick.

"I thought he was an independent film director," I say as James pulls into the valet line.

Wren scoffs as she touches up her lips. "Yeah. With money coming out of his ass," she mutters. "It's how he can afford for some of his projects to flop—*shit*."

"What's wrong?" I ask as someone comes to open our door.

"I can't get my fucking shoe on," she grunts, trying to quickly hook the heels.

I chuckle and get out of the car. "Give," I say, kneeling down in front of her.

"I'm fine. I just need another thirty seconds," she says.

I sigh as I look up at her. "There's only one other reason for me to be on my knees in front of you, so unless we're saying to hell with this party and getting on with the after-party, I suggest you give me your shoes."

Her lips twist. She tosses me one of her shoes and shoves my shoulder with her other foot. "There's no after-party," she says.

I snicker as I slide her perfectly manicured foot into the slim heel.

I half expected to find a butterfly tattoo on her ankle or just above it just so I could make fun of her, yet instead, all I find is a few freckles dotting her pale skin. These pants fit snugly on her legs, and I can't fucking wait to see her stand up out of this car so I can get a good look at her outfit. The lacy bodysuit she's wearing beneath her black jacket has been calling my name the entire car ride.

I hear the click of a camera, and it makes me smirk as I slide her other shoe on.

My eyes lift to hers, and when I have the hook in place, I lean down to kiss her ankle as if the kiss is a seal.

"Please don't tell me you're one of those guys that likes feet," she says as I straighten before her.

I chuckle and extend my hand to her. "If there was a set of feet on this planet that might get me to have a foot fetish, it would be yours," I say. "They're pretty cute feet."

Wren rolls her eyes and steps out of the car. I gulp as she's revealed, as her long legs step out onto the driveway, the height of the heels bringing the top of her head to just below my nose. Fuck, these pants hug every curve of her generous hips and thick thighs, the lace bodysuit she's wearing accentuating her waist and tits. I feel my jaw tighten as I hold in a groan.

She grabs her purse and tucks it under her arm, then glances up at me.

"Something you need to say, Matthews?" she asks. "You're staring hard enough."

"It's hard not to," I say without thinking.

Her lips tighten into a thin line. "Rule—"

"I know, I know," I say quickly. "It slipped. Kill me."

"That's strike two," she adds.

I blink, my lips curling upward in a suggestive way. "What happens after three?" I ask.

The sideways glare she gives me is somehow relaxing. I can't explain it. And as she slides her arm through mine, I swear I see the faintest whisper of something not hatred gleaming in her emerald eyes.

"Let's go, poser," she says, and together, we head into the mansion.

I quickly realize that I'm a fish out of fucking water in this crowd.

No amount of parties that I've previously attended could have prepared me for this. Every person who she interacts with feels like a business deal. I make it a point to act more casual than usual, going as far as making sure to keep my hands in my pockets, my voice low. I hang back and let her chat instead of crowding her, allow her to choose when we touch, if she wants to lean into me or hold my hand.

Any friends we encounter feels like a weight off of my chest, even if our conversations don't last long.

Wren keeps asking people where Sean is, and I assume she means the director she's here to see. We turn in the directions of where people point us, eventually leading all the way into the largest fucking kitchen I've ever seen that overlooks the hills.

"There," Wren says, leaning into me.

"What?"

"The man there. Silver hair. Three o'clock," she clarifies. "That's Sean."

"Are you okay?" I ask, seeing her start to pick at the skin around her nails. "Need me to get you anything?"

"No, I'm fine—"

"Wren Kelly," Sean drawls, heading toward her with a soft smile on his face.

Wren immediately straightens, a faux sense of relaxation pouring over her outer shell. I still feel her tense, yet all this director will see is a confident woman.

"Hi, Sean," she says with a sigh.

Sean brings her hand up to his lips to kiss her knuckles when he reaches her. "You are…" He steps back and peers over her. "I know the compliment people like to give is that you light up the room, but dear, you are a black hole sucking all of us into your orbit. Stunning, as always."

Wren mumbles a "Hm," with a sardonic smile. "You have always been one for shit flattery," she says.

"And one day, you'll learn to take the compliment," he replies. His gaze moves to me, and he draws away from her.

"Lead singer from Young Decay?" He raises his brows at Wren like he's impressed, then looks up in my direction. "Bravo to you, sir. She's a hard one to land," he says to me.

"Even harder to hold onto," I say, my hand sitting at the small of Wren's back.

Sean chuckles, peering slyly between us. He speaks again, but I barely hear what he's saying. There's a man on the other side of the partition staring our way. I wouldn't think anything of it normally, yet something about him makes me uneasy. He's wearing the right clothing to fit in, though somehow, he sticks out.

"—I wonder if I might steal you for a moment, dear," I hear Sean say. "I want to personally give you the script I've been working on with Barbara."

I blink and look down at Wren when she squeezes my side. "You'll be okay by yourself?" she asks.

Sean laughs. "Dear, he's Reed Matthews. He'll be fine," he says, reaching for Wren's arm.

I glance back to the wall where the strange guy was leaning, only to find that he's disappeared.

Uneasiness worms its way into my bones, the memory of the model party coming to mind.

"Reed?"

"Yeah," I breathe, looking down at her again. "Yeah, I'll be fine. Screening starts in fifteen?" I ask Sean.

"I'll have her back to you before then," Sean promises.

I don't like letting her go, but I can't exactly say that without appearing like an asshole. So, I lean over and kiss her forehead, then flick her chin with my knuckle, making her look up at me.

"Don't forget me," I say.

I release her with a nod to Sean, gaze shifting to where the stranger had been, and I make my way out in that direction.

I pull out my phone and open it to Mads's number, shooting him a quick text and my location.

> If you don't hear from me later, here's where I am.

Mads texts back almost immediately.

MADNESS

Yeah, fuck that man.

I'm not above crashing some rich asshole's party.

What's up?

Where's James?

> James is outside. I'm good.

> You remember the weird vibes from the party? That creep?

Is he there?

> No. Could be anything. Jealous ex. Weirdo stalker. Just someone watching us.

Don't get involved. Leave it.

> Yeah, I know.

I peer around me for any sign of the guy in question, though most of what I find is simply a few leering gazes and smiles that I remind myself are off limits.

MADNESS

You're going to find him, aren't you?

> Yep

Call me before you do anything stupid.

I close my phone and push it into my back pocket as I reach the makeshift bar where I only ask for a bottle of water. I try to keep an eye on Wren as I also glance around for the guy, making note of anyone else I don't recognize—which is quite a few people. Though most of them look harmless enough.

The sound of someone laughing as they approach the bar draws me out of my daze, shifting my attention fully. I step out of the way as the man clumsily steps up and leans over to the bartender, a grin on his face, and I recognize him as the costar of Wren's upcoming film, Chris.

While I did hear her speaking pleasantly about him at the festival, my sister got a different story from Wren.

"—oh, shit—sorry, man." He's laughing as he knocks into me.

I step away from the bar and wave him off. "No worries," I reply, trying not to pay him any attention.

Has it been fifteen minutes, yet?

People seem to be making their way outside to the makeshift setup Sean has on his ridiculous lawn.

"Wait, I know you. You're the guy Wren's dating now, right?" Chris says once he has his drink.

"That does seem to be my new title, yeah," I answer him. "Reed," I introduce myself.

"Reed…" Chris's grin makes my jaw tense, though I try to stay casual. "Hey—has she told you about that night when we got snowed in on set?" Chris asks, sliding closer to me. "Talk about lighting a fucking fire—"

I already want to throat punch this guy.

"—stopped us and said we couldn't because it would ruin us on set," Chris is going on. "Guess it makes sense she's gone after some chump rock kid."

"Hey," I interrupt him, talking with my hands, "I don't… I

don't really care," I say. "Who she's fucked is her business. I don't care how she turned you down. I'm not into kissing and telling."

"No?" Chris laughs. "I thought you were some hot rockstar or something. Most rockstars like talking about who they're fucking."

"You've been talking to the wrong rockstars, then," I reply, thinking of every respectful musician I've met. I give him a slap on the shoulder and start to walk away. "It was good to meet you, man."

And just that quickly, I've lost Wren.

Shit.

"Hey, pretty boy. I'm not done talking to you," Chris calls out.

I scoff and glance back over my shoulder. "Yeah? I'm trying to find my girl, so let's just call this the end of the conversation you were trying to have. Enjoy the screening."

I need to get the fuck away from him before I lose my cool.

The strange man I'd had my eyes on five minutes earlier catches my gaze. He's ascending the stairs in the middle of a throng of people who appear to be going up there to watch the screening. I can hear Chris saying something else behind me, but I ignore him as I make my way across the room, all the while looking around for any sign of Wren.

People begin to settle outside in the chairs along the deck and the balcony. I spot Sean and a few others we'd chatted with earlier as I also make my way outside. Sean is standing next to the projector screen, and as people take their seats, he begins talking.

I barely hear him. I'm too focused on finding out where Wren has gotten to, and where the sketchy guy from the corner is lurking.

Though, as I glance upstairs, I spot the guy standing with a woman, arm wrapped around her shoulders.

I realize maybe my creep-o-meter might have been off.

So, where the hell is Wren?

I take a sip of my drink and pretend to listen to Sean's speech, standing at the back of the deck where I can see everything. The other two redheads attending this party have their hair pulled up, and in a sea of actors and models, Wren has completely disappeared.

"Did you know…"

God fucking help me.

If this guy doesn't leave me the hell alone…

"Sean's place has three levels," Chris goes on, sinking an arm around my shoulders.

"That's great, man," I say, sliding out of his grasp. "Always glad to get a lesson in Hollywood home architecture when I didn't ask for it."

Chris laughs. "You're funny. I already knew I didn't like you, but now I just feel sorry for you."

The sentence makes my gaze narrow. "Yeah? Why's that?"

Chris leans over and jerks his chin in the direction of the house. My gaze follows the gesture, and as I see what he's pointing out, I feel my jaw set.

Wren is upstairs on the third floor balcony with two men, away from the rest of the crowd. My fist curls at the way she's looking at them, the smile on her lips that I've never seen before. They corner her against the railing edge, her back hitting it as one of them reaches out and touches her arm. I expect her to swat him away, yet all she does is sip her drink.

Chris claps on my shoulder and shakes me slightly. "I think that was a record for her," he says. "What, you two were together… a month? She usually drives guys away after the first date."

"Fuck off, man," I mutter.

I set my drink down on the nearby table and glance up at the balcony one more time. The movie is starting. I have half a mind to leave her here for making me look like an idiot. I know we're not really dating, but that doesn't mean she can fuck around in front of the rest of the industry.

I have to maneuver through one of the bedrooms on the third floor to reach the balcony off of it. I can't fucking fathom why the hell she was up here anyway, unless Sean brought her up here to give her the script.

She's wearing a smirk on her lips that appears entirely flirtatious. I take a few deep breaths just to keep the person I'm becoming from rising to the surface. The rage she draws out of me is unlike anything else, and I can't figure out why.

"Hey, babe," I say loudly when I open the glass door.

Wren's smile drops the moment our eyes meet. I can't tell if it was forced or if she's terrified that I've caught her. At this point, I don't know that I care. If these guys are some of the goons she's running from, she should have texted me. I'd rather cause a fucking scene getting her away from them than her flirt and make both of us look like idiots.

"Reed," she says, her voice breathless. "I wasn't sure where you'd gone."

"I thought I lost you, too," I say. "I trust these guys were keeping you company," I add. I give the two men glaring looks, and they step back from her, allowing me to slide in and wrap my arm around her waist.

The kiss we share lingers. I pause when we part, my nose brushing hers. "Everything okay?" I ask softly.

"Yeah," she answers. Her palms push slightly on my chest, throat clearing. "Chester and Paul are old friends." She introduces them, and I swear I hear a twinge of annoyance in her tone. "They were just catching me up on the happenings back home in Connecticut."

"Yeah?" I lean my hip against the railing, pulling her tighter. "How's Connecticut, then?" I ask them.

The taller one scoffs and takes two steps back. "Chilly," he says.

"It's August," I say. "Try again."

However, the pair share a sly grin, hands stuffing into their pockets, and both their gazes narrow in on Wren.

"Lovely to see you again, Kelly," the other says. "We'll tell your brother you said hello."

Wren tenses.

"Looking forward to the reunion," the first says.

"Reunion?" I glance down at Wren. "You didn't tell me about that."

"Special invitees only," the first says. "Cost you an eye to get in," he adds, and I hate the way he grins at her.

"Oh yeah?" I jerk my chin toward the stairs. "How about you get fucked instead? Shove your reunion up your ass on the way."

"Reed," Wren hisses.

The pair chuckle. "Until next time, Kelly."

They turn to disappear down the stairs, and as they do, nausea creeps into my throat. I don't know what the hell that was about, but something tells me she's hiding a lot more than what people see on the surface.

I round in front of her, seeing a flicker of fear in her eyes that quickly disappears when she looks up at me.

"You want to tell me what that was about?" I ask, trying to keep my rage down.

"No," she affirms.

I blow out an annoyed breath. "Yeah, I didn't figure you'd be fessing up to anything."

"What are you—"

"We need to talk," I interrupt her. "*Now*."

I CAN HARDLY CATCH my breath as Reed drags me inside Sean's glass-walled bedroom.

I can still feel the ick of Chester and Paul's hands on me, hear the sound of their voices taunting me, telling me to be quiet or else. Threatening to expose me right here if I shout. I've never seen them anywhere except in cars outside of my home before tonight, and hearing Damien's name was enough to have me seething through my fake smile. If I'd shown fear, who knows what kind of security might have been called, what kind of scene they might have displayed.

And Reed…

"Why are you so upset?" I manage when he closes the door, forcing my voice stern. "Why are you acting like I've somehow hurt you?"

"Because you just made me look like a fucking idiot out there," Reed snaps, rounding on me.

"You do that just fine by yourself," I seethe without thinking.

His tongue darts out over his lips as he presses his hands to his hips and paces in a circle, head shaking toward the ceiling. I sink my arms around my chest.

It wasn't my fault.

I didn't have a choice.

"How did I make you look like an idiot?" I ask, pretending to be dumb.

"Because you were out there flirting with those two guys as if you forgot how to be mean," he says. "What—did your bitch badge suddenly disappear? Are you doing this out of some twisted desire to see how far you can humiliate me?"

"Not everything is about you," I grind.

"Then enlighten me," he says. "Tell me what the fuck that was all about. Who were those guys? Were they part of the goons trying to scare you? Should I be worried?"

You should be running.

"I told you, they were old friends. And I don't have to explain anything to you." I grab my purse from the table where I'd left it earlier and start for the door. "I have to go. People are waiting on me."

"Hey—" He grabs my arm and whirls me back into him, catching me at the small of my back so that I can't break away. His eyes are wild, barely a fraction of blue around his swollen black pupils. It's devastatingly hypnotizing, and I feel my nostrils flare as he continues speaking.

"Rule eight: It doesn't fucking matter whether this is pretend or real… When you're with me, you're *mine*."

The claim makes me nauseous. It settles uneasily in my core and alerts my every muscle. I'm ready to flee, ready to run away from his flagrant possession.

I shove him harshly, nails catching on his collar as I do. "Don't do that," I snap.

Reed gives me a downcast glare, his jaw tight. "Do what?" he asks.

"Claim me like some *possession*," I argue. "I'm not some play thing you get to toss around."

A scornful huff leaves him. "I'd like to do a lot more than just *'toss you around,'*" he says deliberately.

Our eyes meet, combined rage giving way to something more aggressive and licentious beneath it. His stare is eating me alive, and I'd like to take that anger and see how far I can stretch it, how aggressively he'll 'toss me around.' I'd barely been able to breathe earlier when he massaged all the way up my leg, treading too close to my inner thigh.

I swear, he barely noticed how close he was to me.

"Tell me," I say.

"Tell you what?" he growls.

"Tell me what you want to do to me," I dare him.

Reed looks as if he wants to swallow, as if nerves sit on the very tip of his tongue but he's pressing them deep down into the very depths of his soul so as to appear entirely confident in what he's about to say.

That same sick sense of pride fills my gut.

I've made him nervous.

I've burrowed beneath his precious good-boy skin.

I've brought out an anger that only those close to him have ever seen.

Empowerment dances in the goosebumps that rise on my arms as he peers me over.

"I want to make you regret having ever looked at me," he says, and the hatred in his rasp forces me to inhale a jagged breath. "I want to hear you beg for forgiveness for every shit word you've ever said to me," he goes on. "I want you on your fucking knees and staring up at me with a mouthful of my cock, mascara-filled tears falling down your wrecked face as you gag—"

"As if your dick will come remotely close to choking me," I challenge.

A muscle feathers in his jaw, and I roll my eyes at his frustration.

"What else? Get creative, Matthews. I'm waiting," I go on. "Tell me what you *really* want to do to me."

In a snap, he thrusts his hand around my throat and throws me into the wall. I jerk against his grip, but it's tighter than it was the night at Anne's party—as if he's no longer afraid of what I might do in retaliation.

Like he means to make it hurt.

"Let go of me," I manage, stretching my chin upward in an attempt to free my windpipe of his crushing grip.

"No," he says, his mouth an inch from mine.

"Reed—"

"If you wanted fucking gentle, you should have found some other idiot who you knew would be too scared to push your buttons," he says, fingers digging in the soft space beneath my jaw. "You should have dug a little further into who I really am or either found someone willing to worship you out of fear of pissing you off. Because that isn't me. Keep talking, bird. I don't fucking care."

My breath catches as he leans forward, his nose dragging across my cheek.

"You send me to my absolute limit," he says, an obvious restraint in his voice. "To the edge of my will. I want to lick the tears from your face when you bleed beneath me… I'm going to make you hurt, bird," he swears, and my chest caves at the promise. "I'm going to steal, rattle, and break every part of you," he hisses against the shell of my ear. "And you're going to take it like a good little princess—"

"I'm not your fucking princess," I seethe.

"No," he agrees, staring into my eyes. "You're the annoying melody that I can't get out of my head. You've wormed beneath my itching skin, and the only way I know that I'll ever be able to cure myself of your sickness is to bury myself within you." He leans forward, breath skimming my lips. I feel my eyes flutter at the tickle of it, at how he's suddenly staring at my mouth as though he's going to devour me whole.

"Tonight, I'm going to fuck you until one of us collapses," he swears. "Until neither of us can lift our limbs, and we're pleading for the other to stop. Long after we're covered in bruises and blood from fighting over how much we *don't want this*…"

His lashes lift, and as our eyes meet, he increases the pressure on my neck again, and this time, I don't try to get away.

"If you're truly trying to hurt me, the joke's on you," I say.

"Why's that?" he whispers.

"Because I'm into that shit."

His lips crash onto mine.

The kiss is somehow more aggressive than the public ones he's met me with before. Somehow more consuming and mind-numbing. Maybe it's his grip on my throat that has me light-headed enough to see stars, but for whatever reason, I believe his promise. I can feel it in his tightening fingers, see it in his rage-fueled eyes.

I claw my fingers down his neck and wrap them into his hair, pulling and tugging to the point that he groans into my mouth. The groan does something to my insides—whether it's pride at drawing this out of him or delirium, I don't know.

I want to hear it again.

He grabs at my waist, my hip, my ass, chipped nails digging into my skin and bruising me like he means to rip my skin off. At some point, my thigh wraps around his waist. I'm pulling him closer and closer with a sudden, overpowering need to feel his body pressed to mine.

And when we part, I swallow at the darkness in his gaze.

"Why did you stop?" I ask breathlessly.

Don't stop.

A light flashes into the room. It averts my attention before I can say anything about the kiss or the way he's grabbing me. I turn slightly in its distracting direction, and my insides sink.

We're making out in the middle of a glass-walled room, a hundred people able to see us a floor below.

"Shit," I say under my breath.

"I didn't figure you wanted anyone to see," Reed says roughly.

The gaze he meets me with raises the hair on my arms. The look is dark, sensual, and makes me feel as if he would have no problem if everyone watched him rail me sideways in this glass room—might prefer it even.

Reed releases me and presses his phone to his ear, a number already dialed. "Hey—no, can you pull around really fast? Yeah, we're leaving. Hey, and call Stella. I need a hotel room nearby for tonight."

He hangs up and looks toward everyone who's staring, then holds both arms up, his middle fingers flashing on both.

"What—" I narrow my gaze at him. "No, we're not leaving. The screening isn't over."

Please make me leave.

Reed hauls me into him and kisses me harshly. It catches me off guard, though not nearly as much as the way I respond to that kiss with as much fervor as his. I find my fingers ripping at his hair and leaning into his body when he pulls me tighter. I'm breathless when we part, and he doesn't let me go at once.

"Do you have your script?" he asks.

"Yes."

I don't want to be here any longer.

"Did you need to kiss Sean's ass and tell him how amazing this dumb film is?"

"No…"

"Then unless you'd like for all of these people to watch you get fucked against a glass wall, we're leaving."

I gawk at him. "You need to work on your patience," I say.

Reed laughs. "I have zero fucking patience with you, bird," he says as he slips his hand into mine. "Let's go."

I barely have time to glance back at the crowd still staring outside as he drags me down the stairs. I don't know where Paul or Chester have gotten to, if they watched our display, or if they decided to take a fucking hike.

I don't even have time to apologize to Sean.

Whatever.

I'll text him later.

James gazes at me for a longer moment than I'm used to when we reach him. "Everything okay?" he asks, and somehow I get the feeling he doesn't just mean between Reed and me.

"Just fucking peachy," Reed says.

Reed gets into the SUV, and as he does, James meets my stare. "Anything I should know about?" he asks me.

I don't know why the question strikes me in my gut, and it bothers me that I can't tell if he's just being protective of his client or if he knows something more. Either way, I shake my head and climb into the vehicle behind Reed, ignoring the look James gives me when he closes the door.

We're pulling up to the hotel when it hits me that a hundred people just watched Reed choke me.

"Goddammit," I mutter.

"What?" Reed practically snaps as we come to a halt.

"Pretty sure people just recorded you with your hand around my throat," I say, glancing sideways at him.

"I'll be right back," James says, hurrying out of the front.

"They also just recorded the most real appearance they're ever going to get," Reed says, opening his own door.

James is already inside chatting with the front desk.

Reed holds out his hand to me. "Come on."

I swat him away. "The moment is over," I argue. "You can take me home."

"That's not going to work for me," he says.

"Why's that?"

"Because I'm giving away free face rides to sexy redheads that infuriate me."

I stare at him flatly. "Odd time to joke."

"Odd time to choose not to like your pussy eaten," he retorts. "Are you going to come with me or should I tell James to park the car in the garage and stand outside?"

I don't speak, and Reed sighs, his hands pressing to his hips.

"Wren, if you really want to go home, then just say so," he says defeatedly. "Tell me to go fuck myself. I'm not forcing something you're not interested in."

I consider him for a short moment.

I should tell him to go fuck himself.

I should tell him he's an ass, and that I hate him.

Fuck this.

All I want right now is for him to angry-fuck me into the next life—or at least until I can't remember my own name.

I grab my purse and slide out of the vehicle.

REED'S EXPRESSION doesn't change when I step up to him, my chin rising so that our faces are just a fraction apart.

"You talk a lot of shit, Reed Matthews," I say. "Don't think this changes anything. We're not going to be friends after this, nor will this get any more 'real.'"

A smirk tugs at his lips. He entwines our fingers together and leans down to my ear. "You can tell me how much you still hate me after squirting on my face," he rasps.

I laugh sardonically and shove him. "You're so fucking full of it. You can't make me do that. *No one* has ever made me do that."

Reed scoffs. "I'll take that bet."

He pulls me out of the way of the door and closes it behind me. James appears out of the hotel, keycard in his grasp that he hands off to Reed and me, ending the exchange with a fist bump. It's the only goodbye Reed gives his bodyguard before the SUV pulls away, and Reed leads me through the hotel to the elevator.

There are too many people around us. Between the bellhop and other guests glancing in our direction, I feel my neck heating. *What the fuck am I doing?* Thirty minutes ago, some goons were threatening my life, and now, I'm going to a hotel to get fucked?

God, what is wrong with me?

Reed's hand tightens on mine, and as the guests exit on the next floor, he pulls me flush, knuckle beneath my chin.

"Stop overthinking it," he breathes, squeezing my waist. His mouth brushes over my jaw, teeth tugging at my skin. "It's just sex."

I curse the way the hair on my neck stands with his breath against my ear.

"I'm not overthinking anything," I manage.

"No?" His teeth drag over my jaw, tongue following the nipping line. "I can't wait to see you undone over me… How wet this pussy is… " He kisses the soft space beneath my ear. *"All for me."*

It doesn't matter that my mouth is dry or that I can't stop my eyes from fluttering at the tease of his touch.

I'll make him earn me.

"You'll need to work harder for that," I tell him. "I'm not one of your groupies. I don't start dripping at the sound of your voice."

"Hm," he mutters as his thumb swipes over my lip. "There's a goal to reach."

"There's no goal—"

The elevator dings. He grabs my hand and whisks me out of the elevator without another word. The suite is at the end of the hall, and Reed doesn't hesitate before putting the keycard in and throwing open the door.

I give him a sideways glare as he shuts it behind us, his gaze dragging over me as if it's taking every restraint he's capable of not to throw me onto the kitchen island right then and there. He shrugs his jacket off and advances on me after I toss my bag into a nearby chair. My jaw clenches, a glaring hatred resting in my gaze as he reaches beneath my chin and his thumb swipes my lips.

"You're trembling," he breathes.

"You're mistaken," I hiss. "You see what you want through that fat ego of yours. Not everyone wants to get on their knees to worship you."

"I don't ask that you get on your knees or that you worship me. All I want is to watch you eat your fucking words," he says.

"And now, you'll get nothing out of me," I seethe.

His lips land aggressively on mine. I don't close my eyes, and neither does he. Our eyes are locked through the kiss—the challenge present in our entwined bodies. He pulls back from my mouth, biting my bottom lip hard enough to split the skin when he does. I wince at the surprising sting, and Reed licks the blood away.

I can see the scarlet color on his tongue when he hisses, *"Watch me."*

The iron tang hits me with our next desperate kiss. I claw my fingers down his neck, fighting against every part of me that wants to give in and see how far over the edge he can truly take me.

But I won't willingly succumb to him.

I refuse to give him any kind of satisfaction.

"Pick a safe word," he says as he tears at my pants. "Something completely ridiculous."

"Your name, then," I reply. "Because it's ridiculous that you think I might say it while you're trying to find my clit."

A smirk licks at his lips. "Bananas," he says.

I stare at him flatly, trying to ignore the way my thighs tighten when he drops to his knees to take my pants off. "Really? That's the best safe word you can come up with?"

"Shit," I hear him mutter under his breath. I frown at him, noticing that he's staring at my hips and swiping one hand over his face, his other squeezing the outside of my thigh. "Jesus, fucking hell—is this a thong bodysuit?"

My brow quirks at the outline of his already hardening cock when he stands, the memory of the guitarist barely able to fit his lips around it springing to mind.

I haven't even touched him…

I lift my eyes to his, meeting his dark stare. He looks like he's going to pounce on me, like he's going to eat me alive if I give him the chance.

"Bed. Now," he tells me.

"You don't tell me—"

Reed grabs me by my jaw and shoves me into the wall. His free hand pins mine beneath it by my head. I twist, but he has me wholly at his mercy.

I want to hate it.

Even still, something about the move prompts goosebumps to rise on my arms. Warmth floods between my thighs. And when he puckers my lips between his fingers, only an inch from his, I hear a noise leave me that can't be mistaken for anything else except desperation.

"You're going to get your ass on that fucking bed and sit on my face before I lose my goddamn mind over you," he says in a strained voice. "Or do you need me to fuck you right here against this wall?"

I wiggle my face out of his grasp. "I think I like you losing your mind over me," I hiss.

Reed huffs. "You'll like it even more with my tongue in your pussy."

His lips crash upon mine again, and this time, I scratch his bare chest, his neck, his cheeks.

I *do* prefer him losing his shit like this. He's manic and unhinged, and as much as I detest being told what to do, when he says it, I almost comply.

I want to ruin him.

He tugs me with him toward the bed, his ass hitting it after his knees. I start to straddle his lap, but he halts me standing with his hands beneath the thigh hems of this bodysuit.

"Off," he says, slapping my ass as the word leaves his lips.

I peel the straps down, keeping a look at him as the lacy fabric rolls over my skin and reveals my breasts.

"Jesus fucking hell," I hear him mutter. He grabs my tit with one hand and sucks my nipple into his mouth, his other hand dragging the snug suit off. And once I'm bare, Reed pauses to groan.

"Shit, you're fucking incredible," he breathes.

He slides his hand between my thighs, the other wrapping behind my neck, and he pulls me into a kiss as his finger dives into my pussy.

God, I haven't been touched in so long that one long digit is enough to make me wither into his grasp. I bend my knees and straddle over his lap, hands bracing against his shoulders as he slides his finger into my pussy, dragging the wetness that I hate my betraying body for to my clit.

"What was that about my voice not making you wet?" he says into my mouth.

"Just shut up already." I shove him backward, and the smirk on his lips makes me want to scratch it off. Even so, he slides up toward the headboard and gestures for me with only a crook of his finger.

I wonder just how much talk he actually is, or if he can live up to the hype he's created around himself.

Without speaking, I move toward him, and when I'm straddling his face, Reed blows out an audible groan and wraps his arms up around my ass. The sensation makes me jerk, though not nearly as much as I do when he licks me.

Thank fuck for this headboard.

Oh. My. *God.*

I thought when he said he wanted to eat me, he meant it

like every other guy I've ever been with. A few licks, maybe suck on my clit for a moment just to make me feel as if I'm special. Tell me he's done with me after a couple of minutes because his jaw is getting tired…

However, just like the kiss he met me with on that field, he's a surprise.

Reed Matthews *devours* me.

I can hardly stop myself from whimpering pathetically with every suck and drag of his tongue. He's squeezing my ass and hips, holding me in place when I try to move my hips or jerk away. It's almost too much.

He's almost too much.

But fuck… too much feels *too fucking good.*

Every thought in my head evacuates. I forget whose face I'm riding, whose tongue is inside me. I forget that I should be pushing him away, not letting him see me in this raw state.

Because there's no hiding what he's doing to me, how he's making me feel.

I grab onto the headboard and cry out, my eyes shutting tightly as tears prick the corners. I don't think I've ever been as pathetic and at someone's mercy as I am right now. All I can see are his eyes on me, his chipped black nails digging into the tops of my thighs as he holds me in place.

I'm beginning to teeter on the edge of my will, my orgasm rising up and up. It's in my goddamn throat, stretching out to my fingertips and my toes.

"Holy fuck—*shit*—" I almost fall backward in an attempt to stop him from sending me over this edge that I've never reached before.

"Oh my god—*Reed*—*Fuck*—"

He doesn't let up. He slides two fingers in me as I stop breathing, as I jerk in his grasp. Those digits curl inside me, the motions brushing my spot, his lips puckered around my clit and dragging me further and further into his clutches.

I try to stop it.

I try not to whimper. I try to stop the tears streaking down my face.

But fuck, it's too much.

I can't—

My entire body shakes. Chills pour over my skin. I release in such a way that I haven't done before, and when I feel a warm wetness escaping me, I almost scream.

Son of a fucking bitch.

I come and come, wave after wave. Sound mutes. Tingles erupt inside me. It's a crash and hit like nothing and everything all at once.

I think I'm genuinely crying.

Reed grabs me by the hips and pushes me backward. I fall onto my back without any kind of argument, my body unable to begin recovering from whatever the hell he just did to me. I feel my back arch, and another whimper leaves me when he stands from the bed to take his pants off.

Triumph rests on his smug, glistening face. The sight of it is sobering. I blink and wipe my eyes, refusing to let him see all that he's pulled from me.

"You're flushed and crying, bird," he says. "Are you embarrassed of the way your pussy responds to me?"

"Nothing *responded* to you," I manage, trying not to stare at the sight of his now fully naked body in front of me. The tattoos at the defined vee of his hips. The blacked out parts of his muscled thighs. The motion of his hands as he folds his black pants as if he's deliberately taking his time right now because he knows I'm staring.

And—*fucking hell*—the tip of his hard dick is glistening with precum already.

I force my gaze to his face, trying not to think about him and the guitarist. "I was enjoying a perfectly good fantasy."

He crawls back over me and chuckles against my neck. "Liar," he bites out.

"How would you know?" I ask, feeling his cock slide against my abdomen.

I'm still shaking.

"Because you've already said no one's ever made you squirt before, and yet... *fuck*. You squirted beautifully," he rasps. "I might have to buy the hotel a new mattress when I'm done with you."

I shove his face back, and he catches my wrist before I can slap him. A smile licks at his lips, his shaggy hair falling over his eyes. He tauntingly kisses my palm, causing my blood to boil, my body to squirm.

"There's something you should know about me," he says, his hoarse voice like the vibrations of a bass line. "The angrier you try to make me, the harder I get. So, keep fighting me. Keep slapping me. Until you say your safe word, I'm not stopping. I promised you would break, and I intend to rake out every last bit of your soul and rage—even if it means stealing it in tiny little shreds. I'll *claw* my way into you."

I want to choke him.

I want to watch him beg me for air.

He leans down and pushes his pelvis up, his dick brushing along my pussy. "Do you feel that, bird?" he hisses. "Do you feel what your bratty little attitude does to me?"

I glare at him. "You have issues, Matthews," I say plainly.

"You don't know the half of it."

"My pussy isn't going to solve any of them," I go on.

"That's a shame," he says. "Because I think..." His tip tickles my entrance, and for some reason, I find my hips rising to meet his. "I think fucking you until you can't feel the rest of your body will make me feel a lot better."

I already can't feel my body.

"You're full of shit," I say.

He smirks over me. "Resist me, then."

Thank god my cunt is still salivating from his tongue. Because when he rams inside me, I feel him in my throat. A high-pitched squeak leaves me. I fist the sheets, legs hiking higher.

Oh my—

"Oh, *fuck*—" My jaw drops as I squirm to adjust, to take him without completely falling apart and whimpering at his fill, but he pulls out, his tip tickling at my entrance—

I gasp when he slams relentlessly inside of me again. No mercy. No ease. No care for the way he's stretching me.

Just fucking *him*.

"That's it… Take it, little bird," he growls. "Take every last fucking inch of me."

The cry that leaves me prompts a smile to split his lips. He wraps his arm beneath my thigh and hikes my leg higher, allowing him deeper and deeper with every unfaltering thrust.

Mother fuck.

Why does this feel so fucking good?

He's hitting my spot every goddamn time he pushes inside, and the way he's angled has me gulping and struggling to remember to breathe. I can't stop my hips from rising to meet his, my back from arching into him. He bites my hardened nipple, tugs it into his mouth, and I shove his face away and pull him back within the same second. His lips land on mine. I dig my nails into his cheek, scratching him off of me and somehow begging him for more.

The tears are back in the corners of my eyes. Whimpers and cries leave me that only make him drive harder.

His snicker vibrates in my ears. "You might hate me, but your pussy fucking loves me," he says against my throat.

"Shut *up*," I manage, fingers pulling in his hair. My mouth drops as he sinks his head between my breasts, sucking my skin into his mouth and nipping at my freckles. I feel him move his hand between us and slide down my stomach until he reaches my clit.

"*Oh my god—*"

I barely get the words out before Reed grabs my face with the same hand he'd just had between us and forces me to look at him. A darkness rests in his cold eyes, vacant of amusement and swelled with a smugness I don't think I've ever seen on anyone else.

"God is a construct put together by people who needed an explanation for things they couldn't explain," he hisses. "In this bedroom, *I'm* the one making you feel those things. So, the next time you call out for your *god,* remember I'm the one answering."

My nostrils flare. "I don't have a god, and if I did, his name sure as fuck wouldn't be Reed Matthews."

Reed chuckles, then captures my bottom lip between his teeth as if accepting the challenge. He slaps my ass and pulls out of me, then jerks his chin toward the headboard.

"Grab it," he says.

"Cute," I snap. "I don't need to—*fuck*—" My words cease. I bite my tongue, a pathetic sob sounding from me when he picks my thigh up onto his chest and slams inside me once again. My hamstring is stretched, body pulling at the state he has me in.

I grab the rails of the headboard without thinking, and I hear him snicker triumphantly.

"Music to my fucking ears," he says.

I'm throbbing, holding my climax at the edge already. I don't want to admit how far gone I am, how much I need to release.

"Fuck you," I grit out.

Reed wraps his arms around my thigh, his pace picking up. He sticks his finger in his mouth, wets the digit, and I realize on his next thrust what he's doing. He reaches between us, the pad of his middle finger dragging over my clit, and I jerk at the added sensation.

"Mother fuck—"

I can't feel my arms.

I need to come again. I'm trembling. Between the deepness of his dick and the pressure of his teasing finger, I'm once more on the verge of withering and crying beneath him.

I hate him.

I hate him.

I fucking—oh— "*Fuck!*" I screech in a voice I don't recognize.

I think I black out.

The release rocks into my bones and has me squirming voraciously against his continued motions. I come and come, unable to stop my pussy from throbbing around his dick, unable to form coherent words.

"That's it—oh, *shit*, that's it—Shit, that grip—"

His eyes scrunch, mouth dropping. His grasp on my leg has it numb.

He comes with a groan that sends a chill down my arms. I feel him release deep inside me. He drops my leg and bends over me, his face still askew when his forehead lands on my breasts. I gulp the dryness in my mouth, feeling our chests rise and fall against one another as we struggle to regain composure.

"If you think we're going to cuddle, you're sadly mistaken," I finally manage.

He scoffs against my chest, kisses my sternum, and sits up, slowly pulling his dick out of me as he does. The vacancy makes me feel empty. God, the pit he's left behind has my chest caving in response.

A smirk lifts his lips when he peers down at the cum leaking from my pussy.

"For two people who hate each other, we make one hell of a sexy mess," he says.

I shove him backward, making him fall on his ass at the foot of the bed, though it doesn't phase him.

"I'm taking a shower," I say, standing. "You can let yourself out."

Reed scrambles up from the floor and reaches for my hand. My eyes narrow when I look back at him. Even so, he isn't looking at my face. His gaze is wandering down my bare body as if he means to devour it just as wickedly as he did minutes earlier.

"Come to my concert when I'm back in LA," he says.

"Why?" I ask.

"Because that's what girlfriends do, in case no one told you."

"I missed the memo," I mutter, turning back around to go to the bathroom.

Reed tugs me into him, my wobbling legs giving way despite my want to fight. I shove him, fighting to get away, but he grasps the bend of my hips so tightly that I have to suck air through my teeth.

"You're the one who needs me, bird," he practically growls, long fingers holding me in place. "I don't know what you're running from, and I haven't decided if I care. But I know that I enjoy testing your every limit—" He grabs my hair and tugs my head back, exposing my neck to his lips. "—and once I break through this exterior you're clinging so *desperately* to, I'll have you begging for me—"

"Don't think this is happening every time," I seethe.

He chuckles deeply and kisses my collar. "We'll see."

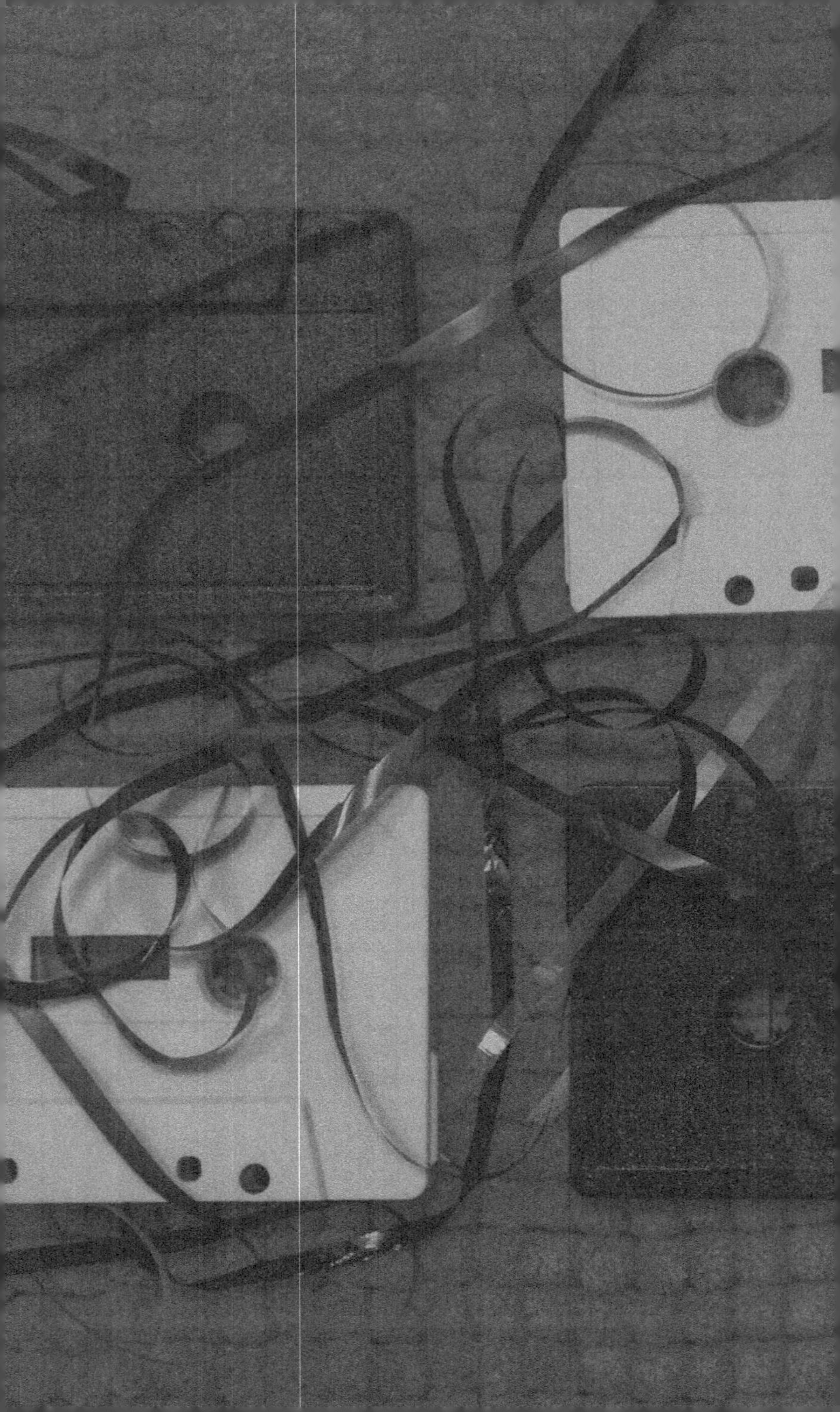

CHAPTER SIXTEEN

I THOUGHT there was nothing like the restlessness that the stage brings me.

I thought the only way to get this fitful feeling out of my bones was performing.

But *god fucking dammit*… Being with Wren… It comes fucking close.

I can't get the taste of her out of my head. I can't get how her pussy felt gripping around me off of my mind. I hear her whimpering every time I close my eyes. God, I haven't slept in a week. Watching porn and jerking off isn't enough. I need to see her. I need her fight. Her anger. Her hatred.

That *smart fucking mouth.*

Jesus.

I'm a moron for getting involved with her.

I run my hand behind my neck and lean over my knees, still staring at a photo of her and I from the charity concert. It's hard to believe so much fire rests beneath the surface of the coy smile she has on her lips in this picture.

The sound of Mads talking on the phone nearby makes me look up. He's pacing with one hand in his pocket, his hood up over his head, yet that fucking smile on his face…

Andi will be at the Las Vegas concert this Friday. I'm excited to see her, and yet, for whatever fucking reason, it also punches a hole in my gut.

A hand squeezes my shoulder before I can dwell too much over my own solitude. "Hey—you ready?" Rock, our sound guy, asks.

"Yeah," I answer as my phone buzzes. I see the number on the screen and immediately hold a hand up to Rock. "Just give me a second."

It's Wren.

I glance back up at Mads who's laughing, and suddenly, the thought of talking to Wren makes my heart twist in a way that confuses me.

And yet, when I read back the texts she and I sent each other the day after the screening, a warmth blooms in my chest, and I shift in my seat.

BIRD

You stopped by the front desk and gave them
money for a new mattress?!

The look on the manager's face had been worth it.

Bird... did you not feel how wet the bed was?
It would be bad manners to let anyone else
use that after us.

You're obnoxious.

Do you buy a bed after every rendezvous?

Honestly, no one's ever squirted as
spectacularly as you did. I think I need to see
if I can do it again.

For research purposes.

And I think you got lucky. That will never
happen again.

Challenge accepted.

That wasn't a challenge.

We'll see.

The new message and photo catches my attention then, and I stare at it for a moment before replying.

BIRD

Have you seen this?

It's a photo of us the night of the screening… Kissing against the wall with my hand on her neck. My insides reel at how fucking sexy it is. Another text comes through, this one a link to a video. I click it and realize it's a segment from a notorious gossip channel on YouTube. And as it starts to play, I push my headphones on.

"—this one today from a private screening in the Hills," one host is saying. "Now, this was a party put on by indie film director, Sean Livingston. The anonymous person who sent in the video and pictures says Wren Kelly and Young Decay lead singer, Reed Matthews, were seen entering the party together, hand-in-hand—you know, the whole nine. Looking very cozy right? Then, Kelly starts flirting—"

"Flirting?" the other host scoffs. "Are we… are we sure we have that right?"

"Yeah, even sources say that Kelly was acting off," the first replies. "Anyway, Matthews finds her upstairs, and they argue in Sean's bedroom away from everyone, apparently not realizing that almost everyone at the screening in Sean's backyard can clearly see

them through the glass walls. The guy pushes her against the wall, chokes her out, and then, in a twist—they start making out."

"Some kinky shit, bro," the second laughs.

"Yeah, you know, people in our comments this morning when we posted about this went wild. A lot of them were on the side of 'this is hot,' but a select few were telling Kelly to run for the hills."

"Just fucking get out of there," the second says, arms animatedly moving his arms in jest. "Looks to me like Kelly was into it."

"I mean... Let's be honest. If Reed Matthews pushed you against a wall and started making out with you, you'd be into it, too," the first replies.

"Yeah, I would," the second says. "I think we'd all be into it."

"My wife would give me a pass," the first says.

"You would give your wife a pass, too," the second adds.

"Only if she lets me watch," the first says. "We were talking a few weeks ago about the interview these two did after the charity concert. People were still unsure of whether this wasn't just a publicity stunt then. I mean, still could be, but I think most of those people are doing some backtracking. How about you?"

"I definitely am," the second says.

I pull off my headphones and hit the video call button on her contact. I don't know if she's going to answer, but for some fucking reason, I feel like torturing myself by seeing her.

She answers with an annoyed look on her gorgeous face. "What?"

"That's no way to greet your boyfriend," I taunt.

Her lips press together thinly, and she props the phone on

something in front of her. "Fine. Hi, honey. Are you getting ready for your little band gig?" she says sarcastically.

I chuckle at the mockery. "Yeah, something like that," I say as I reach for my tea. "I watched that video."

"I'd like to punch them in the face," she mutters, reaching for a cracker and sitting back in her chair. "At least speculation is calming down."

"What are you eating?" I ask when she crunches down on the cracker.

"Wheat Thins and cheese," she says. "And wine."

"No real food?"

"Forgot to go shopping," she answers. "I'll order takeout later and send Larry for groceries in the morning—Why are you being nosy?"

"Just trying to figure you out," I say.

"Yeah. Well. You shouldn't. People around me have died for less," she says with a fake, flat smile. "Where are you?"

"I have no idea," I admit. I glance over my phone toward where Stella is standing. "Hey, Stels. What city are we in?"

Stella looks up from her phone. "Dallas. Do you need anything?"

"Ah… more tea," I say, holding up my nearly empty mug.

"You can't get your own tea?" Wren asks me.

"You can't get your own groceries?" I say, looking back at the phone.

She twists her lips and points at the screen. "Right," she mutters as she grabs a slice of cheese.

Something about her relaxed state has me wondering if she's just had a good morning, or if she's actually getting used to me.

I'm willing to find out.

"Are you coming to my concert this Friday?" I ask, only knowing that we'll be in Vegas because Andi is supposed to be driving out, though she may not stay for the concert since she'll have she and Mads's new dog, Zero, with her.

"The one in Vegas? Do you really want me there?" Wren asks.

"Why wouldn't I?" I ask.

"Because you'd have to act like you like me along with putting on your own performance," she replies.

"I do like you," I admit, to which she furls her entire face in disgust.

"Ew. Why?"

I don't really know myself.

Yet something about her is entirely addicting—even if we're fighting most of the time.

"What happened to licking my tears while I bleed?" she taunts, tilting her head. "Making me hurt?"

A chuckle leaves me. "I still want to make you hurt," I reply. "It isn't one or the other. Besides, it's fun breaking you down," I say, and the annoyance slides from her face.

"As much as I hate you saying that, it's much better than you telling me I'm a likable person," she says.

I grin crookedly. "So you'll come to my concert?"

"Why do you want me there?"

"Because I want to fuck you sideways after and hear that little noise you make when I'm drawing out your stubborn fucking orgasms."

"*Jesus fuck,* dude," I hear Zeb curse nearby.

I smirk at him over my shoulder, and he shakes his head, chuckling at me.

"There's no noise," Wren argues. "And you should also know, you cannot choke me out anytime you want."

"And you should know, you have my full permission to choke me any time *you* want," I reply.

"I'll remember that next time you get on my last nerve." She brings her glass of white wine to her lips and downs a large swig. "I told you the sex isn't happening every time we see each other."

"Fine," I say with a shrug. "I'll climb the rafters to kiss you during the concert instead."

"Oh god," she drawls. "Hell no. Please don't."

"What is it with you and dramatic gestures?"

"Because I don't know what to do with myself," she argues. "Am I supposed to smile? Blush? Pretend to be surprised?"

I almost laugh at the anxiety in her voice. "You're literally an actress," I say.

"Acting gives me a script. A person to pretend to be. It's difficult being that person without a camera on me," she replies. "Hence, our current situation."

"We have to keep up appearances, bird."

"Appearances, my ass. If I go to your concert, and you do that, I'm leaving."

I laugh at her annoyance. "Definitely doing it now," I say.

"Reed—"

"If you don't want me doing crazy things to prove myself, then you should post on your socials more. Next time I'm in LA, we should go out. Get more photos together than just the ones on the red carpet at events."

"Like a date?"

The way her nose curls up at the suggestion makes me smirk.

"I don't know which would be worse," she mutters.

"A date means you get to listen to my witty jokes for hours on end—and you have to pretend like you think I'm funny just in case someone is watching," I grin.

"Ugh. You're exhausting. Fine. A kiss at the concert, then. But do not sing to me," she says as she crunches down on another cracker.

I punch the air in a celebratory way.

"—you can't make that one," I hear someone shout from Wren's side of the conversation.

"What?" Wren shouts back at them.

The other person replies, but I can't make out what they're saying, and Wren makes a face.

"Who's there?" I ask.

"Just Larry," she says. "What are you talking about? This Friday?" she asks him. "Oh. Oh, no I didn't know that. God, did I miss an entire week?"

"What's up?" I ask, confused.

Larry comes around Wren's side and waves. "Hi, Reed."

"Hey, Lare," I reply. "What's going on?"

"Wren won't be able to make the concert next weekend. She has an audition," he answers.

"What time is the audition?" I ask.

Wren rolls her eyes. "What he means is, I have to go read for a part, and then do dinner with one of the producers to try and kiss his ass," she says against her wine glass.

"And what *she* means is, she *gets* to read for a part in an upcoming romcom piece, then is having dinner at a fancy restaurant with one of the most prominent producers in Hollywood to seal the deal," Larry says. "She makes it sound so drab," he adds tauntingly.

"So, next Wednesday, then," I say. "We'll be in San Fran."

"I'm surprised you know your own dates," she says.

"Only because my sister will be there again," I say.

"Hey yo, Chaos!" Zeb calls out. "You ready?"

I glance up over the screen. "Yeah, just a minute," I reply.

Larry has disappeared from behind Wren by the time I look back down, leaving her alone at the table again. "Aw, too bad, you have to go," she says with a pouted lip.

"Get Larry back," I tell her.

"Why?"

"Humor me," I say.

She pauses to eye me. "You're so fucking weird," she mutters. "Hey, La—oh, you're right here."

"I heard my name," Larry says, peeking around the corner.

"Hey, take a photo of her lunch, wine, and me on the phone, then post it with some sappy caption," I say, and Larry beams at me.

"Oh, he's *good*," he says. "Let me get out of this."

Larry slides out to the side, and I smile at the camera as if she's just said something funny, Wren's face in the corner appearing mildly amused.

"What are you, my social media manager?" Wren asks once Larry has the photo done.

"I have millions of followers," I shrug. "Maybe you should take a few suggestions."

"You have millions of followers because people think you're hot," she argues.

"So… all of your followers like you for your outstanding personality?" I tilt my head with the question, and she presses her lips together thinly.

"Goodbye, poser," she grunts.

A grin slides onto my lips. "Yeah, okay. I'll text you pictures later."

"I don't need pictures of your body when I can find them on social media," she argues.

"You don't have pictures of the dick you squirted around last week, though," I say in a low voice.

"That was your tongue, *not* your dick."

Wren hangs up without another word, and a victorious laugh leaves me.

"The hell is so funny?" Zeb asks when he reaches me.

"Ah, nothing," I say, hopping to my feet. "Just fucking with bird. I'm ready. What are we—"

My phone buzzes again, and I turn it over, expecting a text from Wren telling me not to send her any photos. However, it's a phone call coming through, and I don't recognize the number on the screen. I frown and pause, gawking as the device continues to ring.

"What's up?" Zeb asks.

"I don't know this number," I say.

"Ah, fuck," Zeb groans. "Here we go again."

"Everything okay?" James calls over to us, apparently having seen my face.

"Ah… yeah." I hold up my phone. "Number I don't recognize. Doubt it's anything to be concerned about."

"First time?" he asks, coming toward me.

"Yeah. Yeah, I've never seen this one."

James gestures for my phone, and I hand it to him so he can take a picture of the screen with his own camera. "I'll check it out," he says.

It isn't the first time James has acted odd like this about a strange number. Just a few months ago, Zeb was being harassed by a rogue fan who got his number. James took it upon himself to take care of the entire situation—going as far as filing the restraining order for Zeb and hiring extra security just for him.

Not to mention the shit Bonnie's been in with her own stalker that she's had since before she even joined the band.

"Think it's nothing?" I ask James.

"Could be," he sighs. "Don't go anywhere without telling me for a few days, though."

"Wouldn't dream of stepping out of your sight," I tell him, and James smiles.

"What's going on?" Mads asks as he comes up to us.

He shares a look with James that makes my brows narrow, though I don't question them. If these two know something, I'm honestly better off staying in the dark about it.

"Ah, just a weird number," I say. "Probably nothing."

Mads nods, one hand in his pocket, the other out to smack me on my gut. "You ready to warm up?" he asks.

I toss my phone over to the end of the stage and jump a few times to amp myself up for this sound check.

"Tea," Stella says as she comes sprinting up behind us.

I take a single sip and set it down on the edge of the stage before following Zeb, and when I start my vocal warm-ups, every other thought evacuates from my mind.

CHAPTER SEVENTEEN

REED

NO ONE ever tells you how much more a concert means when the people you love are in attendance. I hear it in Mads's bass line when Andi is at a show. I see it in his face when she's standing backstage or on the balcony. I know I perform a better show when my family is waiting, yet somewhere in the back of my mind, I've always wondered what it would feel like to see my person staring back at me.

I used to dwell on it all the time—especially when we first started out. And maybe that was because I used to be in relationships a lot—short as they might have been—so there was always someone there to greet me after, someone to applaud and tell me how amazing the show was.

Somewhere along the journey, I stopped getting into relationships that I couldn't stay faithful to, and in that, I became numb to the feeling of wanting someone backstage.

I love my fucking family. I love the family that the band has given me. And staring out into the mass of people watching us play tonight, the love I have for this stage and our fans is affirmed.

Even so, I feel fucking empty.

It wasn't until the charity concert that that feeling of

longing began to creep back into my bones. It wasn't until I saw Wren on that balcony that I remembered how much someone being there had once meant to me.

And maybe that's why seeing her standing in the backstage VIP box above us right now makes me want to vomit—in a good way.

She didn't tell me she was coming.

I shouldn't feel the way I do upon seeing her. It doesn't even have anything to do with liking her or not. I know it's purely the adrenaline coursing through me, the elation of having someone there for *me*—real or not.

She came to my concert.

She's standing in the box beside Andi, at least appearing like she doesn't entirely hate her life right now. I get the urge to climb the lighting rig to her, but I won't embarrass her this time. I know it's a hard boundary for her, and as much as I love pushing her, I'll do that later.

For now, I'll settle for pointing to her.

I'll settle for the extra adrenaline suddenly swarming my blood and hiking my heart rate. I'll settle for the sweat pouring down my face, and the wet of my hair. The screaming fans singing our lyrics back to me in a way that swells my heart and takes me to the verge of tears.

Because even if our relationship isn't real, I don't feel as hollow as I did just one show earlier.

You're going to need luck to stay above water, I can hear my sister saying.

I glance up at the VIP area again and swallow when I meet Wren's gaze.

My sister can kiss my ass.

I'll ride this fucking feeling until I crash into a brick wall.

During the last song, I see someone usher Wren and Andi down. And when Wren is finally in my peripherals, when she's standing at the edge of the stage in the wings, I swear I see her singing along. The realization makes me grin side-ways at her, and before I know it, I'm running in her direction.

She came to see my show.

A lump lurches into my throat. She's watching me as if she knew I would do this, as if she's prepared to act her dutiful part, and when my lips land upon hers, I hear the crowd scream behind us.

I've missed having someone here for me.

God, that sounds sad.

I keep my hand on her cheek when we part, holding her cheek lightly, dragging my thumb beneath her chin.

I wish she wasn't so fucking devastating.

It would make it so much easier to pretend none of this matters.

"You came," I manage.

"Bored at home, honestly," she says in a deadpan voice.

The retort makes me smile. I hear the bass line behind me. I don't have time to say anything else, but I hold onto her finger-tips a moment longer, bring the mic to my lips, and finally turn back to the crowd.

"Are you ready?!" I shout at them, one arm in the air.

Bonnie leads into the second chorus. I belt out a scream, a renewed sense of excitement seeming to surge and surge and *surge* out. I can't feel my face anymore, especially not as I hold my mic out to the audience, and they sing the song back to us.

Tonight feels fucking amazing.

A few stagehands come up to me and clap my hands when I come bouncing off after the last song, congratulating us on a show well done. I try to pay attention to what my friends are saying to me; however, Wren is chewing her bottom lip as if she's forcing herself not to appear like she actually enjoyed herself tonight.

I think my feet run faster than my heart. Because the next

thing I know, I have my hands pressed to her face, and I kiss her hard. Damn her little rules.

My stage. My territory.

She can fight me about it later.

The nip on my bottom lip and the way she yanks at the roots of my hair tells me she will.

"I really wish you wouldn't kiss me like that," she says against my lips.

"Why? Do you like it?" I ask.

"Because you kiss like you're desperate," she replies.

"Maybe I am."

Wren pushes slightly on my chest, making me chuckle.

"I didn't know you were coming," I say.

How is she so much prettier right now?

It must be the fucking lights.

"You never answered me," I add.

Wren sighs. "Ah…" She glances behind me at Mads, who's cornering in on us while Andi chats with Bonnie, presumably showing her photos of their dog as I can hear Bonnie cooing at the photo Andi is showing her on her phone.

"Hey, Wren," Mads says with a grin.

"Mads," she says. "Hell of a show."

I balk. "The hell—you haven't even told me you liked the show," I say.

"No, you were too busy kissing me," she says with batting lashes.

I huff amusedly. "Fair trade, honestly."

"Hey—" Mads slaps my stomach. "—No parties tonight. We have a flight at two."

"Oh, good, you're telling him," Avie says as he walks up to us, phone in his hand. "No parties. No groupies—"

Wren clears her throat, and Avie stares at her like he's just noticed her there.

"Sweetheart, your being here means shit to me," Avie says.

"I don't know what you two do or who you invite into your little relationship behind closed doors. So no groupies."

Her nostrils flare, and she folds her arms across her chest. I expect her to say something smart back, though she just watches him for another moment like she's trying to play nice, and Avie looks at me again.

"And no lingering too much out back. Autographs. Showers. Actually, I don't care if you fucking shower. We're leaving here at one, got it?" Avie asks us.

He doesn't wait for an answer before he turns on his heel and presses his phone to his face to yell at someone else. I turn back to Wren, who's watching Avie walk away.

"Stick around tonight?" I ask her, and she looks my way. "Wait for me to finish doing what I need to do?"

"Why?"

"Because I have a lot of energy, and no one else to annoy. And because I know you didn't just come here to watch me play."

"Look at who became a mind reader," she says, though her voice isn't lined with anger, and the jeer makes me smirk. She huffs amusedly and nods. "Yeah. I'll hang."

Zeb comes up beside us then and strategically hands Wren a vodka mini bottle without looking away from me. "There's a line already out back. You want to shower now or later?" he asks me.

"Ah, later," I reply.

"Good choice. I think Mads is fucking your sister in the dressing room anyway," Zeb says, grinning.

"Oh, *come on*," I say to him. "I didn't need that image—"

Zeb claps my shoulder and laughs. "Let's go, then. Kelly, I'll try to bring him back in one piece."

"Pieces is fine," she says. "I just need him to look pretty."

I beam at her taunt.

By the time I get back from signing and showering, I find

Wren standing on the empty stage. There are still a few people hanging around backstage. Zeb is crashed on the couch in the dressing room, Bonnie taking a longer than usual shower.

I'm pretty sure she has someone in there with her, though I don't intend on finding out since Avie told us no groupies.

I pause at the side of the stage to watch Wren for a moment. She's just standing there, staring out at the quiet venue. The only people left are a few of our crew hanging out in the audience, well out of earshot. I take the bottle of champagne in my hands and slowly twist the cork. It finally pops, making Wren jump, and the crew yells back at me.

I grin at the surprised look on Wren's face.

"Yeah, Reed!" someone shouts, another whistling.

"Pop the bubbly!"

Wren is watching my every move as I come toward her, and something about the way she's watching me twists my already knotting stomach.

"Do you want some of this?" I ask her, gesturing with the champagne.

She squints at me as if she knows it comes with stipulations. "You're not spitting that in my mouth," she says, only low enough that I hear her.

I chuckle as my friends continue to whistle. "Come on, bird. We still have an audience."

"And you think that is going to complete our ruse, do you?"

"I definitely think it'll help," I reply. "One taste, and I won't kiss you again the rest of the night."

She takes out her phone and looks at it. "The rest of the night is only an hour."

"I didn't know you only came for a repeat of the last time we were together."

Her lips press into a thin line. "Will spitting in my mouth get you to shut up faster?"

"It'll get me to tell these guys to leave us so we can get on to why you really came here," I reply.

Wren breathes in a heavy breath and slides her hands up my chest, taking a fistful of my shirt into her fingers. "The only reason I'm entertaining this is because it's champagne. If you ever try this with only your spit, I'll put a cage on your dick and edge you until you ugly cry."

"Kinky *and* mean," I tease, squeezing her hip. "I told you I liked you."

Before she can respond, I press the champagne bottle to my lips and take a long swig, holding it in my mouth as I pull her mouth open with a tug on her chin. However, just as our eyes meet, and I see her gulp like she's opening her throat, I swallow the bubbly and grin wickedly at the crew staring at us.

"You fuckers thought!" I shout.

The whole group laughs and boo's, playfully bashing me for teasing them. I shake my head at their insults, then jerk my head toward the stage door. "Why don't all of you take a hike?" I say, trying to get rid of them.

They start moving, and I pull Wren into me again, swaying with her slightly as she glares.

"I can't believe you were going to let me do that," I say, smirking at Wren.

"I was going to spit it back in your face," she replies.

My head falls back, faking hurt. "You would do that to me in front of my friends?"

"It would've been funny," she shrugs.

I scoff. "I didn't know you knew what funny was."

Wren shoves me off, and I laugh, making sure to make it look like we're playing. The crew is nearly packed up and out of our sight, and as the last person disappears backstage, Wren's gaze staggers on me again.

"You should know, I didn't come here because of the sex," she says, hugging her chest.

I take a drink of the champagne. "I don't care," I say. "I just care that you came. It's nice having someone here just for me. Real or not."

Wren squints at me as if she isn't sure how to take the sentence, then grabs the champagne bottle from my hand.

"You have thousands of fans here for you every night," she says.

"It isn't the same," I reply.

I don't know why I even admitted it to her.

God, I must be fucking tired.

I run my hand through my hair and wipe my face, feeling my adrenaline slowly start to wane. I need a fucking coffee if we're heading to the airport soon.

"Why did you come?" I ask as she drinks.

"My publicist says we appear rigid. Also, she's pissed about the leaked video from the other night," she answers.

"Rigid?" I repeat, brows narrowed. "I've never been called rigid before. That's new."

"Considering I'm constantly being called rigid, it was no surprise to me," she mutters. "Anyway. I thought… I thought it would be a good idea to see you in your territory."

"Does that make things easier for you?" I ask.

"Something about it does, yes," she admits. "I don't feel like a puppet on a string."

I consider her a moment, noting how she's avoiding my eyes, and I can't tell if it's nerves or something else—or even just her default. She usually makes a point to look at my face, so much so that it feels like she's peering through my soul.

The complete opposite of what she's doing right now.

"What do you need from me?" I ask.

There's a pause where she looks down at her feet, then

throws a fleeting glance my way. "I was told it might help if I got to know you."

I almost laugh. "You make it sound like work."

"Ugh," she grunts. "For me, it is. I hate small talk."

"Who said anything about small talk?"

"You know what I mean," she sighs. "I hate the questions about where I came from or about the person I was in high school. The weather outside and my favorite color—"

"Which is?"

"Black like my heart, but that's not the point," she goes on.

I smile at how annoyed she is about it all. "What is the point, then?" I ask her.

"The point is, I'm not who I was fifteen years ago. So, why bring it up?"

"Some people like putting together puzzles," I reply.

"I'm not a puzzle."

"Yeah, that we can agree on," I say. "You're a fucking Lego set with ten thousand tiny parts that no person has ever figured out how to put together," I say, and she looks at me over her shoulder.

"Funny," she says.

"Am I wrong?"

She drinks again from the bottle and starts heading downstage, her heels clacking on the wood. I stare at her for a few moments—at the woman who looks like she's tired of life itself, but doesn't think anyone will notice. She pauses at the edge and hangs her head back, inhaling a deep breath like she's trying to breathe in the lingering smell of pyrotechnics and sweat.

"When's the last time you were on the stage?" I ask her.

Wren opens her eyes and stares out at the empty venue. "Senior year high school," she answers. "We did The Secret Garden," she goes on.

"Do you miss it?" I ask.

"God, no," she says tiredly. Wren sighs and sits on the edge of the stage, and I follow. "Gawked at by live audiences? No, thank you. It's easier playing a part behind a camera."

"How is that so different?"

"Behind the camera, I can fuck up and do another take."

I chuckle softly. "We are the opposite, then," I say. "I love the fucking stage. Nothing like the adrenaline there."

"I think what you do is a little different from memorizing a play," she says. "At least you get to improvise. Not the set list, but everything else."

"Is that why you hide so much? Why you don't like surprises or dramatic gestures?" I ask. "Because the real world feels like a stage you don't have a script to?"

Her sideways gaze meets mine, and she reaches for the bottle again. "Thank you for not climbing the rafters tonight," she says as she takes a drink.

"I thought I would be easy on you," I say.

"Nothing about this is easy," she says under her breath.

Silence swells between us as I watch her, noting the solemness in her eyes and the way her lips tug downward as if they've forgotten joy.

"When is our next event?" I ask her.

"Private screening in a couple of weeks," she answers.

I nod. "I have no idea what my schedule is like, but if I have a couple of days, I could come over. We can go on that date we talked about."

She wrinkles her nose up at me again.

Shit, she's cute when she thinks I've lost my mind.

"We didn't really talk about that," she says, and I sigh in response, head hanging.

"Let me guess. You have rules about that, too?" I ask.

She pauses, an apparent tug trying to lift those perfect red lips. "Fine. No rules, then, if that'll make you happy."

I try not to grin. "No rules?" I ask. "I can kiss you anytime I want?"

Wren makes a gagging sound. "Why do you have to say it like some hopeless teenage girl?"

"Sometimes I feel like a hopeless teenage girl," I say thoughtfully. "Wondering when my crush is going to text me back. Wondering why they haven't liked my social post yet or commented to tell me how much they miss me."

Only her eyes shift in my direction, and I grin.

"Don't you have a plane to catch?" she asks.

I pick up my phone to check the time. "Ah… fifteen minutes," I say. "Bonnie is probably done fucking that groupie if you want to crash the dressing room for a quickie."

Wren gives me a flat look. "I told you I didn't come for sex."

"Are you really telling me that you came all this way just to tell me your publicist wants us to stop being rigid?"

"Not entirely. You asked me to come to your show. I came to your show," she says. "That's what girlfriends do, right?"

A lump sits in my throat, and I'm reminded once again that this is nothing to her. The feeling I'd felt when I saw her standing in the VIP box is only a reflection of my staggering loneliness, of the void that I've filled with mindless sex and attention from anyone I could get it from over the last few years.

"Yeah," I answer stiffly.

The sound of someone approaching at a fast pace averts our attention before either of us can say another word.

"Hey—leaving in five," Zeb says from the wings. "Avie is getting antsy."

I glance over my shoulder at him, somewhat crestfallen that the night is over. "Okay. I'll get my shit."

Wren stands before I do, and I rise to meet her. "Do you

know what else girlfriends do?" I ask, and Wren huffs like she can read my mind.

"What's that, poser?"

"Sometimes they hop from one city to the next and go to multiple shows," I answer.

"I can't do that," she says. "That isn't a good idea."

"Why? Do you have plans tomorrow?" I ask.

The way she looks at me then makes my gaze narrow, though I don't push it.

"A kiss goodbye, then," I suggest.

She sighs heavily. "You are… relentless," she says, and she steps up to me anyways.

"I'd never get anything if I wasn't," I say, tilting her head back.

The kiss I meet her with isn't filled with the passion and bite that our past kisses have held. And maybe that's because I'm too fucking exhausted to fight.

When I open my eyes, she's already staring at me, and it makes me wonder if she held her eyes open the entire kiss, and I was the only chump feeling anything within those few seconds.

Wren drops her hands from my chest and steps back. "You should get going," she says as she pulls her phone out.

"Do you need a ride somewhere?" I ask, my stomach trying to unwind.

"I have it," she replies, wiggling her phone.

I want to wring this standoffishness out of her, or at the very least, find out why she's so determined not to let me get to know her, even when her job depends on it.

The decision I make is going to break me, but only if I can break her first.

CHAPTER EIGHTEEN

THINGS ARE TOO QUIET.

I haven't heard from Damien or seen any of his guys for a few weeks now. Not since Sean's party—which is surprising considering the video of Reed and I from that event.

I don't like it.

It's affecting my nerves more than it would if they were constantly on my ass.

I stare at Damien's number on my phone, the last texts from him now sitting with a date and not just the day of the week like usual.

Maybe he's dead.

Wouldn't that be amazing?

There's a light tap on my door. It's so light that I barely hear it. It doesn't startle me. I already know it's Reed. I've been panic cleaning this place for the last two hours after putting it off for two days. I know I probably left chips in the cushions; however, at this point, there's little I can do about it.

I glance around the condo one more time before saying, "Fuck it," and going to the door.

I open it as he's knocking again, and as I do, he staggers, and I nearly start at the sight of him.

Dammit.

He's really fucking cute in this checkerboard flat bill hat.

Some of his shaggy black hair sticks out from under it, somehow totally messy, and yet perfectly in place. He's changed out his eyebrow and lip piercings from bright pink to matte black, and the difference is staggering against his pale blue eyes.

There's something about the way he looks today that appears freshly polished.

"Did you get your hair trimmed?" I ask, looking him over. "And… what, was it pampering day in the Matthews household?" I say as I notice his freshly manicured nails.

Reed smirks and takes his hat off to run his hand through his hair. "You said I needed to wear more than a crop top," he says about our texts last night. "Thought maybe that included cleaning the road off of me."

I open the door wider, letting him inside. He has a bag in his other hand. The smell of something spicy wafts in my direction, and I remember his Thai food suggestion for lunch.

Which I forgot about.

It's part of his 'get to know each other' plan he's cooked up. It's a little annoying and out of my comfort zone. Even still, at least there is something about Reed that doesn't make me feel like a show pony. I've even been texting him back within a reasonable timeframe as if he, unlike everyone else around me, doesn't suck the energy out of me with the straw of a single sentence.

Ugh.

Is he becoming my friend?

Gross.

I want to gag at my own inner monologue.

"Do you have any stalkers?" he asks as he pushes past me. "Besides that guy from the party that you still won't tell me about?"

My stomach drops. "No more than any normal actress, I guess," I lie. "And it's better you don't know about him. Wait—why do you ask about stalkers?"

"Ever since we started this, I feel like I'm being watched," he answers.

"Are you sure they're not *your* stalkers?" I ask.

"Could be," he says with a shrug.

"It's probably photographers looking to get a photo of us," I say, though my nerves are shot.

"Whoa," Reed says, and I pause to frown at him.

"What?" I ask upon seeing his wide eyes.

"You have... damn, you have a lot of fucking plants," he answers.

I glance around my condo, ready to retort and tell him he needs to learn to count because I only have a few.

But he's right.

I do have a lot of fucking plants.

Hang on. *Why is he asking about stalkers?*

"Wait. Did someone follow you here today?" I ask him.

"Ah, no," he answers. "Just a general icky feeling. Hair standing on the back of my neck. Weird phone calls—"

"Weird phone calls?" I repeat in panic.

He waves me off. "James says it's nothing. He looked into them."

"Is this just when you're in LA?"

"Pretty much all the time," he replies. He sits the bag in his hand on the counter. He's still staring at the plants around the place like he's never seen someone with so many.

"How do you keep up with when these get watered?" he asks.

I tap on the chart I have attached to the fridge, but Reed is already onto the next thing.

"Are these twinkle lights?" he asks as he steps up to touch

one of the strings of amber lights that I have instead of over-head lights in every room.

"Hey—" I swat at his big hand before he can uncurl the hours it took me to get those damn things where I wanted them. "Don't mess with my twinkle lights."

Reed grins. "But I like twinkle lights."

My lips press tightly together at the innocent look on his face. "You are a cat," I tell him.

"If anyone is a cat in this equation, it's you—*oh shit!* You have a dog?!"

Anita jumps down from her orange couch then, and Reed's face lights up at the sight of the Australian Shepherd trotting happily toward him, tail wagging.

"Hello, gorgeous," he coos, squatting down to greet her. "What is your name?"

I stare at my dog for betraying me. "This is Anita," I tell him. "She's a hoe. And a traitor. Smile at her, and she'll wiggle her ass in your face." I look poignantly at Anita. "I told you to bite him," I say to her.

"What? This beauty? Bite me?" He threads his fingers into her long hair by her face and puckers his lips like he's going to kiss her. "I think we're going to be best friends."

"Stop kissing my dog," I say.

"Why? Are you jealous?"

I eye them one more time before turning back to the food still in bags on the counter. Reed's claim that he feels like he's being watched still rings in the back of my mind. It distracts me from listening to him love on Anita and causes the back of my neck to itch. I'm so distracted that I keep tapping my phone to make sure Damien hasn't sent some threatening message or texted me about my 'pretty new boyfriend.'

"Hey, I had an idea," Reed says, suddenly beside me.

I almost jump at his unexpected proximity, but pretend I

didn't notice instead. "You should slow down with those. You're going to hurt yourself," I tell him.

I can see his grin from the corner of my eye, and I decide to give him a chance.

"What was your idea?" I ask.

"I was thinking we could shake things up a bit," he goes on. "Make the tabloids and online speculators go wild."

"Are they not already?" I ask. "After you choked me? I got a message last night from an ex costar concerned for my well-being."

"What did you tell them?"

"I told them to mind their own fucking business," I reply. "And that I had asked you to do it, and you made sure to take gentle care of me after."

"Liar," he says. "Okay, but think of that, though *not* so angrily this time," he adds, smirking.

There's a knot that twists my stomach. It's nerves and anticipation, yet wickedness all at once. I don't know what he's thinking; however, the darkened look in his gaze tells me it's something my publicist probably won't approve of.

Though the fact that he just said he's being followed has my anxiety turning into spite.

"I'm listening," I say.

He grins crookedly and grabs his phone. "Have you seen any of my videos?"

I stop fidgeting. "You mean the ones of you shirtless doing things with your hands?"

"That feels like an oversimplification, but yes," he answers.

"What about them?"

"You could be in one."

I blink, gawking at the confident musician in front of me. "What?"

"I have an idea, and it involves you. Naked. On the bed."

"I told you you shouldn't think so hard. You'll break your brain. This idea being clear evidence," I say.

"It'll be hot," he adds.

I give him a dull look. "I can't do that, and you know it," I say. "As much as my publicist wants me doing more with you, she'd kill me for something like that. I'm already in trouble with her for getting filmed at Sean's party. She wasn't thrilled about the other night."

"What did she say?" he asks.

"She told me I shouldn't let my anger about this entire thing ruin it for me," I admit. "To remember a little classy kink will sell, not rage."

"This is a classy kink," he says.

I roll my eyes over to him, and he beams.

"It's only fun," he says. "What's wrong? Afraid you'll like it?"

I stare for a beat too long—chew on my tongue a bit *too* hard.

Reed smirks and fumbles with his phone a moment, bringing up a video he took just days before. He moves behind me and wraps his long arms around me, bracing one hand on the counter lip at my hip, the other holding up his phone so that I can watch the clip.

I don't have to watch it to know exactly which video he's showing me. I should know. I've watched them more times than I would ever admit to anyone. Since our rendezvous after the party a few weeks ago, I actually got off to one of them.

Something Reed will *never* find out about.

This one is of him shirtless and toying with his microphone —wrapping the cord up around his elbow, his hands, knotting it and untying it, stroking the microphone itself. This video was all I could think of watching him perform the other week, all I could see when he sat beside me on the stage. He talks with his hands so much that they're hard to ignore.

I'm so consumed by the images that when his breath skims my ear, I almost jerk.

"What do you say?" he rasps. "Want to create a little chaos?"

The video plays again, this time my focus going to the darkly shadowed tattoos around his neck, the flex of his muscles in his long fingers.

My tongue is stuck to the roof of my mouth.

I shouldn't.

I *really* shouldn't.

However, my gut is telling me to throw caution to the wind. Impulsivity writhes beneath my suddenly restless fingers. I feel my hand begin to move side-to-side in an almost twisting motion as I debate my move.

I think I've been around Reed too long.

Or maybe it's that I'm tired of people telling me what I can and can't do.

Reed presses his chest into my back. He brings his free hand around my waist as he flips to another video, and slides his fingertips just below the waistband of my leggings. I hate what his touch does to me. I hate that it reminds me of the way he tossed me around the last time we were truly alone together, the way his fingers feel around my neck, how they seem to worship every inch of my curves like he isn't afraid of me.

His breath skims the top of my head, prompting me to draw my bottom lip between my teeth in a final attempt at talking myself out of this.

"Let's play, little bird," he breathes against the shell of my ear.

I glare sideways at him, head shifting just enough that I can see him out of the corner of my eye.

"You are the worst influence," I finally give in.

He hisses a celebratory noise and pulls away from me,

though not before slapping my ass so hard that my feet clear the floor.

Holy sh—

"*Jesus mother fucking hell, Reed!*" I yelp, nearly screaming. "Oh my—" I struggle to keep my composure as Reed laughs. A restrained noise sounds from my throat. *Goddammit—*

My ass is on *fire*.

"I'm going to fucking—if you *ever* do that again—"

"Your bedroom is down here, I'm assuming?" he asks, pointing to the hall.

"Yes, but—" I start to follow him, wincing with every step, and I have to stop at the end of the kitchen island. "I should fucking murder you—"

Reed is snickering at the end of my bed and looking at his phone. I blow out a forced, audible breath, trying to push the pain to the back of my mind, hands twisting and stretching as I itch to work this pain out.

"Your dancing is cute," he says.

"Oh, fuck off," I snap.

A devious, mocking chuckle sounds from him as I lean my palms against the countertop and take a few deep breaths in an attempt to calm my racing heart. I can still feel every inch of his hand on my ass, his handprint permanently scarred on my skin.

"Mother fuck, I hate you," I grunt.

"Come here," he says in an off-hand voice, and I glance over my shoulder in his direction.

He's bent over the mattress, shirt already removed, one hand on the bed and the other holding his phone. He slides his hand up the sheet and then grips it hard between his fingers, his muscles flexing, videoing the entire thing. He does it two more times before straightening in my direction.

I hate the way my mouth dries at the sight of his hip vee and the tattoos that I suddenly have the urge to lick.

Fuck, what is wrong with me?

Reed crooks two fingers and gestures me his way. "Get over here," he says.

I tuck my arms around my chest. "I need to know what exactly you're planning," I say.

"Why?"

"So I know what to expect, how to react," I answer.

He scoffs, eyes drifting to the bed and then back to me. "Take your shirt off and lie down on the bed," he says.

My brows raise. "Excuse—"

"If you're scared, just say so," he jeers.

Lips pressing firmly together, I flip him off and step into the bedroom. Our eyes stagger on one another. I'm forcing myself not to look at his trim, bare chest, the blacked out areas of his arms, or the dark designs that wrap up and around his neck. I grasp the hem of my shirt and pull it over my head, hoping it will distract me from my current predicament. Even still, all I see in my head is him over me, holding my face and my neck as he slams inside my now throbbing pussy and pushing me into submission beneath him.

His gaze drifts down my front in a predatory way, tongue swiping over his dry lips as if he's imagining the same thing, and I can't deny how much I enjoy the way he stares at me. Like he's eager to please, consume, and praise every inch of my generous curves.

The dominance suddenly resting in his rounded shoulders somehow makes him seem taller.

I don't know how he does it.

"Lie down," he says hoarsely.

There's a beat where I don't move. A fraction of time that I know is less than a second, yet with our eyes locked, feels like forever.

Until, finally, I do as I'm told.

Reed's chin lifts just noticeably when I sit on the mattress and scoot back.

"Just lie down?" I ask.

He nods and swallows, though his eyes are so dilated that I wonder if he's already fucking me in the back of his mind.

A heavy breath leaves me, and I lay back, settling my entwined hands over my stomach. The ceiling fan is on low above me. I try to concentrate on it as I feel the bed shift.

"Can you at least tell me what you're going to do?" I ask, refusing to watch him crawl up the bed toward me—no matter how tempting the display appears in my peripheral vision.

"I'm going to wrap my hand around your throat," he says.

Simple enough.

I'm hyper aware of how high my chest is raising as he straddles over me and settles on my hips. I can feel his dick on my abdomen, and I try not to think about the fact that he's mildly erect already. He's barely watching me, so absorbed by his phone that he's only looking at me through its lens.

"Do *not* get my face," I tell him. "I swear, Reed. If you get my face—"

"When we're done filming, I'm fucking that mean girl attitude out of you," he interrupts me.

I scoff. "Have fun trying," I taunt.

His wrist flops, and he turns his attention directly on me instead of through his phone, smiling. "Oh, bird... I will," he says, his voice vibrating.

He swipes his tongue over his lips again and moves the phone over me, his palm coming to a rest on my sternum. I find my gaze drifting to the phone, suddenly nervous of him filming me so close.

Cameras rolling rarely get to me. But this... This feels raw. Unfiltered and void of a character I'm supposed to portray, even if I'm still supposed to be 'his girlfriend.'

"Don't look at my phone," he says. "Look at me."

I do.

Concentration clouds his icy eyes. He taps his screen, and I feel my breath catch. His palm moves up my chest and whispers over my collar. And when he reaches my throat, he grasps me so quickly that my mouth drops with a gasp.

Fuck.

When he'd said he was going to wrap his hand around my throat, I didn't know he meant *that.*

Reed's pupils look as if they blow entirely.

"Do that again," he says.

"Do what?" I manage.

"That fucking little moan," he replies.

"I didn't moan," I argue.

He huffs, his white teeth gleaming in contrast to the shadows cast over his features. "We'll see."

He taps his screen and moves his palm back to my sternum, and this time, I swallow at the intensity of his gaze. He positions the phone again, and I don't look away as he drags his hand up my chest.

Every hair on my body raises with the movement of his palm. I don't know why this time his touch pricks my skin with heat and tension, why his gaze seems even more devious and pleased about my being compliant and going along with his little game.

Heavy breaths make my chest rise and fall beneath the graze of his fingers. I try to gulp as they tickle over my collar. I know he's going to grab my throat at any second. I feel the tension rising, the anticipation nearly unbearable—

And when his hand launches around my neck, my jaw drops again, and a soft, uncontrollable whimper leaves me.

Reed chuckles a deep, triumphant laugh. "I didn't know I was getting mixed up with a *good* little slut," he rasps.

I strike his chest so hard that he winces, and just as I open my mouth to retort and tell him what a dick he is, he throws his phone over his shoulder, yanks me off the bed by my neck, and kisses me hard.

Fucking asshole.

CHAPTER NINETEEN

I DON'T UNDERSTAND how every kiss from him numbs my mind and makes me forget what century I'm in. It's maddening the way my body responds to his, how I'm already arching my back and hiking my legs around his waist.

However, this is all I've thought about for weeks, and so, I claw at his chest and shove his shoulder, relishing his tightening grip when he tries to suspend my fight.

Reed pins me into the mattress, body aligning on top of mine, hips holding me down. A groan slips by me as I feel the outline of his hardening dick press against my pelvis. I reach for the button of his jeans, but he takes my hands away, fingers tight around my wrists when he takes his kiss to my jaw, my throat, my collar.

"You should know," he says, straightening over me. "I *did* come for sex."

I almost smile. "And you should know, I came for sex at the concert, too. I was just seeing how hard you would work for it." I lean up and bite at his lip, nose brushing his cheek. "You failed," I breathe at his ear.

A low growl leaves him, our tongues licking against one

another. He grabs the waistband of my leggings and tugs them down aggressively without breaking away from my lips.

I swear, I feel goosebumps rising on his arms.

"We'll see how much of a failure you think I am when I'm done with you today," he swears.

And in one swift motion, his tongue is between my thighs.

I shove at his face and thread my fingers into his hair, pulling him closer as he sucks my clit into his mouth and holds my thighs with such a grip that I feel the pressure in my bones. I don't hold back from rocking against his mouth, the motions and desperation driving me faster to that addictive end.

Reed's lips twist against my pussy. "Someone's fucking greedy today," he says in a pleased voice. "I'll make you a groupie yet."

I would love to refute him; however, I've been wet since he walked in, and the only noise I can manage in response is a high-pitched cry, my free hand fisting the sheet as I throw my head back into the pillow.

Shit, his tongue feels fucking amazing.

I hear him fumbling with his pants, trying to get them off without drawing any attention away from what his mouth is doing to me. He hums a note, the vibrations on my pussy making my thighs hike. The noises of his tongue flicking and sucking me are as devastating as it feels. And as he sides two fingers inside me, I take the pillow from behind my head and shove it over my face.

"Shit," I hear him curse. He moves his mouth from my cunt and begins kissing up my stomach, lingering on my stretch marks and licking the length of a few. I feel his hard dick ready at my entrance when he's back over me, and as I take the pillow from my face, I'm met with his gaze.

"Do you know what I've been dreaming about for weeks now?" he says as his tip teases over my clit.

"Figuring out how to suck your own dick?" I say, and he laughs.

"No, bird. I've been dreaming of watching this ass of yours bounce on my lap," he says. "I want a front row seat to the view of your pussy stretching and taking my dick an inch at a time."

"Now who's being greedy?" I taunt in a low voice.

He grins and smacks my thigh, then rolls over onto the mattress, his curved dick lying on his toned abdomen. I sit up and reach over, taking his thick cock in my fist and stroking up and down. Reed curses under his breath, chin jutting toward the ceiling.

I want to see the look he had on his face when the guitarist was sucking him off.

I want to see him hide his face as he whimpers and sucks air through his teeth.

I want him whimpering out my name and begging.

Pushing my tits together, I sit at his side and take him with both of my hands. Precum glistens on his tip. I watch it bead down his slit, and as I'm mesmerized by it, I gather spit in my mouth. A hiss sounds from him as the spit leaves my mouth and drops onto his tip, and I look at him as I work it down his shaft.

"Do you want my mouth first?" I ask, leaning down. My tongue flicks over his slit, and his abdomen flinches.

"No," he admits.

A smirk dares to toy on my lips. "No?"

"If you come anywhere near me with that fucking mouth, I'll lose my mind," he breathes.

I give him a fake pout. "Poor little Reed. Can't control his own urges."

He leans up and puts a few pillows behind him, then reaches for my chin, pulling my face to his.

"Turn around and straddle my lap, but don't get on my dick yet," he rasps.

I do as he says. His hands are everywhere the moment I'm sitting atop him—my hips, my ass, my tits, my neck. It's a massage that sends shivers down my spine, and when he begins toying in my hair, goosebumps rise over my arms.

"Are you braiding my hair?" I ask when I feel him tugging it.

Reed finishes tying it off, then wraps it around his hand and gives it a hard yank. Air hisses through my teeth with the wince, and I hear him chuckle.

"Perfect," he declares. He sits up and pushes his arms around me, his chest flush to my back, hands cupping my breasts. "Put me inside you," he breathes against my ear.

I reach between us and sit up on my knees to allow him enough room, and as I slide onto his dick, I'm reminded of how fucking full he makes me feel. My mouth drops despite myself as I start a slow rhythm, guided by his hands. He bites my shoulder, the nape of my neck, and when he finally relaxes back on the pillows, I grab his thighs and go to work.

"Fucking hell, bird," he moans. He grabs my ass with both hands and squeezes to the point that I know I'll be bruised tomorrow. The pain licks at my greed, causing me to slow my riding motions and roll my hips so that I'm taking him inch-for-inch with every stroke.

"Jeez, you're fucking sexy like this," he hisses. "This fucking body… *Shit*… You take me so well."

Reed groans, thrusting his pelvis up like he needs more. I dig my nails into his thighs, angry red welts rising in their wake, and the sight of them remind me of his promise to crawl beneath my skin.

The thought makes me shift onto my feet, squatting over him and leaning backward against his chest. It's a different angle, and shit… I don't know how he gets harder, but with his groan, he does.

"Oh my—*fuck*, Wren," he whines.

That's right.

Call my fucking name.

He slides his hand down my stomach and finds my clit with ease, his other hand wrapping beneath my chin. He tugs my jaw down and presses his fingers inside my mouth. I taste myself on those digits, humming pleasure around them.

The pressure of his finger on my clit makes my thighs clench. I'm struggling for composure, to keep my rhythm going as he begins to break me down.

And when Reed flips us so that my face is in the mattress, my ass hiked up and knees beneath me, I slip into the pathetic creature he made me the last time.

His face is between my spread thighs again, full intention of an end this time. It's barely a minute that he's lapping at my cunt before he's sliding his dick into me. He reaches for my braid and yanks my head back as he slams inside. Over and over and *over*. Continuously slapping my ass or teasing my clit. Keeping my back arched how he wants it. It's an anvil on my senses, consuming me whole.

I don't know what day it is, the time, or my own fucking name.

But I know his.

And something about that feels fucking freeing.

Every thrust and slap of his hand drives me further. And when I come, I feel it sliding down my thighs. I feel the dopamine hit, crack over my skull and wash over my skin.

I can't stop coming—*squirting* for him and only him. Even when he curses my name and I feel him explode inside me, my own release continues to roll in waves. Tears fall down my cheeks and soak into the mattress.

Finally, after a few moments, I feel the releases slow.

Reed doesn't pull out of me as he slumps against my back and kisses my spine. "Fucking hell, bird," he groans out. "Your pussy grips."

I pick my head up, feeling him slide out of me with one last slap, and I frown back at him.

"My pussy grips?" I repeat in confusion.

He looks like he might smile. "Yeah," he says as he sinks onto his ass. "God, look at the mess you made," he adds, gesturing to the wet bed.

The wet spot is mildly embarrassing. Even so, I throw my discarded underwear at his face. "Lucky. Once again," I say as I roll to the edge of the bed to get up. I grab my robe from the floor and push it onto my shoulders, hearing Reed get up himself.

Shit, my legs are wobbly.

And now I'm starving.

That curry sounds amazing.

"Oh my god—"

The noise of Reed's exclamation turns me around, and when I see where he is, my stomach drops. He's standing at the door to my closet and staring inside at the clutter like he just found the entrance to Narnia.

"The hell are you doing in my closet?!" I ask, running forward to slam the door shut.

"I was looking for the bathroom," he answers. "Why do you have bags and boxes of random shit piled in here? Did you just move?" he asks.

"No," I reply. "No, they're just boxes of things I might need one day—stop snooping. It's rude."

The smirk on his lips makes me retract. I stare at him for a beat, unsure of why this is amusing.

"What?" I ask.

"It's just... I had a suspicion that you were neurodivergent, but I didn't want to say anything," he says.

"What does that have to do with my boxes?" I ask.

"These are your doom boxes," he says matter-of-factly.

I blink, chewing on my tongue as my hands settle haughtily on my hips. "My what?"

"Doom boxes," he repeats. "My youngest brother, Koen, does the same thing. And my mom. She loves to hoard shit 'just in case.' It used to drive my dad crazy, but I think it's become more of an endearment now. Though, her boxes are a lot more chaotic and all over the house. At least yours are neatly tucked away in a closet."

I just stare at him. "You don't think it's weird?" I ask him.

"Nah. My middle brother, Kamden, is the only one of us that's typical. Dad is the 'neat and tidy' type, while my mom is… *not*," he says fondly, smiling at the ground. "She used to have a color-coordinated board on the fridge and in the hallway in order to remember things like laundry or appointments. We had sticky notes everywhere after Koen was born. Three boys, one teenage girl, plus Mads on most days… It was a lot. Dad helped her develop a system that worked after she broke down one day for missing Koen's first year doctor's appointments and forgetting to pick me up from school. The system helped—eighty percent of the time, at least. Some days, she just didn't have the energy."

"I know how that is," I mutter under my breath. "It doesn't annoy you?" I ask.

He smirks at me, then sweeps his knuckle beneath my chin —which I swat away, and the slap only makes his smile widen.

"I think it's cute," he admits. "Helps me understand you a little more—See? We're getting to know each other already."

I gawk, mouth twisting. "You don't get to think I'm cute," I say.

A quiet chuckle sounds from him. "Why not?" he asks.

"Because that's not how we work," I say as I turn on my heel.

"I think that's exactly how we work. You're the one that just squirted on my dick for the second time, and you're walking around with my cum falling down your thigh," he says, following me.

I flip him off over my shoulder.

"So, what about you, then?" he says when he catches me.

"What about me?" I ask.

"Do you have any siblings like you? Or were you the odd one out?"

Cold air sweeps over my suddenly itching face. I practically feel my walls rise, and within a blink, I can't think.

"What, are you writing my biography now?" I say as I round the corner.

"What about… weird ex-boyfriends that we might run into tonight?" he goes on to ask. "Costar fuck buddies?"

"Will you get jealous if I say yes?" I throw over my shoulder.

"No," he says. "Just make me work harder to make you forget them."

"You already make me forget my fucking name," I mutter under my breath.

Reed grabs my arm and pulls me into him. He's smiling coyly, gaze perusing my robed body like he's already fucking me again in his mind.

"I make you forget your own name?" he asks as if it's news to him.

I chew on the inside of my mouth again, annoyed at his grin, but honestly willing to say anything to get him to stop prying about my family.

"I can't believe I'm saying this, but yes, Reed. You somehow fuck the nerves right out of my body," I say, voice dripping with frustration. "If I keep you around for nothing else during this promo season, it'll be that."

"And because I look pretty?" he taunts.

"And because you look pretty," I feed his ego in a deadpan tone.

Reed hisses a *"Yes!"* and punches the air, making my brows furrow.

"You really don't mind being used like this?" I ask.

He chuckles deviously and kisses my cheek. "Bird… We've barely scratched the surface. Do you know what I think?"

"I'm terrified to ask," I mutter.

"I think your managers chose me for a reason," he goes on, suddenly standing over me as my back presses into the wall.

"And I think that reason was to help you realize that you can be who you really are without consequence. You can be this smart ass, bratty bitch without shutting everyone out, and people will fucking love you. You don't have to put up a wall every time you step outside. So, stop being so scared of me in public and *use me*. I'm waiting to see how the woman who doesn't care what anyone else thinks, not the show she thinks everyone else is wanting."

CHAPTER TWENTY

I DON'T KNOW what it is about Reed Matthews that pushes me over the edge, but I'm fucking falling. I don't know how he's calling me names and fucking the life out of me in one minute, and then empowering my soul in the very next. I don't know why his challenge and drive make me insane to the point that I'm willing to do anything to prove him wrong.

Push.

Shove.

Fuck.

Slap.

Reed Matthews is the exact danger I knew he would be.

Fuck. Why do I like it?

My nerves have never been this calm heading into any meeting or party. I've never felt my breathing so even. I'm tapping on my knee, not out of any nervous habit, but because the anticipation won't let me stop moving.

"Holy shit," Reed mutters beside me.

My brows narrow at the exclamation. "What is it?"

He jerks his chin, gesturing me toward him. "Come watch this."

I scoot across the bench toward him until he leans over

with his phone so I can see the video he's been working on for the last half hour.

Holy hell.

It's our video from earlier today, and the moment it begins playing, warmth spreads over my entire body—not only from the actual video, but the memory of our filming it.

It starts out with his hand trailing up the mattress like many others he has posted, but this time, instead of his hand gripping the sheet, it transitions to his piano key tattooed fingers tightening around my throat, the beat dropping with the switch. There's a glimpse of my mouth as it sags, and the pillows of my breasts move with my caving chest.

Why is this so fucking hot?

It plays three times before I can speak.

"I think we're going to break the internet," he says, bringing me out of the stupor.

We're definitely going to break something.

"Are you posting that right now?" I ask.

His gaze lingers on mine for a moment. "Do you want me to wait?"

I consider it. Wait, and it'll post tomorrow. After the screening. When I'm not around anyone. The *safe* option.

Or post it now and walk into this party with people knowing he probably just fucked me into next week.

"Posting now would be a bad idea," I say.

"Oh, the worst," he agrees, though the amusement in his gaze tells me otherwise.

"People would have questions."

"Tons," he says.

"I'll have to turn my phone off," I go on.

Reed's gaze moves to my lips, inching closer. "What a shame that would be."

"The *name* calling," I say.

"I'll call you worse after," he says against my lips.

"Promise?"

A huff leaves him, the corner of his lip tugging fully upward. "On my life."

Something flutters in my stomach when his mouth brushes against mine. I barely notice my arms moving, my fingers curling in the ends of his hair at his neck.

"And they thought you would be a *good* influence on me," I say.

"They were wrong," Reed rasps.

I hesitate a moment longer, dodging when he tries to kiss me, when he tries to pull me into him. My mouth opens and closes against his, tension building in the whispers of air between our bodies.

"Post it," I say.

Reed grins, his lashes lifting, eyes locking on mine. "Yes," he hisses. He bites at my bottom lip and squeezes my ass, and I shove him away as we pull up to the driveway.

I'm in such fucking shit.

"Hey James, give us a second," Reed says, his fingers typing quickly on the phone. I stare at his screen, and when he goes to tap 'post,' he hesitates one more second, eyes shifting to me. And without losing my stare, he hits the blue word.

I'm still watching him when my phone rings.

My publicist's name stretches across the screen, and I'm tempted to laugh. Though before I can let it out, Reed grabs my phone, tosses it into the third row, and plants a harsh kiss on me. It catches me off guard. Even still, I kiss him back.

"Let's go fuck something up," he says when we part.

He doesn't give me a second to respond. I can hear my phone buzzing in the third row, but the moment my door is opened, I forget about it.

Music is playing loudly from the back. I see Reed's gaze narrow when he reaches me, obviously confused by the party atmosphere.

"Different," he says.

"That's Felix," I mutter, thinking of whenever the young producer would come on set. "He's a prick, but at least he's funny."

"The producer on this?" Reed asks.

"Felix West," I say. "He was a teenage billionaire. He started on YouTube when it first became a big thing. One of its first comedic stars. But instead of going into acting or touring, he decided he wanted to write and produce. That was after he went to rehab for a gambling addiction—for the *second* time."

"Twice for gambling?"

"I think the first time was cocaine."

Two men open up the doors for us as one recognizes me, and the moment we enter, music floods the space around us.

Fucking Felix.

"Kelly!"

Speaking of the devil.

I look past a few people coming our way, moving my head to try and see where Felix is coming from. I hear his voice again, and Reed leans closer to me. "Balcony," he directs me.

At the top of the stairs, Felix is grinning back at me.

"Mean girl!" he calls as he starts toward us, and I pause to meet him at the bottom of the staircase. "There you are. I wondered if you were too busy to make it," he says, leaning in to kiss my cheek.

"I try to make time for people who throw money my way," I reply, and Felix grins.

"Atta girl," he coos, gaze moving to Reed. "Ah, the boyfriend!" Felix exclaims.

"What's up," Reed says, taking Felix's casual handshake.

"How's it going? You guys are fucking killing it on tour," Felix says to him. "I'm trying to get tickets for your New Year's Eve show, but I think I might have to jerk off some jackass to land them."

"Hollywood Hollow Arena, man," Reed says, returning the grin. "It's jerk off some prick or sell your firstborn."

"Some of them would probably prefer the firstborn," Felix mutters. "Nah, I plan on throwing some money at them for VIP. Unless you want to hook a friend up?"

Reed laughs. "They just let me get up there and talk shit to people," he says. "They know better than to give me access to that. I'd give them away just to get people to the show."

"And I am glad your manager took that power away from you now," Felix says. "Don't give away anything people will pay double resell for."

I scoff. "You're a troll."

"If I'm a troll, then you gotta pay the tolls, pretty," he says, winking at me. "Alright come on. I'll show you the fun shit."

Reed slides his fingers into mine, and together we follow Felix into the next room where the music is bumping, and I finally realize how many people he's invited to this fucking screening.

Jesus hell.

"Drinks. Adderall. Weed. Whatever you guys need, don't hesitate," Felix says, walking backward in front of us.

I eye him. "I thought you were on the up?" I ask.

Felix grins. "Bad manners to remind people they're supposed to be sober, Kelly."

"Just looking out for a friend," I snap, batting my lashes.

A cold laugh leaves him, and he pulls out the necklace where his five year chip is dangling. "Still got it," he says, kissing the chip. "The goodies are for you sick bastards," he adds. "Seriously, though. If you need anything at all—"

"We'll find you," Reed says as he pushes his arm over my shoulders.

Felix claps his hands in front of him, then points to us, still grinning crookedly. "Okay, love birds. Screening starts in an hour. Make yourselves at home. There's food out back—oh,

and if you two get any urges to show out like you did at Sean's
—" he raises a poignant brow at me "—there are several *private*
bedrooms. Try to find one," he adds with a wink.

He skips away then, leaving Reed and I staring after him.

"Am I that chat happy?" Reed asks me.

"You're worse," I tell him.

"How's that?"

I look up at him. "Because Felix only pulls off 'this guy is
definitely an asshole' energy. You pull off 'somehow this happy
emo puppy is also going to fuck my face off later, and I'm
going to thank him for it.'"

"That is the nicest thing anyone has ever said to me," Reed
beams.

"I'm a great actress," I say, and he grabs his chest like I've
hurt him.

"So *mean*. Who can I put you in front of so you can be mean
to them instead?"

A man moving toward us catches my attention from the
corner of my eyes. "One guess."

His jaw tenses like he can see the familiar face approaching,
too. "Mother fuck," he grunts. "Kiss me," he says with a soft
peck on my lips.

"You just kissed me," I say.

"You know how I mean, bird," he replies, his nose nudging
mine.

"Why?" I ask.

"Because I want to see the jealousy on this fucker's face
when I make you moan for me in public," he practically
growls.

His open mouth lands upon mine, and I press my hand to
his face as I let him in.

It's difficult reminding myself not to give in in public as
much as I do when we're alone. Not when he's kissing me like
this. Not when his long fingers are squeezing the small of my

back and my side. And especially not when he has me so flush that I can feel his dick through his clothes.

A groan leaves me at that, and I feel his smile on my lips at the triumph I'd already forgotten not to give him.

"Ahem," Chris clears his throat as he reaches us.

Reed and I part, peering sideways in Chris's direction as if we've forgotten the rest of the room exists, and if I'm being honest with myself, I almost did.

"Man, you are more forgiving than I ever could be," Chris says to Reed, ignoring me.

Reed straightens and slides his arm around my shoulders.

Every time he pulls me into him like this, I feel my body tense at the proximity, the musky smell of his citrus soap. For someone who is on the road most days out of the year and living on a diet of hot tea, salad, and pizza, he smells better than any man I've ever been around.

Though something tells me he probably has a better skin care routine than I do.

"Hi, Chris," I say to him.

I should have throat punched this guy when he was pushing into my dressing room trying to get lucky. Instead, I'd kicked him in the balls with my heel in the hopes it would damage his chances of reproduction.

The last thing we need on this planet is more of him.

"Kelly," he says with a nod, and his gaze moves back to Reed. "I didn't realize you were an idiot as well as a bore."

Reed chuckles. "I'm neither of those things. I'm just not here to entertain assholes like you."

"No, just thousands of screaming teeny boppers," Chris says.

Reed laughs. "You know what? I'm not even mad about that. We sell out places that you'd barely fill up the first two rows to."

I press on Reed's chest, not wanting him to get into a fight tonight—not because I'm being protective, but rather because if anyone is hitting this guy, it's me.

"If we're done comparing dicks, I think it's time to get something to eat," I say. "I'll see you on the tour, Chris," I say, tugging on Reed's arm.

"Doubt that," Chris says, and I pause.

"What was that?" I ask.

"I said I doubt you'll be joining me on the press tour," Chris says.

"Yeah? Why's that?"

Chris huffs and peers between us. "That little stunt you pulled tonight has people scrambling to do damage control."

"What stunt?" I ask innocently.

"Don't play dumb, Kelly. It isn't a good look for you," Chris replies.

"Your face in itself isn't a good look, yet somehow they still let you walk around in public," I reply.

"The video," Chris says, his voice tense.

"Oh, the video…" I look at Reed, who smirks at me and reaches up to my chin, giving it a playful flick.

"You're lucky they're not dragging you into the director's office right now," Chris goes on. "I heard from my agent that people were already pulling interviews for you. A shame, really, that one little clip can cause so much damage—not to mention the video from Sean's. I've had a few people ask what the hell happened to make pretty boy Reed Matthews so *angry.*"

"You smug bastard," I snap.

Fucking typical. Of course, he sent in that video.

Chris smirks. "Maybe you should remember that the next time you think about airing your sex life."

I know it's a lie.

Because if it were true, Felix would be loud enough about it that a scene would already have been caused.

Reed sighs as he steps up to Chris and stretches his arm around the actor's shoulders, his height towering over Chris's. "You know… they say jealousy is actually brought on by some kind of past trauma," Reed says slowly. "A good therapist could help you unpack that. Get to the root of why you're so insecure. It's really not healthy to harbor those kinds of emotions." He pats Chris on the chest twice like he's consoling him. "In the meantime, while you're figuring out your shit, I'll be making that beautiful redhead over there come on my dick. Morning. Noon. Night. Maybe even in the bathroom at this fucking party. Do me a favor? If you hear screaming, just tell everyone it was a coyote." He squeezes Chris's shoulder as he takes his arm away, then starts toward me, still pointing at the tense actor. "You're a good man, right? I can trust you to do that for us?"

I feel my eyes burning a victorious hole in Chris's face as Reed wraps his arm around my waist and kisses me deliberately.

Reed gives my nose a playful nudge when we part.

"Ready to get something to eat?" he asks. "Or maybe…" His gaze moves predatorily over me, lip drawing behind his teeth.

Before Reed can finish his sentence, Chris tips back the rest of his drink, his ice clinking the glass, and he turns around to leave us as if we've just ruined his night.

"I like when you're mean to other people," Reed says, gently toying with the end of my hair over my shoulder. "Makes me feel a little better about being bullied by you."

"Except that you like it," I say, and he smiles crookedly.

"How many people here have watched our video, do you think?" he asks.

"You mean how many people are wondering when we're going to sneak away to fuck in a random closet?" I ask, feeling the stares.

"Are you offering?"

I resist pushing him away, and he grins.

His phone buzzes in his pocket then, and he only releases me to catch the messages coming in.

"Whoa," he says, grinning.

"What is it?" I ask.

"My tour manager," he laughs. "Check this out."

Reed extends the phone to me so I can see the texts, and when I read them, I nearly smile.

TOUR KEEPER - STELLA

Are you with Wren Kelly?

She needs to call her manager.

Now.

I can't believe you posted that.

You have her in so much trouble.

It was hot, though.

"Amanda is probably dialing everyone I know," I say. "I honestly thought she was supposed to be here." I glance around us, looking for any sign of her, but see nothing more than a few people staring back at us.

"Should we get food and seats?" Reed asks, stuffing his phone back in his pocket.

"Ha. No," I say, balking. "God. No. I can't sit through an entire movie with myself in it."

Reed looks like he wants to laugh. "You don't watch your own films?"

"Hell no," I answer him.

"So… why are we here?"

"Most of these assholes working the party have their own podcasts and gossip accounts," I say. "The bartender has a podcast that talks about celebrities' favorite drinks and shows you how to make them. That server over there with the blonde hair, she works for that podcast that I sent you a link to the other day. The waitressing job is just for extra cash, but it has its perks."

"And you know all of this, how?" he asks.

"Felix," I answer. "He hires people like them on purpose so people think his parties are more amazing than they actually are. Always wants to create a buzz around his brand. He has his smarts when it comes to shit like this."

"If that's what you want to call it," Reed mutters.

"There you are."

Oh, here we go.

Reed and I turn toward the woman's voice, finding Amanda coming up to us with a pursed lip smile on her face.

"Let me guess," Reed says. "You're here to jail me?"

"I'd put you in handcuffs, but something tells me you'd like it too much," Amanda replies as she extends her hand. "Amanda," she introduces herself.

"Reed," he replies as if she didn't already know. "And you're right. Though I'd prefer it if she's the one handcuffing me," he says as he nods my way.

I stare pointedly at my manager. "Do you see what I'm dealing with here?"

"I do," she says. "Judging by that little video, I'd say you're starting to like it."

"Guess again," I mumble.

Amanda's smile widens between us before she jerks her head toward the entrance. "Come on. I know you're not going to watch your movie anyway. Let's meet over at your place so we can have a little chat," she says, looking at Reed.

"Am I in trouble?" Reed taunts, but Amanda turns on her heel.

"Not with me," Amanda throws over her shoulder.

CHAPTER TWENTY-ONE
WREN

THE MOMENT we get back to my apartment, Reed curls up on the couch with Anita, and the dog rolls over onto her back and snuggles him as if he's her favorite person ever.

I give my dog a deadpan stare. "Hoe," I call her.

Reed grins wider. "This is now my girlfriend," he says. "You've been replaced."

"And it comes as no surprise that you're into bestiality, *Sasquatch*," I retort.

"I am glad the two of you at least appear to be infatuated with each other in public," Amanda says from the kitchen island. "Shannon will be here in a minute."

I frown and glance at my clock. "Shannon? She's coming here?"

"She wanted to talk to Matthews in person," Amanda replies.

"Oh, a spanking, then. Can't wait," he grins.

The door flies open then, revealing Larry as he staggers inside wearing satin pajamas—two bags in his hands, and a flustered look on his face.

"Half of the reason she has me is to *schedule* meetings like this so that she isn't bombarded," Larry says in an annoyed voice to Amanda. "Who cares if they posted a sexy video? They're going viral—"

"It could have hurt her chances at the indie part," Amanda argues.

Everything seems to go silent around us despite the television going.

My stomach knots, and I hear Reed sit up.

"Wait, what?" Reed asks as he stands.

"What are you talking about?" I ask Amanda.

Amanda's lips press into a thin line, and she hesitates as if she doesn't want to tell me whatever sits on the tip of her tongue.

"I was waiting on Shannon to get here for damage control," she says.

"What do you mean damage control?" Reed asks, and I swear there's more panic in his voice than mine. "It was just for fun."

Amanda looks at me. "Sean called."

Larry tosses me a squishy stress ball animal, though I don't look down to see what animal it is. I'm already squeezing it as if I can rip it apart.

"Sean loves controversy," I say defensively.

"Sean also has the managers of other actors calling him and telling him their clients don't want to work with the Public Mean Girl Whore of Hollywood," Amanda says. "His words, not mine."

Reed snorts.

"Don't ever call me that," I say to him.

"I'm changing your name in my phone," he replies, already taking his phone out.

"This is serious," Amanda says in a warning tone.

"You'll need to gag and quarter him to get him to take anything seriously—"

"That sounds like a fun time actually," Reed interjects.

"—If you didn't know that about him then maybe you should have done more research before pinning him with me," I go on.

"When we chose him, we didn't expect him to actually talk you into something reckless," Shannon says when she comes through the door.

Reed folds his arms over his chest, watching her set her bag on the kitchen counter. "So, what? You want me to delete it?" Reed asks Shannon.

"What did Sean say?" I ask Amanda. "Does he want it down? Erased? A public statement put out so he doesn't feel awkward about hiring me?"

"No, actually, he wants you more," Amanda says.

I hurl the stress ball at her face.

It hits her in the boob and ricochets off, knocking my coffee machine over and spilling the ready ground coffee all over the countertop.

I barely notice.

"What the fucking hell, Mandi!" I snap, but Amanda grins.

"Is your broom in one of these doom closets?" Reed asks me.

"Yes, by the door, but I can clean it—What do you mean he wants me more?" I ask Amanda.

"I mean, he asked if you would be doing any more of those videos and if they were promo for something you were working on because if they weren't, then they should be," Amanda answers.

I scoff. "Yeah, like the romcom would want to use that as a promo," I mutter.

"They wouldn't," Shannon agrees. "In fact, they're not thrilled about it. However, because you're going viral right now and there's no blatant nudity, they're letting it slide."

Reed walks behind me to clean up the coffee and pauses to

whisper against my ear, "Which translates to: they thought it was hot."

"And as far as the leaked video from Sean's—" Shannon pauses to wait for Reed to look at her "—don't *ever* do that in public again," she says to him. "I don't care what you two do behind closed doors, but that display had us in knots. I've had phone call after phone call with your own people, and while we've handled it to say that both of you are passionate adults, if it happens again, you're going to have to put out a statement saying that you're not a narcissistic asshole controlling my client and abusing her behind the scenes."

Reed looks like someone just slapped him in the face.

"Shit," he grunts. "Fuck. *No.* That's not… That's not who I am. That night got tense. I was jealous. I'm… *shit.* I'm sorry. I would never put my hands on her in any way like that— fucking hell." He quickly spins toward me, panic in his voice as he pleads, "Wren, you *know*—"

"Reed," Shannon says, holding up a hand and silencing his ramble. "It's handled. Just keep it in the bedroom or if you two are fighting, make sure to leave the fucking venue before anything crazy happens. I was honestly surprised it wasn't her choking you."

Reed remains quiet for a beat, and I feel him sit on the stool close to me, then sink his head into his hands atop the bar. I stare between Amanda and Shannon, waiting for them to keep going about Sean and the indie part.

"Hang on, if everyone is okay with this—Sean, especially since he's pretty important right now—why the hell would you scare me like that?" I ask. "What was the point?"

"The point was to scare you so you might realize how this could have gone were it anyone else," Shannon says. "Some of these old shits wouldn't want you attached to their films with a video like that."

"I don't want to work for them anyway," I say. "I'm not working for someone who wants to silence me."

Amanda and Shannon smile. "We thought you might say that," Amanda says.

"What does that mean?" I ask.

Amanda filters through her bag and takes out a stack of papers—a script, I realize.

A lump rises in my throat.

"What's this?" I ask as she slides it across the counter.

"This was delivered to me at my home as I was getting ready to go out to Felix's party to find you, along with a note," Amanda says. "It's a script for a Marilyn Monroe inspired picture. From Amber Weisen."

I stare at her.

"Holy shit," I hear Reed say.

"Marilyn Monroe was like a size six," is the only thing I can manage.

"Well, that was my first question after I got over the shock," Amanda says. "I wanted to make sure they weren't going to try to put you on some dangerously ridiculous starvation diet to fit into whatever they might think is right for the picture."

"And?" I ask when she hesitates.

"And, I was told that they don't give a fuck if you're a size two or twenty. If you read well and keep doing what you're doing… it's yours."

My knees weaken. I hear a barstool slide my way, and thank fuck it lands under my ass before I hit the floor.

Which is when I catch what she just said.

"What do you mean, keep doing what I'm doing?" I say, looking at Amanda.

Amanda gives me a sly smile. "You forget Hollywood has eyes everywhere, Wren. Even *backstage*," she says with a raised brow.

I don't like the way she says the word.

"What does that mean?" Reed asks.

My stomach drops as it dawns on me what's happening.

"She knows it's fake," I realize.

"She knows it's fake," Amanda nods. "Something about the two of you talking very loudly backstage about making yourselves look 'less rigid.'"

"Fuck," I curse. "Why would she offer a script after that?"

"She thought the ruse was ingenious marketing," Amanda says, and I know it's an embellishment of the truth.

I look at Shannon and wait for what's really happening here.

"She's using your relationship as your audition," Shannon answers.

"Oh *fuck*." I sink my head into my hands.

I suddenly feel as if the world is sitting on my shoulders, pushing me down and down and down. Tonight had been easier because I'd let go of a fraction of the fucks I should give in public. Before, my future depended on this little charade, and I think I wanted it to fail just so I could prove I didn't need someone by my side to land a gig.

Yet now…

Now my career truly depends on how well I pull this off?

Nausea creeps into my throat.

"I'm missing something," Reed says.

"It means she expects me to really act with you," I say, meeting his eyes. "Sell it like I would behind the camera. Not just appearing less tense or playing nice."

"I have means to help with that," he says, winking at me.

"That also means—" Shannon looks at Reed this time. "Nothing overtly stupid. Keep it classy. This little video is your tipping point. People are going to be asking you a lot of questions at the events coming up—more so than they were before because you've put your sex life out there. So, you need to get your stories straight. Where did you meet? Did you make him work for it?"

Shannon leans closer to us, finger pointing into the countertop when she speaks.

"When I look at a photo of you two, I want to feel like I'm reading a romance novel that I can't put down," she says firmly. "I want more, more, *more*. Make me *crave* the two of you. I want to become the person who obsesses over you for weeks at a time. I want to eat up every fucking picture you post, wondering when you're going to appear at one of his concerts, scoping out airports in the hopes to see you two making out at the gate, needing to know if you've met his parents or not. Give me *everything*."

The walls seem to be closing in.

Why is this shirt so tight?

"I think I'm going to gag," I mutter, pulling at the neck of my shirt.

"I'll pull your hair back if you do," Reed says.

"Reed, why do you look like it's Christmas morning, and you're a five year old who just got his first bike?" Larry asks, leaning his elbows on the countertop.

Shit, is it hot in here?

"Because I like this," I hear Reed reply.

Why is there air blowing on me? Is that the fan? Why is my fan on?

"What part exactly?" Larry asks Reed, his amusement apparent.

"Getting told to put on more of a show," Reed answers. "It's kind of what I do."

My skin is too itchy.

A hand lands on my thigh and squeezes, and I look sideways to meet Reed's gaze. "Hey," he says softly, ignoring whatever Shannon and Amanda are saying. "Okay?"

I wipe my face harshly, making sure that it hurts my

cheeks. "Yeah. Fine—hey, did we need to talk about anything else?" I ask Amanda and Shannon.

Amanda looks at me like she knows I need a few minutes.

"All set," she says, smiling. She turns to Shannon. "Do you want to go grab drinks with me?"

"Let's go," Shannon says.

As Amanda and Shannon file out, and I finally find the floor to stand, Larry comes over to me.

"I didn't know anything about this," he says hurriedly. "I'll send you all the dates for your events tomorrow so you and Reed can plan better. I—"

"It's fine," I say.

I just want everyone out.

"You're not mad?" Larry asks.

"I will be if everyone doesn't leave within the next sixty seconds," I say through my teeth.

"And… we're done." Larry grabs Amanda and Shannon, ushering them to the door. "Okay. Come on. You two can chat later. Bye Reed!" he calls to him over his shoulder.

"See ya," Reed says from the barstool.

I don't know what else Amanda and Shannon say. My hand is on the door. Larry tells me goodbye, but I'm staring at the floor, suddenly noticing the pattern of the wood that looks like a face.

Demons stare back at me.

I know it's my anxiety. I know there are no demons other than the ones hiding under my bed and those that follow me on the street to protect me from myself.

Man, they've been doing a shit job lately.

The moment I shut the door, I pause to take a breath.

The script is staring at me from the counter, burning a hole in my nonexistent soul and threatening to break me as badly as Reed swears to. The pressure of the role has me unable to fill my lungs. My palm is pressing against this door as if the moment I move away, I'll fall down the rabbit hole to Wonderland, never to be found again.

Maybe that would be better than this.

"You're a fucking badass," Reed says behind me. "Did you know that?"

I scoff at the compliment and finally move. "This is insane," I mutter. "I need to process," I admit. "That was… *a lot*. Maybe I should go on a walk—"

"I can come with you," he says, drawing closer.

"No," I say as I continue to avoid his eyes. "No, I need to be alone. I need to wrap my head around this."

"Hey," he says, tipping my face back with his finger. "Don't worry. I have you. You'll get the part."

My jaw tightens as I look at him. "You don't have to be nice to me. This is more than you signed up for."

"I signed up to break you," he says. "Looks like I have full permission to make you lose your mind over me now."

I huff, shaking my head. "Yeah. Right. Okay," I say.

"Besides. I believe it was my idea that got us into a further mess," he adds.

My gaze lifts to his once more. "You're absolutely reckless," I say to him.

His lips flinch upward. "The worst," he agrees, tongue flicking over his lips.

I swallow under his stare, yet just as he leans down to kiss me, I push on his chest.

"You need to go home," I say against his lips.

"Let me stay," he whispers. "We can talk. Figure this out together."

"I need to be alone, Reed," I say, stepping away from him.

He sighs, head hanging. "Okay." He grabs his phone from the counter and dials a number, then holds it up to his ear. "Hey. Yeah, I'm ready. Okay, cool. Be down in a minute."

I barely notice that he's off the phone.

"Today was fun," he says awkwardly.

I curl my nose up, reaching for the door knob. "Oh, no. No, we're not doing that. Don't say that again."

Reed smirks. "Fine. It was a horrible day. I can't believe you're still so fucking mean to me."

Damn him for seeing through me.

"I like it better when you're pouting," I go along. "Groveling on your knees is a good look, too."

The corner of his lips hike higher, and he falls to his knees in front of me without a second thought. "I think between your knees is my best look," he says, leaning his face into my thighs.

"Reed!" I shove him back, and he laughs as he catches himself on the floor.

"Goodnight, poser," I drawl, opening the door.

He stands defeatedly. "I don't get a kiss goodbye?" he asks, stopping at the threshold.

"What is it with you and goodbye kisses?" I ask.

"If it's a good one, you might invite me to stay."

"That's not—no. *No.* Bye, Reed," I say as I start closing the door on him.

"High five? Fist bump? Ass slap?" he continues to beg in the few inches of door he has left to battle. "Wren—"

The door clicks, and as it does, I lean my forehead against the steel, unable to swipe the tiniest fraction of a smile from my lips. A soft chuckle leaves me that feels foreign, and as I sigh, Anita comes trotting up to me.

"I heard that," Reed says on the other side of the door.

"You heard wrong," I call back. "Goodnight, Reed."

There's a quiet beat on the other side, until finally, I hear him tap twice on the door. "Night, bird," he replies.

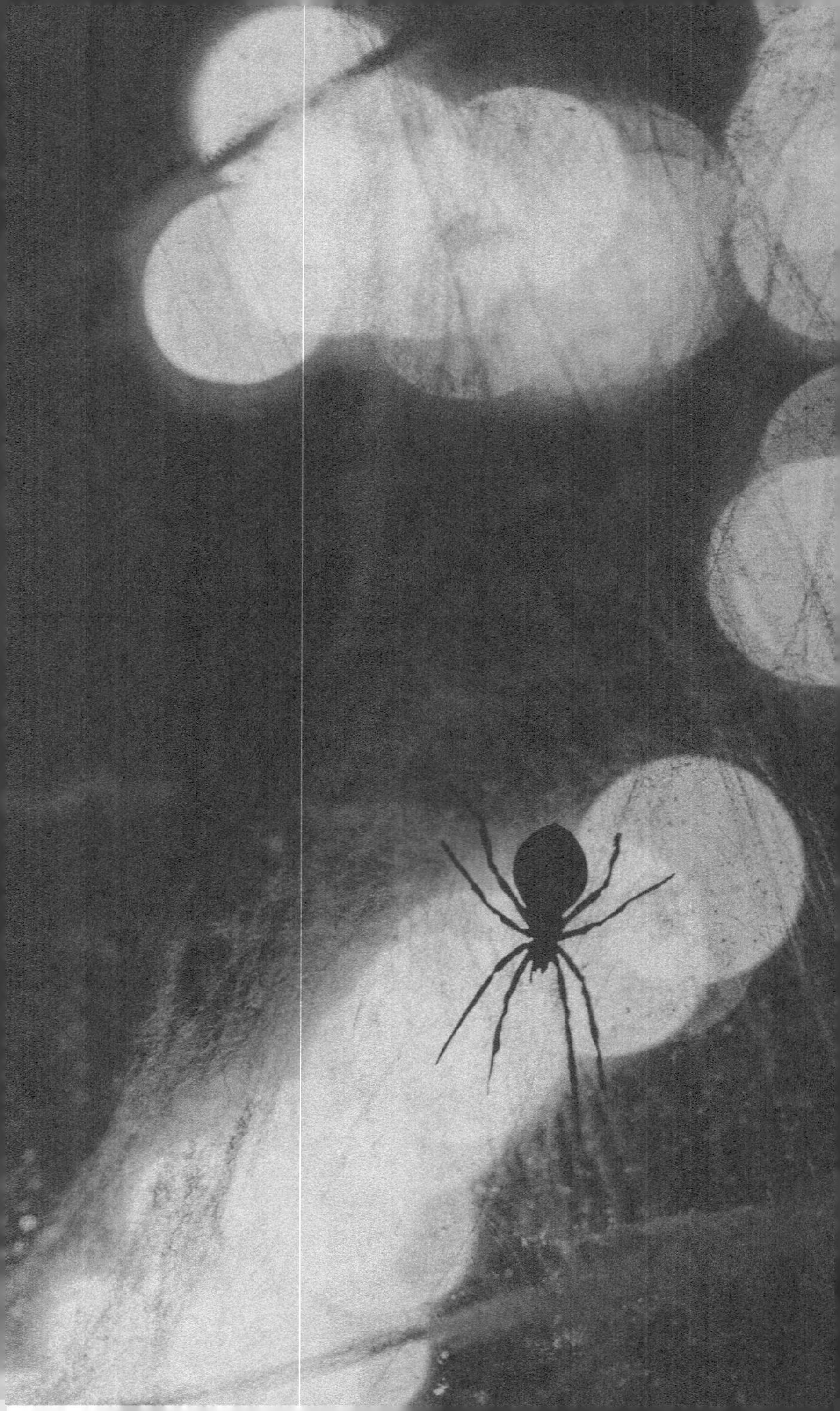

CHAPTER TWENTY-TWO

WREN

I SINK DOWN to my knees and close my eyes. Anita puts her paw on my thigh like she's trying to comfort me, and I finally manage to take in a few even breaths to try and calm the anxiety sweeping through my bones.

When did getting a part become so fucking complicated?

Anita whines and pushes her nose beneath my elbow, prompting a smile on my lips as she eagerly nudges me to take her on a walk.

"Okay, girl," I say, scratching her ears and kissing her nose. I push my hair up into a pony and put a hat on after standing, followed by an oversized hoodie from the chair—only realizing that it's Reed's when I smell him on it.

Ugh. I can't believe I just inhaled the fleece like it's a drug.

I gag and look down at Anita. "Bite me if I ever do that again," I tell her.

She sneezes in response, and we head out of the door.

"Hey, Tommy," I say to the doorman as Anita and I exit the building.

"Miss Kelly," Tommy replies, nodding. "Miss Anita," he greets my dog.

We cross the street and head into the moonlit park across

the way. Anita sets the pace when we hit the sidewalk, and I try not to zone out completely as the cool night air ushers me into a pool of thoughts.

Everything in me wants to shut down for a month. The pressure feels like it's swelling my bones. Times like this, I wish I had a close friend or family member to call to talk myself down from the ledge I'm rocking my toes against. However, that thought alone sinks my heart more than ten seconds earlier. My twin brother's face flashes behind my eyes, and I tug on Anita's leash so we can sit on the bench long enough for me to draw myself out of the stupor.

I know what he'd tell me if he were here. He'd wonder where my smile was. He'd tell me this should be easy, that the number of times we had to act as kids to get out of trouble should have been enough experience to sell something like this with ease. He'd tell me I'm easy to love, but difficult to like, and those that don't care to put in the effort don't deserve me anyway.

I sink my head into my hands as a tear drops down my cheek, and the empty part of me that had once been filled with his presence continues to leak.

Some days, I miss him more than I know how to put into words, and others… Other days, he feels like such a distant memory that I contemplate if he was ever real—if *any* of my past was real.

"Run, raven," Travis begs from his knees, his arms tied behind his back. "Run."

A gun raises to his temple, and he flinches at the touch, his gaze lifting to the man standing over him. "Please, don't hurt her," he says to Damien. "Please. Do what you want with me. Just let her go—"

"No—" I launch against the men's grips on my arms, eyes clouded with tears. "No, please. I'll do whatever you want. Set him free. I can pay you back—"

I gasp, pull out of the haunting vision, and swipe the tears off my cheeks.

Though, stifling my sobs feels impossible as the reminder of my last moments with him repeats like a broken reel.

Raven…

I forgot he used to call me that.

—Anita growls.

My ears perk at the unexpected noise. It sends my body into flight, eyes scanning the dark where she's looking. I scramble for my phone in my pocket, but I don't take it out. Instead, I slide it to the camera screen and tap record on the video, not caring that it may not pick up anything that's about to happen since it's in my pocket.

And when I see the person coming into the light, I force myself to stand.

"No where for you to hide this time, Kelly," Erik says as he pauses on the other side of the walk.

Vomit lurches into my throat. I wrap Anita's leash around my hand and tug her closer. "I didn't think vampires came out during a full moon," I say. "Aren't you afraid of the big bad wolf?"

Erik glares at me. "Damien wants to see you."

"You can tell Damien if he wants me then he can come get me himself," I snap, hating that my voice is already shaking. "Stop sending his little trolls to do his dirty work."

"You're lucky he didn't come find you after the party when you dodged me," Erik goes on. "Even luckier that your boy toy still has a face."

I stare at Erik, waiting on him to continue.

Yet, he doesn't.

"Why does he need to see me?" I eventually ask. "What have I done to warrant a face-to-face? He doesn't like the pictures you all send him?"

"Boss didn't really like the video from today," Erik says.

"I don't really give a fuck what he likes. You can remind him that he swore he'd never interfere with my job—"

"So long as you stay a perfectly quiet, mediocre little starlet," Erik says. "Or did you forget about that part?"

I grit my teeth and set my feet, prepared to run if I need to. "Fuck you," I hiss. "I'm tired of putting my dreams on the back burner because he thinks I'm going to blab about him or what he's done to me," I say. "I have no plans to talk about him to anyone. He needs to stop thinking he's such an important part of my life. He's nothing more than a reminder of how fucking alone he's made me."

"He didn't make you that way," Erik says. "That was your brother's doings."

Tears sting the back of my nose. "Is that it, then? Are you taking me in tonight?"

Go away or get it over with.

"No," Erik says. "I just wanted to make sure you remember that we can take you anytime we want. There's nothing your security can do about it—not that she would anyway."

I swallow because I know he's right. The only thing Tara has tried to do is keep them off my back, protect me from being taken, not get rid of them.

Erik's lips flinch upward. "Goodnight, Kelly. I expect I'll see you again soon."

I don't move as he staggers backward and turns. I don't move as he walks away, my body refusing to even shift from this spot so long as he's in my sight line.

And when he's finally nothing more than a speck in my peripheral, I bolt.

Anita runs at my side. My heart is in my ears. I don't bother looking both ways as we run across the street. I'm too fucking scared that I'll find a white SUV parked on the side of the road. Too terrified to make eye contact with any person who might be staring at us a little too hard.

Headlights flash on me as I reach the steps leading up to the complex's front door. Tommy has the door open, though he's chatting with another tenant. I keep my head down, letting my hood fall over my face as I dart through the glass door.

It doesn't matter that I know I'll be safe past these doors. I don't feel safe. I won't feel safe until I'm upstairs and a chair is under my door handle.

I can't stop moving.

The elevator isn't fast enough.

I'm pressing back the tears that want to fall. Forcing my knees rigid.

Fear that makes me want to scream crashes in on me. I need my room. I need my music. I need something to let this all out.

God, where are my keys?

Get in. Get in. Get in.

I get my key into the lock just as the second elevator dings. I don't look away from the door as I practically throw myself inside. I pretend there isn't a shadow coming down the hall. I ignore the footsteps coming closer on the floor.

My door slams behind me. I release Anita's leash and grab a chair to shove under the handle. It hits my toe, prompting a screech to leave me that I quickly stifle. The pain nearly buckles my knees; however, I can't stop.

The chair tilts under the handle, and I gawk at it for a half second.

It isn't enough.

I take inventory of everything around me.

Table. Couch. Dresser—

Foyer table.

I throw everything from on top of it to the ground, ignoring the shattering glass, and I push it in front of the door.

There's no one coming after you.

You're safe in here.

What if I'm not?

What if they're waiting on me at the elevator?

What if they're biding their time until I'm asleep?

I'm still shaking when I step back from the door, unable to look away. With every second that passes, I'm waiting on a wiggle of the knob. A slam. A knock.

I'm waiting on their threats to be fulfilled.

You destroy everything you touch.

Jaw quivering, I realize I haven't taken a full breath since leaving the park.

My entire body feels numb, all the way down to the marrow of my bones. My knees hit the cold floor, and I sink over them as emotion floods my core.

Do not fucking cry, I tell myself.

Don't you dare cry.

You're better than this.

But I'm so tired.

I'm so fucking tired.

Help.

Help me.

Please help me.

I want out of this.

Yet no one can help me. I know that. I know without getting them killed, there's no way for anyone to help me.

You know the only way out of this.

"Stop it," I say out loud, hands pressing to my ears.

I can't do this right now.

I can't go *there* right now.

My gaze drifts to my bedroom after a while, and before I can stop myself, I'm walking to it.

My hands shake as I open the top drawer of my dresser, as I pull out the antique music box buried in the back of it. There are scratches in the wooden top from the moments I didn't know how to handle my own frustration, when I was mad at my mom for the stupidest shit and thought the best way to get back at her was to mark up the music box she loved.

She never cared that I scratched it.

She just cared that I was okay.

I still smell her dandelion lotion she used to put on before bed every night. Still see her calm smile and hear the smoothness of her voice when she sang my twin brother and me a lullaby at night—all the way into our teen years, whether it was just a hum or the full song.

My heart caves in on itself the longer I stare.

I miss her hugs. Her reassurance. I miss the connection we shared.

I run my fingers over the faded flowers on the box, my heart skipping when my nail snags on one of the etchings. I remember the day I did this. I remember sitting on the bed with her after the fight, the weight of her arm around my shoulders as she tried to help me calm down and talk it out.

"You're going to fly one day," she whispers, kissing my temple. "So high, not even the wind can catch you."

"Mom, that doesn't make sense," I laugh, laying back on her pillow.

She meets my smile with her own. "I know, sweetie. But one day, you'll understand what I mean."

"What about me?" Travis asks, lying down opposite us. "What am I going to do?"

"Probably start a cult," our dad says as he enters the room.

"Richard!" Mom exclaims, though her smile doesn't fade.

Travis sits up and leans on her shoulder, mirroring me, and Mom kisses the top of his head.

"I need you two to promise me something," she says. "I need you to promise me you'll always take care of one another. Even when you get on one another's nerves and want to kill the other one... remember, you've already shared a womb together. Everything else should be easy."

"Mom!" Travis shoves her slightly, and I gag.

"That's so gross," I say in disgust.

Mom laughs and hugs us tighter. "Just promise me," she says. "Promise each other."

I glance around her at Travis, grinning widely, and he meets my grin.

"Promise," he says.

"Promise," I reply.

"Wait—we have to do the thing," he adds, sitting up on his knees.

"Oh, okay!" I follow, knowing what he's going to do.

"Ready?" he asks.

"Ready," I reply eagerly.

"I cross my heart and hope to die," we say together, acting it out with our hands as we do. "Stick a needle in my eye."

I swipe the snot from under my nose and blink back the tears clouding my eyes. It was just a silly saying, something we heard and thought it was both gruesome and funny.

We never really stopped saying it.

Some best friends have a pinky swear. My brother and I had that poem. All the way until the day that…

I shake the thought from my mind, ignoring the memory of his screams pricking at the back of my ears, the feeling of how sore my throat had been from shrieking and pleading and crying, the relentless feeling of helplessness and pain…

If only my mother knew what her beloved music box contained now, she might rise from the grave to take it away from me.

Just open it.

I crack the lid, and as the delicate melody, Once Upon a Dream, begins to play, my heart crushes just as it has every other time I've looked inside. The tiny ballerina spins as beautifully as it did when I was five, even if she's faded a little more over the years.

A crystal heart-shaped jar lays perfectly in a bed of purple velvet inside; however, it's what the jar contains that forces bile into my throat.

A preserved eyeball—a needle struck through it.

It's the only piece of my brother that I'll ever see again.

CHAPTER TWENTY-THREE

REED

TWO EVENTS HAVE PASSED since our little talk with her people.

Talk of her landing the role in Sean's film as well as the rumors of her being considered for the Monroe flick has lit a fire inside her, or at least something has. She feels more at ease beside me, more willing to pretend to be infatuated with me instead of hating every second, going as far as actually playing along to make a few assholes jealous.

Of course, that could be due to the amount of sex we have to try and squash her nerves.

We had the official studio screening when her security had had to pull over so I could eat her out in the back of the black SUV; the charity art gala when I ripped her dress, and we had to find a seamstress before she could walk the red carpet.

She'd gone so ballistic on me that I questioned whether we'd have to issue a breakup statement that night. The limo driver had pulled over to let us finish yelling at each other—and give me enough time to finger her to the point of tears fell down her face. That part wasn't entirely my fault. She was so pissed that she didn't want to 'give me the satisfaction' of her orgasm.

I made her come anyway.

The raging lust in her eyes when she's denying it drives me fucking insane.

And standing next to her on the red carpet?

Fuck.

Performing in front of a crowd is one thing. Standing awkwardly on a runway in front of a line of photographers shouting at you and battling for the best photo is something entirely different. I've gotten pretty good at working the carpet when needed. However, normally, I have the safety of at least one of my bandmates around me. Without them, I feel naked, even if I don't let it show.

Wren, though…

Fuck, she glows.

She's wholly in her element the moment she steps onto that carpet, the flash and click of still cameras everywhere. Even with her mean girl stare and quips, the photographers seem to enjoy every little flinch of a smile or debonair motion.

And when they ask us to stand together? Fucking forget about it.

She's *too* easy to stand beside.

So much so that I'm questioning my own sanity. She might have a hard time selling us when we're in front of people she calls 'friends,' but fuck. She has no problem selling it with the cameras in front of her.

It was at the art gala that she let me hold her hand, the art gala when she appeared amused at the joke I told the table. When she walked around the gallery with me to choose a piece to go in my vacant apartment.

We ate fast food on her living room floor after.

I don't even fucking care that we didn't have sex again that night.

Talking shit with her is a fucking drug.

I've thought more about her goddamn mouth than I've ever thought about anything before.

It wasn't until I got to the hotel after our date a few weeks back that I realized the day we recorded the choking video, I also accidentally recorded something... *more.*

The last video clip we took hadn't only gotten me wrapping my hand around her neck. It continued recording after, and *fuck*... the things on that clip...

I think I've gotten off to the video of us fucking more times than I want to admit over the last few weeks. Watching her take me, hearing her whimper my name and bite her lips as she rides me backward... The pictures of us together don't help matters.

She's so fucking gorgeous that it hurts.

I still haven't sent her the video out of some fear that she'll get more pissed than usual if she finds out I accidentally filmed us having sex.

Mads smacks the back of my head, drawing me out of my daze. I don't have to ask why he's hitting me. One look at his tight-lipped expression says it all.

"Sorry," I mutter, wincing at the sting. "What were we saying?"

We're sitting at a cafe in... Denver? Fuck. I need to look closer at the tour sheet instead of Mads or Stella having to tell me the morning of. I glance around us, noting the glimpse of the mountains in the far distance, not that that is conclusive.

But I really think we're in Denver.

"Come on, dude. Her pussy can't be that good," Zeb says, watching me from across the table.

My eyes drag up from the photo I'm staring at on my phone, brow elevating with my poignant stare.

Zeb mirrors me in disbelief, then takes a drag from the vape he's just purchased nearby, a smirk licking at the corner of his lips. "No shit," he drawls. "Really?"

"Has to be her mouth that has him drunk," Bonnie chimes in, grinning my way. "Is she as mean in the sheets as she is at every other hour of the day?

I slump back in my seat and toss my phone face down on the table. "I don't want to talk about it," I say, hating myself for getting caught up with her. "What's up?"

"We were just deciding where to go sightseeing on our day off," Mads answers, pushing a cup of espresso my way.

"No press?" I ask.

"Nah. Whole day off. Which means phones on airplane," he adds with a glance around us.

No complaints here.

I shoot Wren a quick text. We've started turning our phones on airplane lately because of the amount of press we've had—good and bad—so we can enjoy a full, present day off with one another without any sort of distraction.

> Off grid today in case you try to find me.

If there's one thing I've learned about Wren, it's that she either texts back immediately, six hours later, or not at all. And it's never because she's purposefully ignoring me. I know it's because of how her mind works, how she may not have the energy to text me at the time, or she just forgets.

I hate how cute I think it is.

What I hate even more is the drop my stomach does when she texts back within seconds.

> HOLLYWOOD MEAN GIRL
>
> I won't.
>
> Have fun, though.

> I think that's the second nicest thing you've
> ever said to me

Don't get used to it.

I almost smile at the screen and close my phone as I hear Zeb suggesting a hike with a wilderness guide. I'm prepared to turn my phone to airplane mode and lay it on the table with everyone else's, when I see it light up again with another message.

HOLLYWOOD MEAN GIRL

Video me later?

I frown at the phone. She actually *wants* me to video her? I usually just do it to annoy her.

To discuss the next gala, I mean.

Ah, fuck. I haven't told her yet.

I don't know that I'll be able to make that one with the tour. We'll be across the country.

Oh. Okay.

It's all she says, and something about it makes me restless.

"Okay?" Mads asks, his voice low in comparison to Bonnie and Zeb's conversation going on.

"Ah, yeah," I say. "Yeah, just telling bird not to look for me today."

A smile lifts in Mads's eyes. "That all?"

"Fuck off," I shove him. "I had to tell her I might not make the gala next week."

"Is she mad about it?"

"I honestly don't know," I reply. "She's hard to read."

"So, call," he suggests.

I wave him off. "She hates phone calls. I'll video her

tonight," I say. "We have some crazy shit to see today. Did I hear Zeb say we have a guide?"

Mads smiles and leans back in his chair, laying his phone down on the table. "Honestly hoping we see some fucking bison or something wild."

I chuckle. "Fuck yeah, man."

I glance back at my phone and send one more text.

> I'll video you tonight, bird.

Okay, poser.

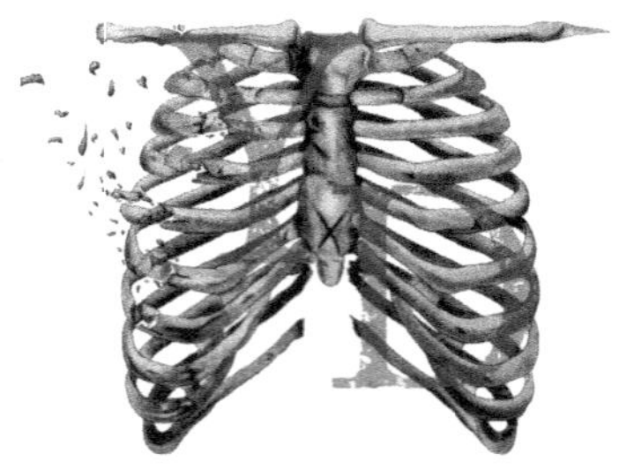

If there's one thing I love, it's getting out and into the fresh air to clear the racing shit in my head. I don't know what the guide is saying up ahead. I think he's talking about the fucking flora on the sides of the trail we're walking on. As we reach a ledge, I pause and let my head sink back, soaking in the warmth of the sun and letting it pour over my tight skin.

God fucking hell, I'm tired.

I crack my neck and glance up the trail, noting a guy

coming down the hill with a little girl sitting on his shoulders. Her laughter causes me to smile, and I watch them continue past us, followed closely by the mom and a young boy.

The images send my mind running—images of a future of one day teaching my kid to play an instrument or bringing them onstage. Showing them music and acting like a child without people telling me to grow the fuck up.

I know I'm nowhere near ready for that. I love my life. I love performing and traveling and doing crazy shit. But one day… One day, I really fucking want it.

Mads pauses beside me, hands stuffed in his pockets, and I notice he's watching the same thing I am.

"We talked about it, you know," he says cryptically. "Me and Andi."

"About… kids?" I ask.

"Yeah," Mads says, swallowing hard. "Yeah, the night I proposed to her."

I glance at the look on my best friend's face. "And?"

Mads meets my gaze, and I beam at him, knowing that little smirk in his eyes. It's a far cry from the seriousness I've seen in them over the years. The pain. The anger and rage.

God, we've come a long fucking way in twenty years.

I try not to think about his past most days. I try not to think that it ever affected me, but fuck. Every time Mads came over with bruises, scars, or a fat lip from his dad beating the shit out of him, I wanted to ride my bike to his dad's house and end him. It killed me to see my best friend in so much pain, just as much as it killed me to see my sister in the agony she was in with her mom.

I reach over and grab his shoulder, shaking him slightly. "You're going to be a fucking amazing dad one day, man," I tell him, and I mean every syllable.

"Probably shit the bed somehow," Mads says, clearing his throat. "It's in my genetics, after all."

"Fuck that," I say. "And you know better. I hear you telling Andi all the time that you'll never be like them," I add, referring to his dad and her mom.

"Of course I say that. But what if there's nothing I can do about it? What if it's somehow fucking embedded in me somewhere just waiting to be unlocked?"

I pause, considering him a minute. "You're fucking scared," I realize.

"Hell yeah, I'm scared," he admits. "Do you know what gets me, though?"

"What's that?"

"I know I'm fucking scared, yet I also know that I'd have ten kids with her if that's what she wanted," he says.

I laugh. "Ten? Jesus hell. Just make it an even dozen."

"Nah, that's what you're for," he grins.

"Have to buy Mom and Dad a bigger house," I say.

"Damn, already?" Zeb says, pausing on the other side of Mads with Bonnie. "Didn't you just buy them that house?"

"Talking about Mads having a whole fucking brood of kids to pack in it," I say.

Zeb narrows his eyes at Mads, still smiling. "Why doesn't that surprise me at all?"

"You ever think about it?" I ask Zeb.

"Nah," Zeb says. "My sisters have enough kids for all of us."

"Oh yeah, your youngest sister just had her third, right?" I ask.

"Fourth," Zeb answers. "My oldest sister keeps asking. I just tell her it isn't for me. I like the uncle life. My oldest sister likes to say I'll change my mind with the right person, but the right person for me is supposed to want the same things, aren't they?"

"Agreed," Bonnie says. "Can't imagine having a little rugrat, honestly."

"Aunt Funbags," I tease her.

She grins and looks at Mads. "Anytime you need a crazy aunt, I'm here for the job."

"Replace Kamden with her," I tell him, and Mads chuckles.

"Is there like a form I can fill out to make that official?" Mads asks.

The guide motions us to join him at the next bend, and each of us squeeze Mads's shoulder as we pass. I linger to walk with him, and when we turn so that the sun flickers on his eyes, I note the glisten in them.

Mads is the strongest fucking guy I know. Even so, something about my sister breaks him entirely.

I don't know that I'll ever understand what it means to love someone as much as he loves her.

But fuck… I hope I do.

CHAPTER TWENTY-FOUR

REED

THE HIKE WEARS ME DOWN. Even still, when we reach the hotel and head to our respective rooms, it's all I can do not to immediately call Wren. I at least hold myself together long enough to shower first, and by the time I lay down on the bed, I hear my stomach growl.

Fuck, I should have gotten a snack.

It's already too late.

Wren answers on the third ring.

She's sitting at her kitchen island looking in a mirror, mascara in her hand.

"Hey, poser," she says without looking away from the mirror.

I sigh and lean back on the pillow, arm up over my head. "What are you doing?" I ask.

"Putting on makeup," she replies.

"I thought people did your makeup for you," I say.

"That's why I'm trying to do it," she says as she screws the mascara cap back on. She bats her lashes at me, then takes her hair out of the ponytail, letting the ginger waves cascade over her shoulder. I swallow as I watch, imagining her looking up at me with those doe eyes, her hair in that same wave as she takes my dick deep down her throat, her dark nails stark against my skin and stroking up and down.

Shit.

I adjust on the bed and clear my throat, brushing off the fact that she's staring at me as much as I'm staring at her.

"So… wait, why are you doing your own makeup again?" I ask in an attempt to get the fantasy out of my head.

"For the absolute fuck of it," she says.

"Liar," I accuse.

Her lips press thinly together as she glances toward the phone. "My publicist wants me to take more selfies."

"Why?"

"Because she wants raw photos and videos posted. Casual. Everyday. Simple."

I snort at the thought of Wren posting random, seemingly unplanned, videos. "You don't know how to be casual about anything. Don't you stage most things?"

"I didn't ask for your help," she says.

"Maybe you need it," I say.

She purses her lips and rifles through her bag again. "Did you genuinely just get out of the shower and haven't bothered to put on clothes, or do you have a groupie hiding in there sucking your dick?"

I frown, my ears burning at the comment. "We're dating. Why would I have another person in here with me?"

"You're a rockstar on tour. I thought that was like a rule or something," she says.

I blink. *The fuck?*

"Seriously?"

Wren stops putting on lip liner and glances my way. "What?"

"That comment—Real or not, I'm not a jackass, bird," I say defensively.

"Did I upset you?"

"A little, yeah," I say, sitting up. I push my wet hair off my face. "Do you really think that shitty about me?"

"I… it was a joke," she almost stammers. "I didn't mean… I mean, we never talked about—"

"Are *you* seeing anyone else?" I ask.

Wren wrinkles her nose. "God no. I don't have energy to spend on someone else."

"So, why would you think I'm seeing other people?" I ask.

"Because you're… *you*," she says, like it's obvious. "I'm sorry. I didn't realize you would get upset."

I am upset.

I'm one more comment away from being pissed.

Wren avoids looking at the camera and pretends to file through the makeup bag at her side, carefully putting the brush she was just using back into its place.

"I guess now would be a weird time to tell you that I'll be in New York City next week," she says in a quiet voice.

My insides twist at the knowledge that she's coming where I'll be instead of the other way around. "You're traveling to see me?" I ask.

"It's Fashion Week," she corrects me. "I always go to Fashion Week. And, Shannon booked a few last minute interviews and things so, I'll be doing that instead of the charity gala next Saturday."

"What days are you coming?" I ask.

"Ah… Thursday to Wednesday, I think," she answers. "Shannon wanted me to try and convince you to go watch me walk on Saturday, but I told her I wasn't sure with your schedule."

"You're walking?" I ask.

"One of the models dropped out a couple of days ago," she says. "I used to work with the designer when that's all I was doing. He called in a favor."

Shit.

Getting to watch her strut down a fucking runway might be the highlight of this entire relationship. I've seen videos of her at previous Fashion Weeks.

It'd be worth being exhausted the next day over.

I run my hand over my face. "I have off Saturday," I say. "I might be a fucking mute and sipping tea all day, but I do have the day off."

Because at least there wouldn't be any traveling involved with this event.

"Having you mute for an entire night sounds enticing," she says.

The comment almost makes me smile. "You'd like that," I say. "Does Larry have your schedule? Or do you know what time you'll be needed on Saturday?"

"It's usually all day," she says. "It isn't mandatory to see me," she adds quickly.

Something about the pink on her cheeks makes me hesitate to answer. And after the groupie comment, I just want to know something.

"Hey, do you think we can just talk to me for a minute?" I ask her.

Wren's gaze narrows, but she sets her things down and focuses on the camera nonetheless. "What's wrong?"

A heavy sigh leaves me. I'm not sure what's wrong. Maybe it's the conversation on the mountain today that's wormed its way into my head. "Maybe I *want* to see you," I tell her.

A muscle in her jaw feathers. "What's wrong with you? Why are you being a sad boy today?" she asks, and I know it isn't a jab, but rather the most sincere question she's ever asked me.

I set the phone down against a pillow and wipe my face again. "Do you ever think about having a family?"

The words blurt out before I can stop them. Wren gawks at me, eyes widened beneath her furrowed brows.

"Jesus, Reed," she says. "You can't just ask people if they want to have a family. And that is by far the weirdest, most terrifying question you have ever asked me," she says. "Why are you thinking about that? We aren't a real couple—"

I scoff. "I'm talking to you as a friend," I say. "Don't friends talk about this kind of thing?"

"We're not friends," she says.

"We're fucking friends, bird," I almost snap. "I know that grosses you out for some reason, but we are. Accept it."

"I don't want to," she says, rolling her nose up again.

"I'm going to smother you with my friendship if you don't—"

"Smothering me might be better."

"Some days, I just want to fucking choke you out with niceness," I go on. "Slap your ass harder than last time so you feel our friendship for weeks after."

She glares. "I still have a mark on my ass from that," she says.

"You'll have a permanent handprint next time, and a tattoo next to it that says, 'Reed Matthews's BFF.'"

"Yeah? What does that stand for?"

"Best Fuck Friend," I tell her.

The corner of her mouth twitches, and her silence causes my frustration to swell.

"Come on, bird. Pretend I'm drowning. Offer me a lifeline," I almost beg.

Wren is quiet for another beat, mouth twisting as she considers it, and then finally, she stands.

"What are you doing now?" I ask her.

She sits the phone on her kitchen island and goes into her cabinet. "I'm too sober for this conversation," she says as she pours herself a shot of vodka. She kicks it back without making a face, a shiver rolls over her shoulders, and then pours another.

"Okay, why are you asking about having a family?" she asks. "That seems serious for you."

Thank fuck.

"My sister is getting married next month," I say. "Mads is talking about them starting a family soon after. We chatted about it earlier, but I can't stop thinking about it."

"Are you worried about the band?"

"Nah," I shake my head. "Andi would never make him feel like he had to choose. Music is too important for them."

"What's the worry, then?"

I shrug. "I honestly don't know. The talk of it just... it kind of hit me in the gut today."

Wren doesn't speak for a moment as she unscrews the cap on her reusable water bottle. "Would showing you my tits make you feel better?" she asks.

An unexpected chuckle leaves me. "Funny," I say.

"It's a genuine offer," she goes on.

"I'd rather see them in person next week," I tell her.

"Is that why you want to see me? To play with my tits?"

"You're using me for publicity," I say. "I think it's fair for me to use you for steady sex."

"Touché," she agrees.

I laugh softly at her. "Why is it hard to believe that I just want to see you?"

"Because you shouldn't," she answers.

"If I don't see you next week, I won't see you again until Halloween."

"And that's a bad thing because..."

"If I'm not mistaken, you're the one making time for me," I say.

"I regret having said anything to you," she says.

I feel my mouth flatten into a line, jaw twitching. "Would it make you feel better if I told you I just wanted to fuck you?"

There's a smirk in her eyes that catches me off guard. I bring the phone closer to my face and squint at her expression.

"You're *trying* to frustrate me, aren't you?" I realize.

She brings her cup to her mouth, but I swear there's a fucking grin on her lips when she wraps them around the rim. "No idea what you're talking about," she gargles.

"Wren."

"Of course, I'm trying to frustrate you," she says. "You were sad. I'd rather you be mad at me than wallowing in whatever self-pity party you were having."

I gawk at her as an aching warmth wraps around my chest.

"Why are you looking at me like that?" she asks.

"Nothing," I say, terrified that anything I might say about her caring enough to try and drag me out of my slump will send her running.

"Okay, well, I have to go before I lose motivation to do these dumb fucking videos," she says, looking annoyed.

"Send them to me first for approval," I tell her.

Her mouth twists like she wants to tell me no. "Yeah. Fine. Try not to use them to jerk off to. I have better photos from the swimsuit issue I did."

"Yeah, those are already saved on my phone," I say, unwilling to tell her about the secret sex tape yet.

Wren scoffs. "Bye, poser. Have fun onstage at Red Rocks tomorrow. I hear it's amazing."

I beam at her. "You remembered where I'm playing?"

Her expression falters as if she didn't realize what she said. "No," she says fast.

"You can't remember to put your clothes in the dryer, but you remembered what venue I'm playing at," I go on taunting her.

"Okay, but who actually remembers to put their clothes in the dryer?" she argues.

"A lot of people," I say.

"Not you," she says.

"Clearly not me," I agree.

"Let's not make a big deal out of this," she says.

A knock sounds on my door then, and I glance at my clock. *Shit*. I should be ready to go out to eat by now.

"Is that your groupie?" she asks.

I glare at her, and this time, an actual *devious* smile rises on her lips.

Holy shit, that's cute.

It's so fucking cute that for a few seconds, I forget what she said.

I can't let her know that I saw it.

Act cool, dude.

"Ah… yeah," I say, taking the phone with me as I go to the door. "Yeah, you want to see them? You can meet the groupie I'm cheating on you with. Hang on."

"Only if he's bearded and has a tongue ring," she says.

I whip open the door, find Mads on the other side, and I turn the phone around so that she can see him.

"Hey, man, why aren't you—oh." Mads grins and waves at the camera. "Hey, Wren," he says.

I turn the phone back to me. "Satisfied?"

"Isn't there a rule that says your groupie can't be hotter than you?" she taunts.

Mads snorts.

I stare at her for the comment, chewing my mouth as I debate how to answer that. "That was cold," I finally reply. "You're in so much trouble next week."

"She's coming next week?" Mads asks.

"Not by choice," she says.

"She misses me," I tell Mads, and he scoffs.

"Hang up and get dressed," he tells me. "You know how Zeb gets about being late."

Ah, fuck.

"Yeah. Okay. I'll text you later, bird," I say, knowing better than to argue if Zeb is involved.

"Night, poser," she says, and before I can think of some excuse to keep her on the phone just to annoy her, she hangs up.

Mads is smirking at me when I look over the phone, and I flip off his knowing face. "Shut up," I say.

"I didn't say anything," Mads says. "But you're fucked, you know that."

I don't need him to remind me.

CHAPTER TWENTY-FIVE

TELLING Bonnie that Wren had tickets for the four of us for Fashion Week on Saturday, and basically any party we wanted to attend the entire weekend, resulted in the drummer nearly having a meltdown from excitement. So much so that she and Zeb went out after our concert on Friday night to meet Wren at one of the parties.

Wren even sent over clothes from the designer she's walking for.

It's Saturday, and I still haven't seen her despite the fact that she came in early on Wednesday. We've texted every night, and she's continuously asked if I'm sure I'll be up for her show, and I'm making sure that I am.

I'm a fucking mess, and it's killing me.

Thursday, Stella put me on bedrest for my voice. Yesterday, I didn't leave the hotel until sound check. I would have went out with Bonnie and Zeb, but Mads practically threw me into the SUV after we signed autographs and told James to carry me into the hotel room if he had to—especially if I was still planning on attending Wren's show today.

It's the only fucking reason I went without a fight.

The sun is peeking through the drawn curtains and as I lift myself up onto my stomach, I groan inwardly.

Water.

I need fucking water.

And a hotter than hell shower.

I hate being confined into the hotel, but it's better than getting onstage and being unable to perform.

HOLLYWOOD MEAN GIRL

Morning, poser.

The text is from Wren—an hour earlier.

Shit.

I need to get my ass going if I'm going to see her before her show this afternoon.

Hey.

Her text back is almost immediate, and my stomach does that twisting thing it likes to do when that happens.

HOLLYWOOD MEAN GIRL

Oh good. You're alive. I thought I was going to have to grieve on the runway for you.

Aw, you would grieve for me?

Maybe one tear.

Do you think you'll make it today?

Yeah. I'll make it. I'll come see you soon and bring breakfast.

Fruit.

When do you think you're coming?

I frown at the screen and sit up.

Need to shower first. I didn't think you wanted me there until ten. Should I rush?

If you can.

Is something wrong?

I haven't walked in a year. My nerves are shot.

What does that have to do with me and my fruit?

Do I need to spell it out?

I'd love that.

Three dots strum across the bottom of the screen, and I smile at her apparent fluster.

Just get over here

Such a demanding little bird. Bad morning?

Do you actually care?

I do. I'd care more if it means I get to fuck that frown upside-down.

The dots flicker on and off the screen longer this time—long enough that I lay back on the bed again and grin, wondering what her bratty mind is thinking.

HOLLYWOOD MEAN GIRL

Play nice or I'll spit.

Oh, *fuck* yes.

I don't think I've ever showered so quickly. I text both Mads and Stella before I get in—asking Stella if she can get breakfast for me to take over to Wren's, and letting Mads know where I'm going.

MADNESS

You sure you feel better?

I wouldn't be going anywhere if I didn't.

No shot I would jeopardize performing for this.

Okay. I trust you.

Maybe try to limit your talking today.

Definitely.

I really do intend to try.

Stella, being the excellent manager that she is, presents me with two paper bags full of breakfast foods simply because she said she isn't sure what models eat. I laugh and take it, then load into the SUV with James after.

"How's it going this morning, Matthews?" James asks.

"Fucking exhausted," I reply, stretching my legs in the back seat. "Do you know where Wren—"

James holds up his phone. "Reached out to her security this morning," he replies as he pulls out of the hotel.

I sink back and lay my head on the rest, my eyes closing. The tea Stella made me is warm inside the thermal cup in my hand, and I think it might send me back to sleep if this drive is too long.

"Have you had any more of those unknown calls lately?" James asks after a few minutes.

"Ah… not this week at least," I reply, opening up my phone to text Wren that I'll be there soon.

James turns off the road. "Let me know if they do. Especially if you're with Wren."

"Why especially if I'm with her?"

"Because losing one of you would get me in enough shit," James says, smirking at me through the rear view. "Losing two of you would get me fired."

I scoff. "Mads murdered a guy nearly two years ago, and you're still with us. I think you're stuck."

James pulls up to the front, puts the SUV in park, and turns around to look at me. "Just stay vigilant. Let me know if you see anything."

I frown. "Should I be seeing anything?"

"With the publicity surrounding you, yeah. You might." He turns back to the front and unlocks the door. "Tara is coming around to pick up Wren when she's ready. I'll swing back to get you."

I stare at the back of his head, gaze narrowing; however, I don't question him.

HOLLYWOOD MEAN GIRL

Room 3534

Wren's room number.

I clap James's seat twice and mutter a quick, "See ya," to him before pulling my hood over my head and exiting the car.

Everything around her is fucking weird.

When I reach her door, I knock twice, and she answers it as if she was standing in front of it waiting on me. Her eyes are wide, almost fearful, and she peers quickly around me and down the hall.

"Hey—"

"Were you followed?" she asks, cutting me off.

The fuck.

I pause, brows knitting together. "What… Okay, James just told me to watch out for stalkers, and now you're asking if I was followed. Is there a reason you think I might have been?" I ask.

Her jaw sets for a beat before her shoulders finally sink, and she opens the door enough for me to come inside.

I hesitate, lips pressing together as I fully look at her.

She's not wearing much makeup. Her hair is pulled up as if she just rolled out of bed, and yet by the look of the coffees on the counter and the noise of the television going, I know she probably never went to sleep.

I wonder if that was because of nerves for the show or whatever has her freaked out on most days.

"You know, one day, you're going to tell me what the hell is going on with you," I say.

"The less you know, the better," she says. "Get in here and take off your clothes."

I balk slightly. "What—no hello kiss? No leading foreplay or lube? You're just going to take me dry?" I ask.

"Yes, actually, hearing you speak makes me dryer than the fucking Sahara," she snaps.

"Ah, you're *mean* today," I drawl. "I thought we were getting better. What the hell—"

Wren drags me flush with fistfuls of my shirt before I can say another word, and when her lips crash against mine, I throw the door closed behind me, drop the food on the floor, and latch my arms around her waist and her neck, kissing her with all the pent up tension I've been holding onto since the last time we saw each other.

Shit, I needed this.

"This is the last time this is happening," she says between our kisses.

I chuckle against her lips. "Tell that to me next month when I'm balls deep in this tight little cunt before the Halloween party."

She shoves me and pulls her shirt over her head, a glare in her eyes when she throws it to the floor and reveals the black lacy bra she's wearing beneath.

Every time she undresses, I think I lose another fraction of myself. I intend to lick and bite every stretch mark on her stomach, her thighs… bite the curves of her stomach and her tits, the cute creases at her ribs when she's arched and taking me from behind.

Jesus fucking fuck, she's sexy.

"We still have to figure out our costumes," she says impatiently. She pulls me down to her lips again, teeth grazing my bottom lip, her short nails scratching at my cheeks. I start to wrap my hands around her bare waist, but she swats my face and drags back to look at me.

"And if you say Joker and Quinn, you can go home with blue balls right now," she warns, finger in my face.

Fucking hell, the *fight* today.

That's okay.

I'll fuck the funk out of both of us.

I bite at her hand, teeth clashing at the edge of her nail, and then yank her into me. "I'll go as a dog on a fucking leash if that's what you want, bird," I tell her, licking the corner of her lips. "I'll be your pet. You can be my Cruella."

She scoffs. "Why would you do that to yourself?"

"Because watching you break beneath me after, might be worth crawling on my hands and knees for a few hours," I reply.

Her nostrils flare. "You're such a dick."

"Yeah?" I kiss her chastely. "What are you going to do about it?"

I can't get enough of challenging her—of the wild display in her raging, dilated pupils. Of the aggression in her kiss, her touch. I want to push every single button she has just to see what she's capable of.

Although, looking into her eyes right now, I wonder if I've just made a mistake.

Her eyes stay open this time when she kisses me. She

wraps her hands around my belt and tugs me along, walking backward to the bedroom of the suite. I start to reach out to her, to throw her onto the bed so I can worship every line of her soft body, kiss every freckle stretched over her pale skin.

But she grabs me by the chin before I can make my move, and I'm stunned when she forces me to look at her.

"Everyone else around me wants to control my strings. Tell me who and how to be. Shut me up and close me off," she says darkly. "Everyone except *you*."

Her nails rake against my cheek, and I turn my head so that I can kiss her palm, never losing that direct eye contact with her.

"And I fucking *hate you* for it," she hisses, open mouth brushing against mine.

"You don't," I manage. "You crave it, bird. You crave the cracks I've chipped in your walls. The push and pull, and the fact that I'll fucking drag you out kicking and screaming from under this mask if I have to." I kiss her harshly, groaning into her mouth when she nips at my tongue. "So, tell me."

"Tell you what?" she breathes.

"Tell me how you'll punish me for making you feel this way," I almost beg.

Her tongue meets mine, the lick almost claiming in nature. *Fuck*. I'll get on my knees right here if that's what she wants. I'll crawl across this bedroom to her and let her stab my chest with one of these pretty fucking heels she'll be wearing on the runway later.

"Will you punish me from your knees?" I go on, jaw trembling as she lets me grab her waist. "Or would you rather I get on mine?"

Wren's nails drag down the sides of my neck to my shirt, ripping through the collar and the thin fabric.

God, I'm already fucking hard.

Her hands trail down my chest, leaving behind the prettiest

red welts in their wake. She drags her short claws over my tattoos, outlining some of the dark marks. And when she reaches my jeans, unbuttons them, and strokes my dick, I almost fall to my goddamn knees right there.

Her voice licks my ear when she leans up and whispers, "You come when I say so."

Abso-fucking-lutely *yes*.

I barely get my groundings before she's sinking onto the floor in front of me. I make myself back up against the dresser so that I have somewhere to hold myself up, because the moment that she spits on my dick, my legs jerk like they're going to give way.

I'm so fucking weak.

Her lips wrap around my tip, tongue dragging through my slit as she pushes her spit over the entirety of me. I grow harder in her soft hands, my jaw clenched at the delicate feel of her. I swallow the dryness on my throat and push both hands through my hair, feeling my hips shifting in response to her motions. My arm crooks over my face, a smile tugging the corner of my lips upward as she rakes her nails over my abdomen, my dick hitting the back of her throat.

Open your eyes.

Stop fucking hiding like it isn't Wren goddamn Kelly sucking your dick right now.

I wipe my face and look down to watch, and as I do, I groan.

She looks so fucking sexy like this.

On her knees in nothing more than her lace bra and panties. My dick stretching her mouth. A smile threatens to rise at seeing her struggle to take all of me, at the drool trickling from the corners of her lips.

She draws those delightful lips down my shaft, her lashes lifting so that our eyes meet. God, her fucking eyes…

Her tongue slides through my slit as she cups my balls, and my head falls back onto my neck.

"Goddamn it, bird," I manage.

She reaches for my hand and guides it into her ponytail, and I have to peer down again with the permission she's giving me to push her right now. I push on her head, forcing her to take more of me, and she hums a groan in response.

"Fuck, do that again," I whimper.

I don't think I've ever whimpered before.

But no one's ever had me in a chokehold like this.

God, am I about to cry?

Wren draws back, her hand working the end of my dick. "Where do you want to come?"

I swallow looking down at her. "I get options?" I ask.

A smirk flickers on her red lips, and she leans forward, her tongue outstretched, and drags it along my slit. "Anywhere you want," she says in a sultry voice that has my fist curling. "So long as you do it when I tell you to."

"Fuck," I hiss, my head hanging. "Okay. I can do that."

Wren rocks back onto her feet and stands slowly, her entire body on full display in front of me as if she's auctioning herself off—one space to coat with cum to the highest bidder.

I think I would sell my soul for her.

She reaches behind her and unhooks her bra, watching me the entire time. The black lace falls to the floor, her underwear following, and just like the very first time I saw her naked, I forget how to breathe.

A pathetic whimper leaves me at the sight of her bare body.

Shit fucking hell.

Her nails rake my stomach as she tilts into me and meets my tongue with her own. I'm stiff, yet as her full tits brush my bare chest, I reach out to gently squeeze them. She groans into my mouth, her own hand moving to my throbbing dick and stroking me languidly.

"Here," I manage as I bring her taut nipples between my fingers, tugging on the peaks. "I want your tits covered in me."

She drags her bottom lip behind her teeth. The motion makes me want to spank her for teasing me like this. A coy look rises in her eyes, and she leans up to place a lingering kiss on my lips.

"I want to try something," she says. "If you're game."

I press my palm to her cheek, barely breathing as I reply, "You could tell me to walk around this city naked, and I'd risk getting put in jail if it would put a smile on your face."

"There's a thought for later," she jeers.

I'm drunk for her.

She releases me and goes to her bag on the floor. From within it, she takes out a small clear jar, and I narrow my eyes at the white substance.

"Coconut oil?" I ask as she opens the lid.

"It's a great lube," she replies. She sits the open jar on the bed and crawls up the mattress until she's propped onto the pillows near the headboard. The most pathetic whimper I've ever heard from myself sounds as she dips her fingers in the oil and drags the glistening lube between her tits, watching me the entire time. And when she slowly cups her breasts in her hands, thumbs swirling that lube over her peaked nipples, I feel my hard dick twitch.

"Straddle me," she says. "Fuck my tits."

I don't need telling twice.

I remove my pants completely, trying not to look like an eager kid on Christmas as I crawl over her. She leans up and pushes her oiled hands into my hair and pulls me down into a hard kiss when I'm over her. I cup her breasts and squeeze gently, eliciting another soft moan from her as we part.

And when she positions my dick between her lubed tits, I whine out her name.

Fuck, they're soft. She has them pushed up in a way that

overlaps my entire dick, and as I come in contact with her lips, she licks my tip.

I don't know how long I'm lasting here either.

Precum spills from me after a few steady strokes. I'm resisting leaning down and biting her tits or reaching back to find out how wet she is from this. The thought crosses my mind over and over, with every time I pinch her nipples, and she sucks air through her teeth.

Another few strokes, and she snakes her middle finger up to my mouth, and says, "Suck." The digit parts my lips and pushes into my now open mouth, and I suck her finger when she drives it down my throat.

She adds a second finger, her eyes lit up with delight while watching me. I squeeze her tits harder, groaning as I continue sliding my dick up and down her sternum. I can taste the coconut on her fingers, resisting my own gag reflex.

It isn't until I see her dip those two fingers into the coconut oil again that I realize what she meant by 'try something.'

"Bird…"

She slides her lubed finger between my ass cheeks, and I fucking wish I had something to bite that wasn't my lip. My mouth is already on the verge of bleeding from holding back, and now she's doing *this?!*

"Oh fucking hell—"

I don't know how she knows exactly where to massage my prostate, but *fuck.*

I'm going to collapse. I'm a pathetic mewl in her clutches.

I slump over her, my pace picking up, and she matches my movements with her finger.

"Wren," I whimper.

"That's it," she coos triumphantly. "Say my fucking name, poser."

"*Wren,*" I beg.

Tears prick the corners of my eyes. It's fucking overwhelming in the best way. I can't control my strokes. I'm erratic. I'm on the verge of begging her to end me, and also telling her to never stop. Trembles and chills rake over my body. I'm holding my release at the very edge, barely able to catch my breath when I feel her toy with the idea of adding a second finger.

I feel her thumb on my cheek, swiping away the tear rolling down it.

"You look really pretty when you cry," she says in a painstakingly erotic voice.

I must be dreaming.

The absolute empowerment in her eyes and voice is hypnotic. It has me desperate to throw her on her stomach so I can watch this ass bounce when I rail into her, but more than that... *Fuck.* More than that, I wonder how fucking sexy she would look standing over me wearing leather lingerie, a bunny mask, and a flogger in her hands.

God fucking dammit.

"I need to... Shit. Bird. *Please,*" I beg.

I've completely lost control of this.

My head hangs, hair falling over my eyes as she tauntingly wipes my cheek again. I feel her lips wrap around the tip of my dick, her finger brushing inside me in just the right place. I squeeze her tits tighter around my cock, shaking at trying to deny the release threatening to spill.

And when she tilts my chin up with her knuckle, our eyes meeting, she finally says, "Come for me," in a voice that completely sends me over the edge.

I pull from between her breasts as I come, and the milky white coats her. I come and come, spilling everything I'd denied over her skin. Even after I'm done, I can't catch my breath. I can't stop twitching.

I've never seen anything sexier than her lying on this bed beneath me with my cum splattered over her tits.

"Holy shit," are the only two words I can manage right now.

Because *holy shit.*

"You made an absolute mess," she taunts, almost smirking up at me. "I expect you to clean it up."

I grin crookedly. "I like the idea more of you walking down that fucking runway covered in me," I say.

"I bet you would like that," she says.

I kiss her hard, not caring that she gets my cum on my own chest when we're flush, not caring that she has it on her fingers when she threads them into my hair.

I don't think I'll ever get over what just happened.

I pull away from her lips and keep her gaze as I drag two fingers through my cum, and then slide those two fingers inside her.

Wren inhales sharply, apparent that she didn't expect me to reciprocate. She's soaked. Swollen. Her clit hard. I press the pad of my thumb to her clit and curl those digits inside her, making sure to memorize every moan she meets me with.

"Did you enjoy making me come?" I ask.

"Yes," she says, rising her hips to meet my hand. "Are you going to make me?"

I drag my nose down her cheek and kiss her jaw. "In about thirty seconds," I swear.

"Yes," she hisses.

She starts riding my hand as if she's forgotten she's supposed to refute me, and I take full advantage.

"I want you over me in a leather bunny suit the next time you do that to me," I breathe in her ear.

She drags her fingers into my hair and nips at my bottom lip. "The next time I do that to you, it'll be with a strap-on," she bites out. "We can come together."

Oh my god.

Am I in love with this woman?

"Is that okay with you, poser?" she asks, biting my earlobe.

"Sounds fucking perfect."

Our lips crash together. My fingers slide in and out of her in rapid motion, the noise of her pussy music to my fucking ears. She groans into my mouth, jaw sagging, chest sinking as she grabs for me in an attempt to bring herself over that edge. Her pussy grips my fingers. She's so close. Just one more…

I fucking love making her squirt.

She trembles against me and rides her orgasm. Wave after wave. Whimper after whimper. And I finally slow my motions, lingering to slide her release over her clit, over her abdomen, finally dragging it through my cum now drying on her tits.

Wren takes a moment to catch her breath, gaze moving to the ceiling, and then she taps my shoulder.

"Breakfast," she says, as if the one word is enough. "I need… shower."

I chuckle and kiss her collarbone. "Yes, Madame," I answer, and I swear I see a flicker of amused delight in those dark green eyes.

I suck our cum off my fingers as I head into the kitchenette to retrieve the discarded food I threw on the floor. A smile lifts my lips as I take the food out of the bag and reveal the smorgasbord Stella was nice enough to give me.

As I try to sort through it all, a box on the counter catches my eye. It has a bow on it, the sides taped down, and I feel a pang of jealousy in my gut as I wonder if someone sent her a gift.

Wren comes out of the shower a few minutes later, wearing a long sleeve tee and shorts that I've never seen before. She appears so casual with her hair still up in the same pony that now looks fully sexed up.

"What?" she asks as I hand her a water.

"Somehow you're even prettier after that," I answer.

Wren purses her lips, though I swear I see amusement in her gaze. "Rules," she says.

I slide her the tray of fruit without losing my smile. She goes for the strawberry first, and I force myself to look away and take a bite of French toast.

"That's yours, by the way," she says, jerking her chin toward the box on the counter.

I gawk. "You got me a gift?"

"Don't get sappy," she drawls as she comes around to push it my way. "I thought it was funny."

"*You* thought something was funny? Jeez. Someone call fucking security. I have the wrong Wren Kelly."

"Shut the fuck up," she almost chuckles, rolling her eyes. "Just open it."

I shove my food out of the way and bring the box toward me, carefully picking at the tape on the sides like I'm almost scared that something is going to jump out at me.

"Why are you looking at it like it's a bomb?" she asks.

"Because it's a gift from you. It might be," I say as I finally get two sides off. I start to struggle with the last, but Wren taps the knife near me, and I give her a look as I take it and pry the last two pieces of tape off.

Glitter.

Oh, mother fuck––

Glitter and confetti explode in my face.

"You little bitch," I mutter, hearing her snort on the other side of the counter. My lashes lift, and I meet her devious, amused stare.

I'd be mad except it's cute as hell.

It's then that I realize the tiny confetti now sticking to me is actually––

"Are these tiny dicks?" I ask, holding one up to my face.

"They are," she says proudly. "I have a supply to ensure extra annoyance when I give people shit gifts."

The real gift in the box catches my eye then, and I chuckle as I take it out. It's a blue penis, a little stiff in the middle and curved. "What… What is this?" I ask her.

"Thought you would know a penis when you saw one," she replies.

I frown at it. "Really, though. What is it?"

A smile plays in her eyes when she takes it from my hands and bends it to resemble a C. "It's a neck pillow," she says, modeling it for me. "I thought… with all the traveling you're doing for me, it would be helpful to have on the plane."

"A penis neck pillow?" I repeat, taking it back from her.

My stomach knots as I stare at it, unable to swipe the smile from my face.

"You hate it," she says defeatedly.

"No, I fucking love it, actually," I say when I meet her eyes. "Thank you."

She curls her nose up in the most disgusted, adorable way. "Ugh. Don't say thank you. You just ruined it," she says, popping back a piece of melon.

"What do you want me to say instead?" I ask.

"I don't know. Tell me to go fuck myself with it or something," she replies.

I laugh, knowing how she is with compliments. "It's fucking disgusting," I say.

"Ah, yes," she hisses in a celebratory way.

"Absolutely horrendous," I add.

"That's the stuff."

"Who in their right fucking mind gives someone a penis neck pillow?" I go on, grinning. "It's disturbing. What will people think when they see me with this on the plane?"

"Yes. I ruin *everything*," she says, throwing her head back as if the words are edging her.

"And the dick glitter? I'm going to be washing it out of my

hair for weeks. That's going to be fun to explain to the press later today."

The quietest, most melodic laugh leaves her then, as if she forgot to squash it down. It makes her pause enough that it shakes her shoulders, lifts the corners of her mouth, and when she looks up at me again, the smallest of smiles lingers there, and I gulp at the sight of it.

I pause to stare at her for a beat long enough that the image can become ingrained in my mind.

"How do I make you smile like that all the time?" I ask.

The smile fades softly, and she quickly lets her hair hide her expression. "I think it's time for you to leave," she says, closing the lid of the fruit tray.

I tap twice on the countertop, cursing my heart for the way it's aching right now. "What time should we be there?" I ask.

"Ah… I'll tell Larry to let you know. I have to be there in an hour to start getting ready. He'll have passes backstage and everything," she answers.

"Do I get to see you after?" I ask.

"For all the ass kissing," she says with a bat of her lashes. "Do me a favor today?"

"What kind of favor?"

"Wear the floral pants that Albert sent," she says, almost smirking.

I haven't even looked through the clothes she sent over for the bedrest I've been on. "Why those?" I ask.

"Just trust me."

CHAPTER TWENTY-SIX

THE CLOTHING CHOICES Wren's designer friends sent over are about to become my entire fucking personality.

I might never take these floral skinny jeans off. I have them paired with a long sleeve sheer shirt that I'm pretty sure might have been meant as an oversized mini dress for Bonnie to wear, but let's be honest.

It looks better on me.

"Hey—I was looking for that," Bonnie says when we meet in the lobby. "The hell—trade shirts with me."

I stare at her tiny top. "I don't think that will even pass as a crop top on me," I argue. "Way too tight."

"Then just wear these necklaces and your leather jacket," she says, holding up the bunch of necklaces hanging between her petite tits. "You almost have enough tats, it looks like you're wearing a shirt anyway."

"I might get cold," I smirk, guarding my chest. "You know I have sensitive nipples."

"Matthews! Look here!"

Cameras flash in front of us, drawing me back to the carpet the four of us are posing on. Bonnie and Zeb have already made Fashion Week news; however, with me and Mads added today, I know the questions are about to reach new heights.

"Matthews! Over here!" another photographer yells.

"Tourning!"

"Are you excited about seeing Kelly on the runway today?" someone shouts at me.

There is a line of interviewers waiting before we can even get in the door. Thank fuck for Larry navigating this for us, pointing to where we need to go, and telling certain people that we're not talking to them—well, that *I'm* not talking to them.

Most of them just shout their questions to me anyway, and I try to answer as many as I can, in the fewest words that I'm able.

"Hey, Matthews! Are you excited to watch Kelly return to the runway today?" someone asks.

"Oh, is that what we're calling it? Her return?" I ask the journalist as Larry continues to push us through. "Yeah, I'm excited. I've never seen her on the runway."

"Matthews, over here! Have you seen her new film yet? What do you have to say about the rumors of her and costar Chris Suthers having problems on set?" someone else asks.

I grin, knowing full well not to get into that drama. "Next question," I answer, prompting a few of them to laugh.

"Who are you wearing?" someone shouts.

"Whoever the hell my girlfriend told me to wear," I reply.

"He's wearing Matteo and LoRocco," Larry shouts out. "As is the rest of the band!"

"Will we see you on the runway at some point?" another asks.

"I don't think you guys can handle me walking on a runway," I reply to their amusement.

"Did you get to see Kelly earlier today?" someone asks.

I smirk at the ground as the memory from earlier fills me, and then meet the journalist's gaze. "Yeah, I got to see her."

"How's she doing? Is she nervous?" the same person asks.

I chuckle softly. "Wren Kelly doesn't get nervous. She's a fucking badass."

Mads leans over to Larry and says something that I don't catch.

"How do you get your hair to look messy but hot?" a different person asks.

"My girlfriend pulls it," I answer, and someone whistles.

"Will we see you at the afterparty tonight?" the next person asks me.

"Yeah, and we expect all of you to be at our gig tomorrow getting your faces fucked off," I answer.

"That's all the questions!" Larry shouts out, making a few people boo him. "Nope. Sorry. If there's one thing we all want to protect, it's his voice! That's it—Addison, don't look at me like that. I will take you off of Wren's favored list," he adds to an annoyed looking brunette at the end of the line. "You can chat with her at the afterparty."

"I expect five minutes," she says.

"You get three—Let's go, lovelies," he says, ushering us out of the line of questions.

This part is always a blur.

Faces. Questions. Small talk. Hand shakes. Kisses. One person after the other and the other. I pay more attention to the faces of our fans after a concert than I do the people I barely know who think they know me.

It's all good fun, though.

Four seats are reserved right beside the runway for us. When I turn around toward Mads, I notice he's pulled his mask up, and I smile at my best friend.

"Hey—" I say, nudging him as we sit down. "I'm glad you're here. I know it's not your scene."

Mads sighs and sits back, his gaze moving around the space as if he's searching for something. "I fucking love you, man," he finally replies. "Whatever you need, I'm here. Besides, I think Bonnie is enjoying herself," he adds with a nod to Bonnie, who's chatting with a model at the end of the seats, a finger twirling in the woman's hair.

I laugh. "She has the most game out of all of us," I say.

Someone yanks on a piece of my hair in the back. I wince and turn, finding Zeb staring at something on his finger that he's just pulled off of me.

"Is this dick glitter?" he asks, showing me.

I laugh. "Yeah, man," I reply. "I'll explain later."

"Some kinky shit, dude," he grins, and I flip him off.

Zeb flicks the glitter to the floor before sitting down beside Mads, and as they start to chat, I look out at the runway again. My stomach begins to twist, heel tapping nervously. I don't know why I feel the need to fidget more than usual. Maybe because I know how big of a deal this is for Wren, how uneasy she was about walking despite the confident face she put on.

I take my phone out of my pocket and stare at the blank screen. I shouldn't text her. I know she probably won't answer.

But I do it anyway.

> I don't know if you're supposed to say good luck or break a leg when it comes to this kind of show. So, whatever good luck salutation I should use, let's pretend that's what I'm saying.

I flip over to my camera, turning it front-ways so I can take a selfie of Mads, Zeb, and I, and before I can post it, Wren texts back.

> THE DEATH OF ME
>
> Larry is bringing you a scarf.

I glance toward the stage, eyes narrowed, and I see Larry darting my way with a large scarf in his hands.

THE DEATH OF ME

I read somewhere that it helps singers when
they're sick.

Larry helps me wrap it around my neck and fix it properly, and when he's satisfied, he runs backstage without another word.

You looked up how to help my voice?

Don't think too hard about it.

I don't want your fans mad at me if you get
onstage hoarse tomorrow.

Rocco heard me saying you were resting your
voice and had an extra one.

I smile at the screen.

You've been talking to your friends about me?

No.

I want to tease her about it, yet I'm too scared that I'll spook her or worse—make her realize she's done something nice.

I'd say thank you, but then you might tell Larry
to set the scarf on fire.

Just put on the scarf and look pretty for the
cameras.

I chuckle.

Yes, ma'am.

The lights dim then, and I put my phone back in my pocket as the designer walks out onstage.

The other models are a blur. I follow the direction of the others around us, clapping when they do; however, I can't stop myself from moving a little to the music playing, especially with Bonnie sitting beside me.

Fuck anyone judging us for not being 'proper.'

And when Wren walks out, I can't take my eyes away. Wren's walk appears like she's moving in slow motion. There's a look in her eyes as if she owns this stage—the entire fucking world. It's a different confidence than she the one displays anywhere else. I hear a few people higher up whistle and shout. Bonnie nudges me in the ribs, and I realize when Wren reaches the end that I'm staring at her thinking of the look on her face when she had me in her clutches this morning. The power in her gaze. The laugh she'd given me after.

Her gaze shifts just noticeably in my direction when she comes back down, lip twitching the slightest bit.

I don't even know what the hell she's wearing because I can't look away from her face.

I finally exhale when she disappears.

She changes looks twice more, and by the time she goes back down the third time, the designer meets her at the stage, grinning widely, and he pulls her into him for a hug before the pair walk together out once more, the rest of the models following in a line as the show wraps up.

I stand with the crowd and whistle, locking eyes with Wren. And as she reaches me, she slows. My heart lurches into my throat. She pauses in front of me, reaches for my scarf, and drags me to her for a kiss that causes the audience and entire fleet of photographers to lose their minds.

Fucking hell.

I nearly lose my *own* shit.

Her bottom lip draws behind her teeth when she smirks

and swipes away the transferred lipstick from the corner of my mouth. And when she joins the designer again to finish walking, I can't stop fucking grinning.

There's a weird feeling swirling inside me as I watch her, as our eyes meet once again on her walk back. I don't remember the last time I felt this, and it pains me more than it fills me with joy.

Shit.

Larry is there to escort us to the afterparty when everyone is offstage and the room begins to clear.

Thank fuck. I'm *starving*.

As we head back, I run into several people who I have to stop to chat with. Someone shoves a warm drink in my hands at some point, and it's the reminder I need to slow down my chitchatting.

This scarf is definitely making me feel better, though.

"Hey—" Mads nudges me. "I'll be right back. Don't leave from here."

"Yeah, man," I reply. The people around us keep talking, though I barely hear them. I stare after Mads as he walks over to two guys who I've never seen before, hands in the pockets of his coat.

A knot forms in my gut as I watch. Mads sees more than anyone else I know. If he's approaching two strangers, something has to be up—whether that's to do with me or something else, I'm not sure.

The exchange is barely a minute, but at the end of that minute, another man approaches with his arm around a model, and the first two guys look between each other, hold up their hands, then turn around to leave.

I frown at Mads when he joins me again.

"What was that about?" I ask, seeing one of them turn to look at me over their shoulder.

"Taking care of something," Mads says. A smile slides on

his lips and he claps my shoulder. "Let's go find your girl."

I don't know if I want to know what just happened.

I notice as we move through the space that some people have flowers in their arms, and I realize when the models come out that they're for them.

Son of a bitch.

I should have brought her flowers.

How did I not think of that?

Even as pissed as I am at myself for the mistake, the thought escapes me when I see Wren coming toward us.

She's wearing an oversized dress that makes her appear so casual despite the stage makeup still on her face. Her gaze meets mine across the room, lips twitching upward like they did on the runway, and I start to rock back and forth on my feet, unable to stay still and itching to run to her.

I won't because she'd fucking kill me.

A few people stop her to speak. I try not to show how anxious I am to see her, though I can barely look away from her.

And when she finally reaches me, I don't hesitate before kissing her.

"Hey," I manage when we part.

"You taste like ginger," she says. "Are you—Oh, you're drinking tea."

"I think Larry handed it to me," I say.

She stares at me. "You don't know who handed you a drink but you're drinking it?"

"It's a bedazzled thermal with ginger tea that says 'Wren's bitch,' on it," I say. "The only people going by that name are either me or Larry."

"I guess it's fitting that he's letting you borrow it then," she says.

I beam at her for a beat, taking in the sight of her in the exaggerated stage makeup, and it does something to my insides. Not because the makeup makes her more beautiful. She's fucking stunning with or without it. But because walking on that runway… that was her original stage. The stage that made her name and let her soar.

And I can see that euphoria in her eyes.

It's the same euphoria I see in mine after a concert.

"You were insanely amazing, by the way," I say, squeezing her waist. "I've never been obsessed with someone's walk before. Now though…" I glance her up and down, whistling suggestively. "You might have to do that for me again. Maybe I'll get something sexy you can model for me."

She gives me a look. "Rules," she says.

"Fuck your rules." I lean closer to her ear. "The kiss was brilliant."

She almost smiles, yet instead pats my cheek mockingly. "I know."

I laugh then, and as I glance around us, I notice every model receiving flowers except for her, and it makes me want to send for a bouquet larger than she can carry just to make up for it.

"No one told me I was supposed to bring you flowers," I say as I hang onto her.

"Yeah, that was on purpose," she says. "I didn't want you to bring something as large as my face for me to carry around."

"Aw, look at that. You know me so well," I tease her.

Her lips press together thinly, and she sighs, swaying slightly in my arms. "I think I'm breaking up with you," she says, and I grin at the statement.

"No, you're not," I say.

"I might. I don't like what you're doing to me."

And I swallow at the confession.

"What am I doing to you?" I ask, my voice suddenly thick.

"I don't know. I was talking about you backstage without someone bringing you up. I've sent you two gifts. I actually kept my phone out so I could see if you texted me before the show." She frowns at me. "It's disgusting, and I hate it. Go away."

I laugh and flick her chin with my knuckle. "It's called having a friend, bird."

Though I'm screaming at myself that it might be more.

Stop.

You can't think about her like that.

Wren's gaze moves past me as I'm trying to figure her out, and the next thing I know, she's pulling me down to her lips.

Fuck the way my chest tightens with her kiss.

However, when we part, I see her glaring at someone past me, and I realize the kiss wasn't just because.

"I'm scared to ask what that was about," I say as I pull her closer.

"I forgot how much fun it is making people jealous," she says, her fingers in my hair.

My brows raise. "Oh, is that what we're doing tonight?" I kiss her fleetingly. "That changes everything. Let's have some fun."

CHAPTER TWENTY-SEVEN

WREN

THERE'S a man wearing mirror sunglasses on the other side of the outdoor restaurant where I'm waiting on Larry and Amanda. A man who—despite the glasses—I know is watching me.

I should be used to it by now.

Tara is waiting over by her SUV, leaned against the side of it. I know she knows he's there, too. I've already texted her.

Even if he isn't here to hurt me.

Not in broad daylight. *No.* Damien is too cowardly for that.

This guy is more than likely only here as a reminder from the night Erik cornered me, or to make sure I'm not meeting with anyone they don't know.

So fucking annoying.

I glance down at my phone, noting that Reed hasn't texted me yet today, and I shift when I don't see his name on the screen. I haven't seen him since New York City, and as much as I hate to admit it, I kind of miss his stupid face.

I'll never tell him that.

The movie press tour is picking up lately. I've been doing so many talk shows and appearances that it's all blurring together.

I always get at least one question about dating Reed Matthews.

All of them show the photo of me kissing him on the runway at Fashion Week, and each time they show it, I think my face gets redder and redder. Reed has poked fun at my near smiles and pink cheeks each interview. The photo blew up in the tabloids and online. It was everywhere I looked—is *still* everywhere I look. To say that people went wild over it is an understatement.

Shannon even sent me a vase of roses the following day.

I shake the memory of the adrenaline that had flowed through me to work up the nerve to kiss him that day. My stomach had been in my throat. However, it was too good of an opportunity to miss, and I knew Rocco wouldn't care, so I pushed through.

It was worth the anxiety.

Clips of Young Decay have been playing on my phone for the last twenty minutes. I've been watching short videos from their concerts at Red Rocks and venues across the east coast as I wait for Larry and Amanda, even watching the videos posted of Reed blowing me a kiss from the stage during the New York City concert the night after the runway show.

I hate how fucking cute the look on his face is when he does it.

He'd had a goth, patchwork bunny plush and single black-tipped white rose waiting on me at my apartment when I made it home—thorns intact. And when I'd videoed with him later that night, he told me he'd asked the thorns to remain so I'd prick my finger on one.

Just so he could be my Prince Charming and kiss me awake.

I'd gagged, corrected his knowledge on the Sleeping Beauty fairytale, and closed the video chat. Though it was the comment after we hung up that still has me smiling.

POSER BOY

Sleeping Beauty can fucking stay in a coma.
I'll take my redheaded Maleficent instead.

I should be studying for the Marilyn Monroe picture. Or basically *anything* else.

Though, since our time at Fashion Week, I've found my free time more and more consumed with him.

A notification about the girl who went missing at Fashion Week comes up as I start to rewind a video of Reed crawling down the stage walk to launch water at some desperate fans' faces. I've heard the story about the missing girl on the news a few times, though the media here isn't covering it much. I flip back over to the video of Reed again just as a text comes through. At first I ignore the message, too entranced by watching the footage of Reed smirking and whipping his wet hair off his face, but another text comes in, and I finally glimpse at the number.

UNKNOWN

I am.

I'm more interested in who you're meeting.

You could have just asked instead of having your goon follow.

That wouldn't be as fun.

What is it with you? Why the increased bullshit?

Increased media presence on your end means
an increase in keeping an eye on you from
mine.

> So, if I get these parts, I should expect people
> following me wherever the set takes me?

Fire your bodyguard and hire Erik, then you
won't have to deal with so many different
followers.

> I'm never doing that.

Suit yourself.

By the way, if any of your new friends threaten
my guys like that one did in NYC again, you
can kiss your little boyfriend goodbye.

You can add his eye to your collection.

Or do you two share a different little saying
than you did with your brother?

I stiffen.

> Leave Reed alone.

> He hasn't done anything.

> And maybe if you didn't want him questioning
> me or snooping into why I have stalkers, you
> should keep your distance. What did you think
> would happen? Of course, he's going to ask
> who your people are.

I can't stop my fingers from pounding on the screen. Can't
stop the words from vomiting out of me at the mere mention of
the band.

Thanks to Erik's little scene at that party, he
knows I'm not telling him the truth.

And no one threatened you. You're not that
fucking important.

Another text comes through, and my heart does a little skip when I see Reed's name. I stay on Damien's screen and text him back one more time.

If you fucking touch him, I'll go public.

It's the first time I've ever threatened Damien.

However, the thought of him touching anyone in Young Decay has suddenly unleashed something within me.

I'll probably regret it later, but right now, I don't care.

I wait for his text.

I wait for the anticipatory dots on the bottom of the screen.

Yet even a full minute later, Damien doesn't respond.

I hesitantly flip to Reed's messages, and even though it's only his texts, something about the words helps me breathe a little better, deters the nausea in my twisting stomach, and even lets my jaw release.

POSER BOY

I know you don't watch your own films, but
this is one I think you should consider.

I've been hiding it for a few weeks.

I don't know what he's talking about, and I'm not sure I care. He could be telling me he saw a dog taking a shit by a fire hydrant, and I'd probably read it like a romance novel.

Ugh.

What is he doing to me?

What are you talking about? What film?

It's the rest of the video from the morning we
filmed the clip for my socials.

My stomach drops.

Oh god. What do you mean the rest of the
video? What did you do?

I didn't realize I forgot to stop recording when
I threw my phone across the room.

Were you ever going to tell me about it?

Honestly I was scared you'd break up
with me.

You're not scared of that now?

Nah. You told Morning America that I'm the
highlight of your day. I think you like me.

My jaw tenses.

That's not what I said.

That's basically what you said.

I huff and lean back in my seat.

Send me the video.

I don't know if I should. It's pretty hot. Maybe
too hot for you.

I'm mildly insulted that you think a video of us
fucking is just 'pretty hot'

I can practically hear his chuckle.

> I'll see you at the Halloween party next week.
> After, I'll show you my definition of 'pretty hot.'

> Big promises for someone with average
> equipment.

It's a flat-out lie, but it's fun teasing his pride.

> We'll see how average you think I am when
> I'm fucking that bratty mouth of yours again.

> Did you get my leash?

> I did. Larry had fun bedazzling it.

> That's fucking perfect.

> What do you think of these to match my
> costume?

A picture comes through of three sets of painted nails, and I bite my lip to keep from grinning outright.

> You have scary movie ones right now,
> don't you?

He sends back a picture of his current nails—ghosts, black cats, and headstones. The last time I saw him, they were ghost face masks and blood.

The piano key tattoos on his fingers make me shift. They seem to disappear into smoke as they travel down his hands, warping into skulls and fading into the full sleeves on his arms. I know most of his tattoos are music related, including the guitar strings on the inside of his left forearm that appear as if his skin is peeled away to show the strings instead of bones and muscle beneath.

I force myself to look at the nail options instead of fantasizing about what I want those hands to do to me.

> Matte black and white ones. You're not allowed to upstage me.

> I don't think that would be possible.

> And before you tell me off, fuck your rules.

I reply with the middle finger emoji, and he sends a tongue and the wet emojis back.

It doesn't surprise me that he 'accidentally' recorded us having sex. Especially that day.

I glance around me as I open the video and put my headphones in. It starts out with the last part of him recording the bit for his short, then continues recording when he throws the phone across the room. It lands sideways on the chair as Reed kisses me.

Holy shit.

This is *hot*.

Heat creeps up and up my chest with every passing second —until my face is fully flushed and my breaths shorten. I've never watched myself fuck someone, let alone someone who looks at my body as if it's the answers to every prayer he's ever sent to a desolate god. Shit, the way he grabs my ass and stares at me while I'm riding him… The noises he's making in response.

It's almost better than experiencing it myself.

I squeeze my thighs and run my hand behind my neck as I continue watching. I shouldn't be watching it right now. It's too early for this. I'm in too public of an area. Anyone could come up behind me and see that I'm literally watching rockstar porn.

Still, I can't take my eyes away.

He's pulling my hair and sliding into me from behind, his hips hitting my ass. The sound of his motions and my pussy taking him skitters chills along my arms. I know he's close. I can tell by the strain on his face. He's waiting on me to find my end first, his groans filling the room along with my disjointed whimpers—

"Whatcha watching?"

Larry's voice makes me jump. My phone flies out of my hands and lands on the other side of the table, face up. I scramble to grab it, but Larry is already on the other side to get it for me.

"Wait, don't—"

"What? What are you—*oh my god!*" Larry's eyes light up, his mouth dropping. He drops into his seat and picks up the phone, ignoring my pleas for him to leave it.

"Oh my god. Is that… *Oh my god.* This is… *Wren, this is hot!*" he finally hisses.

I slump back in my chair and give up.

It's over.

I'm done for.

"Oh my god," he keeps saying.

"Can you please stop repeating that?" I mutter.

"You know, I hoped he was fucking you into next Tuesday, but I think a small part of me thought his swagger might be all talk." Larry slides the phone back in my direction. "I'm glad to know he's taking care of you."

"Shut up," I mutter, closing the video.

I'll have to finish watching later.

Larry smirks at me as the waiter comes over to take his drink order.

"Oh, that reminds me! We have a fitting today," Larry says.

"What kind of fitting?" I ask as I take a chip from the basket and dip it into the spiciest salsa.

"For your Halloween costume," he answers.

My phone buzzes, and I pick it up just as I see Damien's minion stand from his seat and leave the restaurant.

TARA - SECURITY

That SUV is leaving.

Did you talk to Damien?

> I did. Maybe we won't have to deal with them for a few weeks, I tell her.

Fingers crossed. Screenshot the texts and send them to me.

The waitress comes over, and as Larry begins chatting with her about lunch specials and more, I flip back over to Damien's text and quickly do as she asked before deleting the message altogether.

TARA - SECURITY

What does he mean that one of Reed's friends threatened him?

> I have no idea.

> I only saw them once the morning of the show from my hotel window.

> Nothing after.

I'll chat with their bodyguard.

Don't bring it up to Reed.

Let me handle it.

> Okay.

The very last thing I intend to do is talk to Reed about it.

I throw my phone in my bag and give Larry my full attention as two margaritas hit the table.

"It's barely noon," I say to him.

"It's a jalapeño marg. Shut up and drink it," he says as he pulls his planner out and basically slams it on the table, sending the silverware clanking. He thumbs through the pages until reaching October, then opens it to run through the promos I have this week.

"Okay, fitting tonight. You have tomorrow off. I thought we could go through those two scripts to get you ready for the official reading with Sean's people on Thursday—"

"When is my meeting with Amber?" I ask.

"That is… November 1st. So, I know you and Reed have a party night planned for Halloween, but try to pack it in early," he says, and I stare flatly at him.

"A party night?" I repeat, voice deadpan.

"Is that not what you're doing?" Larry asks.

I scoff. "He's coming in that morning, we're going to the party, and then he's leaving the next day for like fucking Canada or something. I don't know how much partying will be had."

"Aww," Larry coos, pouting his lip.

"What?"

"It's just so cute that you know his touring schedule," he tells me.

I sip my margarita, the extra spice hitting my tongue, and simply stare at my assistant. "You know I could fire you," I say.

Larry laughs. "You couldn't remember which days you're supposed to wash your hair if you fired me."

I take another sip and let the drink sit in my mouth as I try to come up with a retort.

I have nothing.

"Touché," I mutter, sitting up.

"Will Halloween night be the first night you let him stay over?" Larry asks.

I make a gagging face. "You say it like we're teenagers talking about my first crush," I say.

"Sweetie, for me, this is your first crush," he says. "Therefore, I'm treating it like so. And you were just watching a video of the two of you having sex," he adds pointedly.

I chew on my tongue. "Yes," I finally answer. "Halloween will be the first time I'm letting him stay over."

Larry squeals.

"What is the celebration?" Shannon asks as she and Amanda approach.

"It's nothing," I say, drink to my lips and staring at Larry like I dare him to tell them what we were just talking about. "Larry was just going over my schedule this week."

"Add in a fitting with LoRocco on Saturday," Amanda says. "And you'll need to let Reed know Matteo wants to send over a few items to wherever the hell he'll be this weekend."

I look between them at the mention of the designers. "Why?"

"Because they're designing your outfits for the LA premiere," she says as if I was already aware of it.

I blink. "What?" I manage.

Amanda smirks. "He took your measurements at the show," she says. "Wanted it to be a surprise."

I've never had a dress designed specifically for me.

I've never had a dress started from scratch with me in mind.

Normally, Larry shops different designers to find one that he likes and it's tailored for me.

"He's making a dress for me?" I ask, feeling my jaw tighten.

Larry squeezes me beneath the table, knowing how big of a moment this is.

Amanda nods. "Yes, girl. We're doing it," she says.

"*You're* doing it," Shannon corrects her. "I don't know what it is about that shaggy haired rockstar and his tight pants, but he's certainly pulled something out of you that no one else has been able to touch. And I'm not saying this as a praise to him at all. He's played his part well, but… what he's done is frame you. You're the stunning art piece, he's just made you look more expensive. I think it's safe to say he's paid off," she says smugly, sipping her drink.

"The studio is pleased, nonetheless," Amanda adds. "When do you see him again?"

"Halloween," I answer. "Movie premiere a week later."

"You'll be free of him by Christmas," Shannon says. "It won't matter then if you're with him or not. You'll have your parts and the two of you can be whatever you want. Stay friends. Go back to hating each other. Enough people love you that they won't care."

I should be happy.

I should be cheers'ing with them and thanking fuck that this is almost over.

I should be thinking about keeping him safe from my chaos and the shitty situation I'm in.

But I'm toying with my fingers and shrinking into this seat, my ears burning and one eye on the phone in my purse. Reed's smile flashes behind my eyes. I hear his laugh, feel his poke in my side when he's trying to annoy me, feel his hand around my throat as he brings me to an end that no one else has ever reached.

I raise my glass and lift it to meet theirs, a celebratory sip to the winning scheme.

And yet, I'm hollow.

CHAPTER TWENTY-EIGHT

REED

I DON'T THINK BEING DRESSED as a dog and led around on a leash by my fake girlfriend in front of cameras at a red carpet Hollywood party was on the BINGO card for this year.

But it's fucking fantastic.

I press my hand to the small of Wren's back when photographers ask for a photo of us together, and when she needs the space to show off her black and white gown, I linger back a few paces for my own photos.

Thank fuck one of us isn't being interviewed at this one.

I'm sure someone thinks I'm humiliated. That the collar around my neck and the chain leading into her hand somehow emasculates me.

Absolutely fuck that.

"Give us a kiss!" someone shouts at us.

Wren looks up at me as we join one another again. She tugs me down to her face by the leash, and when our lips are breaths apart, we lick our tongues together before giving them the kissing display they're itching for.

I have full permission to take our public display from PG-

13 to NC-17, to make people question their sanity, and whether they think we're sexy or disgusting tonight.

Wren's words, not mine.

"Now who's the one into bestiality," I murmur against her mouth.

The corner of her red-painted lips tugs upward, and she jerks my leash. "Sit."

I hear someone scream as I sink to my knees, and the light-bulb flashes go off so quickly that they stagger in my vision.

Even on my knees, the top of my head comes up higher than her waist. She threads her fingers into my hair and tilts my head back by my chin. I'm mesmerized by the dark look in her pupils, blinded by the camera flashes and her confidence tonight.

So much so that I stick my tongue out just to see if she'll spit on me.

She drags her thumb over my tongue to open my mouth wider, and when her spit falls into my mouth, I think my dick twitches.

"Swallow like a good boy," she tells me.

I do.

God, I fucking do.

And the cameras go fucking nuts.

Wren smirks and starts walking, the train of her dress dragging, and I fall onto all fours to crawl along beside her.

When we reach the end of the carpet, Wren gives me a smile that feels almost genuine and holds out her hand. I take it and rise to my feet, dragging her into my arms when I'm up.

I'm probably smearing our makeup, but I don't fucking care.

She's on another level tonight, and I can't get enough of it.

"Tell me to swallow in public like that again, and we'll be escorted out of here in handcuffs for public indecency," I tell her when we part.

Mirth dances in her eyes as she straightens out my shirt with her palms. "Hm," she mumbles smugly. "Let's get through tonight before we make any future plans."

"Hey, lovers, let's go," Larry calls us.

I don't know what to expect at this party, but the music is thumping. I immediately feel my energy rising upon entering. The DJ is set up in the far corner, standing tables scattered by the bar, seated tables upstairs, and a dance floor that's already packed.

Friends come up to us. I don't know how long we walk from group to group and chat with her friends or mine—all of whom compliment the costumes and talk to us about either the tour or Wren's recently landed role in Sean's indie film.

However, the more we speak with people, the more I notice Wren's energy waning, and I can't discern if it's from the socializing or something different. She's barely touched her first drink, and by the time we finally reach a table on our own, I see her stagger.

"Whoa—" I say, catching her by the arm. "Okay?"

"Yeah," she replies. "Yeah, I'm fine. Must be the Spanx," she jokes.

I know better. She's a fucking pro. It's definitely not whatever tights she has on under this perfectly snug dress.

"You didn't eat before this, did you?" I realize.

Wren stares blankly at the wall for a beat. "Um. No, actually,"

"No?" I repeat.

"No, I think I forgot," she says, pressing her hand against the table. "That explains a few things."

I huff, almost amused at the look on her face. I should have known, especially with her nerves and the fact that we only had a few minutes before leaving to see each other.

I should start packing snacks as this isn't the first time she's done this.

Leaning over, I kiss her cheek, tell her I'll be back in a few minutes with something, and Wren nods—waving me off like she hardly hears me. Though, I barely take more than a few steps before she launches after me.

"Wait—um… nothing sticky. No weird vegetables. Preferably something really spicy—"

"Bird," I cut her off, on the verge of smiling. "I know how you eat."

She relaxes the faintest bit, and I kiss her softly, dragging my knuckle beneath her chin as I do. "I have you, remember? Just don't go anywhere."

At least the food at this place looks fucking amazing.

While Wren eats, Foster from the metal band, New Dawn, comes up to us to chat. His band is opening for us at the New Year's Eve show at Hollywood Hollow Arena.

It's fucking weird because just a few years ago, we were opening for them.

"I can't believe you guys are opening for us," I say to him. "Isn't that fucking weird?"

Foster laughs. "I think we always knew you shits would go on to do some sick things, but getting the call to ask if we'd open the show was pretty wild. I like that the label is putting on a whole day, though. I heard you guys were bringing on the orchestra for your set."

I grin. "Hell fucking yes, dude. Mads and Zeb have been working with a composer to get music ready for all the instruments and shit. They have a meeting with the guy tomorrow to work on some tracks they've already recorded. It's insane. I can't wait."

Foster eyes me. "Tell me they're giving you a real piano, bro. Like a big ass grand piano."

A quiet chuckle leaves me. "Listen. They didn't fucking believe I played when we were first chatting with them about it. I felt like I was auditioning for the orchestra when the guy told me to get up there and play."

"You were like 'fucking watch this,'" Foster laughs.

"Fucking eat your words," I grin. "They did, too. I said, 'I don't have piano keys tattooed on my fingers for no reason.'"

"It's all aesthetic," Foster teases.

I laugh. "All fucking aesthetic."

I glance over at Wren then, noticing that she looks a little less pale than she did five minutes earlier, and I reach out to flick her hair. "How you feeling there, bird?"

"Much better," she says, wiping the corners of her lips. She glances at Foster and gives him the tiniest smile. "Hi, Foster."

"What's up, Kelly," he says, the right corner of his lip quirking upward as he watches her sink her arm around me, her hand settling into my back pocket. She lays her head on my side, and I try to keep my composure as I hug her into me.

This is nice.

"Will we see you at the New Year's Eve show?" Foster asks her.

Shit.

Wren stiffens, though it isn't noticeable to any onlooker by the way she smiles.

"New Year's? Maybe. I'll see what I can manage," she answers.

However, the vacant look in her eyes when she looks up at me tells me I should hug her a little tighter.

Foster holds out his fist for me to bump. "Catch you guys later," he says.

Wren turns into me once Foster is out of earshot. There's a twinge of pink on her cheeks, a look of mild panic in her eyes.

"Hey," I say, tipping her chin up. "We don't have to think about anything except tonight," I tell her. "Until you say the word, this is as real as everyone else thinks it is."

"It's just pretend," she breathes.

"It's the most realistic game of pretend I've ever played," I say, and she looks like she wants to laugh. But her jaw sets, and she sighs heavily. I can't discern the expression, and it makes me shift on my feet.

"Why are you looking at me like that?"

"I was just thinking about how much I hate you," she says.

I scoff. "That seems to be plaguing your thoughts a lot lately."

"It has," she admits. "It burns me inside that I think of you when I'm alone."

I brace my hand against her neck and pull her closer. "Yeah? Why's that?"

"Because I wake up in the middle of the night wondering what you're doing, what city you're in," she breathes. "Because I see something weird on the street and immediately want to send you a picture, and I want to buy you stupid gag gifts just because it's funny."

Every word has my insides screaming.

"Dance with me," I say, taking her hands.

Her lips twist slightly as she weighs her options. "Three songs," she decides.

I punch the air before kissing her hard. "I'll fucking take it."

I don't think I've ever had a worse idea.

Every move of her body against mine is hypnotizing. Every lift of her lashes and gape of her mouth drags me further beneath the water that I'm already struggling to navigate.

During the first song, we jump. We shake it out, matching those around us. I hear her laugh, and it's enough to pull her into me. And by the time the second song wraps up, she's dancing in my arms.

And the third…

The third has me kissing her. It has me drunk and unable to think—even though I've only had two drinks. Forget the people around us. Forget the cameras. Forget everything in this world except the two of us.

It's three fucking songs.

Three fucking songs, and I'm helpless.

Because all I can think about is the fact that I don't know how much longer I have with her. I've been so consumed with trying to help her sell this and making sure she got the parts she wanted that I lost track of fucking time. I forgot that this had a timeline. I forgot that this would have an ending.

And no one promised it would be a happy one.

I feel my jaw quiver when the third song wraps up, and it takes everything in me just to whisper, "Are you ready to leave?"

Wren's lips brush against mine. She swallows, her chest heaving, and finally she nods.

I can't get her back to her condo fast enough.

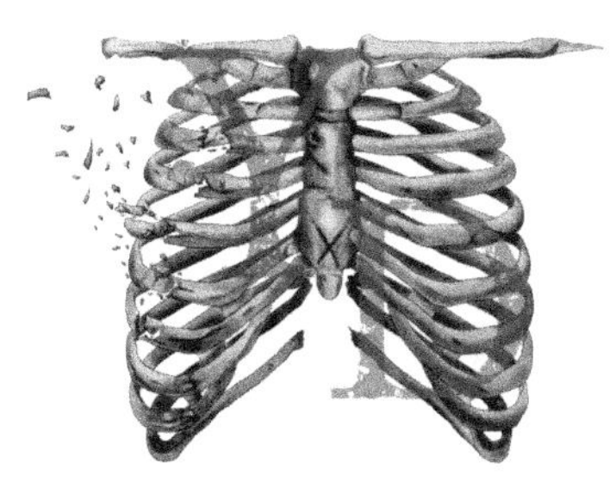

We barely make it through the door of her apartment before we're on one another.

The door slams behind me. She's clawing at my shirt and tugging the roots of my hair. I kick my shoes off and shed myself of my shirt, reckless emotion bubbling beneath the surface of my eager drive for her. The fact that this is waning has me on the edge. The fact that I've completely abandoned my own sense of reality has me desperate.

I'm pissed about it.

I grasp her wrists and pin them behind her back. She's struggling to stay on her heeled feet as I advance, forcing her to walk backward, forcing her shoulder blades together with the deliberate strain I'm putting on her.

I don't fucking care.

I hope she feels this stretch in her shoulders for days.

I hope her pretty porcelain skin bruises beneath my tight grip.

I kiss her with every step, relishing the nip of her teeth on my tongue as if it's the only way she thinks she can fight back.

I want her to fight me. I want her to feel as if she's being ripped apart when I fuck her tonight.

But most importantly…

I want to fuck the word 'pretend' right out of her goddamn vocabulary.

She pulls back, sucking on my tongue as she does, and looks up at me. "I can't take you seriously in these things," she says, snatching the dog ears off my head.

"How attached are you to this dress?" I ask, tugging down the stubborn zipper.

"I kind of like it," she says.

"That's too fucking bad."

I feel the fabric rip beneath my hands. She gasps and peers at me with wide eyes when she hears the noise, but I crash my lips against hers before she can slap my face or tell me off.

Her wilt and surrender into my arms sends me.

I unclasp her bra and snatch at the support and shape

wear she's wearing, peeling it off and exposing her sexy body in its stunning glory. I weave my fingers into her hair at the nape of her neck and pull, walking her backward into the bedroom as my other hand finds the heat between her thighs.

Mother fuck—

"Have you been this wet for me all night?" I ask as we enter the bedroom.

"No," she says, sharp claws digging into my chest.

I almost snicker.

Yeah, she has.

She slides her fingers onto my face and puckers my lips, forcing my mouth to hers. Her back hits the dresser and rattles the lamp atop it, sending it crashing to the floor. She's unbuckling my pants and tearing them off with as much aggression as I had with her clothes, though she doesn't stay on her feet and let me take them off myself.

She's on her knees, my hardening cock in her mouth, and pushing my cigarette jeans down to my ankles.

"Oh fuck," is the only thing I can manage when her claws tickle my balls, and she greedily sucks me. The noises her mouth is making, the drool threatening the corners of her lips… There's nothing slow about this. It's sloppy and slutty and indelicate, and I fucking love it.

She's going to have me coming in her mouth before I can even touch her if she keeps this up.

I grab her by her hair and pull her off her knees, relishing the wince on her face and the way she falls into me when she's on her feet. Our lips meet as if we're starving for one another, and I finish kicking my pants off before throwing her sideways onto the mattress.

Crawling over her, I pin her wrists to the bed by her sprawled hair, elbows bent out at her sides, my knees on her thighs and holding her in place. She whips her head back and forth, chest rising with every heavy breath like she wants me off.

Though the smirk on her lips and darkness in those swollen pupils has me fucking feral.

"Reed," she begs, squirming, trying to lift her hips.

"How do you want me to fuck you tonight, little bird?" I ask, nose skimming her cheek.

She turns and licks my cheek, bringing my eyes to hers, and I pause to watch her say in a breathless whisper, "Finish breaking me."

In the back of my mind, I wonder if we were hit by a rogue driver on the way home, if we were knocked out of the car, and I'm dreaming all of this from a coma in a hospital bed miles away.

Fuck that noise.

I slide off her thighs and hike her knees up to my ribs, the strain causing her to arch her back. My lips land on hers as I thrust relentlessly inside her. She cries into my mouth and bites my tongue, leaving welts behind on my cheeks from these fucking nails.

I can't stop kissing her.

Not even when she rolls me onto my back and sinks onto my dick. Not when her chest is flush to mine, her rolling, riding motions making me whimper in her mouth. She sucks air through her teeth when I bruise my fingers into her hips and slap her ass, the unfiltered noises causing me to forget myself.

"Fuck, Reed," she cries out. "You feel so fucking good *—right there—*" She sits up and presses her palms to my chest, weight teetering atop me. *Jesus fuck…* I'm going to come just looking at her on top of me like this. I press my hands in the creases where her waist meets her hips—accentuated at this angle, and guide her back and forth. Her clit sits on my pelvis, and watching her find that rhythm is fucking fantastic.

I sit up and kiss her again, our chest flush as she wraps her arms around my neck. Her fingers are tugging in my hair to the point that I gasp and groan into her.

She suddenly shoves my face and pushes me away. The fight sends me. I pin my arms around her back and throw her backward. She lands with a bounce as I slam inside and grab her wrists.

Pushing. Pulling. Kissing. Biting.

It's all a blur, a kick to my senses.

All I know is that I'm fucking doomed.

After a firm slap, I pull out of her and flip her on her stomach. She starts to sit up, but I shove her back down. Her face buries in the mattress. I knot my fingers in her hair and spread my wide hand across her exposed cheek, my thumb hooking into the edge of her open mouth, and I slam into her wet pussy.

Fuck, how did that make her wetter?

I hear her cry, feel her bite down on my fingers, but I don't stop. My free hand is pressing her left wrist into the small of her back, holding her steady as I thrust harshly inside her. I feel a tear hit my hand, feel her mouth moving as a struggling noise sounds from her, and I move my thumb just so I can hear how much more she wants.

"Reed… Reed…" She whimpers out my name and squirms under my weight, free hand white-knuckling the sheet. "Oh my god—*shit*—bananas—*Jesus, fuck*—bananas!"

I think the world just stopped spinning.

Fuck.

Fuck. *Fuck.*

I think my eyes are about to bulge out of my head. My heart rate is out of control from panic spreading throughout. I'm already out of her and jumping off the bed, yet she's still lying there. Still hasn't moved. Still clenching the sheets.

"Shit—Are you okay?" I ask. "Wren?"

Her breaths are deep, and each one pulls her into the mattress further. I don't know what to do. Oh fuck, *have I hurt her?!*

I sink onto the floor in front of her to see her face. My hand is trembling as I start to reach out, hesitant because I don't know if she wants to be touched or left alone.

Shit.

"Wren?"

"Yeah," she finally manages. "Yeah, I'm… *Shit.*" She starts to roll over onto her back, and I help her into a sitting position before kneeling in front of her again, my hands on her bent knees dangling off the bed.

Fuck, I hope I didn't hurt her.

It's all I can do to watch her every movement, fixating on her breathing specifically.

"Wren?" I repeat, squeezing her thigh.

Because she still hasn't looked at me.

"I'm sorry," she says, hanging her head.

My gaze narrows. "Why are you sorry?" I ask, completely bewildered by the apology.

"I just… I'm sorry. You didn't do anything. It was me. I got in my head." She presses her hands to her face and pushes her hair back. "Oh god, Reed. I'm sorry."

"Hey—" I take her wrists in my hands and pull them down into her lap, thumbs caressing her palms. A lump sits in my throat. "Are you okay?"

She sniffs back what I realize are actual tears on her face.

"Jesus fuck, Wren," I mutter, tipping her chin up. "Did I hurt you?" I ask, panicking.

"No," she manages. "No, you didn't."

Her eyes finally lift to mine, and I swallow beneath that glistening stare. "Are you sure?" I ask. "Did I have you in a weird bind? Too much pressure on your back? What—"

A small smile creeps onto her lips. Even just the sight of it slows my words. She braces her hand on my cheek and kisses me softly, cutting off the ramble I was about to go into.

My mind is a blank canvas waiting on her to paint.

Our eyes meet when we part, but I hold her face a moment longer. "You didn't do anything wrong," she says assuringly. "The opposite, actually. I'm sorry I stopped you."

I don't entirely know what she means, but I don't want to pressure her. I don't want to push her to say anything she doesn't want to.

"Don't ever be sorry for using your words," I tell her. "I'd rather you tell me to stop than let me hurt you."

She nods softly, eyes closing as she leans her forehead against mine.

I have no fucking clue what's happening right now, but I'm going to soak up every second.

I kiss her one more time before heading into her kitchen for bottles of water from the fridge and stopping by her bathroom for the two robes she has on the back of the door on my way back.

"What are you doing?" she asks when I push my arms through one of them and start to wrap her in the other. "Don't you want to finish?"

"You invited me to stay the night, bird. I have hours to do that again. But first, water," I say as I hand her an open bottle of water.

She takes a long swig, the bottle crinkling as she gulps it back so hard that some of it trickles down her chin. "So… what are we doing?" she asks once she stands.

I tie the belt around her waist and lean in to kiss her nose. "We're going to shower, order late night munchies, and share a bottle of gin."

"I don't know that you should be drinking that much. Don't you have a gig tomorrow?" she asks.

I smirk at her. "Have you been doing more research on what helps singers' vocal cords?"

Her jaw tenses. "No."

I chuckle. "Yeah, okay," I say. "Come on. You can tell me what else I should and shouldn't be doing after we shower."

The costume face makeup I'm wearing swirls around the drain as the hot water pours over us just minutes later. I have her against the wall, my dick buried inside her—long, slow strokes this time. No rush, especially when the pizza said it would take over an hour to get here.

They can leave it at the door if it comes early.

I'll heat it up when I'm finished with her.

Her sudsy hands thread in my hair, tightening as she reaches the end this time. No frills. Nothing except the two of us.

Even when the water is cold and we're towel drying off one another, it takes all of my restraint not to kiss her. It still stings that she had to use her safe word on me, though if using that word leads into this every time, maybe I'll push her more often.

A joke, of course.

I have more respect for her boundaries than that.

"What are you doing?" she asks as I bring my travel bag out of my duffle.

I almost grin as I remember we've never spent the night together. "You don't know my nighttime routine," I say.

"I wasn't aware you had one. You're a twenty-eight year old rockstar from North Carolina. I thought your nighttime routine consisted of turning your shirt inside out and calling it clean."

My lips split crookedly. "You're not wrong. I don't get to do this every night. Which is why it matters so much more when I do get a night off."

Wren leans over the bag and starts taking out the vials of

skincare one by one, reading them and asking what each one is for, and when she has everything—including the face masks—out on the counter, she stares.

"Reed… you have more skincare than I do."

"How do you think I stay this sexy? It isn't just the sweat and stage lights."

Wren eyes me as she slides a few more jars her way, including one of the face masks. "I'm listening."

I think we both forget about the pizza.

She follows my routine, ending with us both in face masks and headbands to hold our hair back. I had to braid her hair for her, making sure to give it a generous tug that led us back into the bedroom. Though, with the masks on, it was hard to kiss her.

I settle for a couple of selfies against the pillows.

"One kiss. One natural," I say, and something of a grunt sounds from her.

"This is so time consuming," she says, but doesn't pull away when I twist to kiss her.

"You taste like aloe," she says when we part. "Did some get on your lip?"

I laugh and lay my back against her, head lying on her soft breasts. "I might have," I answer. "Lean closer," I tell her.

She threads her hair into my hair and shifts a little so that we're fully entwined. Dammit, her fingers feels amazing. The way her nails scratch my scalp makes my eyelids flutter, breaks goosebumps along my flesh.

I force my attention back on what I was doing and take a few photos of us. She's such a fucking model. I see it every time the camera comes out. She slips into a different persona, each one as gorgeous and sexy as the one before.

I swallow as I look at the two of us together.

"What's wrong?" she asks, and I realize I've hesitated for too long.

"Nothing," I say, staring at the picture. "That's nearly too sexy for social media."

A quiet huff of amusement sounds from her. "We're wearing face masks and matching makeup headbands."

"Exactly. We might break the internet," I say. "Caption?"

"Find someone who will braid your hair and pull it, too," she says without missing a beat.

I beam, shifting slightly so I can see her. "After we eat, I'm going to take full advantage of having you in the same bed all night beside me," I tell her.

"In other words, you're forcing me to cuddle?" she asks, her voice deadpan.

"Yep."

There's a knock on the door, and for a moment, I think about letting the food get cold. But the grumble of her stomach makes me smile.

"Feed bird. Got it," I say, jumping out of the bed.

We take off the face masks and wash our faces before grabbing the pizza from the hall.

Wren is searching for glasses from the top cabinet when I return from the door.

"I haven't been looking up singing things, by the way," she says as she grabs two short glasses. "Some of the other models were talking about their singer boyfriends at Fashion Week and mentioned things they do."

I smile at her and open up the pizza lid. "I was just giving you a hard time," I say. "It's fun."

"I'm glad vexing me makes you happy," she smirks.

"It really does," I grin.

My gaze snags on the butcher's block behind her, and an idea pops into my head.

It's a stupid one, but I'm curious.

"How do you feel about games?" I ask.

Her mouth twists, and she cracks the top of the bottle of

gin. "Depends on the game," she replies. "Why? What were you thinking? Spin the bottle? I have some stuffed plushies that might like making out with you."

I almost laugh at her retort. "The first time we had sex, you said you were into some shit, which I assume you meant kinky shit. I'm curious what that entails."

She squints at me and pours the alcohol into our glasses. I glance at the butcher's block again, and this time, she follows my gaze.

"You want to play the knife game?" she asks, brows lifting.

"You already used your safe word on me once tonight," I shrug. "I wonder if I can get you to do it again."

The words have barely left my lips when I see the look in her eyes shift. She glances at the knives again and back to me, and the way she's staring has my insides growing cold, like she's just invited a ghost into the house.

Or plans on murdering me.

Neither of which would be surprising.

"Okay, poser. Let's do it," she says. "I could get into a bit of blood play."

Oh.

Oh, I was fucking joking—

Why am I not saying that?

Why is my mouth not moving?

Are we really doing this?

I gulp upon seeing her grab the largest knife from the block.

Not *that* fucking knife.

"Don't you have a smaller knife than that one?" I ask.

"What's wrong, Matthews?" she taunts, stepping toward me. "Afraid I'll hurt your precious hands?"

I straighten in the seat, staring at her as she comes around the counter in my direction.

Why did I think this was a good joke?

"If you stab my fingers, just remember, they're my liveli-hood," I say.

"Here I thought your face was your moneymaker," she says, tilting her head.

"I mean, my face definitely helps, but if you take away my ability to play piano, we will have a problem," I say.

My stomach has never been in so many knots.

"That's cute," she says.

She's barely three feet away from me.

"What is?" I ask.

"The fact that you suggested this, and now you're scared."

"I'm not scared," I say, though I hate the nervous sound in my voice. "That's not what this is."

She pauses at the seat beside me, wraps one arm over her stomach, and bends her elbow at the opposite wrist so that the blade is touching her chin. The sight of her holding that knife shouldn't have all the blood in my body rushing to my dick—

Fucking hell, though.

Her brow lifts when she spies my already hardening length.

She comes to stand between my thighs in such a swag-gering manner that it's all I can do to swallow.

I'm starting to think she's fucking with me.

"Come on, wolfie…" she says as she drags the back of the knife across my cheek. "Let little Red Riding Hood show you how she bites."

She's *definitely* fucking with me.

I back against the counter like it might save me. "Ah… okay," I say, unwilling to back down.

Her gaze drifts to my lips, the tip of the blade pressing into my chin. "You're trembling," she says.

I don't remember the last time my heart thumped this erratically.

"I'm not," I argue.

"You're really cute when you're scared," she goes on. "I wonder if you're this cute when you bleed."

"I think the point of the knife game is *not* to stab the other person," I manage, my throat dry.

Her leer turns into a grin larger than I've ever seen on her, and she bites at my lips.

I hate that I flinch.

A chuckle leaves her that I've never heard before.

"I'm fucking with you, Matthews."

CHAPTER TWENTY-NINE

HOLY *SHIT.*

A heavy breath leaves me. "*Jesus, bird,*" I blow out. I press my hands to my knees, nearly nauseous from trying to put on a brave face. "Holy shit. You had me."

I hear her snicker. "I would never call you 'wolfie.' You're a cuddly lap dog that likes to nip and bark. No where near a 'big bad wolf,'" she says.

"I can be a wolf," I say as I gather my wits.

"If anyone is the wolf in our situation, it's me," she says as she turns on her heel toward the block. She slides the large blade back into it, then opens the drawer beneath and pulls out a small pocket knife instead.

"What are you doing with that?"

"Oh, we're still playing," she says. "If only to test your resolve."

My chest caves, but I try to keep my cool. "Okay. As long as it's just that knife."

The corner of her lip twists upward at the corner, and I feel the change in her in the pit of my stomach. Shit. That little glint has me itching to touch her again, to make her laugh however I can.

"I'm suddenly glad I sent Anita away to Larry's tonight," she says.

"I wondered where my girlfriend was," I reply.

"I'll send you a picture of her when I get her back tomorrow. I know you need a new one for your phone background."

"I actually do," I reply.

She pulls the small blade from its sheath, twists it between her hands, then nudges her head toward the living room.

I follow without a word, bringing the pizza and gin along with me.

"Have you played this before?" she asks as we settle on the floor in front of the television where she has metal music playing instead of a show.

"Ah…" I want to tell her yes, even if just to stroke my own ego. However, sitting here nearly naked and vulnerable with her, my pride seems to deflate.

"No," I admit. "Have you?"

She bites her lips together. "Once," she replies. "However, that game ended with me stabbing him in the thumb, so if I stab you—"

"Do not fucking stab me," I interject.

"—don't worry because I know first aid," she finishes.

I eye her, then take the pocket knife from her hand. "I'll go first," I say. I start at her thumb, jumping over her spread fingers and puncturing the wood table with every steady strike. "Want to make this interesting?"

"What—avoiding puncturing each other's hands isn't enough?" she asks.

"For every successful pass, we get to ask a question," I say.

Wren considers me as the knife lands on the outside of her pinky. I see the hesitation in her eyes, and there's a split second when I think she's going to tell me to get out of her apartment. Yet instead, she reaches for the gin, unscrews the cap, and takes a long swig.

"Okay, nosey pants," she says, gesturing for the knife. "As long as you're aware that if you ask something I don't like, I'm the one holding the knife."

I smile. "Deal," I agree. "How do you know first aid?" I ask.

Wren's eyes daze a little with the question, and she carefully takes her first stab. "My brother played lacrosse," she says. "He was always getting hurt."

A sadness lingers in her gaze that makes my heart knot.

"I didn't know you had a brother," I say, though now that she mentions it, I vaguely recall those guys from Sean's saying something about a brother. "You never talk about your family," I add.

"Twin brother, actually," she admits, her gaze shifting to the bedroom.

"You're a twin? Where is he now?"

I instantly regret asking.

Wren stabs the wood, almost scratching my finger, and she pauses as if she can't pick the knife up again. "Ah, he died," she says.

My heart falls at the sorrow in her tone, and it instantly hollows my stomach. "I'm sorry," I say.

She shakes her head, waving me off as she reaches my thumb and hands me the knife. "It was a few years ago," she says, continuing to avoid my eyes.

"What happened?" I ask as I take my first stab.

Her lashes lift, head tilting. "I believe it's my turn."

"Ask away," I say.

She stares at the table, and by the time I'm passing over her ring finger, I have to laugh. "You can't think of a question."

"It's kind of hard," she admits. "Most of the things I'm curious about have been posted online—with Mads going to jail last year and everything."

"You could ask me if all of that is true," I suggest.

"Is it not?" she asks.

I shrug, my turn to stare at our hands. "I think people exaggerate the truth for a story," I say.

"What exactly happened?"

"That… is a very long story. And it starts over twenty years ago." I hand her the knife. "Do you have any other siblings?" I ask her.

"I had two sisters," she replies.

"Had?"

A muscle feathers in her jaw. "Younger one died with my parents. Older one… I don't talk to her anymore."

Missing Lego pieces found.

"You don't… You don't have any family that you talk to?"

I ask because I can't imagine not having family around when I need them.

She doesn't answer as she hands me back the knife. "How did Mads become a part of your family?" she asks.

I almost smile. "We were in grade school. There's some debate on the story, but from what I remember, some kids were giving him shit because he had like stains on his shirt or a bloody lip or something, and I, being the hero that I am, stepped in to defend him."

Wren takes a swig of gin, looking like she wants to smile. "And Mads's version?"

"He says that I was about to get my ass kicked for telling another kid that he was wrong about a band I used to be obsessed with. He says he punched the kid before he could take me out, and my mom took pity on him when we were suspended together."

"That sounds more accurate," she says.

I take the gin from her and gulp back a shot. "He was welcome at our home any time he wanted. His dad… fuck, his dad was an asshole. He used to beat the shit out of Mads for no fucking reason. Sometimes his excuse was just that he went to my place after school or took a ride from my mom instead of walking home like he was supposed to."

"I don't think I realized any of that," she says. "I always thought his dad was just in jail—or that's how the articles last year made it sound."

"Mom tried to get Mads out, but his dad had so many people in the city that covered for him that it was almost impossible. Finally, when Mads turned sixteen, he just stopped going back. I don't think his dad really noticed, and then the bastard was arrested for multiple rapes soon after so it didn't really matter."

I pause to run my hand through my hair, barely noticing that we've passed the knife between us twice in this time. "It fucking hurt seeing my best friend abused like that," I admit.

"Why?" she asks.

"Because watching something like that—happening to someone you love, especially—it just makes you feel so goddamn helpless, doesn't it? All I wanted was to get him out, but I didn't know how to help him or if I even could. I remember begging my mom for him to move in with us when we were in middle school, and I didn't understand what the fuck she meant when she said she couldn't make it official. I tried getting his mind off of it with music, video games… It was one of the reasons we started the band. Music was something that felt like a way out—for both of us. It became a crazy dream that he was hanging onto even more than me. I don't think I ever even considered another career choice once he saved up and bought that fucking bass. If I could make him happy, I'd be happy."

There's a pit in my stomach that I haven't felt in years as I recall each time Mads came to school—or didn't—with a bloody lip, cigarette burn, or worse.

"I feel like I sound like such an asshole talking about this," I admit, a nervous huff leaving me.

"Why?"

"Because it didn't happen to me," I answer, my voice suddenly tense. "I wasn't the one getting beat up at home or called trash at school. I wasn't the one who started wearing a mask when people worked out who his dad was. I had the perfect fucking parents. Great family. We weren't rich or anything, but we made it work. Our parents always made sure we didn't want for anything. They would put together enough money for my piano lessons and Koen's baseball gear. Kamden wasn't really into much. He had debate team on the weekends just to get out of the house, I think."

"What about Andi?"

I run my hand through my hair and take another stab between her fingers. The mention of my sister empties the rest of my body, leaving a void that nausea quickly fills.

I drink another gulp of gin and take the knife from her.

"Andi was running from her own shit and trying to take care of all of us in the same breath. Her mom was as bad as Mads's dad… Sometimes I think watching Andi shield us, pretending like she wasn't hurting… it made me want to do the same for Mads. I didn't want him feeling like he was alone or didn't have a place to go. He had a family that loved him, even if we weren't blood."

Another heavy sigh leaves me as I stare at the space between my fingers where the sharp blade is. "I think you owe me a couple of questions," I say, changing the subject.

"I don't know. I think I like you in this whole sad boy state you're in right now," she replies. "It's kind of hot."

I feel my lips drag upward as if I can't stop my smile. Even so, when I look at her, I wonder what the hell she's hiding.

"I'm not the one avoiding talking about her dead parents," I say, and a familiar glare lifts in her eyes.

"I should stab you for that."

I extend the handle of the blade to her. "Do it."

She eyes me and takes it from my hand. The wood is starting to wear from our game, and I'm kind of surprised neither of us has hurt the other yet.

"Ask me, then," she says, avoiding my eyes once more.

"How did your brother die?" I ask.

"Next question," she says.

"That's not how this works," I argue.

The blade comes down against my skin, and her gaze meets mine as a drop of blood trickles down onto the table. She doesn't move. Doesn't flinch. I'm not even sure she knows she just cut me.

"That's exactly how this is going to work," she affirms. "Next question."

I don't dare push the subject, not with her tone. Not with the glisten suddenly in her eyes or the cut that I refuse to react about.

She releases a steady breath and looks at my hand again, resuming her motions, and I realize the cut was on purpose—a warning not to push anything about her brother.

"Do you miss them?" I choose to ask instead.

Wren pauses with the blade between my ring and pinky fingers. "I used to," she says softly. "But over the years, the memory of them has sort of become a dream. Occasionally I'll see something that reminds me of them and I'll miss them for a little while. However, most days, I forget they ever existed. It's like I've become numb to even the idea of family. At some point, I started wondering if the childhood I remember actually happened or if it's something my mind cooked up to make me forget something worse. Like am I really this person? Or did one of my suicide attempts actually succeed, and this is all part of my consciousness drifting through space to protect me from the fact that I'm already dead?"

Somehow, the admission doesn't surprise me.

It's the most real thing she's ever admitted to me, maybe

the most real thing *anyone* has ever admitted to me—apart from Mads and Bonnie.

I know she didn't say it for sympathy.

I know she didn't say it for attention.

I've been in the trenches of those thoughts with Mads—when he thought the ghosts of his dad's actions would never allow him to live a normal life, and he swore the only escape was leaving this world. I know Andi went through something similar, though I wasn't the one who talked her down. She began going to therapy soon after. And with Bonnie... She nearly drank herself to death before making the decision to go sober.

Wren's jaw tenses as she continues staring at the table, and it's a few seconds before I find any words to say.

"Why do you think it was a dream?" I ask.

Wren swallows. "What I remember about my family was that they were amazing," she says, her voice beginning to shake. "We were an upper middle class family in Connecticut. I was in theater and dance. My brother played lacrosse. Older sister was really popular. Class president. Our younger sister played softball—"

"Did you have nicknames for each other?" I ask, desperately hoping it prompts a happy memory.

Her eyes narrow. "What?"

"Nicknames," I shrug, like I don't have an alternate agenda. "Family is how Mads and I got our nicknames in the band. Madness. Chaos."

She stares at the table for another beat. "My brother used to call me raven."

"Why?"

Wren almost smiles, and goddammit, the sight of it makes my stomach flutter.

"Ah... it started out because I used to collect sticks and feathers as a little girl," she says, and I chuckle. "As we grew up, it became more about my being different and the odd-one-out when it came to friend groups. He actually had a list going of all the things I had in common with them."

"That's cute," I say.

A heavy sigh leaves her then, the happy moment fading as a glisten clouds her eyes. "Looking back on it, everything about my childhood just seemed so ordinary." She twists the knife into the wood by my pinky. "Maybe I think it was a dream because of how abruptly it all ended," she admits.

"What happened?" I ask.

Wren clears her throat and sits up on her knees, then drinks from the nearly empty gin bottle. "Tell me something happy instead," she says as she gives me back the blade and flattens her hand on the table. "Tell me what makes you happy," she goes on.

I take a small sip of gin this time as the drink is beginning to catch up with me.

My face is already numb.

I run my hand through my hair and scratch my neck. *Things that make me happy…*

"Hearing fans sing lyrics back to us," I answer. "Just performing in general."

"Performing is your happy place?"

"Performing is where I belong," I say. "It's the only place I feel… weightless. I don't have to think about it anymore. I just get up there and *do*. I know most people wouldn't say it's their job that makes them happy, but fuck. I love my goddamn job. I wouldn't be who I am without it."

"What about things other than your job? What are the little things that make you happy?"

"I don't know that I follow," I say.

"I mean… something that makes me happy is waking up with Anita in the bed at my feet," she admits. "And flying."

"Flying?" I repeat.

"I went skydiving once, and it… god, it was amazing," she says with a sigh. "The weightlessness and freedom is something I've never been able to find again. I've always wondered if flying a plane might feel similar."

"I didn't know anything made you happy," I say, and she purses her lips at me.

"I'm still holding the knife," she warns.

I snicker and take another shot. "Rain, then, if we're talking about the little shit. Fresh, cold sheets after a hot shower. Dying leaves. Laughing with my friends. Hugging my mom—"

"Aw," she taunts me with a pout.

"And right now," I say. "Here. Sitting on the floor with you."

Her hair falls slightly over her face as she looks at me. "Gross," she says, though I can hear her amusement. "You shouldn't say that."

"What's so wrong with saying that?" I ask, leaning forward.

"Because you shouldn't enjoy this. You should be hating me for dragging you here," she answers.

"Tell me why," I practically beg.

Her gaze shifts to my lips, her own parting the smallest fraction. "Why don't I just kiss you instead?"

I smile against her mouth. "Is this your way of distracting me?"

"I think it's working."

An exhale leaves me when our lips meet. Maybe because I'm pretty fucking drunk, and she's not exactly sober. Maybe because I can't stop myself from giving in to her, especially when I hear her soft groan.

Chills ripple over my skin like warm water pouring over my body.

I don't even know if I can get it up right now, but I can sure as fuck make sure she's taken care of.

However, the moment I press my palm against her throat, a searing pain stabs through my opposite hand. I rip away from her lips at the abrupt agony, the pain suddenly shooting from my pinky up my arm.

Mother fu—

She stabbed me.

"Oh my god—*Reed!*"

She fucking stabbed me.

"Oh *fucking hell!*"

"Reed—oh my—oh my god, *I'm so sorry!*"

I can't stop staring at my hand, the small blade pierced through the top by my pinky finger. It really isn't bad, but fuck, I'm bleeding. Wren grabs the pocket knife and throws it onto the couch, her panicked words an echo in my ears as she tries to think of what to do. I clutch my hand to my chest and fall sideways on the rug.

I can't stop laughing.

My finger is throbbing. I'm bleeding all over her rug.

And I can't stop fucking laughing.

"Reed! Why are you laughing? I just stabbed you! This is serious," she says, even though I can hear her own amusement.

"You *bitch*—I can't believe you stabbed me," I say through the laughter. "I was confessing myself to you."

"Well maybe you'll think about that next time you say you like me," she says.

I sit back up and shake my head, still laughing to stop from crying. "That's not stopping me."

The words have no sooner left me before I'm kissing her again. I don't care that I'm smearing my blood on her face when I grab her, and by the way she's touching me, I'm not sure she cares either.

Fuck, I could make out like this for hours.

The pain of my hand slowly wanes the longer her lips are on mine. She's scratching my scalp and straddling my lap, and

I lose track of time around us. She feels fucking perfect on top of me, her wide hips in my hands, tits brushing against my chest. I don't know at what point I take my hand from her neck and slide it down her front, pausing only to cup her breasts and tug at her hardened nipples. And when I reach between her thighs, I feel her smile against my lips.

She pushes my hand away and places it back on her bare tit instead. "I don't do drunk sex when I can't feel my body," she says. "And I can't feel a thing right now."

I chuckle against her lips, honestly not complaining a bit. "Yeah? What about…" I move my fingers on her ribs, and she jerks violently at the soft tickle.

"Reed!"

A howl of laughter leaves her as I go all in and tickle her to the ground with my good hand. She bats me away and squirms against the play, my name leaving her lips in shrieks of fitful giggles. It's another minute before I let up, and it's only because the look on her face is so fucking mesmerizing that my mind goes blank.

And when she's lying beneath me trying to catch her breath, she manages to say, "Rule one," through her smile.

I snicker and kiss her nose, though I think my lips land sloppily on her eye, making her laugh more. She pushes on my chest to shove me away, and I grin.

"You know we still have pizza. In case you want to sober up," I tell her.

Her eyes widen. "Oh my god—*pizza*." She groans and pushes me off of her. "Honestly that sounds better than an orgasm right now," she says as she sits up.

She opens the box of pizza and grabs a piece as if she's starving, and it's all I can do to sit back and watch her devour the food in her tipsy state.

"I think this is the best food I've ever eaten," she says. "Am I going to have to feed it to you?"

I chuckle and lean up to take a piece. "I have two hands."

"You do, but I figured you would act broken," she taunts.

I smirk at her. "I'm still waiting on you to fix me."

She takes another piece of pizza out and slumps against the front of the couch. "I'm too tipsy to bandage you right now. You'll just have to bleed out."

"What a way to die," I say. "Stabbed by Cruella on Halloween. Left to bleed out on the living room floor while she ate pizza beside me."

Wren nudges me, but doesn't reply, and I sit up to grab my phone from the table.

A few messages from both Mads and Zeb are waiting, along with an email about the New Year's Eve gig from the composer we've been working with—sound files attached.

"Oh shit," I mutter. "Hey, you want to hear something?" I ask her eagerly.

"What is it?"

"So, we hired an orchestra for the New Year's Eve show, and Mads and Zeb have been working with the composer to build on our music instead of it just being a replica of the album. Zeb sent over some of the recorded files."

Her brows lift. "I can hear it?"

"If you want to," I tell her.

"Want to?" She scoffs. "You're asking if I want to hear metal music being played on violins and piano and bass and… It's like asking me if I want to breathe."

I squint at her. "Why?"

"Do you remember how music made you feel when you were younger? When you put on your headphones and stared out of the window thinking no one else understood what you were going through, yet somehow the music did?"

"I still feel like that, but yeah."

"Everyone else around me was listening to whatever was popular, and I was listening to horror orchestra music."

"No shit," I chuckle. "Horror orchestra?"

"I wanted to play violin so fucking badly. But the girl that lived next door played, and I hated her. I always knew she would have said I was copying her if I told my parents I wanted to play, so I never did."

"That's a shitty reason not to play," I say.

"That's teenage girls," she says with a shrug. She looks down at my phone and jerks her chin toward it. "Will you play it for me?"

And for the next few hours, we listen to every section of every song that's been recorded so far.

Wren sinks her head onto my shoulder, listening to the music and to me as I hum along to it and softly sing a few lines here and there, and throughout the session, she hardly speaks. The pain in my finger fades as her breaths even and she seems to surrender.

I can't remember the last time I sat up with someone who wasn't the band or already family.

And I think the very last person I ever expected to feel this with is her.

I'm so fucked.

I hear Wren sniff, and as I look down, I realize she's crying.

I don't bring it up. I don't know what she's thinking or why it's brought out this emotion. So, I hold her a little closer and kiss her forehead, only shifting slightly when she turns to hug against me fully—her ear on my chest, my arms around her back and sitting on her hip.

"Did you ever think your music would be the music someone turned to when they felt they couldn't turn to anything else?" she asks softly. "That it might be what saves someone from thinking life isn't worth the pain?"

The question hits me straight in my gut.

I haven't.

It's what we've always wanted to do, even if we thought

we might not ever get there. We've always made music for us, hoping someone might connect with it and love it as much as we do, but I don't think I've ever thought that it might impact someone the way some of the bands we listened to growing up ever did.

"I don't think I've ever thought about it like that," I manage. "Not because I don't think we make music that could, but because that would be a silent dream come true."

"Maybe you should," she says.

"Why?"

Wren shifts and sits her chin on my chest, glassy gaze staring up at me. "Because I think it would have helped me feel like I wasn't alone."

Let me help you.

Tell me what you're running from.

I swipe away the tear that's spilling down her cheek and mingling with the bloody hand print I left behind earlier. "You're not alone," I tell her. "You never have to be again."

Her teeth set, and she picks her chin up to look down again, this time taking my injured hand in hers.

"I think you need a stitch," she manages.

I feel as if I'm about to ignite.

Every muscle in my body seems to be on edge. There's an emotion pressing behind my eyes and writhing in my stomach, fluttering around my heart, and I don't know what it is. I have this sudden urge to tell her I'll run away with her if that's what she needs to do. I'll hide her, change her name, cut her hair, fake her death. Whatever she needs, I'll take care of it.

Let me take this pain away from you.

Let me show you that I mean it.

You're not alone.

The words scream at me as I watch her clean my wound and place the butterfly sutures on the cut. And when she's done, she kisses my finger, then leans her elbow on the table and sinks her head sideways onto her palm, staring at me with a quiet sigh. Her eyes are tired, and yet she's still awake, still entertaining me.

I open my mouth to speak, but suddenly her eyes widen, and she sits up, staring out of the glass walls.

"Oh my god," she exclaims. "Is that… is that the sun?"

Holy shit.

She's right.

"Damn. No wonder I feel fucking tired," I say as I sit up with her.

"Wait—" She throws her hand against my chest, eyes widened with panic. "What day is it?"

"Ah… that would be November first. Why?"

Her entire face pales when she meets my gaze. "Oh my god."

"What?" I ask.

"I have a meeting with Amber Weisen this morning."

She jumps to her feet, suddenly distraught. "Oh my god—I have to shower. Find something to wear. I have *blood on me*—"

I almost chuckle at her. "Sounds like my cue to leave," I say as I get up.

Everything is starting to hurt.

"Oh shit—Reed—I—"

But I grab her face with both hands, pull her into me, and kiss her hard. Kissing her in the hopes that she feels all the emotions I'm swimming with right now. Every drop of blood and tears and fear we shared. And when we part, our foreheads rest against one another for a beat.

I don't want to let her go, and my insides twist when she doesn't push me away.

"When do I see you again?" I ask against her lips.

Her mouth opens and closes against mine. "The premiere," she answers. "Next week." Her lashes sweep up with the words, framing her sleepy doe eyes.

Shit.

I need to get out of here.

I need back on my fucking tour bus. The safety of my lone-liness. Anything except this.

Anything except falling for the one fucking person I'm not supposed to be.

"I'll text you later," I say.

"Mm. I might not answer," she says, pushing me away. "Busy day."

"Yeah you will," I say, and she actually fucking smiles at me.

She fucking smiles at me.

"Bye, poser."

THE MORNING OF THE PREMIERE, I can't stop pacing.

I don't like that I've already texted Reed this morning at three a.m. hoping he was in LA already. I hate that I know he's going to be fucking exhausted, and yet he's coming anyway.

Most of all, I hate that I'm going to be a fucking mess in front of him.

I can't turn off my brain.

I tried meditation. I tried music. I tried a vibrator. I tried a comfort show. I even went on a fucking run with Anita this morning. My thoughts are on a hamster wheel spinning, spinning, spinning, and I don't know how to get off.

Four soft taps sound on the other side of the door. Anita barks, even if her tail is wagging, and I force my legs to move toward it.

Reed is glaring at me when I open my door.

"Tell your fucking stalkers to get off my ass," he says before pushing past me.

My heart drops. I gawk after him, barely able to comprehend what he just said.

"What?" I finally ask.

Reed runs two hands through his hair and sits his bag on the counter. I don't ask what's inside it. I don't have the capacity to be curious.

"What are you talking about?" I ask again.

"A white SUV followed me from the airport to my hotel, waited outside, then followed my ride here. James isn't with me this weekend, so I was pretty fucking freaked about it." Reed grabs his phone and holds it up, showing off the missed calls he's gotten from a number I know.

A number that makes me want to vomit.

"Do you recognize this number?" he asks.

"I…"

I don't have the mind for this right now.

"You do, don't you?" Reed shifts on his feet, tongue swiping over his lips in an annoyed way. "Wren, who are they?"

This cannot be fucking happening.

Damien is calling him now?!

"Who are they?" he repeats, coming closer.

"No one. They're no one," I eventually say. "Just leave it."

"They've been on my ass the entire time we've been dating—"

"We're not dating," I assert.

"—whatever the fuck you want to call this then," he snaps. "Who are they?"

"They're friends of my brother's," I admit fast.

"What the fuck does that have to do with you? I thought you said your brother was dead," he argues.

"He is," I answer.

"Then… what? Did they have to do with him dying? *Who are they?*"

"I'm not doing this right now," I say, glaring at him. "We're not doing this today. I told you—*multiple times*—the less you fucking know, the better."

"Wren—"

"No, Reed." I snatch out of his grasp when he reaches me, my heart pounding in my ears. "No, I told you. We're not fucking doing this today. I'll take care of them following you. Just… god, can't you leave it?"

"When talk of them makes you this scared? No. It's kind of hard to drop it."

"God, why are you so invested in this? Why does this bother you?"

"Because you're my friend, and I fucking care about you," he says. "Every time you look over your shoulder, you look like you've seen a ghost. You tense every time your phone vibrates. You're constantly scoping out cars and crowds as if you expect someone to jump out and drag you away. *Who are they?!*"

"I can't tell you," I almost plead.

"Why?"

"Reed, please."

"Why can't you fucking tell me?!"

"Because if I tell you, they'll do more than just stalk you," I break down, meeting his bewildered eyes. "They'll take you, and I don't know what they'll do to keep you quiet."

My jaw is shaking.

"So, no, Reed. I'm not telling you who they are or why they're following me. I'm just… I can't. And I need you to respect that. *Please.*"

I'm on the verge of tears.

Please understand.

I can't watch them hurt you.

I avoid his gaze and run my hands over my face, ready to collapse on the floor at any moment. I expect Reed to tell me we're done, that he can't do this anymore.

And I would let him walk out of that door.

Because he doesn't deserve to be treated like this.

I flinch at his unexpected touch, trembling when I feel his even breathing. Reed pulls me into him, ignoring my fight, and he wraps his arms so tightly around me that the pressure seems to squeeze tears from my eyes.

This is nice.

Okay. This… *Why is this helping?*

He runs his hand against my face when we part, and I hate the pathetic way he's looking at me.

"Don't look at me like you feel sorry for me," I say, barely audible. "I don't want pity. I just want you to understand that I can't tell you. It's for your own good."

Reed swallows. "Don't worry about my safety," he says. "You can tell me." His eyes close as he presses his forehead against mine. "Every time you get scared talking about them, all I want to do is take you away from this place. I want to know what we would be up against if I did that."

I meet his eyes. "Someone who thinks he's God," I manage.

Reed scoffs. "He'll have met his match then."

"This isn't a joke," I say. "This isn't Andi's ex-boyfriend."

"I don't care who he is," he replies.

I press on his chest, wishing to hell that I could tell him why. "I need to go to the bathroom," I say, stepping out of his grasp. "I need… what did you bring?"

His jaw feathers, and I know he isn't happy about me changing the subject.

Anxiety presses against my throat as I grip my phone in my hand.

"It's nothing," he says, sighing. "I'll… Just do what you think you need to do."

Because he knows I'm lying, and it stings me to the point that I want to cry.

I don't want you to get hurt.

"Reed…"

"I need a minute, too," he admits as he sinks down to pet Anita. "We're fine. Just go."

Nausea rifles through my bones. I rush into the bathroom and slam the door behind me, tears overflowing onto my cheeks. And when I take my phone out, my thumbs bruise against the screen.

> Stop fucking following him.
>
> Leave him alone.

Damien replies as if he had his phone open and waiting.

UNKNOWN

But he's so cute.

> Fuck off. The charade is nearly done with.
> Leave him alone.

If you're done with him, what do you care if
we follow?

> Because he doesn't know anything.

What's there to know?

I want to scream.

> I told you to leave him alone. Fucking do it or
> else.

I'm starting to think you care for him.

> I don't.

Good. Because you know what happens
when people get too close.

Tears prick my eyes.

I fucking hate this.

              I want out.

Not a chance. You belong to me, Kelly.

Remember that next time you try to threaten
me, too.

          I don't belong to anyone.

The moment you bargained for your brother,
you became mine.

      As far as I'm concerned, that bargain was
      broken when your goon carved him up.

Would you like to discuss this in person?

Knocks echo from the front door.

My heart drops. Blood evacuates my face and pools in my feet, making my legs too heavy to move.

Fuck.

Fucking *fuck*.

I lunge for the doorknob, throw the door open, and run back into the kitchen where Reed is standing stiff by the end of the kitchen island. He has a knife in one hand, his phone in the other, and I see James's number pulled up on the screen like he's ready to dial it.

"Wren…"

Three more knocks.

I grab Reed's arm as he starts for the door, shaking my head in his face.

"No," I mouth.

But Reed kisses me hard. Hard enough that my mind blanks for a split-second, and when he pulls away, I can't look away from his dark eyes.

"I'm not fucking losing you to this," he whispers.

I don't know what he means, and I don't have time to argue. His hand is on the knob. He's twisting. Fear threads through my bones. I clench his arm and press myself in front of him as he fists the hem at the back of my shirt as if he's ready to snatch me backward into the apartment if need be.

Black and gold balloons fill the space in front of us.

"Hello!"

"Larry," I breathe, the relief apparent in my voice.

Larry stands on the other side, a vase of roses in his hands, along with a paper bag and a balloon that reads 'bad bitch.' It's all so big that I can't see his face.

Reed's chest collapses. I take the knife from his hand and toss it onto the counter just as he turns into me and sinks his arm around my waist, his hand behind my head, and he kisses my forehead before holding me once again.

I won't lie.

I'm holding onto him to keep from shaking.

"Well… this is cozy," Larry says, looking between us.

Reed huffs, his breath skimming my hair, then opens the door wider. He doesn't release me as Larry strides inside, and instead tilts my chin up with his knuckle.

The look in his eyes is so different from what it was just moments earlier. It's soft and concerned, no inkling of rage present—as if for a brief moment, he had genuinely feared what might be on the other side of the door.

I'm paralyzed.

Unable to look away from him.

Unable to stop the warmth from spreading through my chest when his hand cups my neck.

"I didn't realize you'd had a sleepover," Larry says.

I blink and drag my gaze from Reed's. "We didn't," I reply.

"I'm just here for breakfast," Reed says, finally peering over to Larry.

"Well, I will leave you two to that," Larry says as he sits the roses on the counter. "I just wanted to come over and bring this, make sure you were okay, see if you needed anything. I'll be back this afternoon for hair and makeup."

A cold sweat breaks on my neck.

"What time is hair and makeup?" Reed asks as he sits on a barstool.

"Noon," Larry answers.

"I'll make sure to be out of here by then," Reed replies.

Larry looks at me again. "Do you need me to bring anything with me when I come back? Or take Anita with me now?"

"No," I manage, sinking my head into my hand. "No, I'm okay. If I think of anything, I'll let you know."

Larry smiles between Reed and me. "Okay. I'll let you get back to breakfast, then," he says with a wink.

"See you, Larry," Reed says.

"Yeah, bye," is all I can manage when I see him heading toward the door.

And when it clicks behind him, I press my hands into the kitchen island and exhale heavily.

I have less than six hours until hair and makeup.

I don't know why that seems so long and yet somehow so short. Anxiety creeps into my chest and tenses my shoulders at the thought.

I wish I could turn my brain off.

Reed is staring at me from the barstool he's sitting on. His tongue darts out over his lips as he peers me over, then nods his head in my direction and says, "Come here."

My feet move, and before I can refute him, I'm standing at his chest. Reed slides his hand through my hair before resting his palm against my neck, his other taking a rest at the small of my back.

I'm not used to how vulnerable he makes me feel. It's almost like he can see through me—like he's seen me all along and not gone running to the hills in fear of all my sharp edges and rough sides.

"I'm sorry I added to your stress this morning," he says softly. "I don't know why I pushed. I just wish you would trust me."

"It isn't about trust, Reed. It's about… Fuck, I should never have gotten you into this—"

"I'm glad you got me into this," he says, and I stare at him. "Why?"

"Because it meant I got to know you," he replies.

It's so cheesy that I feel my face curl up in disgust, and Reed huffs an amused breath.

"Right. Compliments," he says defeatedly.

"It's just so weird when you say things like that," I say, halfway joking.

Another quiet laugh sounds from him. He moves my hair back, his throat bobbing as his gaze wanders over me.

"I'm going to take care of all this racing bullshit going through your head right now," he says. "If you'll let me."

It sounds amazing, though I'm not sure he can actually do it.

"Good luck with that," I mutter.

The corner of his lips flinch upward as he leans in. "I don't need it."

I try to shut my mind off when he kisses me. I try to block out the vision of the texts, the sound of Reed and I arguing with each other. The possibilities of the premiere that night.

The thoughts are so consuming that I barely notice Reed leading me into the bedroom and peeling my robe away. I barely register his hand between my thighs or the moment when my back meets the unkempt bed.

Focus on him.

He feels good.

He'll take care of this.

Wait, his hand—

"How is your hand?" I ask as his mouth captures my nipple.

"Well enough that you don't need to think about it," he says as he hovers over me.

"I still can't believe I stabbed you," I say, my nerves unable to let me shut off. "I can't believe I—*fuck*—"

Reed slams inside me—so forceful that my words turn into a gasp, and I cry out as I arch toward the ceiling.

Even still, I can't keep my mind from racing.

I wasn't even aware he'd taken his own clothes off.

Everything around me is crumbling, and instead of keeping it inside as I usually do, it's seeping out of me like a broken tap that I don't know how to fix.

"Is Mads mad? God, I bet he was pissed about your hand. He's never going to let me live it down—"

"Are we really talking about my best friend right now?" Reed asks.

"I just meant with the tour wrapping up, and—"

Reed groans, his forehead slumping onto my chest. "Mother fuck," I hear him mumble. He pulls out of me and slaps my ass, and I immediately tense.

He's digging in his bag by the door already.

I sit up, hands bracing on the mattress as embarrassment swims through me.

He's frustrated because of me.

Because I can't keep my mouth shut and let him handle my anxiety with a release that will numb me the rest of the night.

Because I'm rambling.

Because I've lost my fucking cool.

Reed turns around, and I feel myself shrink back slightly at the sight of the black tie, headphones, and blindfold in his hands. He stands at the edge of the bed and wraps the tie around his wrists, using his teeth to help tie off two loops. He does it so swiftly and with such ease that I can only gawk at him. Dominance rests within his strong shoulders, and I shift as he kneels onto the end of the bed.

"I thought you might need a little extra help this morning, so I packed reinforcements," he says. "Lay diagonal for me."

"What are you—"

"Just fucking do it, bird," he says exhaustedly.

I swallow, yet obey without question.

He straddles over me, his now semi-erect cock coming to a rest on my stomach. Lifting my arms over my head, he slips the silky tie around my wrists and secures the fabric with a knot to the bedpost. There's a twinge in his jaw that makes me squirm, and I can't help it when I blurt out, "I'm sorry."

"For what?" he asks without moving his gaze.

"For not being able to turn off my brain," I say. "Are you mad at me?"

A quiet chuckle sounds from him, and he smiles as he grabs the blindfold. "No," he says, though I don't entirely believe him, and it causes a new anxiety to writhe behind my eyes.

Fuck, I don't like this.

How has he gotten this far?

How has he broken me down to the person I am behind closed doors?

"Lift up your head," he says softly.

I do, and he places the blindfold around me. Just when I think he's going to pull it down over my eyes, he pauses.

"Hey—" he says, bringing his knuckle beneath my chin to tip my head back. "No more apologizing. I'm not mad at you," he repeats.

"You can be," I say. "You *should* be."

He chuckles again and bends closer. "Frustrated, yes. It's my job to fuck the thoughts out of your head," he says, his lips brushing against mine. "If I can't do that, then what are we even doing here?"

I can't look away from his gaze. "What are the earphones for?" I choose to ask.

"I told you, I packed reinforcements," he says. His lips land on my cheek, my jaw, the soft space beneath my jaw, and his kisses prompt me to close my eyes.

"Reed…"

"Shh…" he whispers before catching my earlobe between his teeth. "Here's what's going to happen right now… I mean to pull your soul from your body and make it jealously watch from above as I touch you. *Tease* you. As I wring out every anxious thought and fear that's ever possessed you. And when we hit the red carpet this afternoon, the only thoughts in your head will be of *me*," he swears. "My lips. My touch. My hands. My tongue. My dick."

He drags his nose down my bare chest as he speaks. My eyes close at the motion. His lips press to my stomach, and, a fraction at a time, he kisses all the way back up to my face, taking extra time to suck each of my nipples.

Our eyes lock, and I don't understand the sensation in the pit of my stomach. The ache and warmth and chills… Something about his eyes in this moment has me wanting to thread my hands through his hair and kiss him until I can't feel my face.

My mind is somehow blank to everything except him.

"How are you doing this?" I manage.

The right corner of his lip quirks crookedly. "Superpowers," he says before his mouth encloses upon mine.

Every inch of me ignites with the deliberate way his tongue slides against mine. Goosebumps trickle down my arms from my shoulders, the hair on the back of my neck standing. I wish I could touch his face, his body, his hard dick grazing against my abdomen.

Sucking on my tongue, he eventually pulls back, and I find

my chest lifting off the bed as if to chase him down and kiss him again.

The small movement prompts the corner of his lips to flicker upward as he places the headphones over my ears, and the very last thing I see before he tugs the blindfold down is his dilated blue eyes.

And in my ears?

It's the orchestra music of their songs.

It's loud and thrilling and entirely overwhelming and *everything*. Every part of my senses seem to heighten behind that mask, my mind succumbing to the weight of his mouth, his hands.

And as he begins softly kissing down my front, I think a tear slips from my closed eyes.

Damn him.

The music steadily drowns the voices in my head. I don't know what he's done to the tracks, but they seem to move between the headset from ear-to-ear. The notes scratch my brain like nothing else ever has, completely calming my nervous system.

He's at my navel, his tongue sliding along my soft belly and sucking the sensitive, neglected areas into his mouth like he means to leave a trail of hickeys from my stomach to my pussy. He scratches my side with his short nails, prompting a moan to leave me. My back arches at the sensation, the way the scrapes are both pain and pleasure.

I can't even complain about how slow he's moving.

He picks one of my legs up and lays it across his shoulder, and when I start to move my other, he slaps my ass like he's telling me off for moving.

I feel his finger moving across my stomach.

'STAY,' he writes on my skin.

Another song comes on, and I inhale deeply in an attempt to

see if it will help ease the tension in my muscles. He kisses the inside of my thighs and rubs my leg, going down, down, down the limb and massaging my thigh and calf the whole way. Reaching my feet, he attends to one with his thumbs pressing into the middle before licking up the center. I jerk at the tickle, but he holds me steady enough that I realize he's smiling against my arch.

Ass.

He repeats the exact motions on my other leg, yet in reverse. And when he's back between my thighs, the bed shifts. He lays sideways across the end and throws my right thigh over his side, my left between his head and his arm in a way that makes me wonder if he's using my leg as a pillow.

As if he's getting comfortable for a long session.

His broad hand splays on my abdomen as the other deliberately strokes my cunt, fingers splitting on either side of my clit in a teasing way that makes me swallow. He dips one digit into my pussy, and I groan at the wetness he then drags over that bundle of nerves, at the feel of his steady breath on my labia. Spit lands on my clit, and somehow, I sink further into the bed.

I wish I could see him. Even so, in the same thought, I'm glad I can't. Every touch and motion is a surprise that has me weak.

I normally hate surprises, but I think I'm too drunk on this to care.

Each song pulls me in further. He flicks his tongue on my clit as one finger finds my entrance again, and the moment he begins tasting me, I know I'm going to lose whatever is left of my mind.

Goddamn Reed fucking Matthews.

He's eating and licking and sucking on me so slowly that I nearly every stroke has my breaths getting heavier. Shit, he feels so damn good. I squirm slightly, moving my hips toward him as a silent plea for more.

Reed grins against my pussy and clenches the back of my thigh.

Worry of whatever might happen tonight evacuates my mind as my arms strain over my head.

"Right there," I say, though I hardly hear my own voice. *"Reed."*

My orgasm is already rising.

Yet, the way he's taking his time tells even though I'm about to come, he's nowhere near being done with me.

The thought makes me whimper.

He crooks two fingers inside me, brushing my spot each time they move. Sucking my clit. Dragging his tongue over me. I rock and groan and try to breathe through the pleasure. Each time I think I'm about to topple over, he slows. Switches the motions of his tongue. Releases the pressure on my spot.

"Reed, please," I beg.

Every muscle in my body ignites and strains. I try to shift beneath him, to move my legs up, but he keeps my left under his head. My toes are pointed. I'm trembling as he edges me.

Again. Again. *Again.*

I'm *crying.*

"Reed, please," I repeat, my voice muffled. "I can't —Please—"

The words have hardly left my lips when he adds a third finger. The jolt and slap of his palm against my clit makes me squeal. He leaves them inside as he nips and sucks on my clit again, and this time, he doesn't stop.

I come. *Hard.*

My legs jerk and writhe against his grip. I'm squirming in his grasp, desperate to wiggle away from from the overwhelming sensation of his touch.

Because he doesn't stop.

I'm still coming when he moves his fingers in and out of my pussy, palm slapping over and over against my clit. My back arches off the bed, arms a weak mess above my head. My fingers are tingling, yet with the way he's finger fucking me right now, I barely notice I even have arms.

I scream his name and pull against the bindings. I can hardly breathe. He's moving up my stomach and kissing me as I come again. And when he begins sucking on my nipples, not letting up his motions, I succumb to another.

Every part of my body is numb. My mind is blank.

There's only one word that infiltrates the totally dark space behind my eyes.

Reed.

I'm coming down from my fifth orgasm when he shifts atop me and his lips crash into mine. I taste my release on his tongue. He slams inside me, and I fucking wish I could wrap my arms around his neck, feel his soft hair between my fingers.

Reed is always everything, though somehow, in this moment, he's more.

And the way he's fucking me?

I think I've died.

His lips are all over, hands touching and caressing my body like he's making sure no space is neglected. And when he settles his hips against mine, slowing and deepening his strokes, his tongue licks away the drying tears on my cheeks.

I feel him in my throat. I'm so full. Spent. Weak.

"Reed, please," I whisper, but he swallows my words with his mouth on mine.

I don't even know what I'm begging him for. I'm shaking and numb as another orgasm somehow looms. I've lost count of how many times he's made me come now. Hit after hit of dopamine clouds my mind, my perception of time and space. I don't know how I'm going to come again, but I know I am.

"Reed," I cry out.

He pulls out of me slightly and shifts forward, and suddenly the air evacuates my lungs.

Oh. My. *God.*

Shit, this position. Tears stream down my cheeks from the incredible pleasure. Everything lines up perfectly. I tug and strain against the bindings on my wrists, my orgasm rising to the point that even his name blanks in my mind.

And I think I black out as a wave of pleasure practically envelopes my entire being.

Cool sweat and tingles brush over my skin when I eventually open my eyes. He's resting his forehead against mine, his body lying flush atop me as if he can't find the strength to move. I can feel his heartbeat, and the steadying thumps relax me into the mattress.

I definitely blacked out.

I don't remember coming. I don't remember him releasing inside me, but I can feel it.

Reed kisses my nose, each tear-stained cheek, and finally my neck before shifting to pull out of me. Fuck, the pit he's left behind. I'm empty in his absence, my pussy numb, legs made of jelly.

The vibration of the bathroom fan going seems to swallow my hearing when he slides one of the earphones up to my temple.

"Well done, little bird," he says in a vibrating rasp against my ear.

DO NOT

CHAPTER THIRTY-ONE

WREN

I CAVE, swallowing hard with the anticipation of which restraint he'll remove next. My arms break out in goosebumps. He reaches for my wrists, and with one hand, loosens the loops. My arms fall onto the pillows, a whimper leaving me that I can't control.

"I've got you," he says.

Because I can't move.

One at a time, he brings my arms from above my head and places my hands on my stomach. God, the *ache*—painful, yet somehow entirely satisfying. I squirm a little in an attempt to get comfortable as he pushes his finger beneath the blindfold's band.

I didn't realize he had turned off most of the lights in the room.

A dim amber hue illuminates his handsome face above me when I open my eyes. Shadows have settled around him, and the sight of him so dominant and yet empathetic in this moment forces a lump in my throat.

I don't know what to say as he wraps a soft hand around my cheek, lips brushing across mine.

"Sometimes it's easier to let go when you have someone

there to catch you," he says.

My bottom lip trembles, and it has nothing to do with how spent and exhausted I am right now.

"Let me take care of you this morning," he says.

"I thought that's what you just did," I manage, still drunk on pleasure.

He chuckles softly. "I mean, I don't want you looking at a clock. It's eight a.m.—"

My heart drops. "Fuck, it's already eight?!" I start to sit up, but he pushes me back down.

"Lay down or I'm tying you to the bed again," he says.

Tempting.

Another huff of amusement leaves him as he bends down and kisses my jaw. "Hair and makeup are coming at noon," he goes on. "Which means you have to start your shower routine by… ten-thirty—eleven at the latest. So, you're going to lay here, let me make your breakfast, and then as long as I have you awake and eating by… nine, that gives you time to eat leisurely and drink two cups of coffee while watching an episode of whatever comfort show you're craving this morning."

I stare at him.

Did he just count back time for me?

His hand squeezes on my hip when I don't immediately respond, and it reminds me to breathe.

"Amendment," I say.

"I thought you might have a few," he replies with a sigh.

"Only one," I say. "I want to lay on the couch while you make breakfast instead of in here."

He smiles and stands by the bed. I start to sit up, but before I can, he slides his arms beneath my knees and back, and then lifts me into his arms. I yelp and grab around his neck, tensing at his blatancy.

"Reed, you can't carry—"

"Tell me you can feel your legs, and I'll put you down," he says as we exit the bedroom.

I look at my legs and try to kick them, but the effort feels like too much.

Reed's chuckle vibrates against me. "Yeah, that's what I thought."

Anita curls up beside me on the couch when he sets me down. The same series marathon is playing on the television that was on overnight. I don't know that I would care if Christmas movies were already playing right now. Not with the state of my body or blurry mind.

I lean back against the couch cushions and feel my eyes drifting, only perking up at the smell of coffee going in the kitchen.

Shit, he doesn't know where anything is.

I start to get to my feet. "The cups are over the machine there. I can get you a pan—"

"Sit your ass down," Reed says.

Because he already has two mugs and the oat milk out from the fridge.

I shrink back into the seat as he drizzles caramel on one of the mugs, and when he has it made to his liking, he brings one of the mugs around to me.

The one he chose for me almost makes me smile.

"How did you know this was my favorite mug," I ask when he hands me the one that says 'cunt.'

"Because I know yours is still pulsing in my absence," he says, smirking when he places it in my hands.

He isn't wrong.

Anita follows him back into the kitchen as I settle into the couch. I'm trying not to watch him move around it as if he knows where everything is, but it's hard not to stare.

Reed Matthews. With his messy black shag of hair that likes to fall into his eyes, seeming to frame those blue daggers when he's serious. Reed Matthews. Tattoos covering his neck, bare chest, and arms. Covering the hands that praise parts of me that I never knew I craved touch upon.

A hopeless fucking romantic that should have told me to go fuck myself instead of kissing me that day.

"I can still feel your mind running," he says as he chops up a small onion.

"At least it's about different things than before," I say.

"Yeah? Is it about me?" He glances up, smirking.

I purse my lips. "Maybe."

Reed punches the air victoriously, and I shake my head.

The onion sizzles in the hot pan. I don't know what he's making, but it smells good at least. Another sigh has me sinking back into the couch again, this time ready to change the channel over to the music station I listen to when I need background noise.

Reed immediately starts rocking on his toes, banging his head, and humming along to the rock music. I watch him air guitar, use the wooden spatulas as his drumsticks and the counter as his set.

"Oh, hey—my sister's wedding is in a week," he says as he flips the food in the pan, still moving to the music.

"Maddox's wedding?" I ask, sipping my coffee.

"Yeah," he answers.

"That should be fun. I'll make sure to put in my calendar not to bother you as much. I know you love your family time."

"I do," he says. "I thought maybe you could come with me."

I nearly choke. "What?" I ask, looking at him over the rim of my coffee.

He meets my gaze, smiling softly. "Come with me to their wedding," he says.

"You want me to meet your family?" I ask.

He turns back to the food he's cooking, avoiding my eyes

when he speaks. "I think it'd be great PR," he says. "If we're pretending to date, wouldn't it make sense that you're at my best friend's wedding?"

Something about the way he says 'pretending' strikes a nerve somewhere deep within me. It's uncomfortable, and while I don't like the way it makes me feel, I'm also not entirely sure how to pinpoint what, exactly, is making me feel this way.

"Besides, it's in the mountains. Small town in the middle of nowhere. It would be a nice getaway from the city. When's the last time you went to a town where paparazzi wasn't on your ass?"

"Do you think that's a good idea?" I ask.

"Why wouldn't it be?"

Our gazes meet, and I wonder if the almost desperate twinge in his tone is real or if I'm still just delirious from his dick and tongue.

"Your family knows this isn't real?"

His motions slow. "Yeah," he answers. "Yeah. They know."

I don't know why his voice sounds sad.

He inhales a sharp breath and plates the omelets. "Means you get to be yourself," he says. "You don't have to mask— because fuck knows the rest of us won't be. Well, you might have to fake it a little at the wedding for photo purposes—and because some of the record label will be there."

"What do you mean I won't have to mask?" I ask.

"I mean, you won't need to worry about putting on the right face, not saying the right thing… being embarrassed, late, traveling somewhere, or even what fucking time it is. You told me once that you feel comfortable around the band."

I do.

"Just imagine the band, but…"

"More golden retrievers?" I ask.

Reed chuckles. "Yeah, something like that."

I consider it.

It *would* be good publicity.

"I'll have to check with Larry to make sure I don't have anything," I say.

"I already did," he says, sliding the plates to the bar. "I didn't want to ask you to go if you already had something planned. You just have a meeting with Amber the day after the wedding, so he said you would have to leave overnight."

"Oh."

That was considerate.

"Okay," I give in.

Reed's eyes light up for reasons I don't understand. "Yeah?"

I frown at him, taking another sip of coffee. "Why are you so excited about me meeting your family? Aren't they going to hate me?"

"I think my sister likes you already—are you hungry?"

"Your sister and I bonded over her threatening me," I say as I make my way to the bar to sit on the stool. "It was nice."

Reed squints at me. "You have a weird sense of friendship," he says.

"I hope it hasn't taken you this long to figure that out." The omelet he's made snags my attention then, and I gawk at him.

"What? Is it not okay?" he asks, voice laced with mild panic.

"Um… actually, it's… wow. How did you know what I eat for breakfast?" I ask.

He smiles slightly. "It was the ingredients in the fridge," he says. "Wasn't hard to figure out."

I feel my eyes narrow. "You've been stalking my socials," I realize.

"Definitely stalked your socials," he says, smiling wider. "I saw you posted this breakfast a couple days ago, thought maybe it was either just routine or a current fixation."

"It's been a fixation for… about six months now," I say, and he chuckles.

"Just that long?" he teases.

"Ah, yeah. Brand new," I reply. I cut into the caramelized onion, capers, and brie omelet, take a bite, and immediately groan at the taste.

"You approve?" he asks.

"I might orgasm again," I mumble. "But next time, you have to take the capers off."

"I thought you liked those."

"I like the flavor. I hate the texture," I say as I push them off to the side. "Anytime they pop in my mouth I want to gag."

"But… you like peas. And boba tea. I've seen you post it," he says.

"I don't make the rules. I just go by my body. And my body screams at the texture of capers. And water chestnuts." A disgusted chill runs over my arms at the thought of the food. "Disgusting."

Reed chuckles softly, but starts cutting his own omelet.

"Where did you learn to cook?" I ask him after a few minutes.

"Ah… my mom," he answers. "We're a big family. Sometimes she needed the help."

"The rest of your siblings didn't help with it?" I ask.

He chews a little slower than just a moment before. "My sister had her own things going on," he answers. "She took care of us as best as she could before leaving for college."

I mirror his slow motions, remembering how he'd briefly mentioned her mom the other night. "How old were you when she left?"

"I was thirteen," he answers. "Mads was living at our place at least five days out of the week by then. My brothers were just ten and eight. Mom worked two jobs for a while when Dad lost his job, before he started writing. He… He went through a bit of a rough patch when Andi left. I started cooking to help them out. And because Kamden and Koen were little shits."

I consider the solemn look on his face. "What happened when Andi left?" I ask. "You mentioned her mom the other night, but… I've only ever heard the rumors about Mads. Nothing about her."

"Ah, you wouldn't hear anything about her. We keep it pretty close," he says.

"What happened?"

Reed's gaze meets mine, and I realize perhaps the answer isn't so simple.

"The summer before Andi went to college, her mom killed herself in our dining room. In front of Andi and my parents," he says.

My stomach drops. "Oh."

Because it's all I can manage.

That's a bit he left off on Halloween.

Reed waves me off as if he doesn't expect any other comment. "Her mom was fucking crazy," he says exasperatedly. "She needed help and refused to get it. Self-medicated with anything she could get her hands on. She used to come over high on pills, steal Andi away for the weekend when Dad wasn't home. It was a fucking mess. I think it was when I turned like ten, she started coming over saying she was sober. Andi never fucking believed her, and neither did my mom." He takes a sip of coffee and pushes his plate away before turning into me.

"So, we had this basement, and Mads and I would play video games down there a lot. Koen and Kamden had like a Legos table down there or some shit. But when her mom would come over, Mom made all of us go down there. Andi would turn the music all the way the fuck up and tell Mads he was in charge of it. And then, while my parents were upstairs screaming and trying their fucking best to get Alice to leave, we would dance and jam out together. Just to drown out the noises. We used to put this wooden chair under the doorknob so no one could get down there. I think at the time, I didn't realize the severity of it."

Every word rips a hole in my heart.

"What do you mean?" I ask.

"I didn't realize when Alice took Andi with her, she was letting her boyfriends hit on her, starving her, just sitting her in the living room like she was some kind of trophy that she could show her boyfriends like, 'hey, you want to be with me because I'm a good mother.'"

"Did you ever have any interaction with her?" I ask.

"A few times. She'd call me a rat, trash, bastard child because I was the oldest of Dad's kids with my mom, and she swore Dad had started seeing her before they ended things. I think she came over once when I was… Six? Looking for Andi. All I knew was that she was there to take my big sister away, and I wanted my sister. So, I shut the door on her fingers and actually broke one of them."

"At six?!" I exclaim.

"Mom gave me extra dessert that night," he says, almost smiling. "I just wanted… I just wanted to protect Andi. I didn't care what happened to me. Seeing the people I love in pain does something to my insides. I can't get rid of the nagging guilt. Like why is it happening to them? *Why them?*" He runs his hands through his hair and pushes it back in a nervous way. "Fuck, I'm back to being an asshole again," he mutters.

For a beat, I watch him. I can see that same shame in his eyes that was there the other night when he talked about Mads. The pain and frustration that I wanted to reach out and take away from him however I could.

"You want to hear something fucked up?" I ask him.

"Yes. Will it make me feel like less of an ass?"

A short huff leaves me, and I poke at the remaining eggs. "I used to know a girl who thought she could take care of everyone around her. And everyone was extremely grateful for her, loved her—she had so many friends because she seemed to focus all of her energy on others. However, it turns out, the entire time she claimed to want to help these people, all she was looking for was praise. She took the phrase 'helping others makes me feel good' too far. She started making people dependent on her as her own form of dopamine. Just for attention, and so she could get people's sympathy."

Reed's brows raise. "That's fucked up."

I shrug. "Honestly, I feel like a lot of people do that and don't realize they're doing it."

"Isn't that like Munchausen syndrome?" he asks. "The 'making them feel dependent on you' part?"

"I don't think so? If anything, maybe similar to Munchausen by proxy," I say questionably. "But, I mean, that is more making someone sick or convincing someone they're sick. Not just what a narcissist does. Narcissists don't have to make you sick in order to control you."

"Is this speaking from experience?" he asks.

I ignore the question.

"Any decent person wants to help people when they can," I go on. "The fucked up part is when they're doing it for the wrong reasons."

"Is that why you don't trust people?" he asks.

I stare at my coffee. "Maybe," I eventually answer. "It's why I don't trust when someone claims to want to help me. Like do you actually want to help? Are you doing it just because you think it's the right thing? Or are you doing it because you think you'll get praise after and then hold me in debt to you?"

"Why do the motivations have to matter? Why can't helping people just be a good thing all around?" he asks.

"Because my misfortunes shouldn't be the source of someone's happiness. I don't want someone helping me to make themselves feel good," I answer. "In my experience, most people want something in return, even if it's just me telling them that I couldn't have done it without them."

"Harsh, bird," he teases me, and it keeps the energy light between us.

I throw a caper at him. "This is why I don't have friends—or one of a few reasons," I say. "Don't get mixed up with me, Matthews. The fire might be on, but it's fucking cold over here."

"Tell me about it," he mutters. "Need a winter coat just to stand near you. The frostbite, though…" He smiles slyly. "The frostbite is worth it."

"Worth losing a finger over?" I ask.

"So far," he answers, holding up his hand.

There's an angry red scar on the back of his hand where I stabbed him.

"I still can't believe you suggested that," I say.

"You said you were into that shit," he replies.

"I am, but I didn't know *you* were," I say.

Reed's smile widens on the right side, his shaggy hair mingling with his long lashes. The devious glint in his icy eyes makes me want to swallow, causes a lump to rise in my throat.

"Do you think my motivations are genuine?" he asks.

Anita plops her front feet into my lap, and I scratch her soft ears as Reed and I's eyes lock on one another.

"Are they?" I ask.

"Fuck no," he says, and I almost laugh. "I'm just here to get good head and slap you around a little."

"So, dopamine-based?" I tease.

"Definitely," he says. "Bonus points if I finally break you down enough for a laugh."

"Oh, we're a game now?" I ask.

"Bird, you're like the big boss at the end of the video game that's killed me…" His voice drifts as he counts on his fingers. "Five times already. At this point, I'm just looking for cheat codes."

I laugh softly, and it feels foreign in my chest. Foreign, and yet relieving. Like I've just exhaled for the first time in ages.

And the look on Reed's face makes me want to laugh again.

Anita jumps down from my lap and takes a few steps back then, barking at me when she does. I turn toward her in surprise, and then my stomach sinks as I realize I need to take her out again. My gaze moves to the clock, noting that it's nearly ten a.m.

"Shit," I mutter, sinking my head into my hand.

"What?" Reed asks.

"I need to walk Anita," I say. "I took her out at four a.m. this morning because I was panicking and trying to clear my head. *Fuck*—"

"I can walk her," Reed says as he stands. He grabs our plates and takes them to the kitchen, and all the while, it's all I can do to stare at him. "You go ahead and shower. I'll take care of her."

"You would do that?" I ask, dumbfounded.

"Well, I mean." He shrugs as he turns on the water and begins washing the plates. "I expect a blowjob after," he says, and I can tell by the look in his eyes that he's at least halfway joking.

"Can't be helping you out for free anymore," he adds, grinning.

I huff and sink back into my chair, watching him load the dishwasher before wiping his hands on a dish towel.

"Why are you being so nice to me?" I ask him.

He whistles at Anita and grabs her leash by the door. "I'm not a monster, bird," he says as he clicks it onto her collar and stands. Our eyes meet, and a pang knots my stomach.

"You needed someone to take care of you this morning," he says with a shrug. "There are a number of things I can't do, but that... that I can do."

Goddamn him.

He's at the door, and I'm on my wobbling feet and making my way across the room as quickly as I can manage. Anita wags her tail and tugs him back, prompting him to turn just in time for me to grab him by his shirt and pull him down to my lips.

I can't count the number of times we've kissed before, but this one... This is a kiss that will stain my mind for days. Weeks. *Years*. It's the kind of kiss that only lost lovers have—longing with a deeper connection that the universe orchestrated long ago.

The thought makes me tense.

His throat bobs when we part. He peers into my eyes, and I take a step back, my cheeks red.

"What was that for?" he asks in a hoarse voice.

Thank you.

I should say it.

I should tell him how much the last few hours have meant.

And yet, there's a hesitation inside me that forces me to say something entirely different.

"It was a good omelet," I reply, and Reed looks at me as if he knows better.

"You're welcome," he says.

It's not for the omelet compliment.

He gives me a small smile and tuts his tongue to signal Anita, then disappears out of the door.

It's a job to hold myself up against the back of the door, forehead leaning on its coolness. I just need to breathe. To clear my now invading thoughts—

Of him.

Only of him.

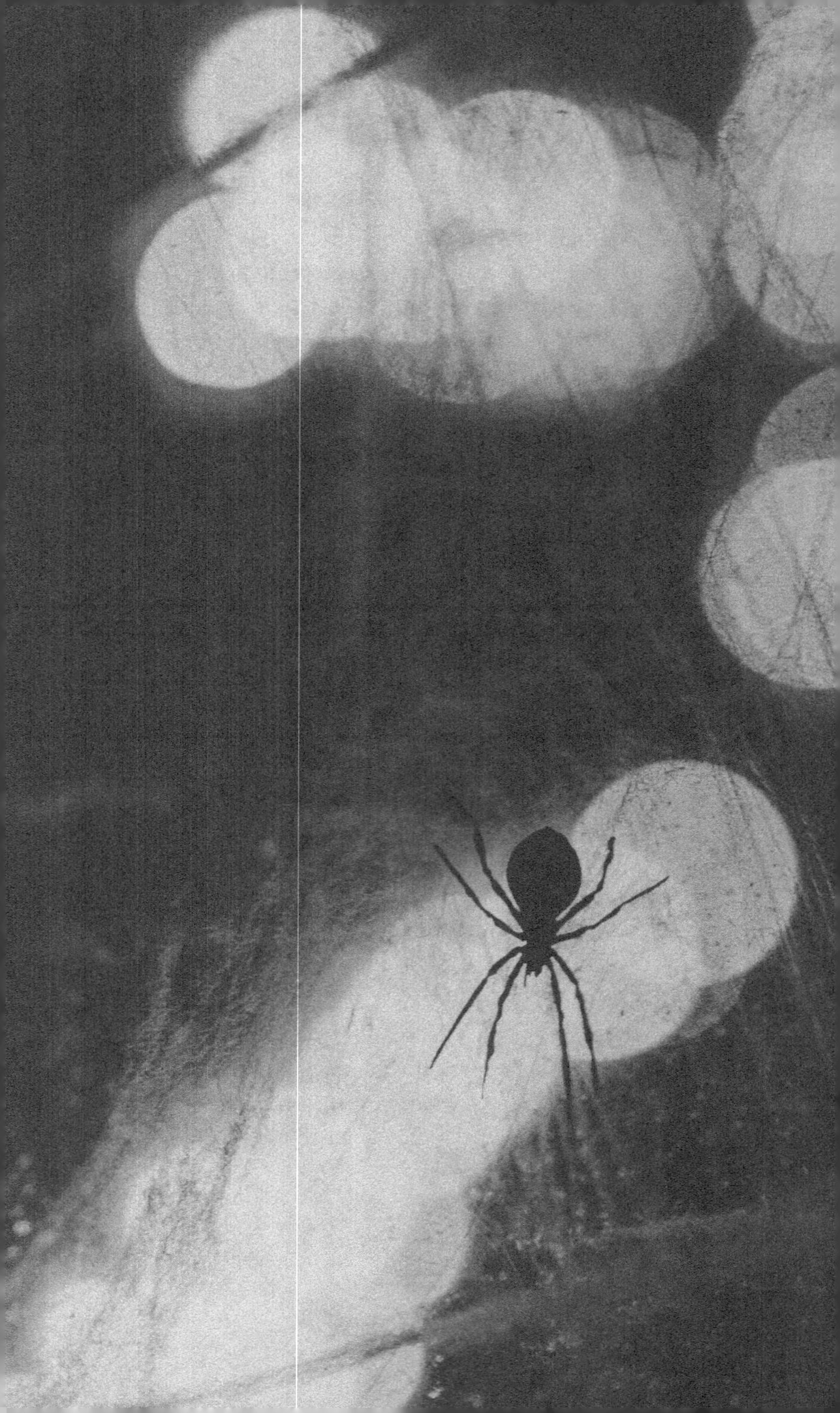

CHAPTER THIRTY-TWO

WREN

I DON'T THINK my heart has stopped aching since yesterday morning.

It started when Reed came back from walking Anita, and I was still in the shower. It bloomed when he came into the bathroom to take a piss, only for our eyes to meet through the foggy glass after, and for him to join me in the shower for a lazy wall fuck that had me seeing stars the remainder of the night—

As if I wasn't already drunk enough on him.

The ache seemed to bleed through me the rest of the night every time our hands or eyes met. I barely remember anything other than him.

Just as he'd promised.

The yoga teacher at the front of the class calls for our second round of locust pose, and I try to focus on my breathing. I'm at a hot yoga class bright and early. The room is a balmy one hundred five degrees, and *fuck*… it feels fantastic.

Exactly what I needed.

And yet, twenty minutes later, as I lay in savasana, there's one moment from the premiere the night before that continues to play behind my closed eyes.

"Kiss!" one photographer shouts as Reed and I make our way down the red carpet.

"Give us a kiss!"

"Hey, Matthews! Over here! Kiss her!"

Reed pauses a few steps ahead of me and reaches back for my hand. I feel a genuine smile rise in my eyes. It's new to me, something I haven't felt in a long while—especially in front of a camera. And while the thought of the movie premiere just minutes away has my skin crawling with nerves, something about the way he's staring at me right now allows me to take an even, full breath.

God, what is he doing to me?

He pulls me into him with a spin that showcases the bottom of my dress, and as he catches me by the waist, he leans over and bends me slightly backward. My modeling instincts kick in, knowing exactly where to place my hands and bent knee to get the perfect angle of my dress. His forehead meets mine, our lips brushing as cameras flash wildly.

The moment is brief. Even so, it feels like forever that I'm in his arms.

And the rest of the night, he didn't let go of my hand.

As the class wraps up, I take a few extra breaths on the floor, my legs crossed beneath me. It's a private, membership-only, studio that Larry found a few years back. I recognize some others rolling up their mats, though after that class, I hope to hell no one wants to chat. It isn't all actors and musicians. There are a few app developers and content creators in the class, too.

I'm wiping my neck with the cool, lavender towel when my gaze snags on the couple at the front of the class chatting on their mats. The woman attending is newer, though her husband has been attending for as long as I have. I've heard that he's a big time dating app developer of... what was the name... Cupid something. There are so many dating apps now, it's hard to keep up with the names.

Thank fuck I never tried them.

The guy says something to his wife, making her laugh, and a pang of jealousy twists my stomach as I realize I'll never have what they have. At least not in the real sense.

I need to get out of here.

The first thing I see when I get to my cubby is missed text messages from Reed—who apparently changed his name in my phone last night.

YOUR FAVORITE PERSON

I should have stayed with you last night.

I should have come up with some excuse to miss my flight.

It was better that you didn't.

There you are.

I was beginning to think you were sleeping in.

I went to yoga.

Yeah? Hot yoga?

Is there another kind of yoga?

That's my favorite, too.

There's a retreat out in the middle of the Mojave Desert that I go to sometimes.

That sounds nice.

Maybe next time you can come with.

I'll have to check my schedule. With any luck, I'll be halfway across the world, and you won't be able to rope me into anything.

Ha, we'll see. When are you done?

> I'm about to shower. I look like a wet dog.

Video me while you shower so I can pretend
I'm washing you like I did yesterday.

> It's a public shower. I don't think they would
> approve.

Fuck them.

I almost laugh out loud.

> I'd have to send them a penis-themed
> namaste gift basket as an apology.

Can I get one of those?

> How about a crystal shaped like a dick?

Yes.

> I might have a guy.

I'm on a high as I shower.

Reed had to take a red-eye flight out of LA not long after the premiere wrapped. We barely socialized at the afterparty, barely got more than a kiss in the SUV when Tara dropped me off at the condo so she could escort Reed through the airport and get him on the plane safely.

I won't see him again until the wedding.

And after that…

My stomach drops every time I think about it. So much so, that I've been ignoring it all morning, pretending next week won't be my last time with him. Maybe Amber Weisen will want to see me act more. Maybe I'll need him for an overseas party. He'll be off the road coming January—

My phone rings as I stride down the sidewalk, hood

pulled up over my head. A fluttering swarms my stomach, involuntary tug at the corners of my lips as I think it's Reed.

It isn't.

The number almost makes me stop walking. My entire body tingles with alert, a rigidness jerking my spine straight, chin high. I glance around the street, noting the people on the sidewalk and at street corners, though I don't see anything out of the ordinary.

I hide the phone under my hood as I answer. "I thought I asked you not to call this number," I snap without so much as a 'hello.'

"That's no way to speak to a friend," Damien says on the other line.

"You're not my friend," I reply. "What do you want?"

"I want to finish our discussion," he says.

"There's nothing to discuss. Leave me alone. Leave *Reed* alone."

A white SUV pulls up to the curb beside me.

I ignore it. Ignore the hair standing on the back of my neck. Ignore the drag in the pit of my stomach. My feet somehow move faster, as if I can outrun a fucking SUV.

The noise of a window rolling down catches my ears. I don't fucking dare look. I know it's probably Erik or one of the other beefy idiots here to scare me.

"I thought we could discuss it in person, Miss Kelly."

Everything within me crashes.

I nearly hurl onto the sidewalk.

I slow to a halt, stubborn to turn. Stubborn to look at him. My eyes shut tight. I will my breaths even.

I'm still laying in the yoga studio.

He isn't here.

"Get in."

I feel my nostrils flare as I finally turn, my jaw set. I have to plant my feet into the ground to keep myself from fleeing down the next street and causing a scene.

Damien sits in the back bench seat of the SUV, a displeased glare on his face. His dark brown eyes seem to pierce into my very soul, cauterizing every bold nerve and sending me faltering into some endless void of no escape. I swallow beneath the stare, breath faltering as my ears begin to warm. He doesn't need to speak for me to know he won't repeat himself.

And the longer I wait outside this car, the higher the chance of him doing something irrational.

I curse myself for going out alone.

"Oh look. You left your cave," I seethe, trying to keep my shit together.

"Get the fuck in this car, Kelly," he sneers.

Erik gets out of the driver seat and opens the door for me, and I take one last glance up the street, hoping to hell *someone* notices me.

However, no one is giving me a second glance.

"Kelly."

"Calm your tits," I snap, clamoring into the seat beside him.

A quiet, devious chuckle leaves Damien. "Dear Kelly…"

The door has barely shut when I hear him move.

He launches forward and grabs me by the throat. I hit and kick, struggling to back myself out of his grasp as the SUV peels away. I manage a strike to his face, a kick to his shin. He winces audibly, hand flying to cover his bleeding nose, and I see the moment when I realize I've fucked up.

Even so, at this point…

I.

Don't.

Care.

A back hand strikes across my cheek and sends me floundering in the seat. Every strand of hair dancing against my skin feels like fire. I'm stunned, and in that second, Damien drags me painfully toward him by my hair, thrusts his palm over my throat again—

Cool metal hits my side.

I know the sensation.

I know the round barrel and square design.

I've felt it before against my temple and my forehead, stared down its sleek silver edge while tears streamed down my face.

The daunting memory of my brother's screams invade my mind as I open my eyes.

"There, now," Damien says as he pulls a handkerchief from his pocket and wipes the blood from his nose. "That wasn't so hard, was it?"

"What do you want?" I say through my teeth.

My face feels like it's broken.

Damien throws the bloody handkerchief into the back before turning his full focus on me."I thought you were smart enough not to try anything by now, but I see I was wrong." He shifts in his seat, moving closer to me and adjusting like he's getting comfortable. The tip of the handgun moves over my tank from my side, dragging down to the hem, and when he presses it beneath my shirt, my jaw begins to quake.

"Do you want to see something?" he asks as he takes out his phone. "I love these little updates."

I peer down at the pictures on his phone with only my eyes, and as I see the ones he's filtering through, I jerk against him.

"You fucking ass—"

But he jabs the point of the gun into my ribs, and I freeze.

Rage and fear pour over me.

The pictures are of Reed. All of them. *Dozens.*

The morning of the premiere. The two of us together backstage at one of his concerts. Andi and I at the charity concert. Reed and I making out in the back of a limo—taken from what looks like the driver's seat. Reed walking Anita with his hood up and hat on. At the fashion show. Reed on the plane with the penis plush around his neck.

And as Damien flips through them, tears prick my eyes.

They've followed him *everywhere.*

My phone buzzes in my pocket.

"This is my favorite, though," Damien says. He switches over to another app, and as a video begins to play, vomit lurches into my throat.

It's a video of Reed sitting outside on what looks like the back steps of a venue by the loading docks. He has headphones in, his phone out, and when my phone vibrates again, I realize this isn't a recording.

"*Leave him alone,*" I shake out.

"Every time I see him, I think… he'd make such a pretty trophy. Even prettier than you. I wonder what I could do with him in my pocket instead of poor little Wren Kelly," Damien taunts.

"You'd never get to him," I spit.

"Oh, I think he'd be easy to get to," Damien counters. He looks directly at me and drags the gun to my breasts. "I think he'd come *running* for his little whore."

"You're wrong," I force out.

"Am I?" He thumbs through the photos back to one of him sitting with his sister and Mads. "What about these two? Do you think he'd come running for them?"

"*If you fucking touch them —* "

Damien throws the phone away, grabs the hair at the nape of my neck, and jerks my head back before I can finish the sentence.

The gun lands beneath my chin. I wince at the coldness of it, teeth chattering when a tear spills down my cheek.

I want to stop trembling.

I want to breathe without fear of somehow causing him to accidentally—or even intentionally—pull the trigger.

I'm paralyzed by the fear of what he's capable of, of what I know he wouldn't hesitate to do.

"What have you told him?" Damien seethes.

"I haven't told him anything—"

"*Liar*, Kelly!" he spits. "I know you have."

"I wouldn't tell him anything. I know better."

"Hm." Damien moves the gun from beneath my chin to between my thighs. "Maybe you'll be more compliant after I fuck you like your boyfriend does."

No.

No. No. No.

My heart drops. A cry leaves me.

"Damien, no—"

I squirm and writhe, trying to back out of his grasp. "No. *Stop*. Damien, please!—*He doesn't know anything!*"

"*Lying fucking whore!*"

Panic.

I slap and shove, squirming under him, unable to stop my tears. His hand is around my throat and crushing my windpipe. I can't breathe. Spots dance in my vision. I throw my hand against the back of Erik's seat, barely noticing that he's pulled into a deserted lot until I feel the vehicle slam to a halt. My foot pounds on Damien's chest. He's ripping at my leggings. They're nearly done for, the seam ripping.

"*Please, Damien! Stop—*"

Metal hits my unclothed pussy. I scream. Kick. *Sob*. God, I can't fucking see. My ears are ringing.

Help.

Please, fucking please, help.

"Boss, what are you—Jesus, *fuck*—"

Erik unhooks his seatbelt. I can hear him speaking to

Damien, but I'm numb and deaf in my fight as the gun presses against my entrance. I keep kicking and shoving.

Another set of hands grab me. Another voice joins Erik's—Damien's. He says something. I finally writhe out of his grasp as Erik pulls Damien off of me. I manage to bring my knees to my chest, curling into a ball against the door—

The gun goes off.

I scream. Glass shatters. Droplets of blood spray on my body. My already ringing ears go fucking numb. My head is between my knees. I'm waiting for the pain. I'm waiting for the reaper.

But it isn't my blood on me.

I still haven't taken a breath when I eventually lift my gaze over my knees.

Damien is sitting back in his seat and looking at his gun as if he's annoyed. He pushes his dark hair back off his forehead, blood mingling with the black strands as he appears to try and catch his breath.

If he's not dead…

I wish I could say that the sight of Erik's blown off head disturbs me.

I wish the sight of his brain and blood splattered everywhere sent me into more of a panic or made me want to hurl.

Yet all it does is tell me how scared Damien truly is of me talking.

Damien presses his phone to his ear.

"Find me," is all he says to the person on the line.

And when his gaze lands on me, I shrink myself as far into the corner of the seat as I can go.

"I'm only going to say this one time, Miss Kelly," he growls. *"Get rid of the boyfriend."*

I swallow the bile in my throat. "I have one more event with him—"

Damien cocks the gun back.

"—just one more!" I almost scream. "It's for my job. You said you would let me have my fucking job!"

A muscle feathers in his jaw as he considers me. "Timeline," he says.

"Ah…" Fuck, I don't even know what day it is. "The event is on the sixteenth. This month."

Damien opens up his phone again to the live video and turns it around to me. "Do I need to explain to you what will happen if I find that you're communicating with him *after* the sixteenth?"

Reed is still sitting outside. Still staring at his phone as if he's waiting for something. He presses it to his ear, tapping his knee, and I hear my own phone vibrate.

"Answer it," Damien demands.

A hot tear drips down my cheek as I grab my phone.

It takes everything in me not to tell Reed to run. To tell him there are people watching and recording him, and he needs to get as far away from me as possible.

I sniff and inhale a deep breath, forcing my voice as even as I can.

"Hey," I manage.

God, do I sound shaky?

I just have a gun pointed at my head. Why would my voice be shaking?

I want to lay under the tires of this SUV and let Damien's goons run me over.

"Hey. I was hoping you would answer," Reed says, and the smile that lights up his face makes my heart sink. "We're heading into sound check. Wanted to call before things got crazy tonight."

"That's cute," I say, trying to sound like myself. "What makes you think I wanted to chat? You know I hate phone calls."

"Intuition," he replies. "Are you walking home? You sound tired."

"Ah, yeah, I'm okay," I say, trying to avoid looking at Damien. "That yoga class kicked my ass. I came out to like ten missed calls and messages. I guess things are just bananas after the premiere, you know? I'll probably lay low the rest of the day. Recover from all the socializing."

There's a beat of silence, and I watch Reed's eyes lift.

Go inside.

Find James.

Stay safe.

"Oh. Okay. I should be heading in to sound check, too. I'll video you after the concert?" he asks as he stands.

Thank fuck.

I wasn't sure he would catch it.

"Yeah," I answer. "Tonight. Have a good show."

I sound so fucking awkward.

I hang up before Reed answers and watch him head through the backstage door.

My gaze lifts to Damien. "Happy?"

He stares at me in silence, then pulls the gun away from my head. The noise of another car pulling up catches my attention, but I don't dare look.

"Chester will take you to your condo," he says plainly. "You have ten days to get rid of the pretty boy. If I have to come back for you, it'll be his head sprayed on the windshield, and you'll find yourself naked on an auction block. Are we clear?"

Someone opens the door, and I nearly fall out of the SUV, but before I can bolt into Chester's car, Damien catches my arm and twists it, forcing me to look at him again.

"Are we clear, Miss Kelly?" he repeats.

"Crystal," I manage.

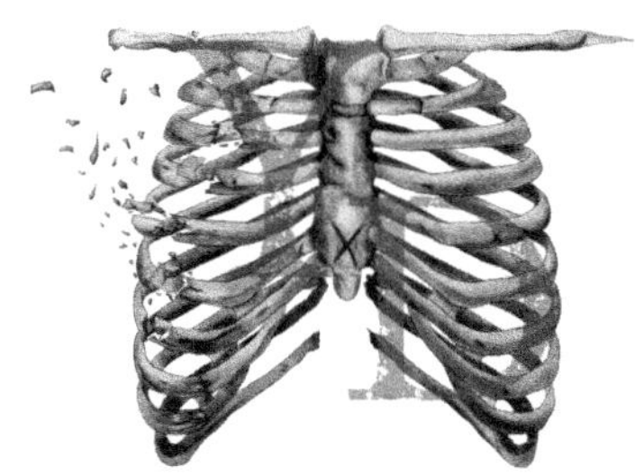

I sit at the bottom of my shower as the blood and scorching hot water swirls around the drain at my toes.

I've only just stopped crying.

Only just stopped shaking.

My insides are numb and cold despite the hot water pounding my skin, and my head is a spinning carousel of light and dark.

I should take myself out of the equation. If I'm not here, nothing else can happen to anyone. If I'm not here, Reed will be safe. If I'm not here, Damien can't hurt me anymore.

God, what have I done?

One more thing that's your fault.

You have more blood on your hands.

First your parents. Then your little sister. Then your fucking twin.

I grip the roots of my hair and start rocking as the invasive thoughts continue trickling in, continue pummeling my mind.

Why did you get Reed involved in this?

Did you need more pain?

I'm so fucking stupid.

You know no one will care if you're gone.

You're all alone anyway.

I am all alone.

I'm so fucking alone.

Send Anita with Larry. She's better off with him.

You don't make anyone's life better.

Just fucking do it already.

Stupid. Stupid. Stupid—

Someone knocks on the bathroom door.

I jump so fast that I slip and hit my head against the glass. It knocks me back on my ass, clouding my vision with white lights as I try to gather my wits.

At least it shuts out the invasive thoughts.

"Wren?"

Larry's voice prompts a sob to choke in my throat. I swallow it and push breath into my lungs, trying hard not to sound like I've been uncontrollably sobbing for the last hour.

Oh, fuck, my face—

"How did you get in?" is all I can think to ask.

"Bitch, I have a key," Larry says. "Everything okay?"

"Yeah," I say. "Yeah. Why? Why are you here? Is something wrong?"

"You have a meeting with Amanda in an hour," he answers. "I'll take Anita out while you're getting ready, if you want."

Mother *fuck*.

Can't this day end already?

"Okay."

Because the word is all I can manage right now.

"Are you sure you're okay?" Larry asks again.

I finally stand and look at myself in the mirror, groaning inwardly at the shadow of a bruise forming on my cheekbone. I grab my heaviest concealer and begin dabbing it over the mark. Fuck, if Larry or anyone were to see this, they'd never let me go on without explaining it to them.

"Yeah," I answer. "I'm fine."

I send a message to Tara for Reed when we're on the way to Amanda's. I don't know if Damien has my phone hacked in a way that he can read my messages or watch my video chats. I don't think he's smart enough for it; however, after today, I'm not taking any chances.

Amanda's office is busy when we arrive. I'm still in a daze, still barely aware of the rest of the world around me as Larry leads me through the lobby, into the elevator, and to her office.

She could tell me I got the part in Amber's Marilyn film, and I don't think I would give two shits right now. All of it seems so unimportant. My choices, my life, all of it. None of it belongs to me. None of it can be what makes me happy.

I just want it to stop.

"Earth to Wren—" Amanda snaps her fingers in my face, drawing me out of the daze.

"Yeah? What? What did I miss?" I ask, sitting up straight.

"I was just saying how successful the premiere was," she says, showing off a photo of Reed and I on the red carpet. "Pre-sale numbers are up. We are a go for release on Friday. I have Amber in my ear, just waiting on the phone call." She leans her hips on the front of her desk. "I have to hand it to the pair of you. You made it look easy."

He made it easy.

He made it *so fucking easy*.

"Wren?" Amanda calls me, her head tilting. "You should be celebrating. What's wrong?"

"Nothing," I say, shifting. "Nothing. I am happy." I force a smile on my lips and make eye contact with her. "You haven't heard anything from Amber?"

"Word is you're a done deal, but I never like to count success until I have it in writing," she replies.

"So… what does this mean? Should we write up Reed and I's breakup?"

Because we have to be done.

There isn't a happily ever after for us.

Not if I want him to live.

Amanda considers me. "If that's what you want," she says. "Nothing says you have to break it off, you know."

"I'm going with him to his sister's wedding this weekend. You can post it the Tuesday after," I tell her as I stand. "Amicable. No drama. Was there anything else?"

"Are you in a hurry for something?" Amanda asks.

"Yeah, I was just going to slit my wrists in the car. Why?" I say, and Amanda gives me a doubtful glare.

"I'll have Shannon draft the breakup, but I'm not sending anything out until you give me the word."

"This is the word. I'm not changing my mind," I argue. "It's done. I have the part. The movie is a success. People think I'm likable—"

"Wren…"

"Are we done?" I ask, this time not leaving any question of my seriousness.

Amanda exchanges a look with Larry, then nods. "Yeah. We're done."

CHAPTER THIRTY-THREE

"WE NEED TO CHAT," James says, clapping me on my shoulder after the concert.

"Someone's in trouble," Bonnie coos.

I frown at James. "What about?"

"Found something on those numbers you gave me." He releases my arm and jerks his chin over for me to follow him.

After the call with Bird today, I'm not arguing.

"What's up?" I ask when we're alone.

"I got a message from Wren's guard during the show," he says. "She said, and I quote, 'keep things bananas until the wedding.'" James stares at me. "Any idea what that means?"

My heart drops a little. Fuck, if she's in trouble… if those people got to her…

"No idea," I say. "Probably a sex thing."

James watches me as if he doesn't believe me. "You get any more of those calls?"

"Same number. Twice today," I answer.

"My people scoping out the cabin for the wedding say reception is shit up on that mountain," he says cryptically. "Maybe the two of you won't be bothered."

James was right.

Reception is shit up here.

I hold my phone in the air again as I stand at the edge of the valley cliff, trying to pick up any bars so that I can find out where Wren is. She's supposed to be flying in today, but I've only been able to get messages from the end of the half-mile driveway.

"Relax, dude," Mads says a few feet away. "I'm sure she's fine."

"This is making me fucking insane," I mutter. "You'd be the same way if she wasn't here yet," I say, glancing toward my sister, who's curled up in an Adirondack chair by the fire pit.

"I'm just glad you don't look like a raccoon carved you up anymore," Mads says about the welts that were on my face and chest after Halloween. "Fucking hell. I didn't know it was possible to get scratched up like that. That would've been an interesting look in the wedding photos."

"I still can't believe she stabbed you," Andi says as she runs her hand through her now dark teal hair.

"He probably deserved it," Mads says, smirking at me. He leans over and gives Andi a quick kiss before saying, "I'm going to take a very long shower. What time is your girl getting here?"

"Ah…" I look down at my phone again and check the time, along with her messages. "Should be here right around when Bonnie is getting in."

"Are they on the same flight?" Mads asks.

"Hell, they might be," I say.

Andi laughs. "That would be interesting to witness. She hasn't been around Bon that much, has she?"

"A little after concerts, parties at Fashion Week. Definitely not an entire plane ride, though," I reply.

"Bon usually tries to sleep on the plane," Mads says. "So maybe Wren won't want to run away."

My phone vibrates then, making my heart drop.

"Message?" Mads asks.

"Ah, yeah. Wren." I look at my phone, only to find a photo message from Wren of her and Bonnie aboard the prop plane that's taking them from the large airport to the local runway.

I laugh. "You were right," I tell Mads, turning the phone around.

"That's fucking hilarious," Mads says, Andi laughing at his side. "Okay, I'm going to shower. What, they're like an hour out?"

"Yeah, something like that," I reply.

Mads leaves Andi and I alone then, and I quickly text Wren back. I don't know if it'll go through, but I'm texting her anyway.

I can't wait for you to get here.

Keep it in your pants, poser. I'm just coming
for the mountain vacation.

I chuckle.

Still. I get to see you.

No cuddling.

Oh, we're cuddling.

There's a pause when I think maybe she's lost connection, though a moment later, her text comes through.

THE DEATH OF ME

Fine. See you soon.

See you.

I smile at the screen before gazing out at the valley below. "What?" Andi asks.

"Ah, nothing," I say, stashing my phone away. "Just… nerves."

Andi laughs. "Yeah, I can imagine. It's been a while since you brought someone home," she says, laying her head against the back of her chair. "You know, I think the two of you are good for each other. You and Wren, I mean. Not you and Bonnie. I love Bon but the two of you together are a dangerous combo."

I scoff. "Why do you think Wren and I are good for each other?"

"I don't know," she says with a shrug. "I guess because she's a challenge for you. She isn't easy all the time. Most of the others you've dated… You grew bored of them because they melted at your feet. Wren… she's a fucking handful."

I snort, running my hand through my hair. "Ah, yeah. Something like that," I manage.

"And as for her… You don't give up. You literally have no quit, and I think she's used to people backing off after a single insult. Maybe not wanting to deal with how difficult she is."

"I don't think she's difficult. She just has her own demons," I reply.

"Maybe that's the difference," she says. "Maddox says he's heard you tell her that you 'have her,' and I thought… I wonder if anyone has ever even tried."

"I'm glad to know you and Mads talk about my love life," I say, glancing sideways at her. "It isn't even real," I say.

"Why can't it be?" she asks.

"What makes you think that's what I want?"

Andi grins. "The photos from Halloween and the premiere did you dirty. It's totally apparent. Everyone can see it."

"See what?" I ask.

"That you're head-over-heels in love with her."

"Ha," I laugh. "You're delusional. That's those fuzzy love goggles you're wearing over Madsy," I tease her.

Andi mutters a "Hm," and stares silently out at the sunset for a beat, and I can feel her holding in her amusement.

I know she's fucking right.

God, I know it.

And I hate her for seeing it.

I stuff my hands in the pockets of my hoodie and slump back in the Adirondack chair. "Fuck you, Andi," I say, and she snorts. A chuckle threatens my insides, and I shake my head at nothing, letting the laughter rise to the surface. "Seriously, *fuck you.*"

Andi howls.

Her laughter echoes in the cold air, ringing out over the valley, and I beam at her. Laughs like this are a sound that I wish I'd heard more of when we were growing up, a sound I wish I'd tried to draw out of her more times than I did.

"You've been chasing love that makes you feel insane your entire life without ever knowing it," Andi says when she's recovered. "An absolute, hopeless romantic. You feel everything. To think you wouldn't fall for this girl was absolutely ridiculous on your part."

"Yeah, well, maybe I thought if I did, it wouldn't be this complicated," I reply.

"Why is it?"

I sigh, thinking about the morning of the premiere, the guys following her, what she swears she can never tell me. I haven't seen the stalkers following me in the last week. Even so, she's acted a little differently. Not as free as she was the night of Halloween.

I wonder if something else happened.

"I'm not entirely sure," I admit.

"Perhaps after this weekend, things will change," she says. "Weddings do weird things to people."

I glance at her. "You sound like you're rooting for this relationship."

Andi shrugs and hugs her blanket tighter. "I think I am."

"Does this mean you like her?" I ask.

Andi smirks crookedly. "I fucking love her. I love that she's not cooing over you."

My mind goes to the night she took control, and I clear my throat. "That she is not," I mutter, and Andi raises a curious brow.

"I'm not entirely sure I want to know," she says.

"I'm definitely not telling you," I laugh. "What about you? Are you ready for the wedding?"

She inhales a deep, long breath, a soft smile on her face as she stares into the distance. "I don't think it's quite hit me yet," she admits. "I'm ready to celebrate and have everyone in the same house, though."

"A noisy affair," I joke.

"I can't wait," she grins. "It's going to be total overload, and I'm going to need to sleep for a week after, but I'll love every minute of this weekend."

"Kids! I made snacks!" my mom, Tina, yells out from the back patio door.

Andi and I sit up, gaze narrowing back at her. "She realizes we're all adults now, right?" I ask.

"Everyone except Koen," Andi says.

I chuckle and help her to her feet, then head inside where my mom is waiting with charcuterie boards and wine.

It's another hour before Wren and Bonnie show up.

I don't know why I'm so fucking nervous standing on the rounded drive. Maybe it's because she's meeting my family or because the last time I saw her was the same day we argued about what she was running from—only for her to use her fucking safe word on the phone with me the next day.

The thought that she might be in actual trouble has had me itching to say something all week. Even still, I knew better. I did like she asked and waited.

There better not be a fucking scratch on her when she gets here.

James pulls into the driveway. I begin to rock on my toes, not entirely sure what to do with my hands. And when the SUV comes to a stop, my stomach is woven into so many knots that I think it might take the rest of the weekend to untie them.

Bonnie bursts out of the backseat—wearing her white skull design cropped sweatshirt, high-waisted joggers, Vans, and Aviator sunglasses. Her hair is a mess, though I doubt she cares as she throws both hands in the air upon seeing me.

"Leading man!"

I follow suit, my own hands in the air so I can catch her jumping out. She launches into my arms, legs hooking around my waist, and hugs me tight. I ruffle her hair when her feet land on the ground.

"Hey, Bon. How was home?" I ask, knowing she spent a couple of days back at her dad's in Southern California.

"Amazing, as always. Got some surfing in. Went to the local dive bar and crashed their drum set—"

I laugh. "Yeah, Mads and I watched that video last night," I say.

"—And then—" Bonnie turns around and nods her chin to Wren, who's climbing across the seat to get out. My heart skips a little upon seeing her, one knot loosening in my gut.

She looks relieved as our eyes meet, her face softening. I swear there's a dark streak on her cheekbone, though I can't be sure with the shadows casting over us right now. It could be makeup from sleeping on the plane ride or dirt from the prop plane.

I'll figure it out when we're alone.

"—then I found this one looking a little lost at LAX," Bonnie says, grinning at Wren. She looks back at me. "I think we're best friends now."

"That is a terrifying proposition," I say, unable to look away from Wren.

"Bon!" I hear Andi say when she emerges from the front door.

Bonnie squeezes my arm and bounds past me to meet my sister, leaving me alone to help Wren.

"Hey," I say, having to swallow at the fact that she's actually here.

"Do not 'hey' me, Reed Matthews," she says. "You didn't tell me I was taking a prop plane to the local airport here. And my phone died right after sending you that photo, so I couldn't text you to shout about it."

I smirk at her fluster. "Did you have fun, though?"

An annoyed smile dares to threaten her lips, and when I extend my hand to help her out of the van, she swats me away playfully.

"You told the pilot I wanted to fly a plane," she says.

I shrug. "I mean… it may have come up in conversation."

"He put me in the copilot's seat and told the copilot to take a nap," she goes on.

My brows lift. "Oh shit," I almost chuckle.

"Yeah, oh shit. He let me *fly the plane,*" she says.

I'm holding in my laughter at her attempt at being mad. "And you're annoyed by that because…"

She finally steps onto solid ground. "Just because—" Her words cease when she looks past me at the cabin. "Holy shit, this cabin is huge."

I take her chin between my fingers and bring her attention back to me. "Why are you ticked?"

"Because you know I hate small talk," she says.

"Besides that," I reply.

She twists her lips, those green eyes seeming to bore through me, and finally she sighs. "Because you're the only one who knows how much I love flying and weightlessness and freedom, and that…" She presses her hands to my chest, another heavy exhale leaving her.

"That meant something to me," she finally says.

Goddamn this feeling in my gut.

I have to swallow beneath her gaze. "And here I was thinking I only did it because you're cute when you're annoyed," I say.

"Oh, is that the only reason?" she asks.

"Yeah, you get all red in the face. It's adorable."

Amusement fills her eyes, and before I can say anything, she sinks her arms around my waist and hugs me closer than she ever has. I hesitate for a beat, caught off guard by the weight of her embrace. Nevertheless, I wrap my arms around her as tightly as she'll let me, and I hang on.

Shit, this feels right.

"Are you okay?" I say into her hair.

"Give me today," she whispers. "I don't want to think about it. I just want to be here."

The words pain me.

Fuck, how do I take this away from her? How do I convince her to let me share it?

My eyes close, and I kiss the top of her head as she eventually releases me.

"What was that for?" I ask. "Did you miss me?"

"I can't hug my friend?" she asks, and my brows shoot up.

"We're friends?"

Wren rolls her eyes and starts to push me away, but I pull her back into me, unable to keep the smile from my lips when I notice the amusement in her gaze.

"I have an urge to kiss you," I say, my voice suddenly hoarse.

"Keep your urges to yourself," she says, and I chuckle, making her mouth tug as if she also wants to smile.

"Why do you want to kiss me? I thought you said they all know this isn't real," she says.

"I don't care," I say as my hand spreads against her neck. "I want to."

"What about what I want?" she manages.

"You want this," I claim.

"Reed, do not kiss me," she says breathlessly, gaze darting to my lips.

"Push me away, then."

Her gaze lifts to mine for a beat, throat bobbing with her swallow.

"Do not kiss me," she whispers, her fists curling on my shirt.

"Why are you bringing me closer?" I ask.

Her chest caves. "Reed…"

My lips land on hers, and within a second, she opens up to me, and it makes my heart drop.

Nothing about this kiss is hurried, rough, or fueled by the passion normally in our bodies. And yet, I know she's still hesitating. I know how much more of herself she hasn't given me, and fuck… I want to know why.

I want to know why I shouldn't feel what I'm feeling right now.

When we part and her lashes flutter upward, revealing the minuscule sliver of green remaining around her pupils, I suddenly want to push her back into the van and shield her from the absolute overwhelming weekend we're about to have.

"Don't do that again," she breathes.

"Next time, it won't be this gentle," I say.

"That's what I meant," she replies.

I can't look away from her, not even when she draws her attention from me and glances past my arm to the cabin again.

"Okay, but seriously," she says, finally parting from me. "How fucking big is this cabin?"

I chuckle, following her gaze. She's right. The cabin has ten bedrooms, complete with a ballroom for events, the largest dining room I've ever seen, a heated pool in the back, theater room, and more that Mads and I didn't get the chance to check out yet.

"Ah… big family," I say. "The entire band. Needed a place to hold the wedding and have a reception. So, pretty large. It even has a music studio in the basement."

"Oh, the wedding is here?" she asks.

"Yeah. There's a cliff overlook in the backyard. They're getting married at an altar there, then depending on how fucking cold it is, might have the reception indoor or out. They haven't decided."

A figure appears at the doors on the other side of the fountain, and my stomach begins to twist upon seeing Koen and Kamden sticking their heads out and grinning like two teenage boys about to meet the girl on the poster on their ceilings.

Which, I'm pretty sure Kamden has one of Wren on his, along with a few other models.

Oh, fuck, why did I bring her here?

"I should have warned you," I say, turning back into her. "My family is… a lot. And when I say a lot—"

"You mean I'm going to be surrounded by the jolliest bunch of assholes this side of the nuthouse?" she asks, and I could kiss her again for quoting my favorite holiday movie.

"Yeah," I chuckle. "Something like that."

She shrugs her bag up on her shoulder. "You underestimate my acting skills, Matthews," she says, patting my chest. "I can handle an entire family of golden retrievers."

"Well, Kamden is more of a Shih Tzu, but—"

Fuck, they're getting way too close.

"Just don't forget your tap-out word," I say upon hearing my mom coming out. "Or if you need a break or anything like that—"

"Reed." She reaches for my cheek and pulls my face back to her. "I know how to say 'no,'" she says.

I eye her. "Do you?"

Her expression flattens. "Let me rephrase. Apparently, I know how to say 'no' to everyone except you. Because you're relentless and somehow, despite your chaos, you're incredibly calming, but we're not getting into that right now—oh my god, your mom is so pretty," she says as her eyes drift past me again.

I chuckle, trying not to get hung up on the words she's just blurted out, and I pick up one of her bags.

"Where do you think I get my looks from?" I say, and we share one more glance before my family descends on her with outstretched arms.

The greetings are a blur.

My mom hugs her like she's known her her entire life. I wait for Wren to give me a weirded out look or push Mom away, but she doesn't even shove off my brothers when they also try to hug her.

I bump Kamden away for good measure.

"Not you," I say, much to his chagrin.

"That's fine," Kamden says, trying to appear charming as he looks at Wren. "I knew the two of you couldn't be actually dating the moment I saw the pictures. No fucking way this guy is scoring with a beautiful girl like you."

Wren gives him an amused stare. "Actually, your brother is scoring pretty frequently with me, so. Sorry, I had to be the one to tell you you're wrong," she says, giving him a mocking pout.

Mads gives me a high five behind her back.

"That's enough, Kamden. Don't crowd her," Tina, my mom, says. She turns her attention to me. "Sweetie, I didn't know whether to leave an extra bedroom for Wren or not given..." Tina glances between Wren and me, and I chuckle.

"I said we're not dating, Mom," I say as I take the luggage out. "I didn't say other things were off the table."

Wren gives me a flat stare, then shakes her head. "What he means is that we're both adults," she says. "I can stay in the room with him so long as he doesn't try to cuddle."

"Someone better find sheets for the spare bedroom," Andi says.

"Regardless of where everyone is sleeping," my dad, Randall, says, calming everyone down. "Tina is in the middle of cooking dinner for all of you, so I need to take her away right now so that nothing burns."

"Oh no—the oven!" Tina darts back into the house like she left something on fire, and as everyone starts filing back inside the cabin, I turn to Wren.

"Are you hungry?" I ask.

"Starving actually," she answers.

"That's great because Mom likes to make extravagant snack bars," I reply. "Do you want to eat or do you need a bit to recover from traveling?"

"I'm great, Reed," she says.

"Are you sure?"

"Cross my heart."

CHAPTER THIRTY-FOUR

WREN

DINNER WITH REED'S family was overwhelming in the very best way.

I found myself on the verge of tears more times than once, and yet every time I felt it, I also felt Reed's hand on mine, his smile in my direction, or even him filling my drink. The acts, as small as they were, reminded me where I am. Who I'm with.

We were both too drunk to do any more than makeout in the bed last night, and I realize as I feel him moving around me this morning that he did, in fact, cuddle me. And as much as I hate it, I also can't bring myself to pull out of his arms.

All I want to do is take you away from this, I can hear him saying.

I wish I could steal him, too.

The thoughts lull me into a state of conscious unconsciousness. I feel him shifting behind me, his hands slowly roaming over my stomach. His lips land softly on my shoulder, one arm somehow wrapped under my side and wrapping up my stomach so he can palm my breasts. I can feel his length hardening behind me, and I wiggle slightly against it.

Reed sucks air through his teeth and bites my throat.

"Shh… go back to sleep," he whispers against the shell of my ear.

I whimper, slipping in and out of consciousness as he slides his opposite hand beneath the band of my underwear and begins deliberately toying with my clit. It's a steady massage on my senses, warming my entire body beneath the heavy blanket we're cuddled beneath. I want to wake up and participate, but *fuck*, this feels too amazing to stop.

"You're so wet for me, bird," he whispers. "Did you dream of me?"

I only groan in response and wrap my arms tighter around my pillow. He kisses lazily down my neck to my spine and moves his hand from between my thighs to rub up and down my side. I can feel my wetness on his fingers as he drags them across my skin.

"Fuck, you're stunning," he mutters when he grabs my ass.

I don't know if it's how tired I already am, if it's the morning chill, or just the softness of his motions, but everything is heightened. I'm awake, and yet not. It feels like a dream, and I whimper into it. The warmth of his chest against my back has me entirely melted. I don't want to move, don't want to wake.

The tip of his dick slides between my ass cheeks, precum dragging across my skin, and I groan at the fact that he's already so hard and ready.

I wonder how long he's been touching me.

A drift of sleep takes me as I note his chest rising and falling against my back. I only wake again when he gently grasps my throat. The pressure is minute, and yet, chills roll down my spine with it.

It's then I realize that he's already inside me from behind.

"Reed." I hardly hear myself say his name. He fills me like no other ever has. Slow. Steady. Every lazy thrust seeming longer than the last.

He drags his free hand over my tits before bracing his palm against my abdomen with his next stroke, and the weight of him hugging me closer draws a whimper.

Fuck…

I'll never tell him that he fucks like a god, though I'm pretty sure he already knows. Right now, he's Sandman, lulling me into the realm of a sleepy haze I don't know that I ever want to wake from. I wonder how long he'll keep up this deliberate ministration, how long he plans on driving into me as if conjoined like this is how we'll spend forever.

I don't even have the levelheadedness to backtrack the thought.

"You feel so fucking good in the morning, bird," he breathes against the back of my neck, nose dragging along my hairline. He shifts his hand lower, middle finger whispering over my clit, and I finch at the sensitivity.

It's all I can do to moan out another murmur of his name.

"I love the way this sleepy cunt takes me," he whispers. "Shit, you feel amazing."

He groans into the crook of my neck and increases his grip around my throat. I'm mildly struggling for air, and yet, in this trancing state, I don't care. Not if he feels like this.

I'm in and out of consciousness, and even still, I feel my orgasm rising. He's guiding me through it, cursing into my neck and rocking my hips.

"Reed," I manage, though it's barely a breath. I pull my bottom lip between my teeth and snake my hand back around his neck, my fingers in his hair. I don't know what time it is. I don't care what day it is.

His lips land on my neck, and he wraps his arm around my breasts, securing me tight against his chest. He's so broad, his arms so long that he swallows me into him. And as his pace quickens, I feel myself falling harder.

Breath sticks in my throat when I come. He curses into my

collar, hands squeezing my tits as he finds his own end within a few steady motions. His mouth opens on my neck, biting out his groan, and I feel him finish within me.

I debate falling back asleep in those following seconds, and I think I do, even if it's only for a moment or two. Eventually, Reed shifts, allowing me to turn onto my back when he slides out of me, and when our eyes meet, he lays his forehead against mine.

"Take a walk with me after breakfast," he whispers. "We'll leave our phones here."

I feel my body tense before I realize why. But as his blue eyes pierce me through loose strands of shaggy hair, I know I can't keep avoiding this.

"Please, Wren," he says.

I swallow and press my hands to his cheeks, emotion burning behind my nose. "Okay."

Because he deserves to know why this is our last weekend together.

When we go down for breakfast an hour later, I can still feel the imprint of his dick inside me, and despite the shower that we both took, I feel like everyone can see exactly where he kissed me this morning and all the places his hands caressed. Classic rock music plays from one of the speakers throughout the house, and I sit down on the barstool at the kitchen island across from where Tina is cooking breakfast and humming along to the songs.

"Morning, Mom—These songs are hitting this morning," Reed says, coolly walking into the space as if it's his own home. He leans over and kisses his mother on the cheek before hitting the cabinets like a drum when he passes, then pauses at the coffee machine.

He appears so at ease with his family. More at ease than he is even on the stage. As if he doesn't have to hide anything with them and can be his entire chaotic self without fear or judgment.

"Reed, do you think you can help your dad with his little project today?" she asks.

Reed narrows his eyes at her over his shoulder, taking the caramel stir stick he was just sucking on out of his mouth. "It's fucking vacation. Why is he working on a project?"

"I think he's rented an old car from some guy down the road and wants to decorate the back for the wedding tomorrow. He was on the phone with him all day on Wednesday." She glances sideways at Reed over her reading glasses. "You know I don't ask," she adds.

Reed chuckles softly. "Wren and I were actually going to take a walk after breakfast," he tells her. "Think it can wait until this afternoon?"

"Don't forget we have rehearsal dinner tonight," she says. "I can see if he'll hold off until in the morning so that your brothers can also help."

"What are they doing today?" Reed asks.

"Who the hell knows," she says before turning her attention to me. "Did you sleep well, Wren? This one didn't cuddle too hard?"

I wipe my hand over my face and crack my neck. "I passed out almost as soon as we got upstairs," I reply.

She gives me a small smile. "You'll find the Matthews gang can get a little… *much*. Add in Bonnie and Zeb, and we're a bowl of complete and utter madness. Sometimes I wonder how Randall puts up with us."

"Dad likes it loud, too," Reed says as he dips a spoon into the food she's making. She lifts a brow at the contemplative look on his face.

"If you tell me it needs more sal—"

"It needs more salt," Reed says, beaming at her.

She throws her dishtowel onto the counter and shakes her head.

"Hey—are you using this burner?" he asks as he takes an onion out of the pantry.

"No. Go for it," she says. "Wren, are you hungry?"

I watch her put what I realize is grits into a large bowl.

"Ah… I'll eventually eat," I answer as she adds it to the other end of the large island where she has the rest of what is essentially a southern breakfast buffet. Tina sighs as she looks over the amount of food she's made already.

"I never know what any of the boys are fixating on at the time," she says. "So, I make a lot of different things just in case. Reed was always the best eater. So much better than Koen, and Kamden… well… he liked dipping sauces, is all I will say."

"And Andi?" I ask.

A small, fond smile lifts on Tina's lips. "Oh, by the time I came along, Andi was already a grown woman in her own mind," she says. "She didn't care what we were having, so long as Reed liked it."

The sentence makes her look sad, and Reed reaches out to squeeze his mom's hand. "Go upstairs and take a break," he tells her. "I know you didn't sleep. I'll finish up."

"I never sleep," she mutters. "Are you sure?"

"Yeah, Mom. I've got it. Bacon and cinnamon rolls in the ovens, right?" he says.

"Yes, and they're homemade rolls, so please watch them." She takes the apron off at the door and hangs it on the hook by the pantry. "I won't be long upstairs. I expect Andi and Maddox will be down soon for coffee. You know they like taking it alone."

"Yeah, they're two peas in the same pod. Go. I'll finish," Reed urges her as he sits a coffee in front of me.

Tina disappears upstairs, and I take a sip of morning brew, noting the caramel taste to it.

It's fucking delicious.

Reed smirks at me. "You like that, don't you?"

"How the hell did you make that, and do I have to buy one of those machines to do it?" I ask.

"I'll send you the link," he says, already tapping away on his phone. "Mads is a coffee nut, so we had to get one for the tour bus."

"You got a special made coffee machine for your tour bus?" I repeat.

"Yeah. Fucking worth it, too," he replies. "And link sent—if it even goes through. Where's your phone?"

"I left it upstairs. I honestly don't want to look at it all weekend," I admit.

Reed's smile falters just noticeably, and he turns back to the sauté pan in front of him.

Kamden comes down after a few minutes. I'm picking at the fruit I packed onto my plate—too overwhelmed by the rest of the choices that I chose to grab safe foods instead of trying new things. Kamden, though… he takes a big plate from the cabinet—after having a slap fight with Reed—and loads up the plate full of some of everything on the buffet.

As I'm gawking at the amount of food he's piling and wondering how the hell he's eating all of it, Reed slides a small plate with a massive cinnamon roll my way.

"Just trust me," he says, tearing off a piece of it and handing it to me. "If you try nothing else from this bar, try this."

I do, and I almost groan at the flavor and texture in my mouth. "That is amazing," I say without bothering to swallow. "That might be better than the orgasm you gave me this morning."

Kamden chokes, and Reed beams at me.

"Yeah, no, you didn't squirt for me like usual this morning," Reed says, almost as if he's in agreement. "I'm just going to have to take you back upstairs and try harder."

He grins sideways at me and turns his attention back to the stove.

"Where's Mom?" Kamden asks.

"Ah, probably showering," Reed replies. "I told her I'd finish up. Wren likes watching me cook."

I know he's trying to fuck with his brother.

"Preferably naked under his apron though," I say.

"Hey—" Reed swats at Kamden's hands coming across the island to the bacon. "Grubs off. It's too hot. You're going to ruin the crunch."

"The only way the crunch is ruined is if you cooked it wrong," Kamden argues.

Reed holds up a knife to Kamden's face. "It's cooked to perfection. Keep your hands off or I'll cut them off."

"Yes, chef," I mutter against the rim of my coffee mug, much to Reed's delight.

Kamden scoffs. "Yeah. Okay, big man. Like you'd ever hurt anyone."

"Yeah, you know, you're right," Reed says. "But she's not afraid of stabbing you," he adds, holding up his hand to show the angry scar.

I smile sarcastically at the look on Kamden's face, and he shakes his head, taking his plate over to the table to eat angrily. Reed smirks at me from the stove as he turns it off and starts checking to make sure everything is done before the rest of the house wakes up and comes down.

I take another sip of coffee, and as I do, Reed slips a plate in front of me. My eyes narrow at first glance, unsure why he would have made me a plate, until I realize what he's done.

He's made the same omelet he made me the morning of the premiere.

And he's moved the capers to the side.

"Mom always makes more food than anyone can eat because… well, you know. And I wasn't sure if you'd eat anything she made, or if it would be so overwhelming that all you ate was fruit—and I was right—but I knew you would eat this," he says.

There's a nervousness in his tone like he thinks I might shout or tell him not to embarrass me.

But all I want to do is kiss him.

Goddamn this restless feeling in my bones.

"You didn't have to," I say.

"I wanted to," he replies.

Reed smiles and sits down on the stool beside me, giving me a sideways nudge when he takes a croissant from the tray and bites down on it.

He's in the middle of chewing when I work up the nerve to lean over and kiss his cheek, anxiety making my heart cart-wheel when he looks confusedly at me.

"Thank you," I say softly.

Reed gulps his food and stares. "How much energy did that take?" he asks.

"Entirely too much. I think I might need to lay down again," I admit as I swiftly turn back to my food.

Reed chuckles and reaches over to squeeze my knee. "You're welcome," he says. "Though I fully expect a blowjob this afternoon," he adds quietly.

"I mean, of course. Why else would you do anything for me?" I reply.

"The special one," he goes on, brow elevating.

"Beggars can't be choosers," I taunt. "You'll get what I give you."

Reed beams. "So, ropes? Flogging? Was that a leather suit I saw in your suitcase?"

He says it a little louder than is appropriate for our conversation, and Kamden glances our way.

I turn my head and fully meet Reed's eyes. "You wanted the bunny suit, right?"

Kamden chokes on his juice.

"Hell yes. You brought the strap, too?" Reed asks, completely fucking with his brother at this point.

I twist my lips, trying to keep myself from smiling, and I coyly take a bite of my food. "An entire weekend with you? Yes. I definitely brought the strap," I say.

"Okay, can you two not?" Kamden asks in an exhausted voice, as if the conversation has him rolling his eyes. "Fuck, I need to borrow Koen's earplugs."

"What happened?" comes a new voice.

Andi and Mads are coming into the kitchen. Andi looks between the three of us and smiles knowingly. "Morning to you two," she says with a wink at me.

Mads stops to squeeze Reed's neck to the point that he winces. Reed jerks out of his grasp, but Mads just slaps him on the shoulder. "The fuck is Kam in a knot about?" he asks.

"They're talking about their sex life," Kamden replies.

"Oh yeah?" Mads glances my way. "Did you get to use those ropes I suggested yet?" he asks me.

"Not yet. Maybe later," I go along. "The cage was fun, though."

"Oh god, there's a cage?!" Kamden asks.

"How are you this bothered?" Andi asks him. "You grew up peeking through the garage door to watch him bang helpless teen girls who also didn't know where their clits were."

I choke on my drink, and Reed slaps my back in some attempt to help me get the water up. Mads stuffs one hand in his pocket and flicks Kamden's ear as he and Andi pass him by.

I still can't get over how pretty Andi is, not to mention how much more olive toned her light skin is in comparison to Reed's paleness. She looks so much like their father in that respect that it makes me wonder if her features are all from the mother that they all want to forget.

And watching her with Maddox... I'm every bit as jealous as I am of the couple at my yoga studio.

I glance at Reed, noting the same longing in his eyes, heavily disguised by his usual happiness, and for the briefest of moments, I wish I was the person who could make him that happy.

CHAPTER THIRTY-FIVE

I KEEP EXPECTING Wren to run away.

Every time my family gets loud or challenging, I'm terrified she's going to excuse herself, and I'll find her packing her bag upstairs, telling me it's all too much or that it reminds her of her own family in some way.

And I can't discern if that's a good or bad thing.

"How are you holding up?" I ask Wren as we head down the driveway toward the overlook on the other side of this hilltop.

She huffs. "Reed, you're so worried," she says, glancing my way. "Why?"

"Because I know my family can be loud and competitive and—"

"Yeah, the pancake eating contest this morning was unexpected, as was the drunken game of charades last night," she says.

I chuckle at the memory. "You fit in," I say, recalling how into the game of charades she got.

She smiles at the ground and starts to fidget with the water bottle in her hands. "We used to play charades on Mondays for pizza and games night. It was my dad's idea of keeping us from getting the Monday blues. My brother and I were always on the same team. It killed our older sister how good we were at it."

"Twin intuition?" I ask.

"Something like that," she says.

I eye her. "You cheated, didn't you?"

"Obviously," she replies. "Travis and I would stay up late on Sunday nights playing in our shared bedroom so that when Monday came, we knew exactly how we would act it out. Everyone pegged it on a twin thing. It always amazed our younger sister. She thought it was the coolest thing. But our older sister insisted we were cheating."

"No one believed her?"

"I think our parents both knew, but they didn't care." She takes a drink of water, slowing as we approach the overlook. "Being around your family... it reminds me of when things were easy and simple in my own."

"This is the first time you haven't shut down when I've asked about them," I say.

A heavy sigh leaves her, her gaze washing out over the vast valley below, and she twists the water bottle between her hands. "Sometimes it's easier to shut down than to have to lie to people."

"Why would you need to lie?" I ask.

"Because of how complicated things got," she answers.

We pause at the edge of the cliff, and I jump onto the rock at the drop-off. It's a flat rock, totally safe as long as I don't slip, but Wren stares at me like I've lost my mind anyway.

"Any last words before you fall off this cliff?" she asks.

I smile back and extend a hand to her. "Are you scared?" I ask.

"No," she says, though I can hear the hesitation in her voice.

"I'll catch you if you fall," I say, and I don't mean the edge of this cliff.

She watches me as if she knows it, too.

Wren steps up to the edge of the cliff beside the rock I'm standing on and pauses, wringing her hands in front of her again. "Do you ever think about what might happen if you just… stepped off?" she asks.

"I expect a full orchestra at my funeral," I say, hands on my hips. "Mads will give the most heart-wrenching eulogy ever known to man. And after, I want to be burned as if my body is a gift to appease the gods, followed by an extreme party."

She eyes me sideways, smiling despite herself. "Not entirely what I meant, but I'm glad to know you have that planned out."

I chuckle. "Nah, I know what you meant. Like the afterlife?" I ask, jumping down from the rock.

"Yeah," she replies.

"I like to think there's some universal energy keeping our souls here until the people we love no longer need us," I say. "Or until that energy transfers to another."

"Like reincarnation?"

"Yeah, something like that."

"I like that," she says. "It would be nice to think that they're not gone."

I consider her for a moment. I can see the nervousness in her eyes as if she's waiting on me to ask her about her family. As if she's working up the courage to say her next words.

"Wren?"

Her teeth clench, eyes blinking back whatever emotion is plaguing her right now.

"Just ask me," she breathes, avoiding my eyes.

I shift on my feet, insides twisting as I finally ask, "What happened to them?"

Wren wraps her arms around her chest, and I see the

moment when she puts on a numb face, when the emotion evacuates from her eyes, and not even the sting of the wind can pull tears out of her.

"A drunk driver hit my parents and younger sister coming home after my senior play," she confesses. "It… It sent their car around a tree, and they all died instantly."

My heart sinks.

Shit.

I don't know what I expected. I don't know what I thought I might hear. But it wasn't that.

"I'm sorry," I manage.

"The driver is behind bars for life. We got some ridiculous payout as if it would make up for what happened to them. Even so, I don't think any of us knew how to handle it."

She pauses for a moment, and through it, I don't move. I know she's working through her words and trying to stifle any true, vivid memories that might prompt an emotion she can't hold back.

"Alice was just fourteen. Travis and I were a month from graduating high school," she goes on as she sits on the rock I was just standing on.

"My older sister is a few years older than us, so even though he and I were already eighteen, she thought our parents dying meant she would have to be our new mother." Wren pauses to scoff. "I didn't need another mother. I needed my sister. And she turned into this overprotective, overbearing *monster*. She wanted to control us. Tell us how to dress, who we could be friends with, where we would go to college, what we needed to do with our money, with our lives… I know she did it because she thought she was helping, and because it probably made her feel better, though all it did was push us away."

"Eventually, Travis and I completely cut ties with her. We moved to LA. I started going to auditions, got a new, *older* boyfriend who wanted to 'take care' of everything for me. And

Travis… He was supposed to be going to school at UCLA. We lived together for a year, but then he started acting really weird. He wouldn't come home for a week at a time. He stopped texting me. I called and called. I even got the police involved, filed a missing persons report on him and everything. Turns out, he was off on a drug bender." She shakes her head in shame, her ears reddening. "I didn't even know he was doing more than weed. Shows you how much I was paying attention to him, right? I was so wrapped up in my own bullshit that I didn't even notice he was doing anything he could get his hands on."

I reach out and squeeze her knee as I see her eyes glistening.

"Police found him sleeping under one of the bridges," she goes on. "When I went down to talk to him, I told him he needed to get clean, and that I would help him, and for the next few years, we repeated that cycle. Over and over and over… I think I kept believing him because who the hell else did either of us have if we didn't have each other? My modeling career started to take off—I was getting jobs wherever and however I could get them, finally landing a few acting roles through contacts I made at different fashion shows. I got my agent, assistant, publicist, a bodyguard… All of them eventually knew what I was dealing with at home, drilled it out of me when they met Travis."

"About five years ago, though, I lost Travis for a good… six months? He'd been clean for almost a year. He was doing *so* much better. He'd started gaining weight. Had a proper job… Again, I called. My bodyguard put out a search through her network. The only thing I could remember him saying was that he had found a way to pay me back the money for rehab and letting him stay with me rent-free for so long. I kept telling him not to worry about it, but Travis wasn't one to stay in debt to family."

The hair on the back of my neck rises when she pauses to gather her thoughts, her knees swaying in a nervous way.

"Then on Christmas morning, I found him on my couch," she goes on, her voice beginning to catch. "He was… *fuck*, he was in a panic. He looked like he hadn't slept in days. I could hardly understand him when he started talking. I thought at first he was back on the drugs, but turns out it was something *so much* worse…"

Wren blows out an audible breath, pausing to swallow and catch her breath.

"He'd *stolen* from someone sketchy back home," she says as a tear drops down her cheek. "Fucking idiot. He'd tried to get into their group and double-cross them on a job. And he apparently succeeded. They'd found him a month after in Miami and told him he had to pay them back, and if he couldn't find the cash, then they'd take it in body parts."

Holy shit.

Another tear rolls down her face. She quickly wipes it away as if the salty drop is an insult. "Fuck, I shouldn't be telling you this," she says. "I shouldn't… You can't get mixed up in this. God, I'm so stupid—"

I grab her hand and kneel in front of her before she can run. "Hey—you're not stupid," I say. "I want to know. If you're willing. Tell me."

A muscle feathers in her jaw as she considers me. "You can't tell anyone about this, Reed. No one. The only reason I'm telling you is because…" She looks away and gulps, and I catch the next tear with my knuckle. She sniffs back her emotion, her voice thick when she says, "The only reason I'm telling you is so you understand why I can't let people close to me. Why this can never be… *real*, no matter how much either of us wants it."

My stomach knots at the words, heart dropping as an inappropriate smirk threatens my lips. "You want this to be real?" I ask.

A smile lifts into her glistening gaze, and she shoves me off-balance. "This is serious," she says.

I almost laugh, but I regain my footing and climb onto the rock beside her, nudging her when I sit.

"Tell me," I say softly. "Why can't I have you?"

She takes a deep breath, still toying with her fingers. "I flew across the country with Travis to try to talk to this guy. I thought I could offer him money, pay back whatever Travis had stolen. I was hoping it might be that simple, and I thought that if it was more complicated, I'd figure it out… There was a white SUV waiting for us when we landed. Travis hadn't told the guy that we were coming. He hadn't been in contact with him in weeks. Yet, there was the SUV. It was like an omen. I knew right then that this was more serious than he'd let on. And that was the day I met Damien Berzatto."

Something about the name makes my skin crawl. My ears perk, gaze zeroing in on her.

"Like mafia?" I ask.

Wren presses her lips together thinly, eyes rolling my way in an unimpressed stare. "He *thinks* he's mafia, but… he's new. I guess that's what makes him just as—if not more—dangerous. He's too fearful of his power being taken away from him. He gets spooked easily, makes irrational moves. He talks a big game, and I don't doubt any of what he says, but something about him doesn't feel as… powerful. It's like he's scared of fucking up and trying to prove to someone else how tough he is."

"What happened with your brother?" I ask.

Wren huffs. "Oh… Just one of Damien's irrational stunts," she says as if laughing about it is the only thing she knows to do. "Damien took one look at me, realized who I was, and decided I was a better asset to him than my brother could ever be. I thought I was bargaining for my brother's life. His for mine. Turns out their definition of 'letting him live' didn't mean letting him go home. It meant letting him live on in the bodies of others."

It feels like the world stopped spinning around us.

"What—like… like *organ trafficking?*" I ask, feeling bile rise in my throat.

She chews on her tongue and nods, her nostrils flaring with emotion. "He sent me Travis's eye a year after and told me he was always watching. Even when I didn't see him."

Mother fuck—

Wren chokes slightly as her tears begin to bubble over. "He follows anyone I'm close with. Any time I make a friend or even have coffee with someone, he sends me a photo. He's terrified that I'm going to get close enough to someone to tell them about him. I don't know what to do anymore. When we started this charade, he threatened you, and I've had to convince him nearly every week that it's all an act… Even just last week, he… He threatened you. He dragged me into his stupid fucking SUV and told me I had until after the wedding to get rid of you—even shot one of his goons while I was in the car."

Bananas.

"It's all my fault. Everything. All that's happened to them —to my parents. My sister. My brother. If my parents hadn't been coming back from my play so late, they would still be alive. My brother would never have gotten into drugs, or eventually killed—"

"It is not your fault," I say, taking her hands. "None of this is your fault."

I don't even know if she hears me.

"I live life in complete fear," she admits through a shaky voice. "Every single fucking day, I'm scared to wake up. A couple years ago, I was at my lowest point. I was so lonely, I—"

Her head drops into her palms, cries unable to hold back. "I don't know why I'm still here. I'm completely alone, and I always will be. And, god, I'm so fucking tired of feeling this way. Damien is the reason I don't allow myself to have friends or date anymore. I keep pushing people away just to protect them from my disaster. *You* especially."

My heart somersaults.

"Why me?" I ask.

"Because you're good, Reed," she says in a tired voice. "You don't deserve to be attached to this—to *me*. Look at all that you have. Your family. Your band. Everything in your life, they could come after it. Do you really want to put your family in jeopardy because of me?"

I fucking hate this.

This isn't fair.

My jaw is quivering as I stare at her. Because I know… god, I fucking know the answer to that question, and I can't bring myself to say it out loud.

"I'll figure it out," I manage, my voice sticking.

Her shoulders droop, and she wipes her tears harshly. "You can't," she breathes. She rises off the rock, and I'm stunned as I stare at her retreating figure. "You can't figure it out because he'll take you—"

"I don't care about me," I say.

"I do," she argues. "What if he takes someone in your family? Mads? Andi? *Your mother?*"

God mother fucking dammit.

She pushes her hands behind her neck and stalks in a circle. "What if he gets to you? Uses all of that against you? You'll be as trapped as I am. We can't be, Reed. We just… We can't."

I don't want to accept this.

I don't want to accept that there's nothing I can do to have her.

But the thought of my family hurting, or anyone getting hurt…

"Then give us today," I blurt out.

Give me today.

Let me love you today.

Wren stops and turns to look at me. "What?" she asks, tone nearly pleading.

I stand and cross the space between us, and when our chests bump, I wrap my hand around her cheek, feeling her soft hair against my fingertips. My chest swells as I stare into her eyes, my inhale jagged when I feel her lean into my touch. She's stunning in this light, the way the sun is soaking into her light auburn hair, and I gulp at the way she's watching me.

I'm pushing my luck; however, if I don't do it now, I don't know that I'll ever get the chance.

"Give us today," I say. "Fuck them. They're not around here. We can have today."

"Reed…"

"Please, Wren."

Because I'm not above begging on my hands and knees for a day of reality with you.

"Let me kiss you," I say, though my voice is barely audible.

She hiccups and starts to pull away, but I hold on tighter. "Reed, this is serious."

"I'm serious," I argue.

Her lips press together thinly. "You kiss me *all the time,*" she replies exasperatedly. "Even when I tell you not to. How is this any different? How is kissing me going to change *any* of this?"

"It won't, and I don't mean any kiss," I say. "I mean *kiss* you, bird."

Her gaze darts to my mouth, jaw twitching as if her voice is as stuck as mine. "What other way is there to kiss someone?" she asks.

I wrap both hands beneath her jaw. "With every fiber of your soul," I reply.

"Joke's on you. Gingers don't have souls," she breathes.

I chuckle, and our smiles lift just breaths apart. I hear the whisper of her own amused huffs, though her eyes are fixated on my lips, and I close the space between us to place a fleeting kiss on her mouth.

Again.

And again.

And *again*.

And with each kiss, I feel the ache in my heart growing.

"I want to kiss you like I mean it," I say breathlessly between kisses. "Like today is our last day. Like *this is real.*"

Her head nudges sideways, dodging my mouth, and my lips land on her cheek, her jaw, her neck. She fidgets with my shirt, head rolling and exposing her throat to me in a way that makes me feel as though she wants to run, but her legs won't move.

"It isn't real," she whispers. "It can't be."

"Maybe today it can," I almost beg.

Because I need her.

I need her to say that I'm allowed to feel what I'm feeling right now.

I need her to tell me that this is real.

Fuck that guy. Fuck being scared. Fuck everything else.

I *know* it's real. Even if it's only today. Even if it feels like we're both dying inside knowing that it's all we have.

I'm willing to part with my heart after this if it means I get to call her mine for one whole day.

She pulls back to look at me, and I see it. I see the same hunger in her eyes that I know rests in mine. Her jaw tightens just noticeably, visible debate running through her head.

I lean forward and press my lips to hers again in a desperate attempt to sway her, our eyes remaining open like this moment might disappear if we turn away from it. As if the reminder of our surrender is all we need to turn this fiction into reality.

"Maybe—maybe just today," she manages.

My heart drops.

She grabs my shirt, and I mutter, "Just today," once again. And when my lips are back on hers, I lose every ounce of restraint that my weakened body was once capable of.

Because I'm a goner.

Our kiss is a shock to my core. The way she's kissing me… it's as if she's allowing herself to be free. As if she's finally remembering what it felt like to not feel controlled by someone in the back of her mind.

Tears mingle on our cheeks. I think my heart might give out at any moment. It's completely irrational to think that this is the answer. But right now, I don't fucking care. She's let me in. She's trusted me enough to tell me she cares, that she wants this, too.

There's a soft smile on her lips when we part that weakens my knees. I curl my arm around her shoulders and pull her wholly into my arms, and she rests the back over her head on my forearm when she peers up at me.

"What can we do with one real day?" she whispers.

CHAPTER THIRTY-SIX

REED

IF I WASN'T ALREADY ENTIRELY TRANSFIXED on her before, I am now.

And if tonight, and maybe tomorrow, is the only time I have for this to be real between us—out of reach from photographers, the people she's running from, and everyone who might try to tear us apart… fuck. I'm taking advantage of it.

She feels… different. A little less guarded. Even her whimpers sound more genuine.

A little more… *free*.

I couldn't even wait for lunch before having her again. And maybe that's a stupid want when the sex is already so fucking amazing, but today, I get to hold her hands. I get to hear her tell me she wants more without fear of saying too much or catching herself when she's calling my name.

I have her spread on the bed, her heels digging into the mattress as she rolls against my tongue. Our hands entwined at her hips, the strength of her grip increasing with every suck on her clit and pulse of my opposite fingers inside her drenched pussy.

"Reed…" she moans, followed by a gasp. "Oh my—*shit*—"

Hearing her say my name while I'm inside her still sends

chills down my spine. Her knees hike as she cries out, her head coming off the bed to look down at me. I glance up, noting that she's biting her lip so hard that she could split it. She's trembling trying to hold back. Every little high-pitched sound coming from her wavers on stolen breath. Her arms are rigid, muscles shaking.

I hold her gaze and go all in, throwing her over the absolute, final whisper of her restraint. And when she spills on my tongue, soaking my face and the sheets, I taste my triumph.

Goddammit, that's amazing.

"There she is," I say, taunting her about the morning sex.

Her body's response to me is stunning, and knowing that I'm the only person who's ever made her release like this makes the victory even more sweet.

I release her hands and rake my palms up her sides as I kiss up her body, listening to her satiated whimpers and short breaths.

My lips meet hers as I reach her face, and she tightens her thighs around my hips, her legs eagerly pulling me to meet her. I grin crookedly against her mouth.

"Such a greedy little bird," I taunt. "You need more?"

"All of you," she breathes as her lashes lift.

The statement makes me pause. It's a surrender I hadn't anticipated, even with the walls down around us, and I wonder if what she's needed was someone to tell her it was okay to feel.

I swallow as my hair falls against her forehead, and I kiss her lightly.

"All of me."

I don't need her to be sure of this right now.

I know I'm hers.

Regardless of how this might end, she's enraptured me. Perhaps one day, if we make it past this, she'll feel comfortable enough to let me have all of her, to let me truly call her 'mine,' and not just in my head.

But today… today, I'll settle for simply being hers.

Our lips meet as her knees bend up to my ribs, and she entwines her fingers in my hair. I'm already fucking straining from watching her come. I grab her ass, spreading her wider, and when I push inside, a shudder rakes over my skin.

I realize we should be getting ready for the rehearsal dinner. Even still, I want to take my time. To slide languidly inside her, making sure to brush her spot with every stroke. To draw out the moans and whispers she sometimes holds onto for fear of giving in.

A groan leaves her as she takes every inch of me. Her pointed nails dig into my sides, and I have to curse at the agonizing pleasure of it. Her hair is blown out around her head on the pillow, chin jutting toward the ceiling as she drops her jaw and whines out the most beautiful little gasps.

I'm so fucking gone for her.

Lips meeting hers, I close the space between our bodies, letting my weight settle onto her chest, and she curls her forearms around my back, her fingers digging into the tops of my shoulders when she pulls me closer. We align as I spread my hand on her thigh and drive deeper.

I think we were made for this very moment.

She moves her hand onto my cheek when our lips part, and as I pick up my steady pace, she holds my gaze. Our jagged breath mingles. I feel her tightening around me. I'm straining to hold on, refusing to give over to this until she finds her own again.

I angle differently, and she sucks in a sharp whimper that ignites the fire in my heart.

"There?" I ask as I repeat.

Her slack jaw trembles, head nodding. "Yes—Fuck, yes, right there, Reed," she says, her chest rising off the bed. "My god, right *there*," she whines. She gasps, and a little laugh leaves her that makes me smile myself.

"Shit, how do you do this?" she breathes, one hand on the headboard, that smile still tugging on her lips.

"If I didn't know you so well, I'd say you were enjoying this, bird," I taunt her.

"Don't stop," she says, arching her back. "You feel amazing."

"You're so tight for me," I breathe. "Are you coming?"

"Right there—yes." Her body curls into mine, her pussy pulsing. She sucks in a sharp breath. "Right there—right there —*fuck*—"

A high-pitched squeal leaves her. She whines and strains, and I feel her coming hard around me. The dig of her nails in my shoulders sends me. I tremble, my body giving out, and I come just seconds after.

My breath is jagged as my forehead drops to the crook of her neck. I can feel her rapid heartbeat against my forehead, feel it slowly come down from the high.

I'm trembling as I slide out of her, and when I see our releases seeping from her spent pussy, my mind goes blank. Before I realize what I'm doing, my face is between her thighs. I lap my tongue in her cunt and lick our cum into my mouth.

"Reed," she gasps.

And with our collective cum trickling from the corners of my lips, the taste of us in my spit, I let the mixture drip from my tongue onto hers.

She swallows like it's the only sustenance she'll taste today, and I have to kiss her again before I lose my shit.

"You like the taste of us, little bird?" I ask breathlessly.

"Yes," she whimpers, licking my tongue against hers.

I reach between her thighs and wet my fingers once more, the milky white cum coating the digits, and I drag them over her throat to her parted lips where she sucks them into her mouth as if she's starving.

"The things you do to me shouldn't be legal," I manage.

She takes my fingers and turns them toward me, pushing them into my own mouth to taste us, and it's then, that I abso-fucking-lutely know:

Wren Kelly is my vice.

She's the addiction that's going to take me out. A fucking weakness destined to disrupt everything I've worked for.

So why am I so *desperate* to keep her?

I wrap my arms around her waist and bring her flush, enclosing her entirely in my grasp as she settles her forearms on my chest. I could stay like this for days. The way her soft curves press against my body is fueling. I love grabbing her, massaging her, burying myself in her…

I lean forward, our noses brushing as she scratches her nails against my jaw.

"I wish I had never laid eyes on you, Reed Matthews," she says softly.

I chuckle under my breath and push the stray hair out of her face. "Success," I tease, and something of a smirk lights up her eyes. I squeeze her tighter upon seeing it and pull her thigh up over mine so I can rake my fingers down the back of it.

"Why do you wish you'd never laid eyes on me?" I ask.

"Because you're debilitating," she answers. "And some-how… somehow, your chaos is my calm," she admits. "And I know that doesn't make any sense because I'm just as chaotic on the inside as you are on the outside, and you're… god, you're *you*, and you don't mind me being as scattered as I am… and… and now, I'm rambling—"

"It's a good thing I speak ramble," I say, and she groans defeatedly.

I laugh at the pink shade rising on her cheeks when she dips her head in embarrassment. "Start over," I tell her.

Her eyes light up when they meet mine, and with a deep inhale, she begins to speak again.

"I meant to say that somehow, you calm me," she says. "You calm my mind and my nerves, and you do it while being entirely yourself. And I absolutely hate you for it."

Another laugh ripples out of me.

"I mean, honestly, who gave you permission to come in and ruin me?" she goes on, and I think my family can hear me laughing ten bedrooms away.

"I was fine being closed off in a prison where no one could get close to me, and you just… You wormed your way in," she says.

"How fucking dare I disrupt the angry bird's life?" I grin.

"How *fucking* dare you," she sighs.

She relaxes into the pillow, her eyes softening to the point that my laughter wanes, and I shift forward to kiss her. And when our lips meet, my heart does that same somersault it did earlier.

"Do you know why I stopped you the other night?" she asks. "When I used the safe word?"

"Why?"

"Because you were *everything*," she says. "And it just hit me as I was laying there beneath you. Everything you'd done for me. Everything you'd *been* for me. From the moment you cornered me in that fucking bathroom to crawling on your knees on a red carpet. And you did it without asking for something in return. You're this person who I don't deserve. I think I wanted you to yell at me for stopping you and saying that word. I think I was hoping that with Foster mentioning the New Year's Eve show that you'd realize you'd tired yourself and wasted months of your life for a woman who would never be able to pay you back for everything."

"I never wanted anything in return," I say.

I just want you.

"Do you want to hear something fucked up?" she asks.

"I love your fucked up stories," I say as I flop on my back.

"When they told me I needed to start dating you just to be more 'likable,' I wanted to quit," she says, meeting my eyes. "God, it fucking hurt so much… It was like, once again, I'd be leaning on someone else to get me to where I wanted to be. Like I couldn't do it on my own. And if I'm being totally honest, I think I wanted it to fail—I wanted *you* to fail."

The rope around my stomach twists and knots, my heart aching for her.

"It sounds so stupid when I say it out loud," she admits. "Especially when I've been dragging you through this with me."

A smirk threatens my lips, and I lean up on my elbows over her. "Yeah. I've got fucking scrapes all over from your dragging. Bruises on my ego. A broken heart… I think you should make it up to me before this is over."

She almost smiles. "How do you propose I do that?"

"Dance with me tomorrow," I suggest.

Wren gives me a confused look. "Dance with you? That's all you want?"

"I don't mean just the slow dancing shit," I say. "I mean, I get to drag you across the floor and actually dance with you. Possibly mosh a little—depending on what music we have going."

"That sounds exhausting," she says. "Can't I just suck your dick by that pretty piano?"

"You'll be doing that anyway," I tell her. "This is my added bonus."

She snickers, and I wrap my hand around her ass and squeeze, then lower to kiss her softly.

"I love when you do that," I say when we part.

"What?"

"Smile because of me."

Her lips draw behind her teeth, though I can see the amusement in her eyes. "You're gross," she says. "Don't say that again."

"I'm the reason you smile—I'm using it to my advantage."

"I have never met anyone so full of themselves," she teases.

I snort. "Yeah, no one except yourself, Miss I-love-when-you-get-angry-because-of-me," I joke.

"It's fun to watch," she teases me. "You're completely bothered by it—"

"Yeah, I know—"

"—It's like pissing off a cat," she ignores me. "One second you're purring and playing wildly, then scratch your belly, and you hiss."

I groan and sink my head onto her chest. "God, you and that bratty mouth."

She snaps her teeth when I look at her, a playfulness in her eyes that I'm fucking feral for.

Maybe I am a cat.

"What are you going to do about it?" she asks.

"Right now?"

"Right fucking now," she dares.

I grab her legs and flip her onto her stomach, making her yelp with the swiftness, and before she has time to gather her wits, I strike her ass—

Hard.

An unexpected screech leaves her, followed by a groan that sends her melting into the mattress. She buries her face in the pillow, her spread knees dragging up beneath her. I slap her ass again, making her jump.

Fuck, that's pretty.

She whimpers at the third strike, and when she groans my name after the fourth, I gently drag my fingers over the tender area. It causes her to flinch, and I smile upon seeing it.

"Do you like your ass turning red, bird?" I ask.

She picks her face up from the mattress and arches her back. "No," she says.

I slowly slide my finger between her cheeks toward her entrance. "No? So, I won't find you soaked for me already?"

"No," she repeats.

My middle finger reaches her already swollen pussy, and I tut my tongue at her. "You're a dirty little liar," I say before striking her ass again.

Again.

"Yes," she whimpers out, her voice nearly sounding like a plea. "Yes. Fuck, Reed—*more*," she whines.

"More?" I chuckle quietly. "Greedy girls don't get what they ask for."

"I'll be good," she begs, and when she tauntingly wiggles her ass, I nearly lose my shit.

I bend over her and kiss my way down her spine, all the while brushing my fingers over her raw, angry ass cheek—the shade of her skin as violent as I've ever seen her skin.

Her timer goes off.

The noise of it causes both of us to groan. I sink my forehead to her ass cheek, closing my eyes and taking one more moment to memorize this bubble we've created around us.

"Hit the snooze," she says, and I lift my head to frown at her.

"Bad idea," I say.

"I allowed an extra ten minutes in the alarm time, so snooze," she tells me.

I almost laugh. "You added in buffer time?"

"I always add in buffer time," she argues.

The grin spreads on my face. "That's cute," I say. "As much as I would love to keep spanking your ass and clit until you come for me again, I know if we're late to this, my dad will have my fucking head," I add, rolling off of the bed. "We'll have to resume this tonight."

Wren sits up, hands pressing into the mattress behind her as she watches me. "Why did you say 'that's cute' as if you know some secret about me that I don't?"

"Nothing," I say as I pick up my suitcase and slam it onto the bed.

One more quirk that I commit to memory.

Zeb shouts down the hall then, asking if we're ready as some of the other guests have started to arrive, and it sends Wren and I into a scramble to get ready.

I don't even have time to fuck her in the shower again.

The entire time I'm getting ready, I'm trying not to think about this too hard. Maybe I shouldn't have told her we could be real today. It feels like an added pressure to try and fit everything into a single day.

Yet, as I look at her in the navy long-sleeve velvet dress hugging every inch of her stunning body, her hair in perfect waves, lashes long and lifting to watch me through them, I forget every thought.

We're halfway down the hall when I push her against the wall just to kiss her again. She responds with a smile against my lips, and I swear, I don't know how much more my heart can swell when it comes to her.

Even so, it somehow does.

"Don't forget your word tonight," I tell her.

"Why would I need it?" she asks.

"Because all of our aunts and uncles and cousins are here," I reply.

"Oh my god, *there are more of you?!*" she exclaims.

I chuckle and kiss her softly once more. "Even more tomorrow."

"I might have to take Mads up on the gummy," she says.

"Honestly, I'm surprised you've lasted this long," I say.

I lean down and kiss her deliberately one more time,

lingering on her taste for as long as it takes my heart to stop doing cartwheels.

A long fucking time.

So long that she chuckles against my lips, and, god, that little smile pressed against mine… it does something to me. Maybe it's that I know it's rare. Maybe it's that I know *I'm* the reason it's on her lips. Or maybe it's the dilation in her green eyes when she finally pulls away from me.

Either way, I'm lost in what we should be.

Fuck, this is going to hurt.

CHAPTER THIRTY-SEVEN

REED

DURING THE REHEARSAL DINNER, I steal every glance from her that I can without appearing too obsessed or protective.

Or at least, I thought I was.

Every laugh and mean-girl comeback she comes up with talking to my family makes me fall a little harder. I don't know how she puts on such a face, or maybe it's that she doesn't feel the need to be as guarded around a group of people who aren't judging her or expecting her to act a certain way.

And maybe that's the difference.

"What if I don't want it to be over?" I say later that night to Mads.

Mads and I are out on the back lawn, sleeping bags set up on the grass in front of us. We promised each other we would spend the night before his wedding outside, just us, like we used to do in the backyard growing up. Leaving Wren upstairs, knowing the fucking lingerie she was wearing beneath that dress, nearly killed me.

But I love my best friend, and there's no way I'd run out on him on his wedding night.

We're leaned against a set of large rocks built into the landscape overlooking the vast valley and mountain range beyond. I wish I could say that we're talking about the universe and being a small, minuscule part of it.

However, I'm the bastard that is only consumed with the girl he can't have.

Mads smirks sideways at me, and I throw a pebble at his face.

"Fuck you, dude," I say. "Don't smirk at me like that."

But Mads just chuckles. "I told you not to get involved," he says.

"Yeah? You knew this would happen?" I ask.

"Dude, *you* fucking knew it was going to happen," he laughs. "You were already halfway obsessed with her to begin with. Angry-obsessed, but still. What—you thought you'd be able to date that beautiful creature, fuck her senseless, and not fall for her?"

I rub my hand against the back of my neck, smiling sheepishly at the ground. "Something like that," I mutter. "Or... I thought if it did happen, it wouldn't be this complicated."

"What do you mean?" Mads asks.

My mind drifts to the secrets she told me earlier, and I push my hand through my hair.

"What's up?" Mads asks as he sits up.

"She told me some things today. Reasons why she's scared," I answer.

"Does it have to do with those guys that follow her?" Mads asks. "Or the ones that follow you?"

I stare at him. "How the hell do you know about that?"

Mads slumps back against the rock and sighs. "Perks of hiding behind a mask for years," he says. "You start to notice the people who also don't want to be noticed. Anyone following my best friend is my business, too."

I huff and nervously scratch the back of my neck again. "Yeah," I say. "Yeah, it has to do with them."

"You don't have to tell me what it's about. That's her business. But if you need me…" His brow raises my way, and I shake my head, mildly amused.

"Newly married man in shady shit? My sister would murder me with her bare hands," I reply.

"Probably," he agrees. "Or she'd be right beside me with a fucking bat."

"Also true," I say with a chuckle.

The cold rock hits my back when I relax, and I gawk at the glittering sky, though I barely comprehend the beauty of the stars and galaxies so clear beneath this cloudless night. Emotions from earlier eat at me—the thought of how alone she's been made to feel. Trapped, even.

I want to pull her out of it. I want to tell her she doesn't have to be alone anymore.

"I can feel your mind running," Mads says without looking my way. "Energy feels like a nervous hamster ball."

I scoff. We've always been able to tell when the other is feeling heavier than normal.

"Weird, right?"

"Really fucking weird," Mads agrees. "Wheels turning about music or just life is one thing. We're usually on the same page, running on the same wheel. This is new."

A smile lifts my lips as I inhale a deep breath. "She was telling me how alone she felt. No family left. No friends…"

"She has us," Mads says. "You."

"I mean before all of this," I say. "I've never really worried about being alone. Big family. You. The band. I've always known you would have my back. And if you weren't there, god fucking help if Zeb or Bonnie were."

Mads laughs under his breath, hands resting on his stomach. "Zeb, man. He listens to all those crime podcasts. He'd be the one you call to clean up the body."

"Give us a lecture on improper disposal technique,

though," I say.

Mads laughs. "Disposal techniques? Is that your euphemism for murder?"

I chuckle. "Can you fucking imagine?"

But Mads sighs and looks out at the stars, head resting on the cool rock. "Yeah, man. I can," he says solemnly.

It's easy to forget what happened to Mads and Andi when you see them as happy as they are together, how well they hide what they went through to be what they are now.

Mads rarely talks about it, and I don't blame him. Seeing him lose his mind in that moment was the hardest thing I've ever watched. And the fight that I had with him after… fuck, sometimes I want to kick myself for it. My best friend was bleeding out, yet all I could think about was him breaking his promise never to sleep with my sister.

I joke about it now because I've never seen him thriving like he is.

Even so, the memory is haunting.

"What was that like?" I ask him.

He toys with the smoke between his fingers for a moment. "I honestly don't remember," he admits. "All I could see was Andi, and how fucking scared she was. I don't know the exact moment when he took his last breath. I don't even remember the look on his face when I started hitting him… whether he asked me to stop or begged for his life. It's all just… It turned into a blur of blood and pain and memories of her mom taking her away as a kid, and I…"

Mads wipes his face with his palm and sits up, the pain of that night shrouding his features.

"Don't ever tell me what happened," he says, eyes rising to mine.

I take a swig of my hard cider as the memory fades, and I block out the noises that guy had indeed made while Mads was beating the life out of him.

"The thought never crossed my mind," I say.

He raises his cider to mine, the bottles clink together, and we relax back to the sound of the crickets chirping nearby. It's quieter than I'm used to—the quietest space I've ever been a part of.

I can practically feel the invasive thoughts beginning to pour in and cloud my mind like the plume of visible breath when I exhale.

"Fucking cold out here," Mads says after a minute. "Too quiet."

"Yeah it is," I agree.

"I thought it'd be nice to clear my head," he adds.

"Nothing about my head feels clear right now." I turn in his direction, noting that he's pulled his hood up over his hat.

"Want to go in?" I ask.

"Yeah, fuck this." Mads rises off the ground, and I laugh when he dusts off his pants and extends a hand to me. "It's pretty to look at, though."

"Better with a bonfire," I say as I get to my feet. "*Best* with someone sitting on my lap to warm me up."

"Ah, tit mitts," Mads says, and I snort.

"Tit mitts?" I repeat.

"Yeah." He places his hands on his chest. "Hands under her shirt between her tits and ribs. Keeps your fingers warm."

A cackle leaves me that echoes into the valley. "Fucking hell, Mads," I laugh. "What about thigh mitts? You get added warmth between those."

"Nah, thigh mitts get me in too much trouble," Mads says as we start back to the house. "Have to leave that for back in the room." He glances back over his shoulder at the open sky and takes a draw from his vape. "How long did we last out here? Like twenty minutes?"

"Ten minutes longer than I thought we would," I reply. "Where do you want to sleep?"

"Ah, I don't care as long as we have some heat," he says.

My gaze narrows in on the mansion of a cabin, thinking about the rooms I'd read about before booking. "Oh, shit, there's a theater room with massive recliners."

"Do they have popcorn stocked in this place?" Mads asks.

"What kind of place has a theater and no popcorn?" I ask.

"Weird places," he replies.

I chuckle and glance up toward the illuminated window in the bedroom where Wren is, and the thought of earlier today causes my stomach to twist with the anticipation of what could be tomorrow. How stunning she'll be in whatever dress she decides to adorn herself in. Her ginger hair in that cascade of waves just over her shoulder and meeting her breast. Fuck, I hope she wears the dark lipstick.

"Tomorrow, man," I say, stuffing my hands into my jacket pockets.

"Fucking tomorrow," Mads says, and I'm sure he's thinking of what Andi will look like when she comes down the aisle.

I clap his shoulder and give him a shake, and he grins at the ground. He blows out an audible breath, swallowing when he looks up toward the room she's in.

"I get to marry her tomorrow," he says softly.

I'm jealous of the elation on his face, of the emotional glisten in his eyes. Even so, I don't let it show.

Mads deserves to be the happiest mother fucker on the planet.

"Yeah, you do," I say as I grasp both his shoulders.

A hiccup of a laugh sounds from him again as if it's just hitting him. "Dude, I get to fucking *marry* her," he repeats, and this time his gaze meets mine. "*Dude—*"

I can't help but to laugh at him, my head throwing back, hands clapping together. Mads looks like he suddenly can't breathe—to the point that he wobbles on his feet and has to sit on the patio steps.

"My god, man—"

"I don't fucking deserve her," Mads interjects over me, his voice full of disbelief and nerves. "The hell is she thinking?"

His eyes lift to mine, and I grin.

"I can't for the life of me figure it out either," I tease him. "I mean you're a homicidal maniac. Beard hasn't been brushed since we got here. You drink as much as you can through a straw so that you don't have to hold back your 'stache. Don't get me started on the way you dress—are you missing a flannel convention this week? Every day you've been in either a hoodie or plaid and a beanie—"

Mads laughs, hauls to his feet, and shoves me backward. "Fuck off, emo poser boy."

I stumble and grab my stomach. "Ah, yeah, little bird likes choking on this emo poser boy now."

"Surprised she's choking," Mads retorts. "You must be using that strap-on."

"Nah, that's for her," I say with a wink, and Mads howls back with laughter. I grin crookedly, delighted hearing him laugh without restraint.

I press my hands to my hips, hair falling into my lashes as Mads comes down from his hysterics. He wipes the tears from under his eyes and shakes his head at me.

"Ah, fuck," he mutters, gathering his wits. "Goddammit. I love you, man."

I chuckle under my breath. "I love you, too, brother."

We bring it in for a hug, clapping one another on the back as we sway for a moment long enough to even our breaths. And when we pull apart, I brace my hand on his bearded face.

"You deserve this, Mads," I tell him. "You deserve her. You deserve every happiness—the entire fucking world, and there's no one who could love my sister the way you do. And honestly, I don't think there's any other girl I'd approve of to love you either."

Mads scoffs as we part. "I thought I was the overprotective one in our relationship," he says.

"You bring it out in me," I say, and he shakes his head, still grinning.

"A long way from punching me in the face over being with her," he jokes.

"Yeah, well, fuck what my immature brain ever thought," I reply. "I've known you were in love with her since we were like thirteen. I think I was just jealous of it. It's like you've always known she would be the one you'd be with the rest of your life because no one could compare to the way you felt for her. And I had no idea what that was like."

"Do you have an idea now?" he asks.

The rope around my stomach tightens, and I scratch my neck. "I don't know that anyone can love someone as much as you love her," I say.

Mads presses his hands to his hips and glances around us for a beat. "You said bird explained that you two really can't be together?" he finally asks.

"Yeah," I say solemnly.

"How does that make you feel?"

"Like I want to vomit," I admit. "Like I want to kidnap her, change her name, her hair, fake her death, and hide her for five years until her name is just a ghost. Until she can walk in the sunlight without fear."

Mads raises his brows. "That's elaborate."

"That's what it would take," I say. "That's the measures it might take to set her free from this just so we can be together."

A smile flinches on his lips. It rises into his eyes, pride and amusement seeping behind it. "Then you're there, man. That's it," he declares.

"What's it?"

"Fucking *love*," he says like it's obvious. "You think I'm the only bastard capable of loving someone so much that you'd do literally anything to keep them? You're fucking there with me."

I feel a lump swell in my throat, and my jaw tightens, yet Mads's eyes seem to be brightening.

"You're looking at me like I'm crazy," he says.

"It's definitely debatable," I say, making him laugh.

But I'm not seeing the amusement. I'm confused, unsure of what I'm feeling or if he's just fucking manic.

"How do you know?" I ask. "What if it's just lust? What if it's only addicting because it's something new?"

Mads threads his hands behind his neck and begins to pace in a circle as if it's the only way to get this sudden energy out.

"Because love like *that*… shit, love like that makes you want to do completely irrational things," he says when our eyes meet. He's using his hands to speak, his excitement and declaration striking me to my core. I can't look away from his gaze, not when he's so certain about this, not when he's losing his mind over it.

"Just fucking… Ah. It makes you want to do things that you think no one else is going to understand. It makes you feel like you're going insane because you don't know if you're even capable of the lengths you want to go to for this person—if need be."

"Like obsession?" I ask.

"Yeah, it's an obsession, and yet… fuck, that word doesn't include the whole of if. Obsession doesn't include the feeling in your gut," he says, pointing to his stomach. "Obsessing over someone is only at the surface. It's all in your head, not your heart. Love… that's in your every fucking fiber. Through your whole soul, dude. Yeah, it'll feel obsessive. It'll feel like every moment with her isn't enough. You'll look at her and think you've suddenly lost your mind because the memory of life before her feels like it didn't belong to you. Loving her is maddening and thrilling and even when you can't catch your breath, it's still what's keeping you alive. And it's the *best fucking feeling there is*. You'll wake up gasping for air and thanking her for it. You'll hate it and want more. It hurts more than any physical pain ever could, and yet, somehow, all you'll remember is the elation. It's fucking chaos on the body, on your heart—on your *sanity*. And *that's* the kind of love I want for you. Because that's how I feel every fucking day that I'm with your sister."

Somewhere through his speech, I stop breathing.

Somewhere in his words, I lose myself.

Because the tear rolling down my cheek is overwhelming. The burning sensation behind my eyes has my jaw quivering.

God fucking dammit.

Mads steps up to me and braces his hands on my face, emotion radiating in his stern expression. "And the thing about you, is that with all that inside you, what you'll do for her will be even more volatile than anything I've ever done."

My eyes narrow. "How's that?" I manage.

"Because you can't hide it," he says. "You wear it on your face. Every fucking person in this house can see it when you look at her. *You're there*, man." He releases me and steps back, hands clapping in front of him.

"What are you going to do about it?" he asks.

I swallow as I stare at him, my hands still stuffed in my pockets. I'm numb, and it isn't just from the cold air swirling around us.

"I really fucking hope those are your vows tomorrow," I choose to say.

Mads scoffs and hangs his head. "Ah… not quite. Haven't written them," he says with a shrug.

"What?" I ask in disbelief.

"I'll figure it out when I'm looking at her," he says, and his face softens like he's imagining that very moment. "God, I can't wait to marry her," he breathes.

I want that.

I want everything he just said.

I want to feel this nervous happiness that he's wearing on the surface.

I want to be so excited about spending the rest of my life with someone who I can't believe chose me. I want to be so surprised by them that I question their decision every day.

And even on the days when I swear I don't deserve them, I want to love them anyway.

Wren's face fills my mind, the lump resurfacing in my throat.

I want it to be her.

Mads looks up toward the house and glances left, then jerks his chin in the direction of the kitchen. "Want to make some snacks? Get out of this cold?

"Like munchie snacks?" I ask.

He grins. "Hell yeah," he says. "Munchie snacks and a horror movie."

I chuckle at his plan. "Let's fucking go, man," I agree.

We walk up the steps in silence, our boots scrubbing on the cold cement, and I see Mads fumbling with something in his jacket pocket. A nervous energy surrounds us both, and it makes me giddy with the anticipatory visions of their wedding.

Because I know that Mads and Andi are both going to lose their shit.

"Listen—" Mads starts, still staring at the ground, "—if I'm a blubbering idiot at the altar tomorrow—"

"If you're *not* a blubbering idiot tomorrow, I'm going to punch you again and give you something to cry about," I interject.

Mads laughs softly and reaches for the door handle. "Just have some fucking tissues ready in case."

CHAPTER THIRTY-EIGHT

WREN

MORNING BREAKS ENTIRELY TOO EARLY.

I spent half of the night binging a reality show on the huge tv in the bedroom, unable to go to sleep out of fear for not knowing what today might bring.

I'm still reeling over admitting so much to Reed, over the way he reacted and how he'd made me feel the rest of the day.

Shit. I want it to be real, too.

I can smell coffee coming from downstairs. I don't know if Reed is coming up to shower or if he's spending the morning with Mads. And my fucking phone is only picking up wifi signals, no bars. Though, I'm not about to try to message him over any social media app. The number of DMs he gets in a day has to be insane already.

It's been nice not being able to receive messages. No looking over my shoulder to see if anyone is following. No SUVs pulling up unexpectedly. No weird phone calls or threatening texts…

I'm petrified that Damien will somehow find his way here or get his hands on an invitation to this wedding.

Stop obsessing about the things you can't control.

One day.

Give yourself one more day of happiness before it's over.

I pull on one of Reed's sweatshirts and my leggings then head downstairs, unsure of what to expect with the security blanket of his presence now absent. Yet even without him, I find myself more at ease around his family than I am around my own colleagues.

Andi is lying on the bench seat of the breakfast nook, her phone in her hands, coffee on the table. She's smiling at something on the screen, though when she sees me coming around the corner, she sits up.

"I'm glad I'm not the only one that slept in," she says.

"Where is everyone?" I ask as I go to the coffee machine.

I have no idea how to work this thing, but I'm going to try anyway.

Andi yawns. "They all went on a hike this morning," she says. "I was instructed not to leave the kitchen until someone told me I could. Mads sent me a couple of pictures. He said they'd be back after lunch to start getting ready. Reed was going to wake you, but then mentioned something about giving you a social break to yourself."

I can't figure out this fucking machine, so I turn on the kettle on the stove.

"I think he's terrified you're going to run away," Andi adds.

I huff amusedly. "I should hide when he gets back just to fuck with him," I say as I take a banana from the bowl and sit on the bench seat across from her.

"Please do that. I think I might pay to see him in a panic," she says. She sinks her temple onto her curled fist, elbow bent on the table, and she smiles at the phone as if she's in a trance.

"I get to marry my best friend today," she says softly, her gaze flickering up to mine. She chuckles under her breath and straightens, sighing as she does. "God, that sounds so cheesy."

"I think I just vomited a little," I say, and Andi beams at me.

"Oh yeah? You'll want to get a barf bag for later, then—I think Tina keeps a few with her. Dad gets sick on the airplane," she explains.

A chuckle leaves me, yet before I can reply to her, I feel my phone vibrating in my pocket. I frown as I take it out, the surprise of hearing it ring making my stomach drop.

Larry's name is on the screen, calling me from a message app.

"Weird," I mutter, knowing it's barely seven a.m. in LA.

"Early for your people, isn't it?" Andi asks.

"Yeah," I reply, suspicious about the call. "I'll just be... Hello?" I answer as I stand to slip outside.

Thank fuck the patio is heated as I forgot my shoes inside.

"Hi, my love," Larry drawls, his voice entirely too chipper for how early it is.

I yawn. "What—is something wrong? I thought I was getting the weekend to myself," I ask him.

"Ah, well, that's not exactly—*hey!*—let me tell her—"

Another voice sounds in the background, an audible scuffle over the phone ensuing.

"What's going—"

"Hi, Wren."

Amanda.

My brows somehow furrow even more.

"Mandy?" I ask. "What's up?"

"Well, I just wanted to personally call and tell you—okay, well, two things actually."

"Which are?" I ask.

"First, you'll be pleased to know that you're officially released from your relationship arrangement on Tuesday," Amanda says. "The breakup statement has been drafted for both parties and approved by PR. You'll be a free bird after."

Now, I really want to vomit.

"Oh," is all I can say.

There's a beat of silence where I know she's thinking I'll be thanking her for the out and celebrating my freedom.

"Wren?" Amanda calls me.

"Hm? Oh. Right. Okay. Yeah. What's the second thing?"

"You got it," she says. "You got the part. It's all in writing."

My knees weaken, and I sink into a crouched position. There's a hollow pit in my stomach where the excitement should be.

"That's amazing," I stagger out, though my jaw is already beginning to shake.

Reed…

"Also, we have you on a red-eye out at three a.m., so Tara will be at the cabin to pick you up around one tonight. You'll take the smaller aircraft out of the local airport like before, and then switchover to a direct to LA in Nashville. As long as there are no delays, you'll make the confirmation dinner with Amber. Larry will meet you at the airport and bring you up to speed on everything you've missed."

I barely hear her.

Because all I can think about is Reed.

Oh, god, Reed…

My heart sinks. I hate the emotion rising behind my eyes. I hate the way my insides seem to be crumbling apart. I don't understand why hearing it from her hurts this much. I knew it wouldn't last. I knew this weekend was all we had.

I should have known better than to let us be 'real' yesterday.

And yet, I want it to be real again today. Damn if my heart somehow breaks further—

Or if I leave this place tomorrow without it.

Where the rest of my life leads, I don't need it anyway.

Not when it belongs to him.

I end the phone call with only an agreement to her plans. My eyes are clouded with tears I didn't realize were forming.

Turning away from the house, I inhale a deep breath, press my hands to my hips, and try to clear the staggering emotion threatening to rip through my exterior.

I need to see him.

I need to talk to him.

My chest is still caving when I find the strength to walk back inside. Thank fuck, it's still only Andi in this kitchen. The kettle whistle is going off, the noise of it barely registering as I rely on my feet to get me where I need to go.

"Everything all good back home?" Andi asks, turning off the kettle.

"Yeah. Yeah, all good. Um… I'm actually not hungry. I'm just… I'm going to lie down for a few minutes." I finally look at her, and Andi gives me a small smile that I wish to hell I could return, and as I start to leave the room, Andi calls me back.

"Hey Wren?"

"Yeah?" I turn.

She stirs the coffee she's making with one of the caramel spoons Reed used yesterday morning, then approaches me with it. "I know the premiere is over," she says, and my stomach drops. "So, if you're breaking up with my brother, do it after tonight. Let him have today." She slides the coffee across the island to me and pauses. "Give *yourself* today," she adds softly.

"Why do you say it like that?" I ask.

Andi gives me a knowing look before taking a sip of her own coffee from a mug with Jack Skellington and Sally on it. It's a look that tells me she can see how much I'm drowning when it comes to her brother, and perhaps that she's seen the same desperation on his face as well.

I stare at the mug, unable to stop myself when I ask, "Why Jack and Sally?"

Andi's expression softens. "Because they each save one

another in the end." She presses her lips together in a thin line and straightens. "Have fun today, Wren. You deserve it."

You deserve him, is what she doesn't say.

I feel my nostrils flare, feel the tears sting the back of my eyes. Even still, I don't reply with anything more than a nod, and I take the coffee back to my room in the hopes that somehow, I'll walk into another reality when I shut the door.

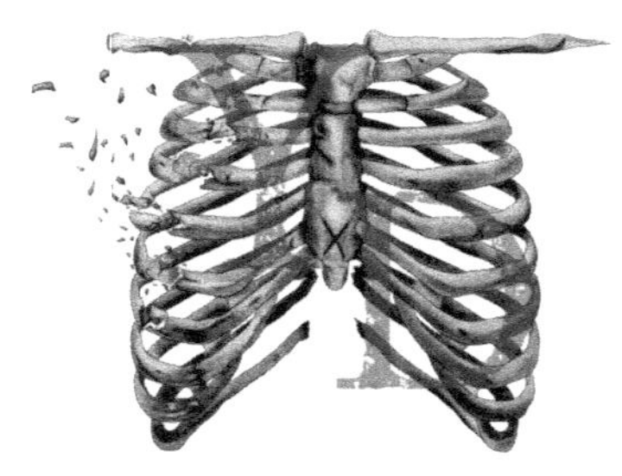

WE'RE REAL

Meet me at the piano?

It's an hour before the ceremony. I stare at the text, wondering when the hell he keeps changing his name in my phone. However, the question drops as the sight of my angry red nail bed catches my eye.

I'm so nervous that I've picked the skin around my nails so bad the last hour that I have more than one bleeding.

I have to tell him.

Fuck, I hope his publicist hasn't called him yet.

I know what Andi said, and for the last few hours, I've

debated even bringing up my agent calling me about it. But I don't think I can get through tonight without talking to him about this, without setting those expectations so that there's no question when I have to leave later.

I already have all of my things packed up, clothes to wear to the airport folded on the bed.

I look at myself one last time in the mirror, adjusting the split of my dress on the left leg and the hem of the long sleeve on my wrist.

As much as I love this dress, I suddenly feel like it's a cage I need to break out of.

Fuck, why am I itchy?

My phone buzzes again, and the words on the screen relax me slightly.

WE'RE REAL

If I have to go up those stairs to find you, my sister is going to be pissed.

Why?

Oh thank fuck text is working.

Because I'll never make it to her fucking wedding.

Be down in a second, poser.

I tuck my phone into the small purse I have for the evening and head down the stairs before I can talk myself out of this.

A heaviness weighs me down, dragging my heels one after the other. The people I pass on the way down to the piano room all greet me, and I try to pay attention to each one, even if in the back of my mind, all I can think about is Reed.

And at the edge of the room, I pause to take it in.

Everything except the food is set up for cocktail hour already, and the entire scene, both inside and outside, looks as if it was pulled out of a gothic wedding magazine. Rich colors of maroon, dark green, blush, and black surround me. Raven skulls dot the floral and vine arrangements. It's old, tall candles, vintage candle holders, and velvet. Lace and moss and scarlet accents. Tree limbs wrap and rise off the tables. My gaze snags on the black, three-tiered cake sitting in the corner of the room, the flowers that travel up the sides in a swirl, and I almost smile at the Jack and Sally, Nightmare Before Christmas, topper on it.

"Holy shit."

Reed's voice makes my heart skip.

I turn around, noticing that he's already standing by the grand piano in all black, the sleeves of his button-up rolled up to his elbows. There's no jacket over his shirt, only suspenders…

And he's staring my way like it's his first time seeing me.

I swallow at how much brighter his eyes are in this room, how much older and tailored he appears today versus any event he's ever done with me. I thought he was sexy at the movie premiere, but today there's something different about him.

He smiles at me like he can see the wheels turning in my mind, like he, too, doesn't know how today is going to go, and even so, he's here.

"Hey," I manage.

"Fuck, you look…" His tongue runs over his lips, and then he gestures me over. "Come here."

The entire way to him, my heart is in my throat. He pulls me in, his hand pressing beneath my hair, and when he kisses me, I can't breathe.

"I missed you last night," he says. "And this morning. I was going to wake you up, but…"

"Reed, we need to talk," I force out before I can lose my nerve.

"We're talking," he says softly.

"No, I mean…" I look up at him, swallowing. "I need to tell you something."

He presses my hair back with his thumb, pain rising in his eyes as if he knows what I'm about to say. "Can it wait?" he whispers.

"That depends," I say. "Have you talked to your publicist?"

A muscle twitches in his jaw, and he releases me to step back. "Don't do this now," he says, voice nearly pleading.

"We have to talk about it," I say.

"Talk about what?"

"My agent called me this morning," I go on. "They're… they're issuing the breakup on Tuesday."

Reed paces in a circle and wrings his hands behind his neck, face looking like nausea has suddenly gripped him.

"The statement was signed off by your people, too," I say as I step toward him. "I thought—"

"Why did you have to do this now?" he says exasperatedly. "Why—why *now?*" He rounds on me, pain clouded by rage in his icy eyes. "You couldn't wait? You couldn't let us have tonight—It's my sister's fucking wedding. My *best friend's* wedding—" He runs both his hands through his hair, and I see his jaw begin to quiver.

"Goddammit, bird," he snaps. "You couldn't let us be real for one more day?"

"I didn't say that we couldn't be," I blurt out.

He stops pacing and goes wholly still, eyes fixated on me.

"What?" he asks.

God, he looks so hurt. I sniff back my emotion, eyes casting out toward the altar in the backyard.

"Wren, what did you just say?" he asks.

"I wasn't asking you about the publicist because I wanted to ruin your day," I say. "I only brought it up because I didn't want you to be blindsided when they called. I wanted to talk to you first. I knew they might call you today—tomorrow if they're nice. I just didn't… I didn't want someone to call you before I could talk to you about it myself."

Reed sighs, his head hanging. "Yeah," he says. "Yeah, they called while we were on our hike. Read me your statement and mine. I didn't want to bring it up because I… I wasn't ready to let you go. I thought if we could just have today, maybe tomorrow might not feel like the worst day of my life."

I want to leap into his arms, but these damned heels—

Thank fuck Reed meets me halfway.

We reach each other, and he wraps his hand beneath my jaw, tipping my head back for a soft kiss that melts my broken heart. And when our eyes meet upon parting, I hope to hell tonight lasts forever.

"We have today?" he asks.

I press my hand to his cheek. A part of me wishes I had never agreed to this. A part of me curses the day I ever thought I wouldn't fall for him.

And yet, I know I wouldn't change a single thing, no matter how much it's going to kill me.

"All day," I whisper.

Reed kisses me so desperately that he bends me backward. It's somehow more desperate than yesterday's. I can practically feel his pain mingling with mine, our broken hearts trying to find their way to each other so as to never let the other go.

Our foreheads rest against each other, and I hear the instrumental piano music playing over the speakers that almost sends me swaying with him. But Reed tips my chin up again, and the way he looks at me finishes crushing what's left of my insides.

"What?" I ask.

"I don't tell you at every event how beautiful you are because *fuck*, bird. You know you're stunning. But today… God, today… Today, I get to say fuck all of your rules. Today, I get to tell you that you're gorgeous and, just maybe, you'll believe me. Today, I get to tell you how every time you walk into a room, I forget the rest of the world exists, how I can't breathe when I'm near you. And when I'm inside you? When you whisper my name like I'm your god?" He groans and pulls me closer. "It's the only time I ever fear death. Because I think my soul wouldn't know how to move on. I'd crawl out of whatever afterlife there might be just to come back to you."

Fucking hell, Reed.

I don't know what my face is doing, but whatever it is makes him smile.

"You think I'm crazy, and that drives me wild," he says.

"I mean, there are a number of things with that statement that I have issues with—"

Reed beams. "Why can't you just let it be romantic?" he laughs.

I lean closer to him and draw my lip behind my teeth, his smile so close to my mouth that I can feel him breathing. "Because I like being the one who makes you crazy," I admit.

He groans. "You're so fucking greedy," he whispers. He bares his teeth and bites the air a whisper from my nose, making me snicker. "I love when you're greedy," he adds, his lips landing on mine.

How do I pause today?

Someone clears their throat nearby.

We part, though our eyes don't move from one another.

"Jesus, fuck," we hear Bonnie's raspy voice. "For two people denying dating, you two always have your tongues down one another's throats."

Reed sighs and turns his head. "What's up, Bon?"

"Just wanted to give you a heads up that photo and video are waiting on you."

"What for?"

Bonnie smiles. "Your first look with your sister."

Reed's smile slips, and it's so adorable that I can't help my laugh. "Go," I tell him. "I'll find you after photo is done with you today."

Zeb comes around the corner then and looks between us, smiling. "I think it's you and me today, mean girl," he says.

"Oh really?" I ask him.

"Yep. Bonnie is with Andi. Reed with Mads." He crosses the space and holds his elbow out to me, and as I take it, he grins crookedly at Reed. "I'm not needed until the actual ceremony," he adds, and I know it's because he's officiating.

Reed looks at me. "Just remember not to play any games with him," he says, winking.

CHAPTER THIRTY-NINE

I'M on cloud fucking nine.

Seeing my sister in her black dress all ready to get married had me in tears. Watching her walk down the aisle toward my best friend sent him into tears. Mads folded over his knees, and I had to clap his shoulder to get him to even stand up straight and take Andi's hands.

Though, not before he signed to her that he loved her when she was halfway to him.

They changed the ceremony up midway, choosing to exchange their vows in private instead of out loud, and Zeb led them through the handfasting ceremony earlier than expected.

Throughout all of it, I couldn't keep myself from staring at Wren.

Photos are a blur. Greeting family and friends… watching Mads and Andi celebrate, the elation on their faces… Fuck, I want it.

By the time photo and video allow us out of their clutches, I'm fucking restless. There are friends from the record label that stop me on my way into the reception, family that all stop to hug me, friends from other bands that I didn't realize were coming. There are so many faces that by the time I think I'll be able to reach Wren across the room, Mads and Andi make their own appearance.

I pause to clap and shout, but once they're dancing and I've wiped the goddamn tears from my face, I find her.

Even so, I don't run.

The lead singer of the wedding band is inviting couples onto the dance floor to join Andi and Mads. It's all I can do to smile at Wren, to take in the sight of her in this fucking dress and truly appreciate how stunning she is glowing around my family and friends.

I try not to think about what awaits us later as I meet her eyes. She gives me a small smile, and I finish crossing the space to her.

"Are you still crying?" she asks, reaching up to my face and wiping my cheeks. I am, and fuck, I don't care. I kiss the inside of her palm, unable to look away, and take her hands into mine.

"Dance with me?" I ask her.

She sighs and swallows, yet she only hesitates for a fraction before squeezing her fingers.

The song is one that Mads has listened to on repeat for what feels like ages. From a newer band that we've performed beside at festivals. It's perfect for this moment, for holding her, swaying with her.

At some point, I wrap my arm around her shoulders and pull her into my chest, unable to look away from the smile on her lips. The lyrics sit on my tongue, and there's a chorus where I mouth the words to her, making her laugh.

And when the song changes into something more upbeat, I completely lose track of time.

We're dancing and drinking and spinning. All of us. All at once. Entirely losing our minds for what I know is hours.

Tonight is a core memory I'll never get over.

However, nothing compares to the moment the beat drops on a song that saved our family more than once.

It's the song Andi played in the basement when the real world cn the main floor was too much. The song that she dragged Kamden and Koen into the middle of the floor to, forcing them to take her hands and dance with her while I played the air guitar on the coffee table and Mads usually sat on the back of the couch, laughing at us and controlling the music.

I lock gazes with my sister, and she grins back at me with glistening eyes.

"Family song!" I shout, cupping my hands around my mouth.

My mom looks as if she forgot how to walk.

Because she's heard Andi play it so loudly that it came up the staircase and mingled with the harsh words and fights happening in the kitchen. Mom stares at Andi, and as she starts tc nod her head, she sets her drink down, then glances my way, and I see the tears in her eyes, too.

It's Andi who reaches her first. She pulls her into the circle, and I run across the room to grab our dad. He laughs when he sets his drink down and I say, "Family song!" in his face. I shake his shoulders, jumping up and down, and together, we join the others in the middle just as Kamden and Koen also drag their asses out there.

As much pain as this song represents, it's also fucking joy. Because we're all here, Mads included, and while we're all fucked up in our own ways, we're healing as a family, and fuck… that's something worth celebrating.

I spot Wren standing beside my mom, smiling at whatever she's saying to her, and I run to her side.

"You'll have to explain the significance of this song later," she says over the music.

I beam at her. "I will," I say. "But right now, I need you to pretend with me."

"Pretend what?" she asks.

"I need you to pretend that this isn't our last night, and that you're now a part of this family," I say.

Wren blinks, smiling nervously toward the others dancing in the circle, but eventually nodding "Okay," she says.

My brothers and I take turns swinging Andi around the space, all of us shouting the lyrics back in one another's faces. Mads and I air guitar back-to-back, even fucking Kamden sings along. I don't know that my heart has ever been more full than right here. Right now.

I swing Andi around the floor again and pull her in for a hug. I'm so fucking proud of her. So fucking in awe of her strength, and I barely register myself squeezing her tight and muttering, "I love you, sis," into her hair.

Andi pulls back and presses her hands to my face, a tear rolling down her cheek. "I love you," she breathes.

Mads slinks his arms around us then, the three of us shouting the bridge of the song. I settle back with the rest of our family, slinking my arm around my mom and dad, and we belt out those final lyrics.

It isn't until the song wraps and goes into the next one that I find Wren again. She's beaming at me, and when I reach her, I thread my hands around her neck to tilt her head back and kiss her.

She draws her bottom lip behind her teeth as I settle my arms around her waist and pull her close.

"You have to stop," she whispers.

"Stop what?" I ask, my fingers spreading wide on her exposed sides.

"Making me fall for you."

A jagged breath enters my lungs, a lump swelling in my

throat. I can't have heard her right. Not when this is our last day. Not when we can't be together after tonight.

Words escape me as I stare into her dark green pools. Our foreheads meet, and I close my eyes to breathe her in. She entwines her fingers into mine, and fuck… I'm begging the world to stop spinning, for time to somehow cease to exist.

Maybe it's stupid to let myself fall into a hole I know I'll never be able to climb out of, to fall for someone unavailable and out of my reach. I've been ridiculed for wearing my heart on my sleeve, for falling too hard, too fast, and for the wrong fucking person too many times.

Call me whatever name you want.

I'm the one who would rather feel my heart shattering into a thousand pieces than to never know what it means to love someone so much that you would throw the world into the fire.

"I'm already fucking gone for you," I whisper back.

A smile tugs on her lips, and she lays her head against my chest, allowing me to hold her closer for the remainder of the song. I can't swallow, can't catch a full breath.

God, this fucking hurts.

"Do you want to get some air?" I ask when the song is over.

She looks down and starts to open her bag to check the time on her phone, but I push it away. "No," I say. "We're not counting down. Just be with me."

Her jaw sets. "Let me set an alarm then."

Mads comes up then, claps my hand, and gives me a hug. I don't know what time it is, but his shirt is soaked in sweat, and I know I don't look much better. My own shirt is open over my suspenders, hair a sweaty mess.

I don't even have on shoes anymore.

"Everything okay?" Mads says, leaning toward me.

I feel my jaw tense. "Yeah. All good. Just going to get some air."

Mads looks at me as if he knows, and he embraces me again. "Here if you need me, man."

I clap his shoulder. "Don't worry about me. Have fun with your wife."

He clutches his chest and staggers off-balance. "Fucking hell, that's weird. I need to find her after that."

I chuckle as he leaves my side and Wren comes up to me again. "Ready?" I ask.

The room with the piano is a calm, quiet hum of background noise when we enter. I snag a cut strawberry from one of the remaining trays and pop it back as we make our way to the piano. I've been itching to play since yesterday.

I strike a few keys, the melody seeming to prick the back of my neck as it floods the air.

Wren is staring into the back beneath the half-open lid, watching it move as I repeat the notes.

"Do that again," she says.

I do, and a little smile works onto her lips that I can't resist. I corner her against the side and press my hands into the top, trapping her there so that when I kiss her, she feels all of me.

She yelps when I grasp her under her hips and lift her up onto the piano.

"Reed—this is not stable. What if we break it?" she asks when I set her down.

"If we break it, I'll buy them a new one," I shrug. I stretch my fingers and crack my neck as I sit on the bench, inhaling a breath before setting my hands up.

"Don't think you're getting me to sing directly to you," I say as my fingers move over the keys. "Unless I have the band behind me or it's just for shits and giggles, I feel awkward."

She laughs softly. "Honestly, I don't know what to do with myself when someone sings out of the blue, especially when they're looking at me for a reaction. And not like, jokingly singing for a laugh, but actually singing. Am I supposed to clap when they're done? Watch them awkwardly? Compliment them? What is the expected social standard here, because I don't know it."

I laugh. "Don't look at me. I have no idea. You know what is hilarious, though?"

"What?"

"Growling, or screaming, when no one expects it," I answer.

Her eyes widen. "Like what you do in your music?"

I nod, grinning up at her.

"Oh, god," she drawls. "What did you do?"

"I was just developing those muscles and figuring out how to do it without sounding like a banshee my junior year in high school. I talked my mom into letting us play the school's Christmas talent show—for the fuck of it. Practically had to drag Mads along. Anyway, it was fine to begin with. I was on piano, he set the bass line—on his new bass that he'd worked all fucking summer just to buy. We got all the way to the bridge, and when I started belting out those lines, some of the younger kids ran out crying."

Wren snorts. "Of course they did. You scared the shit out of them," she jokes. "One second you're singing Jingle Bells, Batman smells, and the next you're screaming? That's the stuff of nightmares. Surprised parents didn't shun you the rest of high school."

"They definitely did. We caused an entire scene," I agree. "Total anarchy. I was fucking innocent enough not to know what we'd done wrong. Some of the people in our grade thought it was cool, though."

"Did you become the popular kids after that?" she asks.

"Nah, we were suspended for a week," I say, and she laughs.

"Oh, I bet your mother loved that," she teases.

"Wanted to murder us," I reply. "But when we got back to

school, suddenly, we were part of the 'bad boys' group, which was pretty fucking weird and cool at the same time. Mads had always been labeled as the troubled kid, but after that, a few girls decided he was the hot, sad boy."

"Hot, sad boy is accurate still," she says. "And you?"

"I was the sexy rockstar," I beam. "I wasn't allowed to go home with anyone because their parents all knew me. Banned their daughters from ever speaking to me, though that just made things worse. No one bothered telling their sons to stay away, though," I add with a grin.

Wren laughs. "Let me guess… You seduced the captain of the football team."

"Abso-fucking-lutely," I say, making her roll her eyes. But I laugh and shake my head. "Nah, no seducing. He was in the closet. Wanted to explore a little. I was a safe person to use. I never told anyone, though. I wasn't one to fuck and brag."

"Did you have a van?"

"Hell yeah, we had a van," I say, and Wren laughs again. "Nah, actually we went to college in the van, but before that, we had my parents' garage."

"Oh, the bad boy band garage," she taunts. "Where you get finger-fucked by a teenage emo poser boy who thinks he knows where the clit is, but doesn't even know *what* it is."

"At seventeen?" I snort. "I didn't know shit. I thought I did, though. I thought I was some sexual deviant badass."

"Of course, you did," she teases. "All boys do."

I chuckle softly and turn my attention back to the tune I'm playing, barely needing to think about it as my fingers run over the keys, feet moving between the pedals.

"What is that?" she asks. "The melody, I mean."

"Ah… it's been in my head since I was a kid," I answer, continuing on. "Never put any lyrics to it, though. Mads is the songwriter. I've never been able to put my thoughts into anything poetic enough for a song. I can put it to a melody better."

"He never found any lyrics to this piece?"

I sigh. "He tells me that it's mine, and I'll need to find the words myself."

"So pushy," she says.

"I know, right?" I chuckle. "It's good motivation, though. Maybe one day all the things battling inside me will come together. Work themselves into words."

"I find it hard to believe that you have trouble putting feelings into words," she says. "You seem to always have the words when you're trying to charm me."

"Not like Mads," I say. "Somehow, he can make eating bread sound like the most romantic thing there is."

"Is that what's holding you back?" she asks. "Because you think anything you put out there won't be as good as his?"

I stare at the keys, slowing the tempo. "That seems fucking stupid, doesn't it?"

"I think it makes you a little less perfect."

Our eyes meet, and I feel my chest tighten.

"I like not being perfect with you," I admit.

Wren doesn't reply, and I play a little louder, adding in notes that seem to flow out of me, an addition to the melody that feels like the missing parts falling into place, and something about it forms a lump in my throat.

She sits up, her feet dangling over the front, then leans down to take her shoes off. I pause playing and gesture for her to let me help.

"Is that what you've been doing to me all this time?" I ask as I unhook one of the heel straps. "Exposing my flaws?"

"Haven't you been breaking me just the same?" she asks.

I hold her eyes as I take the second heel off, then run my hands over her the top of her foot, her exposed calf, pausing to kiss her ankle. And before I can stop myself, I sink my head onto her lap and hug her legs, letting the hum of the music surround our steady breathing.

"I think you were already a little broken," I say. "All I did was tap the pieces that needed to fall to find the real you beneath."

Wren wraps her fingers into my hair and tilts my head back. The look in her eyes has me dragging her off the top of the piano and settling her on my lap between myself and the keys. Even still, I don't kiss her. I hold her. I memorize her scent, her steady breath. Every muscle in my body seems to tingle with the ache of what I know is coming. Of what I don't think has truly hit me yet.

"Wren…"

"Don't," she whispers, pressing her hands to my cheeks, eyes closing as our foreheads meet.

An alarm goes off in her bag, and the noise of it instantly drops my stomach.

Not yet.

Fuck, not yet.

Wren draws a jagged breath, jaw clenching when she pulls back.

"I need to get my stuff from upstairs," she manages.

The walk up the stairs and down the halls feels like I'm walking to my death.

I can't let go of her hand. I think if I do, she'll just disappear. And once we're in the bedroom, my heart gives out at the sight of her suitcase by the door, the clothes on the bed ready for the airport.

I sit on the mattress as she gets her makeup from the bathroom. I can't think as I help her get out of the dress and into her leggings and the Young Decay sweatshirt of mine that she's practically been living in this weekend.

"I should've washed this for you," I say when it's on her.

"Then it wouldn't smell like you," she says.

I huff, smiling just to ignore the butterflies swarming my entire body as she stretches up on her toes to kiss me. And when our lips meet, I wonder how I'm supposed to just go on tomorrow as if none of this ever happened.

Wren pushes me slightly, almost forcing me to pull away.

Because I don't want to.

Maybe if I hold her hostage here, no one will find us.

"I… I have something for you," she says, avoiding my eyes as she reaches for her bag. "I meant to give it to you the other day, but I didn't figure your sister would want it in her wedding photos." She takes out two beaded bracelets and lays them in my open hand.

One says 'slut,' and the other says 'cross my heart.'

I chuckle at the slut one, and she smiles when I hold it up. "Slut?"

"Well, I was going to bedazzle it onto the ass of a pair of grey joggers, but Larry was making these for a concert he's going to, so I had him make it instead," she explains.

"I would've worn the hell out of those pants," I say.

"I know you would have," she says.

I hold up the other one. "And this one?" I ask, knowing I've heard her say the phrase a couple of times.

A muscle feathers in her jaw as she stares at it. "So… cross my heart is something my brother and I used to say to each other," she says. "We would promise each other something, usually something stupid, then say 'cross my heart, hope to die, stick a needle in my eye.' It became our way of saying 'I love you' to one another. And…" She sniffs back a sharp inhale, and I realize she's trembling. "It was the last three words he ever said to me. And I just…" A tear falls down her cheek, and she looks up at me with glistening eyes. "I didn't know how else to tell you goodbye."

My jaw is quaking, fingers shaking when I swipe the tear from her cheek.

I don't know what else to do besides kiss her.

Because I can't let her go.

The kiss is a desperate attempt to keep her here. To remind her that she's safe. To reassure her that she doesn't have to be alone.

Even if it's a worthless shot.

Wren pushes me away again, hand over her mouth as if she forgot herself for a moment.

"I can't do this," she whispers. "I can't… I can't."

She turns to the bed and frantically throws the rest of her things into her carry-on bag, and I'm left standing there watching her like an idiot.

Fucking say something.

Beg on your goddamn knees.

You can't let her go.

Mads's face appears behind my eyes.

"What are you going to do about it?"

The image ignites my fight, and as my heart begins to pound in my chest, I feel a hopelessness weave through me that I have to get out.

"Am I supposed to be okay with this?" I ask, suddenly nauseous. "Am I supposed to just… let you go?"

Wren slows her movements, but stays with her back to me.

"Yes," I hear her whisper.

"Months of getting to know you," I bite out, feeling my eyes swelling. "Months of learning you. Of… of falling…" The four words I want to say stick in my throat. My jaw quivers, and I skip them to keep going.

"And I'm just… I'm supposed to watch you walk away from me in the middle of the night and never speak to you again?"

She swallows as she finally faces me, her bottom lip quivering. "Yes," she breathes.

I shake my head.

No.

I can't.

I won't—

The gamble I'm about to take might cost everything. I'm prepared for it. I'm prepared to put my entire family in hiding just for this. Because she's fucking worth it, and if I don't do something… If I don't take this chance, I don't know that I'll be able to live with myself. I don't know that I can go on not knowing the truth.

"What if I don't want this to be over?"

CHAPTER FORTY

WREN

OH, god, Reed.

Don't do this.

"I thought we went over this," I say. "They will hurt you. Your family won't be safe—"

"I don't care who thinks they own you," he argues. "I don't care, Wren. Fuck—we'll figure it out."

The conviction in his words almost make my knees buckle.

"You can't figure this out," I beg.

Please understand.

He launches forward and takes my hands into his. "I will," he swears. "For you, Wren, I will."

"Why?" I cry, stepping out of his grasp. "Why can't you just let me go? Why do you have to make this so much harder—"

"Because I'm fucking in love with you," he practically shouts.

I choke on a sob and clasp my hand over my mouth, my eyes so clouded with tears that I can hardly see him.

But Reed steps in my direction, and it takes all of my strength not to collapse at the look in his eyes, the tear crawling down his own cheek. The sight has me shaking, and all I want to do is run into his arms and tell him how much I…

You can't.

"I'm so fucking in love with you, bird," he says exasperatedly. "I love…" He swallows as if he can hardly get his voice to work, like it's sticking in his throat and he's carefully choosing each word.

"I love *everything* that you are—*who* you are. Every part of yourself that you think doesn't deserve love. The real *you*. I crave each smile and touch that you let me have. Every goddamn second that we're together—"

"Reed, please," I manage, desperate to stop him. "Don't…"

"Every fucking concert, all I can think about is calling you after so I can tell you how it went," he says, ignoring me. "You've burrowed your way inside my head. My heart. I'm *desperate* for you, bird. The thought of life without you sounds fucking hopeless and empty. You've become so much more to me than just another person in my life. You've become someone I don't want to go a day without. You're everything to me, too, and I can't…"

He swipes his hand over his face, pushing away any stray tears. "I don't know how to simply *give you up*," he says defeatedly. "I can't watch you walk away from me as if none of this ever mattered."

I shake my head as he advances on me further, as he says my name again. His voice is an echo. Everything around me feels swollen. There's a ringing in my ears that I can't stop.

I don't know how to do this.

I don't know how to get him to see that we can't be together.

And maybe that's because I don't want to.

Because I don't know how to give him up either.

"Reed, please," I manage. "Please don't make this any harder than it is. We *can't*."

Even if my body is begging to stay.

I can't let him do this to himself.

"Wren—" He grabs my arms and pulls me into him again, ignoring my struggle.

"Reed, stop—"

"No."

"Reed, please," I choke out. "Don't—"

He manages to get his long arms around me, trapping me against his chest. I'm sobbing, and when he tilts my chin up with his thumb, his hand splayed against my wet cheek, a wail leaves me that I can't stop.

"I told you I wasn't losing you to this, and I fucking meant it," he says firmly.

I stop struggling and meet his red, swollen eyes. My tense shoulders slacken, body sagging against him.

His throat bobs when he swipes a tear from my cheek, and one of his drops onto my jaw.

"I fucking meant it," he breathes.

God, I can't do this.

I shove out of his grasp before I can do anything stupid.

He stumbles and hangs his head, the muscles in his jaw feathering when his eyes lift to mine.

"You're not making this any easier," I force myself to argue.

"Good," he says, and I can hear the frustration rising in his tone again. "Good because this isn't fucking easy. Letting you go isn't easy. *Love* isn't always fucking easy," he snaps. "But goddammit, bird. I don't care. I don't want easy if it means not being with you. I'm not giving you up—"

"We can't, Reed," I plead.

"We *can*—"

"Do you know how it feels to watch someone you love get *butchered alive?*" I blurt out.

Reed pauses. The air around us becomes still, the noise of the music downstairs nonexistent.

And he stares at me as if I've just punched him in the face.

"Because *I do*," I go on. "And I refuse for that to happen to you. I refuse for them to take the people that you love. Tell me, Reed. What would you do if you woke up to the news that your sister had been taken? That your mother was dead? Tell me how much you would love me after that."

His teeth set, body frozen.

"He will steal everything you love if I don't walk away from you right now," I cry.

Reed's head drops. I can see it on his face. He knows I'm right.

And yet, he's still fighting.

"I can't do this," I whisper.

I grab my suitcase from the door, not caring if I've left anything behind.

I have to get out.

If I stay any longer, I'll never leave.

I'll drag him down with me. I'll hurt him. His family.

The heartbreak of leaving him is debilitating enough. To see him or his loved ones hurt might be the final nail in the coffin.

If this doesn't take me out first.

You destroy everything you touch.

You never deserved him.

My suitcase drags on the steps as I practically run, Reed quick on my heels.

"Wren, wait."

"There's nothing left to talk about," I say, keeping my head down and trying not to cause a scene.

"We can figure it out," he repeats. "I'll keep you safe. You don't have to go back to this—"

Tears hiccup in my throat as I reach the bottom floor. "*No?* What am I supposed to do, Reed?" I ask, rounding on him. "Am I supposed to hide out on your tour bus? Forget my career? Forget all that I've worked for?"

His eyes haze over. "Are you saying all of that means more than this?"

I tense, my teeth chattering. God, I can't breathe, not with the way he's looking at me. Not with every word and confession we've exchanged.

I don't want to hurt him. I just need him to let me go.

I throw my hand against the front door and storm out of the house.

Reed grabs my wrist and pulls me back as the door slams. "Tell me the truth, bird. Don't lie to get me to walk away from you."

I bite out a sardonic huff and step out of his arms. "No," I admit, helplessly letting go of everything. "No, none of that… if I could walk away from everything to be with you, I would," I confess. "If I knew he couldn't touch you, I… things would be so different. But this isn't a fucking fairytale. This is reality, and we… this is why we could never be truly real—"

"This was *always* fucking real," he says, the words choking in his throat as he takes me into his arms.

I'm weak as his hand presses against my cheek, our trembling mouths opening and closing against one another.

"It's been real since the moment we left that party together. Since I kissed you at that stupid fucking festival and the night I choked you in front of a hundred people—"

The memory makes me laugh through my sob, and Reed goes on.

"Through every fight, shove, stab, and lie that the sex was only to get rid of your nerves," he says. "You and me, Wren. Tell me I'm wrong. Tell me this was never real for you, because it was always real for me."

Of course, it was fucking real.

Because I've been falling for him since the very first time I saw Young Decay perform at DeathFest.

Even so, I shove him away one last time.

"We're done, Reed," I manage. "God, we're fucking done. We have to be."

Reed doesn't move, and the defeat in his eyes does me in. I turn away fast and head down the dimly lit drive, not knowing when Tara and her van is supposed to be here to pick me up, but I'll wait for her at the end in the dark if I need to. I can't stay—

Reed screams as if someone is ripping him in half.

I don't look.

If I look, I'll never leave him.

If I look, I'm condemning him.

I can't catch my breath for the sobs and tears streaking down my face. I force my numb fingers to move on my phone screen, choking on the spit collecting at the back of my throat, and I dial Amanda's number.

"Yeah?" Amanda answers.

"Where's the car?" I ask. "Where's Tara? I need… I need the car. *Now*—"

"Wren, is everything okay?"

"No," I admit, my palm pressing to my forehead. "No, I need… It's almost one a.m. Where is Tara?"

"Wren, I need you to calm down—"

"Don't fucking tell me to calm down!" I shout into the phone.

I'm trapped.

I can't be in love with him.

Why can't this be simple?

Why did things have to get so complicated?

"I—"

Footsteps pound on the ground behind me. I force breath into my lungs, just enough to hold myself together. Amanda is saying something, yet I don't hear her. I can't hear her, not for the beating feet on the pavement that seem so urgent behind me, the steps that aren't made of someone casually coming outside.

I turn just in time to find Reed storming up behind me. His gaze is haunting, and when he reaches me, he grabs me by my face and hauls me into him. His lips land on mine in the most mind-numbing way, and I sink into him without any hesitation whatsoever.

Our tears mix as I kiss him as fervently as he's kissing me. Like this is the final moment we'll ever have. I can feel him trembling against me, and it breaks what's left of my heart.

A hiccup of a sob leaves me when we part, and I can't bring myself to look into his eyes.

"We'll find a way," he whispers. "I don't know how to let you go, and I won't. No matter how long this takes or what we might have to face. You have me. I'm yours."

"Reed…"

"I don't need you to say anything," he says desperately, pressing his forehead against mine. "I don't… I don't need you to say that you're mine or that you'll be here."

I want to tell him goodbye.

I should.

"You have to let me go," I whisper instead.

"I can't," he breathes.

I throw my arms around his neck and hug him as if he's the only thing holding me from falling off the same cliff we stood on yesterday. It's a last desperate attempt, a final ending to what we never should have been. His hands brace on my cheeks once more when we part, and I rest my forehead against his, memorizing the outline of his touch on my skin.

"Let me go," I shake out as my hands slide over his wrists.

He holds me tighter, eyes scrunched with tears and mouth pressed tightly together as if he refuses to find the words.

However, as he shakily shifts and his lips land softly on my forehead, I let loose a cry that feels entirely foreign, and I don't know why that's the action that does me in, but it does.

God fucking dammit, it does.

"Reed—"

He releases me before I can say another word, and I fall to my knees at the abruptness of the split.

Because he has my broken heart and shattered soul in his hands, and I'm numb to the rest of the world just watching him walk away.

"Wren! *Wren!*—"

My phone is shouting at me.

"Post the breakup," is all I can manage when I press my phone to my ear.

There's a pause on the other end of the line. It's long enough that I clap my hand over my mouth to keep myself from sobbing all over again.

"Are you sure—"

"Goddammit, Mandi, just post it and get me the hell out of here," I snap before hanging up.

CHAPTER FORTY-ONE

REED

THERE'S something they don't tell you about performing with a broken heart.

Every note feels longer. Every lyric is a punch in the gut.

And within every strobe of light, I see her face.

I think I've pushed my body to its absolute limit these last few shows in an attempt to chase the high, to satiate the need of pure adrenaline and pain over my muscles. I want to feel everything, even if it means throwing myself into a burning building just to see if the flames might ignite the same fire I once felt with her.

The microphone is cold in my hand. The lights flare as they cascade across the stage, the band. And Zeb's lingering note vibrates the tense air.

He's the one that found me on my knees in the driveway, completely devoid of a soul or voice to tell him what was wrong. He's the one that hid me the rest of the night in his room and brought tea, whiskey, and everything else to try and ease me into sleep, telling everyone that I'd just drank too much so that they wouldn't come asking questions.

The following morning, I'd sat at the fucking piano for hours, and eventually cried into my sister's shoulder.

I felt horrible about it after.

Because the best day of her life had been the worst day of mine.

That's fucking selfish, and I still hate myself for even letting it cross my mind.

At least the stage helps.

Sweat pricks the back of my neck as I hang against the microphone for a second, eyes glazed at the set list taped to the floor at my feet. It's December 23rd, our second to last show of the year in Raleigh. We have the next two days off to be with family before it's out to LA for rehearsal with the orchestra for our New Year's Eve show.

I can't feel my face.

As I look into the crowd, the signs over the rails in front tighten the muscles of my chest.

You saved me.

We love you.

You've picked up my pieces.

Each one reminds me of Wren and Halloween night. I can still feel her sitting on my lap as she tells me our music might have once saved her. I can still see the look in her eyes when she smiled at me that night, the whisper of her lips when she kissed me, that quiet little moan when she tried to deny how much she wanted me. Even her fucking safe word.

Every reminder makes me want to jump off a bridge or worship those memories all in the same breath.

My chest tightens as I see the song up next.

I look up, and in the split-second before the lights flicker off, a glimpse of ginger hair catches my eyes. I blink, but I know better than to think it's her. Even still, my heart somersaults.

I close my eyes in the darkness surrounding us and steady my breathing.

She isn't here.

She's back in LA.

She's gone.

The knowledge hollows my gut, and when the overhead spotlight comes back on me, I pull my microphone out of the stand.

"Hey, can we all just sit down a minute?" I ask the crowd, walking to the edge to sit on one of the speaker boxes.

Mads comes up beside me, his eyes narrowed over the mask. "You good?" he asks.

I nod. "Yeah. Trying something new to lead into Falling," I tell him, and Mads walks away to let Zeb and Bonnie know what's going on.

I see some fans squint between each other at my request to sit, and it makes me chuckle. "Yeah, just sit. Wherever you are on the floor. And if someone beside you doesn't want to, then fucking drag them down onto your lap."

Mads comes back around and sits on the box beside me, strumming one bass line when he's comfortable. I watch him, glancing at the wedding band on his hand.

"Hey, did you know that this guy got married recently?" I ask the crowd.

The audience roars back, and I grin at my sister who's down in the pit with her camera pointed at us. She shakes her head, a few fans calling out her name by the front.

"Yeah, it was to this lovely, beautiful woman right down here. Everyone wave at my sister, now Mrs. Tourning," I say, pointing to her. "Yeah, I said my sister. You heard that right." I grin slyly at Mads, the microphone flipping when I toss it up. One of our roadies rushes onstage then, an acoustic guitar in her hand that she hands off to Mads, switching out the bass.

"Calling an audible," Mads says to me. "Bon said her wrist is in a knot, so I told her to take a little break. We'll pick up in a few."

I nod. "Want to play a little?"

Mads shrugs. "We can jam."

I look back out at the crowd."Do you mind if I talk to you guys about love?" I ask them.

They scream back, and Mads plays a line from the new bit he's been working on.

"No? Okay. Yeah, I thought I could talk to you about it. You seem like decent fucking people." I get a little more comfortable on the speaker, catching Mads shaking his head at me, and I smirk at him.

"You know, the thing about love is that it fucking hurts," I say into the mic. "It's your entire world falling apart and getting put back together one crumble at a time. When it's good, you're on fire. When it's bad… fuck, somehow you're still on fire. But when it's gone… when it's gone, every breath feels like you're dragging the glass left behind in your chest."

I pause, swallowing the dryness in my throat as I catch a glimpse of the two bracelets on my wrist.

I haven't taken them off since the wedding.

"How many of you thought you knew what love was when you were younger, and then when you grew up, you realized it hit ten times harder?"

A few people shout and whistle, and I look at Mads.

"At least it's not just me," I say to him.

I can see his smile in his eyes.

"Okay, well, this bit is about that. It's something Mads and I have been working on a few weeks now," I go on. "It's for the hopeless romantics out there that fall too hard, too fast without even realizing that they're spiraling past fucking Wonderland."

Mads slowly eases into the notes, and when I hold the microphone to my lips, the words flowing out of me, I sing through the lump in my throat, the chills on the back of my neck, and the entire time we sit on the edge of that stage playing fucking acoustic songs like we're sitting in the garage jamming again, I'm pleading for Wren to appear just to make this moment more perfect.

I needed that break.

I needed to feel it again, to remember that sensation when we first started doing this.

Mads hugs me when Zeb and Bonnie come back on stage a few minutes later, and for the rest of the show, I feel like I'm breathing a little easier.

So much so that when we end—after I've jumped in the crowd and screamed a little louder, felt the music a little harder, after I've practically jumped onto my dad's back and picked my mom up off the floor to hug her backstage—the very first thing I do, is send Wren a text.

It's been weeks, and it's fucking foolish to keep trying, but I don't know how to give it up.

The graveyard of my previous texts are pathetic enough.

Don't shut me out.

I mean it. I'll figure out a way.

Please let me know that you're okay.

Wren.

Say something. I'll settle for a fuck off.

I just want to know that you're okay.

You're not alone.

Her socials have been scarce, though I don't know if that's because she's been traveling for the overseas premieres or if it's something else.

I swallow as my thumbs move over the screen to text her tonight.

> I thought I saw you at my show tonight. I
> know that sounds desperate and reaching,
> but I fucking hope you're here.
>
> And if you are, my mom has already said she
> was leaving an open space at Christmas
> dinner. Again, I know that sounds fucking
> stupid.

I run my hand behind my neck as I hit send on the next text.

> But you'd be safe.

I don't expect a reply. I can't. Not now, and maybe not ever, but that doesn't mean I'm going to stop fighting for her.

Thank fuck I remembered to bring my headphones and keyboard home on this trip.

Christmas Eve, I can't sleep. I'm up all night, replaying the notes and the words that I'm trying so fucking hard to put into lyrics. I don't know how Mads makes this sound so easy. Every song he's ever put together has been easily phrased.

Even with his help, I feel like I'm blundering through it.

And when we all sit around the living room to exchange gifts, I can't help but stare at my phone for a few minutes while Koen and Kamden argue over who gets to give Mom her gift first.

Fuck it.

> Merry Christmas, bird.
>
> I wish you were here.

God, I fucking do.

She'd laugh at these two arguing or knock Kamden down a few notches.

I close my phone and lay it on the table next to me, smiling at my mom as she holds up the sweater Kamden got her. My knees sway in and out, hands clasped in front of me when Koen makes a disgusted face.

"That's a bullshit gift. My turn," Koen says. "Here, Mom. It's better than some shit sweater," Kamden says.

"Don't be mean to your brother," she replies. "I love this sweater—it's very cozy, Kamden. I love it. Thank you."

My phone buzzes, and I glance over at the lit-up screen, expecting it to be Zeb or Bonnie replying to my messages from earlier. It's a picture text, along with a message, and my stomach flips upon seeing it.

LOVE OF MY FUCKING LIFE

Merry Christmas, poser.

The picture is of Anita with reindeer ears on her head.

Emotion immediately begins to burn behind my nose. I suck in a sharp breath and slump into the couch as I stare at the photo, noting that she has a few decorations up in the background—something she would normally avoid.

My anxiety instantly kicks in.

Shit.

What the hell I'm supposed to do now?

"Reed?" Andi says, tearing away from the snuggling kisses of her and Mads's adopted dog, Zero. "Everything okay?"

"I…"

Fuck, do I call her? Do I play it cool? Do I try to text her or will that scare her?

I can't think straight.

Mads leans over to see what I'm staring at, and he squeezes my knee. "Go call her," he says.

I glance around at our family. "But…"

"You're going to be in a hole until you know. Just try it," he says. "Andi and I can keep them distracted with pictures of where we're going for the honeymoon."

Andi jerks her head toward the door when I look at her. "Go."

However, I'm hesitant.

"Just… Hang on."

I quickly type out a message to her.

Because the last thing I want is to get her in trouble. I want to see her. I want to know that she's okay. But fuck, I don't want it to mean she gets hurt.

> Would it be bananas to call you?

Wren texts back almost immediately.

> It would.

> Anita just wanted to say Merry Christmas.

Someone fucking shoot me.

And I'm so stupid when I text her again.

> I really fucking miss you.

It's a desperate ploy, but I know if I don't say it, I'll stare at my phone the next few hours wondering what she might say if I did.

> I miss you, too.

Shit.

Emotion burns behind my eyes.

I have to clench my teeth to keep from turning into a blubbering idiot.

Night, poser.

"Okay?" Andi asks.

I toss my phone back on the table and nod, stifling every-thing that wants to spill over. "Yeah. She was just being nice," I force out.

Andi and Mads exchange a look, but I try not to dwell on it.

She fucking texted me.

She misses me.

If I ever get her back, I'm never letting her go.

CHAPTER FORTY-TWO

"LISTEN, *I know that you and Reed aren't exactly… well, dating, and I don't want to sound like a meddling mother, either, but…"* Tina sighs heavily, her shoulders drooping when she smiles at me. *"There's something about the way he looks at you, and it's been a very long time since someone held his attention for longer than twenty minutes. That boy is a hard one to keep track of,"* she mumbles. *"Anyway, I say all of this just to say… I hope this isn't the last time we see you."*

Anita jumps in my lap as I stare at the texts from Reed. Remembering what his mom said to me at the wedding makes me want to video call him just to be a part of their Christmas.

God, I really fucking miss him.

Every time I think about the wedding, I remember my own family.

I haven't had a proper Christmas in years. Haven't celebrated since Travis died. The small black tree on the television stand is brand new, and the antler ears that I coerced Anita into wearing were an impulse buy on a night when I stayed up drunk thinking about Reed, when my fingers sat atop the video call button on his contact info and I had to throw my phone across the room to keep from calling him and ruining everything.

An occurrence that's become all too common in the last few weeks.

All the boxes of gifts on my counter are supposed to be for him.

God, I'm a fucking mess.

I've lost my fucking mind over this breakup. My entire body is exhausted from the amount of crying I've done, the amount of times I've contemplated whether waking up the next day was worth it. I've hardly picked up around the place, hardly eaten anything more than chips, salsa, and wine. And if it wasn't for Anita…

I don't know the state I might be in if I didn't have her—if I would even be here.

The worst part about this breakup is the fact that neither of us did anything wrong. No one cheated. No one said hurtful words or resented the other, made one feel like they were being manipulated or controlled. I think I would be reacting differently had this been like any other breakup. I would have picked myself up and dissociated until I was over it, continued going on like none of it ever mattered. I've done well masking my emotional turmoil at the events, putting on a face that no one can see past…

But this fucking hurts.

I wish he was pissed at me.

I wish when he texted me, he was shouting.

I wish he was calling me names and telling me I ruined his life.

Of course, he isn't.

I thumb through the photos on my phone. Ones of Anita. The photos in Tokyo that I wanted to send him. The photos of him onstage in Raleigh singing acoustically with Mads.

It's the closest I've come to saying fuck it just to see him again.

I miss him more than I've ever missed anyone—possibly more than I miss my brother. And maybe that's because my brother was dying in front of me all of those years battling addiction. Or maybe… fuck, maybe I'm just heartless and numb.

I glance down at my phone again, some sick part of me wishing Reed would ignore me and call anyway. The tattoo on the inside of my finger catches my eye, and it kills me not to be able to send him a photo of it.

I know he would love it.

I walked into the shop last week on a whim and had them tattoo 'little bird' on the inside of my left ring finger, along with two others from their flash sheets.

Because the other option for trying to release myself from this agony was the box of razor blades I also ordered during my drunken stupor—blades that I've already used a few times on my inner thighs just to see if I still feel anything.

Another tear slides down my cheek at the thought, at the memory of the blood circling the drain.

I'm so fed up with feeling like there's only way out.

I'm so sick of feeling helpless.

And I'm so tired of being tired.

I want to be free. I want to live again. I want to walk outside without looking over my fucking shoulder, to hear my phone ring without my stomach dropping.

Most of all… I want to love.

Everything you love disappears.

You destroy everything you touch.

Everything you touch dies.

Even my plants have started dying.

I haven't heard from Damien since the breakup was issued. However, I've seen his men. I've seen them following me to every meeting, dinner, and event that I've been to. I still don't know if they have anything of mine tapped. I still don't know if they're reading my emails or watching my phone calls.

Even so, I don't know that I want to take the chance.

Each time I think about it, I remember the live video of Reed, the moment Damien shot Erik in the car while trying to rape me. And each time, I slump back into my couch in defeat.

My computer dings—an email.

Who the fuck is working today?

I take another drink of champagne and sit up to click on the email, and as I read the subject, I feel my eyes narrow.

---

subj: SAVE YOUR OWN ASS AND COME BACK TO HIM.

I can't tell who it's from. It's an encrypted folder, and when I click on it, it asks for a password. I click my fingers together, squinting and chewing the inside of my mouth.

Bird, I type, hoping to hell I'm right.

The folder opens, spilling picture after picture onto my screen, voice notes, memos, and when I realize what it is, the only words I can manage are, "Oh my fucking god."

It's pictures of Damien's men following Reed. Pictures of them following *me*. Parties. Events. Going back as far as Anne Tober's party. There's one video, and I open it up to a shaky cell phone video.

"—help you guys with something?"

Mads.

Fucking *Mads*.

I take another drink of champagne from the bottle.

He's confronting Chester and Paul at what looks like Fashion Week. The video goes on with Mads questioning who they are and what they want, yet as another man enters the video, I feel my entire body grow cold.

It's fucking Damien.

It's Damien and…

I clasp my hand over my mouth and nearly throw the computer onto the floor.

Damien was at Fashion Week. And the girl that he has his arm around…

It's the missing model.

"Fucking hell, Maddox," I say out loud, my heart pounding.

Has he been sitting on this? Has he told anyone? Oh god, what if Damien realizes Mads saw him? What if he realizes…

What the actual fuck.

I play back the video again and again, making fucking sure I'm right, before opening up another tab and typing the girl's name into the search bar.

She still hasn't been found.

And as I sit and stare at the screen again, I realize something.

When I see Mads again, I'm going to punch him in the throat, then kiss him.

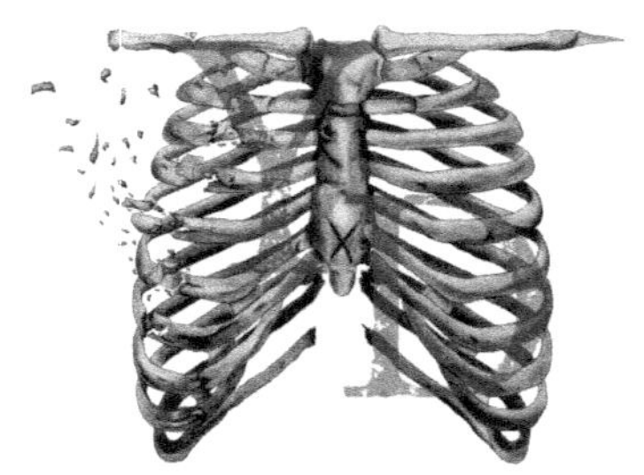

For four days, I get my shit together.

I send Anita to Larry's and give him money to take her out to his parents' farm in Iowa, no questions asked.

I have two backup flash drives along with the first, all with everything I have on Damien, including the black video of him when he threatened, almost raped, and then killed Erik in the SUV.

One drive, I take to Tara, along with my laptop. The second, I put somewhere secure that no one will find it.

And the third is burning a hole in my fucking pocket.

I dial Damien's number and stare at the billboard of Young Decay over me that's advertising their New Year's concert at the Hollywood Hollow Arena.

"This is a nice surprise," he says when he answers.

"We need to talk," I say flatly.

"Cute," he says. "What about?"

"Misha Larén," I say.

Damien goes quiet at the mention of the missing model's

name, and just as I open my mouth to speak, a blue sedan pulls up beside me.

"Your chariot, Miss Kelly."

I hang up the phone and get inside without hesitation.

I don't know where he's taking me. It might be to my death. It might be to a torture more deadly than I can imagine.

But I'm fucking done.

I open my phone and send one more text.

> If I'm not at the New Year's Eve show, you
> know this went the wrong way.

Mads texts me back within ten seconds.

MADS TOURNING

> Send me your location.

I do, and Mads sends back a thumbs-up emoji, along with another text.

> Come to sound check when it's over.

He's definitely more confident in this than I am.

"Hey, no phones," the guy in the front says.

"Fuck off and drive," I snap, pushing my phone into my pocket.

I try to remember the turns this guy is taking, but he's taking some ass-backward way that I quickly lose track. I wish I had someone following me now, someone looking over my shoulder to make sure I say all the right things this time, and that I don't leave anything out.

We pull up to a massive warehouse more than a half hour later, and I turn on the app Tara had me download to record the sound around me, even when the phone is closed. There's no evidence on the phone of the recording other than a small black dot at the top of the screen.

The goon opens the door for me no sooner than I've put my phone in the pocket of my leather jacket. I smack his hand away when he goes to grab my wrist and lead me inside.

Darkness swallows the sunlight as we meet another man at the edge of the loading door.

I don't know what I've just interrupted, but I've never seen Damien look more annoyed.

He's pacing, hands behind his back, an anxious way about his walk that almost makes me smile.

He's fucking nervous.

I shouldn't get so excited to see people nervous when they talk to me, but it does something to my insides.

Damien's gaze lifts when my heels click on the floor. His eyes rake over me, jaw clenching as he pauses, and I'm brought directly in front of him. He stares at me another moment, and all I can do is try not to smile in triumph.

"Search her," he tells one of his guys.

I widen my legs and hold up my arms as the guy rushes up, then I take a look around the warehouse space.

"I see you've upgraded," I say. "This is much better than the dirt road you had us on the last time—*Easy with the fucking hands*," I snap at the one by my legs. "You'd think you don't let these guys get off, Damien. Or are they too busy being your good little subs?"

Damien only lifts his chin in response.

The one behind me finds the flash drive in my pocket, and he pulls it out. "Got this, boss," he says, and he tosses it to a guy with a computer who immediately plugs it in.

"Need a password," he says with a glance over his shoulder.

But I just stare at Damien.

Paul cocks the pistol back and points it at my head. "Password," he warns.

"I'm sorry, is your computer guy not smart enough to hack a fucking encrypted folder?" I taunt.

"The password, Kelly," Damien sighs. "Don't be a hero. I kind of like having you around."

"It doesn't matter what the password is. The evidence is already with the cops," I say.

"You're not that stupid."

"I'm pretty fucking stupid," I argue.

"If you've already given the evidence to the cops, you wouldn't be here trying to strike *yet* another bargain," he bites out.

"I'm not here to strike a bargain. I'm here to tell you that we're done."

His brows lift, and he glances between the rest of his men like he expects them to laugh. "Done?" he eventually repeats.

"Yes. Done. I'm fucking done with you," I seethe.

"That's not how this works, Miss Kelly."

I cool my tremble with an even breath.

"I don't care. I want out," I say. "And this time, you're going to let me out. You're even going to give me a fucking car to go back home, and when I block your number, you're not going to call from another one or come after me."

A sardonic chuckle rumbles from him. "Why would I do that?"

"I have video of you taking Misha away at Fashion Week," I say. "What happened? Did you sell her, too? Along with the other girls who look like her that I've seen missing persons reports for this week? I bet pretty girls like that fetch more money when they're whole, don't they?"

"What do you think your boyfriend will fetch, Miss Kelly?" Damien threatens.

I almost laugh. "Reed? No one would know what the hell

to do with him. You'd end up cutting him like you did my brother just to shut his mouth."

Damien doesn't look away from me as his men shift.

"I mean it. We're fucking done," I say.

"You think I'll let you go over a little video of me with some model who no one gives a fuck about?" he asks, and I can hear the fear beginning to rise in his tone.

"I have a lot more than the model," I say.

His jaw sets. I hear the movement of some of the men as Damien debates his next move.

"You don't have anything," he repeats, voice lower. "You're bluffing."

"Do you want to test that theory?" I ask, head tilting.

Damien blinks. The others around him shift, glancing between one another like they can't believe some dumbass actress is out here threatening their boss.

"Come after me or anyone I love, care for, or otherwise, and we'll find out *exactly* how much I'm bluffing," I warn.

Rage settles on Damien's face—absolute annoyance that I'm threatening him in front of his men.

Damien steps up to the computer guy and says something I can't hear. The guy argues back, prompting Damien to smack him on the back of his head with the handle of his gun. I can't hear all of what they're saying, only whispers of another name —Erik's—followed by Damien almost screaming out of frustration.

"*Who brought me this guy?*" he asks his other men. "Who told me he knew what he was doing?"

"Boss, Erik left everything in a fucking mess," Paul says. "He had it all coded to him."

"And you're telling me none of you are smart enough to *figure this out?!*"

"Tell you what, Damien," I call out, my voice echoing in the space. "I'll give you the password."

He gazes sideways at me over his shoulder.

In a flash, he's crossing the space between us. He points the gun directly at my forehead, and I force my entire body rigid at the sight of his anger getting the best of him.

"You'll give me the password, or you'll die right here," he says through his teeth.

But I'm done backing down from him.

"Kill me, and people will come looking. And you don't know what they might find," I say.

A low noise sounds from his throat as he shifts from foot-to-foot, the gun cocked back. "I should have killed you when you were a lonely little whore."

I don't move. Don't blink.

I have him.

I have his stupid possessive self. If I knew how to make the bastard beg, I would. I'd make him grovel and plead for me to give him the drives.

Though, something tells me he'd bend to no one, no matter what it might cost him.

And right now, seeing Reed again means more than seeing this asshole on his knees.

"Tell me what you want, Kelly," Damien finally says.

My burning ears perk at his deliberate drawl, and I force my jaw to move, force words through the dryness in my mouth. "I want your word that you nor your stupid little minions are going to come after me or anyone I love *ever* again," I tell him. "No more following me around or keeping tabs on me. You can have the password when I have the keys to that car in my hand and I'm halfway down the road. And after I give you that password, you're *never* going to contact me. But if you break that promise… it's fucking *over*."

The last time I stood in front of him like this, Damien had my brother on his knees and a gun pressed to his forehead while Travis screamed at me to run, to leave him.

Run, raven.

I won't see that same thing happen to Reed.

"Ticktock," I taunt him.

Damien rounds on the guys now surrounding the computer again as if a collective of them can figure it out.

"We need more time—"

Damien cocks the gun back and aims without looking. I wince despite myself as it goes off. The bullet flies into the guy's ear, and he falls to the ground.

Damien glares my way, his chest heaving. "That's two you've cost me, Kelly."

"Your issues aren't my problem," I say, keeping myself in check. "My freedom. I want it now."

He's chewing on the inside of his mouth like he's trying to draw blood. The gun trembles at my forehead. He's so angry, it wouldn't come as any surprise if he blew my head off right now.

I need to swallow.

I need to blink.

Every passing second has me on the verge of trembling. Though, each time I feel them, I see Reed's face behind my eyes, and my next breath is even.

"How many more copies do you have?" Damien asks.

A smile tugs on the right corner of my lips. "Come after me and find out."

Damien grinds his teeth, and finally, he jerks his chin in the direction of the guy who brought me here. "Give her your keys," he says.

"Boss…"

"I said give her your fucking keys!" Damien shouts.

The guy tosses me the keys to the old sedan, but I'm not done.

"Your word, Damien. I need to hear you swear it," I say as he starts to turn away from me.

He scratches his neck with the barrel of his gun, other hand to his hip in a frustrated way. "You're free, Kelly," he says.

"What was that?" I ask.

Because I want to fucking humiliate him.

"I said you're free to fucking go! Get out of here before I change my mind!"

"Cross your heart?" I say through gritted teeth.

Damien's eyes widen on me. Paul starts to say something, but Damien is already by the table with the computer. He picks it up and throws it on the floor. Kicks the chairs. Tosses the table.

I slowly back out, my heart pounding in my ears, and as the gun goes off again, I bolt to the car.

Get out.

Go.

"Run, raven."

I do.

I finally fucking run.

The wheels squeal on the road as I peel away. I don't trust that Damien is actually going through with this, but at least maybe I've bought myself a little time.

I have backup plans just in case.

I turn my phone on and call for Tara to meet me outside of town when I'm no more than a minute down the road. I keep looking in my rear view, expecting the white SUV to be following behind. And as I drive, I feel my nerves catching up with me.

I'm rehearsing what I want to say to Reed.

I'm fantasizing about how this conversation might go.

Fuck, I hope this works.

WE'VE BEEN REHEARSING NONSTOP the last two days, and it sounds fucking amazing with the orchestra behind us. Every time the violins start, the hair on the back of my neck stands. I can feel the music in my gut as it works its way to the very tips of my extremities, bubbling out of my mouth like it can't be contained.

Even so, each time I hear it, all I can see is the look of exhilaration on Wren's face when I'd let her listen to the recordings that night.

"We've rearranged a few songs," Mads is saying to the radio DJ interviewing us right now. "Zeb and I've been working with a friend of his, Jaime, to really make something new from our original tracks. I mean, we've been working on this a while now. Had instruments in the studio laying down tracks. But fucking nothing compares to hearing it like this."

"It's insane, man," I agree. "On a whole new level."

"Do you think you'll be adding some of these instruments into your recordings when you get back in the writing caves? Making new music next year?" the DJ asks.

The four of us look between each other. "Yeah, I think so,"

Zeb says. "Third album. We want to make something truly epic that no one's heard before."

"And Reed, does this include getting you back on piano for a few songs? I see they've brought in a grand piano for you."

"Hell yeah," I say. "I'm excited to play on it. We usually only have the board for me to play on. This will be a nice change."

"And that's time," Stella says, coming up to us. "Food is nearly here. I need you to wrap up."

The DJ pouts at her. "Come on, Stels. Five minutes more. It's my job to get all the questions answered."

"And it's my job to take care of the band," Stella says. "Robert, you can come back to watch the sound check, if you like. Right now, I need them to eat something before they all forget."

The DJ wraps up with a couple of questions for Mads, asking to get introduced to the composer who's here backstage. Mads jerks his head in that direction and leads the DJ back, and as he does, I slump onto the edge of the stage, letting my legs dangle down front.

Still no messages.

I run my hand over my face and behind my neck. Yesterday, I was stupid enough to dress in all black, mask and hood, and stand outside Wren's apartment in the hopes that she might come downstairs. Though, she never showed. Not even to walk Anita.

It's eating me not to know if she's okay.

"Hey, sandwiches are here," Mads comes back out to say.

I drink down my water and start to stand, but Mads waves me off. "I'll bring yours out. Wanted to talk to you about the mid-section? Playing your new one?"

"Oh. Okay. Yeah, man."

Weird.

I get to my feet anyway and cross to the piano where I sit

on the bench. Fuck, I don't even know if this song is right. I think it is. It feels more right than the others have.

I let the melody flow from my fingertips, the entire time imagining Wren sitting back on that piano top, smiling at me like I'm absolutely ridiculous. Calling me out on my bullshit.

God, I fucking miss her.

A lump forms in my throat, head hanging as my fingers begin playing harder upon the keys, the restless energy leaving through my fingertips. I barely hear the footsteps coming back onstage, ignoring them because I'm in the middle of a fantasy I know might never come true.

I've wracked my brain these last few weeks for ways to get her out of this. Debated sending my entire family to Australia next year while we're off tour. Debated kidnapping Wren and doing the same with her. I could rent a private jet, take her in the middle of the night somehow.

I just want to get her out.

I don't care about anything—

A gleam of red hair catches in my peripheral.

I don't think about it at first. I'm so consumed in my thoughts of her that it doesn't phase me. But as I hold back what feels like tears, I realize I'm not fucking dreaming.

It's Wren.

The melody falls by the wayside. My heart sinks, breath catching in my throat. Her eyes are swollen and red as if she's been crying. She's wearing a leather jacket, a YD tee, jeans, and heels. She's fidgeting with her hands, her jaw quivering as she stares at me.

I nearly fall off the bench trying to stand.

"Wren."

I don't know why she's here.

I don't know that I care.

All I want to do is hold her and tell her everything will be okay.

"Wren—"

"Wait," she says, taking a step back as I start forward. "I need to tell you something."

"Can I hold you while you tell me?" I beg.

Her chest caves, throat bobbing. "No," she breathes.

I plant my feet on the ground, having to hold myself up on the piano because my knees are fucking weak watching her.

"You deserve better than me," she says deliberately.

"I don't want someone better than you. I want you. You're my person," I say, and she holds up her hand.

"Please, let me get this out before I forget it or trip over my words," she pleads, and judging by the look on her face, I realize she's been repeating whatever she's about to say the entire way here.

"You deserve someone better than me," she repeats. "You deserve someone who will make it on time to your gigs. You deserve someone just as animated as you, someone who matches your energy. You deserve dramatic gestures and someone who's happy all the time and not an absolute scatterbrain—"

I chance another step in her direction. "I like your scatterbrain," I say.

Even still, she backs up again. "You shouldn't. You should want someone with their mind right, with their shit together. There's so much more that someone else could give you. Assurance and affection and all the things that I struggle with. But…. Reed… I'm not ready to be done with you either," she finally admits. "And I want—if you'll let me—I want to try to be better for you—"

"I don't need you to change for me," I say. "I didn't fall in love with you just to ask you to change."

Her jaw visibly trembles. "I don't deserve you," she whispers. "But god fucking dammit, I want to. Because I think I'm in love with you, too."

My heart feels like it might burst at any moment.

"And I say 'I think' because I've never felt like this before," she goes on. "I've never felt this strongly for anyone. I don't know what true love feels like. It's always terrified me. I've run from it for so long…" She fumbles with her hands, nerves visible as she picks at her nails, and when her eyes finally meet mine, my aching heart begins to flutter.

"I want to be *yours*," she says, her voice shaking.

I swallow. "I didn't think you liked that," I manage.

"Any other person who's called me that only saw me as something to take possession of," she says. "Like I was a fucking shirt they could use anytime they wanted. They all meant to take away my autonomy. My body. My voice. My free will. But you… Reed, when you say it, I feel safe. It feels like the last part of me finally clicked. Being around you, your family, your friends… all of them so easy and warm and… it all makes me feel like I'm home again, and that's a feeling I haven't felt in over a decade. I never thought I would feel it again."

I exhale heavily at her admission, unsure of what I'm supposed to say or do right now when all I care about is that she's okay.

"Reed, say something," she pleads.

"What happened with them?"

Because I have to know if I need to hide her right here. Right now. I need to know if I should call James and tell him to take her away.

"It's done," she says, and a tear slides down her face as she says it. "I don't know if it'll last. I don't know if it will work, or for how long, but… that's all you need to know. I'm here. I'm here, and… if you still love me, if you don't hate me. I'm yours."

I've never walked three steps so quickly before.

I've never felt my heart drop into my toes and rise to my shoulders all at once.

But all that and more happens when I kiss her.

I'm yours.

It's all I can hear as I pull her into my arms, as I kiss her with everything that I'm capable of, hoping to fuck that she feels everything that I do.

I'm yours.

Hell yes.

Even if she hadn't said those two words, I would have treated her as if she had. I just want her here. I want her in my arms.

I want her for *always*.

When we part, I wrap my arm around her shoulders and pull her into me, letting her lay her head back on my forearm when she looks up. The small smile on her lips makes my aching heart do a little flip, and I lean forward just enough that our noses graze.

"You're mine?" I whisper.

She inhales a jagged breath as if the fear of saying it is finally working its way out of her body.

"I'm yours," she whispers back, trembling against me.

"Why are you shaking?" I ask.

"It's fucking cold," she says, and I laugh.

She flips her hair out of her face and lays her chin on my chest, smirking up at me. I take my beanie off and put it on her head, willing to get naked if she needs the rest of my clothes, and I wrap my arms tighter around her.

"Because I never thought I would get to do this again," she says. "I never thought I would get to hold you. To talk to you."

"That was never going to happen," I tell her. "I was already plotting an escape to Australia after the tour was over."

"Australia?" she repeats.

"It was a starting point," I say. "The jungles of South America were next."

She looks as if she wants to laugh, and I sigh as I entwine our fingers together, still holding onto this moment with the fear that it might disappear at any time.

Black ink on the inside of her finger catches my eye.

"Did you get a tattoo?" I ask, holding up her hand.

When I see the words, my stomach tightens.

She has *'little bird'* tattooed on the inside of her ring finger.

"I told you I couldn't get you out of my head," she whispers.

A grin flickers on my lips, and I step out of her arms to anxiously wipe my face. "Ah, fucking—"

"What?" she asks.

I lift my shirt to show her the tattoo in the middle of my chest—a skeletal wren in mid-flight, with greyscale watercolor feathers behind the bones, the wings rising up between my pectorals on my sternum.

She gasps, hand covering her mouth. And when her eyes lift to mine, I see them shining with unshed tears.

"I couldn't get you out of my head either," I manage.

I let my shirt fall as she crosses the space to me again, her hands wrapping around my face and bringing me to her lips.

"God, I fucking missed you," I say between our kisses. "I fucking… I have so much to tell you," I add as I feel elation weave through me. I part from her and step back, unsure of what to tell her first, what to *show* her. I can't think straight. "Fuck, I need—There's so much—" I kiss her hard again, barely noticing that she's starting to laugh at me. "Don't *ever* leave me again."

"I don't plan on it," she smiles.

"You have to hear this," I say, gesturing to the violins. "They're on break right now, but it's fucking… ah, you thought hearing it on the recordings was amazing? Hearing it live will make you *cry*—"

"Reed, slow down," she laughs. "You're making me dizzy."

"I can't. I just… Oh, *fuck*, you're here." I sigh and hug her again, face burying into the crook of her neck as she melts and hugs me just as close.

"You can tell me everything. After practice," she says as she steps back. "I'm not about to get in the way of this."

But I'm fucking desperate to keep her in my sight.

"You're not leaving, are you?" I ask. "Stay. You can watch."

"Only if you stay with me tonight."

I think my heart explodes.

"I'm fucking moving in," I say, much to her amusement. "Anita and I are about to be best friends. I'm going to annoy the hell out of you."

"Oh god," she mutters, head in her hand.

"And we're going to yoga together. A *proper* date. You're going to do all the things with me that you pretend to hate," I go on.

"I should have stayed with the mafia," I hear her say.

I slide my arm around her waist and drag my knuckle beneath her chin, knowing she's joking. "And after all of that… When I've fucked you sideways and backward and every way this pretty cunt will take me… we're cuddling."

She squints at me. "I'm taking back all of your gifts."

I feel my eyes widen. "You got me gifts?"

"Too many drunken nights crying over you," she mutters.

Fuck yes.

My nose nudges against hers. "Why does the thought of you crying over me make me so fucking happy?"

"Because you're as twisted as I am," she replies hoarsely, her gaze moving to my lips. "Tell me how much you cried over me."

"Sobbed," I reply.

"Yeah?"

"At the piano on my sister's shoulder," I go on. "On the floor of numerous hotels. Onstage at a fucking concert in Orlando," I hiss.

"Poor little poser boy," she teases me.

"Does that make you wet?" I rasp, breath skimming her lips. "Knowing how devastated I was not to have you tied to me?"

"Soaking," she whispers.

I clear my throat and look over my shoulder at some of the roadies watching us from the wings. "Hey—are we done for today? I need to take care of a needy little bird over here—"

Wren pulls me back and shoves her hand over my mouth, the two of us nearly falling over one another as she shakes her head and says, "No, no—he can be patient! He's not serious—"

I sway with her, my arm wrapped behind her neck, and I kiss her nose. "I'm serious about you," I say. "Now, tell me about these gifts."

She scoffs. "You can see your gifts tonight. Right now, Mads is going to murder me if I don't get you backstage to eat something."

CHAPTER FORTY-THREE

WREN

WHEN REED SMILES AT ME, I want to punch myself in the face for how giddy I get. For the way he reaches into my body and pulls parts of me to the surface that no one's ever reached. For how safe he makes me feel.

And most ridiculously, for how fucking much I love him.

In the last two days, he's made me feel like I'm the only person he's ever loved. He seems to be squeezing in years worth of time into the little moments he isn't practicing. The band took a break yesterday morning to visit the aquarium, and for once, I truly drew breaths that didn't feel like they were made of daggers.

The small stuffed narwhal I fidgeted with walking around is sitting on the coffee table staring back at me.

My face hurts from staying up all night with him because neither of us could turn our brains off. Over the last couple of days, he's had to tell me about every concert, every random dog he petted on the street, every time he looked at a sunrise and thought of waking up with me. He opened every gift I drunkenly bought. Told me about the Christmas I missed, and the fight Kamden and Koen got into. And between all of that, he kissed me. He touched me. He took his time tasting me. Fucking me.

He's put my heart back together and tied it to his.

However, a moment that will forever be ingrained into my mind was the moment when he saw the healing cuts on my thighs.

We were on the bed the first night. I was so fucking excited to be with him again that I didn't give concealing the scars a single thought. Not when he was kissing me the way that he was—from my neck to my tits, and licking down the middle of my stomach. I had my hands in his hair, ready to feel his tongue slide against my pussy when he paused, and the second I saw his face, I realized what he was staring at.

Reed sits back on his knees as heat creeps onto my cheeks.

Shit.

I grab the pillow beside me and start to sit up and close my legs, but his hand stops me. He gapes at my inner thighs, thumb running over one particularly long scar. God, the look on his face, the sorrow in his eyes. I nearly buckle at the weight of it.

"Bird..." His lashes lift, and when our gazes meet, my jaw begins to tremble.

He allows me to sit up and hug my knees into my chest this time, to make myself small against the pillows. My hair falls over the side of my face in the hopes that it hides the shame of those minutes when I drew the blades over my skin and watched the blood mix in the shower water and swirl around the drain.

"Babe, what did you do?" Reed breathes.

I know it isn't an accusation.

I know what he means.

Emotion bubbles up. A lump swells in my throat. I try to sniff back my embarrassment as I search for the words to say...

"I was just so fucking tired," I whisper.

The tears spill over. I can't shut it off despite trying to hold it in.

Reed catches me as I break.

He catches me and holds me and cradles me close, and as he does, I feel every weight I've carried on my shoulders lift.

And I can't stop the words from practically vomiting out of me as if his arms are the passcode to the darkest, most fucked up parts of my tattered soul.

"I wanted to feel something other than the pain I've caused everyone around me," I concede. "I wanted the voices to stop. The guilt. The shame. The loneliness. I've never been able to see a way out. I feel like I can't catch my breath. I'm so stupid, I—"

"Hey—" He pulls back, his own tears streaking down his beautiful face. "Hey, you're not stupid. You're not. You're so fucking strong, bird," he says, holding my face. "So fucking strong. And I know..." He gulps, eyes closing briefly. "I'll never ask if you're okay," he says, and my heart nearly gives out at his promise.

"Not when it comes to this," he goes on. "Because I know, Wren. I know you aren't. I know everything isn't okay. And I know it might never be. What you've been through... fuck, no one should have to go through what you did. It's not okay, and for me... For me, that's okay. I know each second will be a fucking battle. But I'm going to be here. I'm going to be here to remind you that you're worthy of being happy. Of being loved. Of everything in your life that you think doesn't belong, including yourself."

He presses his lips hard to my forehead, and I hiccup on another cry when he tilts my chin up and pushes my hair out of my eyes.

"I love you, and I'm not going anywhere," he swears. "You're never going to be alone again. You belong here. In this world. Right fucking now, bird. No matter what happens, I'm always going to be right here."

I'd hugged him so tightly and remained in his arms for long enough that I'd exhausted every tear in my body and eventually fallen asleep, only to wake up to him kissing every scar on my thighs.

Lying on this couch now, two days later, with Reed asleep atop me, his head on my chest, and my fingers slowly toying with his hair… this might be the happiest I've ever felt. His weight is a comfort, and while he's passed out finally, the sun is rising through the window behind me, and all I can wonder is if this will last.

Fuck, I hope so.

There's a nagging in the back of my mind that wants to pull me beneath the waves of this ocean we're floating on. A nagging that threatens to drag me back to the monsters of my anxiety, the suddenly starving beasts that once constantly told me I would never feel what I'm feeling right now, that after what happened with my family, my brother, I would never deserve to feel this.

Maybe I don't deserve it.

Maybe the reaper will drag him away from me and tell me he was never meant to love me.

But goddammit, I think he was.

I think we would have found each other regardless of the routes life has taken us on. I think our souls would have starved and crawled and fought until they found one another. At least, that's what I tell myself when the detrimental woes begin pressing upon my temples and it dawns on me how much he's not just my lover, but my best friend.

Shit. I've been around him too long.

Never say that out loud.

My phone buzzes on the coffee table, and as I reach for it, I see Mads's name on the screen.

The memory of Mads meeting me outside of the venue fills me. I didn't deserve his kindness or his help, and for as long as I can, I won't tell Reed how much danger Mads put himself in to protect him.

"Where is he?" I ask Mads, practically running into the venue, my heart so erratic that I can barely breathe.

But Mads just pauses in his step and looks me over like he's searching for wounds. "How'd it go?" he says nonchalantly.

"It... went," I reply. "I don't know how long it'll hold them off. He wasn't happy about it."

"You put copies in safe places like I told you?" he asks.

"Yeah," I reply. "You realize they're going to know it was you on the video. Doesn't that scare you?"

Mads shrugs and puts another chip in his mouth. "Not really. What—are they going to take my wife? Let them fucking try it."

"Could take your family," I remind him.

Mads throws the chip bag in the trash and wipes his hands on his sweat towel. "Yeah. Well. That includes you now, and I protect my family." His gaze flickers toward James, and he nods in a way that makes my gaze squint.

"Where is he?" I ask, referring to Reed.

He jerks his chin toward the stage. "Out front. I came back to get his sandwich. I'll meet you out there in a few. Give you time to talk things out," he says as he starts to leave me.

"Hey, Mads?" I call out.

"Yeah, chirp," he says, smirking at me.

My nose wrinkles. "Oh no, you can't give me a nickname, too," I say, nearly forgetting what I was going to say.

Even so, he smiles. "Actually, Andi came up with that one. What's up?"

"Why didn't you take the video to the authorities once you figured out who he was?" I ask, the question burning in the back of my mind for days now.

"How do you know I didn't?" Mads taps his temple twice, walking backward away from me. "Go put my best friend out of his misery."

Add my name to the list of people Mads Tourning has saved.

MADS TOURNING

Is he with you?

I look down at Reed as he squeezes me a little tighter, groaning slightly in his sleep.

Yeah, he's here. Is everything okay?

Big night tonight. Just wanted to make sure
he wasn't on a park bench somewhere.

I mean, he's parked on my bench, but he's
safe at least.

Haha.

Have him at the venue by noon.

Andi says you're treating her to sushi while
we're setting up.

I chuckle at the screen.

Tell her only if she's buying the drinks.

I'll just send you her number.

"You're laughing, and I'm not the one making you," Reed says, his hoarse voice vibrating against my stomach. He picks his head up and sits his chin on my sternum, bright blue eyes glistening sleepily at me. "I think I'm jealous of whoever you're chatting with."

"Just your husband," I tell him. "He wanted to make sure you hadn't been discarded on a park bench somewhere."

Reed groans as he sits up, then grabs his phone and hits the video call button on Mads's number.

The wood he's sporting catches my eye.

"Hey, man," Mads says upon answering. "Don't you look gorgeous this morning?"

Reed pushes his hand through his messy hair and whips it off his face. "What's up?"

"Just making sure you're alive," Mads says, popping a gummy back. "You two disappeared quick after dinner."

Reed glances my way, and images of him fucking me backward over the public bathroom sink fill my mind. We broke the soap dispenser, knocked over the trash can, and spilled the tray of mints and freshening supplies they had on the sink.

It was fucking disgusting.

I loved every second of it.

Reed had given the owner of the bar a few hundreds and his manager's card to let him know the cost of the damages.

"Yeah, sorry about that," Reed says, still watching me. "What time do I need to be up there today?"

"Noon. Bands start playing at two. New Dawn will go on at seven thirty."

"We're up at nine?"

Mads nods. "You guys want to grab breakfast this morning?" he asks as he pushes his beard back to sip from his coffee mug.

Reed sits the phone down so that it's pointing to the ceiling, then leans back over me, quiet as he begins kissing up my stomach. "Maybe," he says as he reaches my breast.

"Hey—don't fuck her while you're on the phone with me," Mads says. "I know this move."

Reed reaches over and tilts the phone back to his face. "You can watch, if you want. Just don't think I want the favor returned because the thought of you fucking my sister still makes me gag."

Mads grins. "Yeah, okay."

"How's the baby making coming, by the way?" Reed asks, sitting up.

"Oh my god, Reed." I press my head into my hand. "You can't just ask people that."

Mads chuckles and flips him off. "If you want to meet for breakfast, we'll be over at Ravenwood Coffee in about a half hour."

"We'll see you there," Reed says. "Later."

"Later, man."

Reed turns the phone over and leans over me again. "Think we can make it in a half hour?"

"I think so." I reach between us and stroke his already hard dick, making him groan into my neck. "First, I think we need to take care of this."

"Fuck yes." He kisses me hard, and I relax into him so quickly that I almost don't care about the fact that he hasn't brushed his teeth yet.

Almost.

I nudge his chest, and when he pulls back, I brace my hands against his cheeks. "I love you, but right now, I need you to go brush your teeth."

Reed snorts and hangs his head, his silky hair falling on my face. "Yeah, that's fair," he says, swiftly kissing me and rising to his feet. "I'm using your toothbrush, right?" he asks as he extends a hand to me.

My eyes widen. "That… *no*," I almost stammer. "No, god, please say you didn't."

"What if I did last night?" he asks.

"That's disgusting. You'd better be fucking with me. I showed you where the extra ones were," I argue.

"Why is that gross? You licked my ass last night," he says, smirking.

"I—*that was different*. You were already clean. And we were *in* the shower," I snap back.

Reed grins. "I'm joking. I would never use your toothbrush," he finally says.

"Oh, thank fuck," I exhale.

Reed pats on the wall leading into the hall. "Shower with me. You can help me with my vocal warm-ups."

"How am I helping with that?" I ask as I stand.

"Well, it's more that you're benefiting from them, really."

I stare at him, confused, and he grins slyly. "Get in here, and I'll show you."

CHAPTER FORTY-FIVE

REED

"SO, TONIGHT IS OUR LAST SHOW," I say, and our road crew boo's in response, making the band chuckle. "And all of us just wanted to bring everyone together back here to say thank you."

The crew all claps and shouts back, a few obscenities amongst them. We're standing out back of the venue while the first band plays so that we have a minute to chat with the crew that's been with us these last three years on and off tour. Next year will be a full year of making new shit, taking time with family, and catching up on becoming a normal human again.

Who am I fucking kidding?

I'll never be a normal human.

"Thank you, thank you from the very bottom of our hearts," I go on.

"Yeah, we couldn't have done this without all of you," Mads says. "It's pretty fucking wild to think about not being around you when we've all been together for pretty much all of the last three years. Like..." He glances over at me, Bonnie, and Zeb. "What the fuck am I going to do after this?"

"Probably fuck your wife," Zeb says.

The crew laughs, and I cover my ears, causing them to howl again.

"Come on, man," I say to Zeb.

Zeb waves me off, and I turn back to the crew. "Anyway, there's nothing really we can say to truly tell you guys how much your support through everything has meant to us. It's been three insane years, and…" I pause to sigh and run my hand through my hair, feeling the emotion of this being the last one for a while catching up to me.

Mads claps my shoulder and shakes me in a comforting way, and I have to laugh to keep myself together. "Okay, I'm done talking. Mads will bring it home."

It's pretty bittersweet to think about, that this is the last stage I'll stand on for a while. The last audience I'll jump into, the last worship I'll fucking lead.

Not forever.

We're not going anywhere.

Even so, my stomach is in knots.

The day goes by in a blur, and now we're less than fifteen minutes from taking the stage.

I left Wren with Andi earlier so I could give today all of my attention. My phone is about to die, and of course, I forgot the charger. It only bothers me because Wren has to leave right after the show tonight to make a red-eye flight out east for something to do with the Marilyn film, and I know I'll be at our afterparty when her plane takes off.

A guided meditation wraps up in my headphones. I don't know what I would do without this hour before the show to clear my head. To get my mind right so that my worries and anxieties of what tonight might bring fades away. And as the birds chirp to signal the end of the meditation track, I start stretching. Bending. Wringing my muscles out of the knots they're in.

I'm on my feet, shaking out my nerves and bouncing on

my toes when I hear a pounding knock on my door. I take out my headphones just in time to hear Stella yelling from the other side. It's muffled, just like the sound of the audience out front.

"—on in ten," I hear Stella saying, continuing to knock. "Reed? Have you wrapped up your meditation? Mads is making his last circle."

Fuck yes.

I'm still bouncing when I reach for the knob, and the moment the door swings open, I hear it.

Young Decay.

Young Decay.

Stella grins knowingly, and I grab my chest like the noise of seventeen thousand fans chanting our name has my knees weak.

"That's fucking beautiful," I say to her.

She shifts her head toward the hall. "You ready?"

"Yeah, let's go."

I can hear fans beating on the stage barrier, some clapping at the end syllable of our name.

"Detour, Stella," I say, pointing toward the stage where I know Mads is probably lurking before coming back from his walk.

Stella smiles and hands me a jacket like she knew I would want to see the stage. "Hood up," she says as I put it on over Wren's bright pink, long-sleeve crop top that I stole.

She doesn't know that I took it from her closet this morning.

The noise of the audience gets louder and louder, and I can barely contain my energy as I find Mads lurking at the edge of the shadows where people can just see his figure. I launch the remaining way to him and jump onto his back. He catches me as if he knew I was coming, which knowing him, he probably heard my footsteps. The force of me sends us stumbling slightly forward, far enough that some fans notice the commotion, and when they spot us, they scream.

I jump down from Mads's back. We clap hands and hug, and I hear Mads laughing at me.

"You shit. You're supposed to be meditating," he says.

"Couldn't help it," I say. I hold up my arms and flash the audience the horns, sticking my tongue out to the shouts of a few people now beating on the barrier. I turn my attention to the orchestra setting up onstage, the musicians warming up in their seats, and it makes my next breath stick a little.

"Fucking hell," I say, bending over my knees. "This is real."

"Hell yeah, man," Mads says, clapping my back. "You ready for this?"

"Fuck no," I admit. "Are you?"

Mads smirks and takes out two gummies from his tin. "Now or never. Cheers," he says as we touch fingers and pop them back.

"Seven," Stella tells us.

Mads and I turn back to the crowd one more time and throw up our arms, eventually finding the mind to go back and meet Bonnie and Zeb in the largest dressing room.

Young Decay.

Young Decay.

Mads hands me one of his earbuds as we walk the hall.

I can't stop moving. Can't stop banging my head to the music Mads has blasting on these headphones. Can't contain myself from jumping and high-fiving everyone on our crew.

This energy needs *out.*

I practically crash into the dressing room where Zeb and Bon are waiting on us. Bonnie meets me in the middle, energy drink shaken and ready to break. She tosses me one, and as we crack the tops, they spray over us.

It's sticky and cold and as much as I hate the ritual, I also fucking love Bon. Laughing and entertaining complete chaos with her makes going onstage so much easier.

The moment Mads puts on our hype music, the four of us circle in. I'm doing vocal warm-ups and bouncing to the classic rock music, completely under the trance of anticipation.

I can already feel the lights, feel the heat against my face.

It's an addiction I'll end up scratching by singing and bouncing around my living room on the off days.

"Five minute warning."

Young Decay.

Young Decay.

It echoes through the space before the door shuts once more.

"Hell yes," Bonnie says, drumming the air. "Chills, every time." She shakes out her body, jumping with me, and Zeb reaches into his back pocket for the things we've been waiting for.

"You ready, bitches?" Zeb asks, holding the small bean bag up between us.

Bonnie's already fighting me, holding me back from catching the drop. I laugh and dodge her, and when Zeb drops it in the middle of us, Mads catches it with his foot instead.

"Oh shit—right here!"

To an outsider, we probably look like four fucking idiots who don't have the sense to be performing in front of seventeen thousand screaming fans. We probably don't look as professional as some other artists do.

But we're not here to be professional.

We're here to fuck people's faces off and have fun. We're here to give fans a concert that they'll talk about decades down the line.

This is our little family. One we chose. One we'll protect over everything.

And nothing can rip that away from us.

By the time Stella comes back around to grab us, I'm on the floor with Bonnie hovering over me and shouting her victory in my face.

"Two minutes," Stella says loudly. "Anything you need before you go on?"

I jump off the floor and swing my arms wide open toward her. "Stella!"

Stella's eyes widen as I engulf her in a hug, even picking her up off the ground. As her feet hit the ground again, the others wrap their arms around us, and we group hug the shit out of her.

"Stella! Stella! Stella!"

"What is this about?" she laughs.

"Thank you for taking care of us," I say. "Me, especially. I know I'm not easy."

"Trust me when I tell you guys that you're pretty fucking easy to work for," she says. "I'd come back if they wanted me to without question."

"Yeah! Hey Avie—you hear that? We want Stella for the next tour," I shout to our manager who's walking by, phone to his ear.

"Yeah, what? Oh. Got it. She's wonderful. Ten fives. Go get your asses on the stage," Avie says fast.

My heartbeat is in my ears as we take the walk to the stage.

I'm clapping and warming up with a few exercises, focusing on my range, as Mads walks beside me, egging me on to my limit.

"Higher."

"Stop being a little bitch."

"You can do better than that."

"*Higher!*"

And when I hit the note I've been working on for a while now, Mads stops to stare at me, awe over his features.

"Holy shit, dude." He claps my hand and brings me into

him for a hug. "That's what I'm fucking talking about. You got this," he says, slapping my stomach.

"Fucking hell, was that you?" Zeb asks when we reach him. "Do it again."

I do, and some of the crew members whistle and shout when I hold it longer. Though, this time, I follow it up with my own scream.

Young Decay.

Young Decay.

The four of us huddle our arms on one another's shoulders and bring it in one more time.

It's the last time I'll have them in a huddle like this until we're recording music, though even that isn't the same as this moment. This feeling.

"I fucking love you guys," I say to them, swallowing hard.

"We love you, man," Bonnie says, grinning.

"What do you say, for our last show, we blow this fucking roof off? We have an orchestra. A goddamn choir. Family and friends flown in from all over. Seventeen *thousand* people—"

"Absolutely insane, bro," Zeb says.

I sigh as I look between them. "I wouldn't want to do this with anyone else. You guys are my fucking family. How much we've grown over the last few years is only the beginning."

"Yeah? What are you dreaming?" Bonnie asks.

"Fucking Best Metal Album of the Year. Selling out venues like football arenas, Wembley Stadium—"

"Win a Grammy," Mads says. "Bring a quartet on tour."

"Multi-platinum records," Zeb says.

"Fuck yeah," I say.

But Bonnie's quiet, and I squeeze her shoulder. "Bon?"

She takes in a deep breath, jaw clenching. "Another year sober," she says.

The statement hits me in my chest.

"Start a fucking family," Mads says, his voice as soft as hers.

I squeeze his arm and glance at Zeb.

"Talk to my mom again," he says.

The three of them look at me, and I don't know what to fucking say. Their goals seem so profound. Meaningful.

"Reed?" Mads calls me.

I swallow, staring at the floor a beat longer as I go through all the things weighing on me lately. The decisions. The turmoil.

The look on Wren's face when she told me how low things had become while we were apart.

"Survive, man," I finally say. "Survive and love and fucking live without fearing that my next breath might be the last."

"Chirp, chirp," Mads taunts, and I shove him sideways.

"Alright, are you bitches ready?" I ask.

"Yeah, man," Zeb says.

"Yeah, let's fucking go," Bonnie says, bouncing.

"Thirty!" someone shouts.

The four of us scream as loud as we can.

I hug each of them tight. Bonnie walks up the steps to her risers. Zeb leaves us for stage left. I hang back with Mads for a few seconds like I always do, and we look at the audience through the slits between the stairs at the back of the stage.

"What are you thinking?" Mads asks.

"I was thinking Wall of Death during Fall tonight," I say.

"Oh shit. Okay. It's been a while since we had a good wall."

"You remember that one from DeathFest?" I ask him.

"That one was fucking epic."

"This is a good venue for it," I say. We've done so many concerts lately with benches or seats instead of pits that it's been hard to have a good mosh.

This venue though…

The thought has me rocking up on my toes in excitement.

"You jumping in the middle?" Mads asks.

"Even if I say no, I know I'll end up diving," I grin.

Mads chuckles. "Fair," he says, shifting on his feet. "What are you really thinking about?"

Someone runs by and hands me a mic, and I toss it in the air once, making sure it's still off. "I was thinking about asking Wren to move in with me," I say.

Mads squints at me, smirking. "Here I thought you were jumping ahead and giving her that little ring that your mom snuck in your carry-on over Christmas."

The ring that's in my bag backstage.

"I don't want to scare her," I say, stomach fluttering.

Mads pulls his mask up over his nose and starts walking backward to his position. "That's the thing about love, man. If it isn't terrifying, the fuck are we risking the pain for?" He points back at me over his shoulder. "One eye on you," he shouts.

"Always," I shout back.

I stand at the back of the stage another minute, staring down at the bracelets on my arm, and I bounce on my toes a few times to shake out the jitters working their way into me.

"Reed! Let's go!" Avie shouts.

I toss the mic in the air one more time and turn it on, and as the intro breaks, I begin singing.

Let's fucking go.

CHAPTER FORTY-SIX

WREN

HE'S FUCKING CHAOS.

He's chaos and insanity and unhinged everything.

The goosebumps haven't left my arms from the very first note he sang.

Andi and I are upstairs over the stage, watching from the side. It's just us. The band's families are all in VIP areas around the arena, but when given the choice, she and I didn't care that we couldn't see the front of the stage. We were both happy watching from the side.

The orchestra sounds insane. I'm in awe of the care taken with the composition, the way the strings and horns have enhanced every single note.

Even I have to blink back emotion when Reed sits at the edge of the stage and looks back at the orchestra like he can't believe they're onstage with him.

"Can you guys fucking believe this right now?" Reed says into the mic, grinning at his bandmates, then at the audience.

Reed and Mads have both pointed and signed our way, the former smiling a little softer at me, gaze lingering a little longer than it has in the past at a concert. Something about the way he glances up makes my chest ache, my ears heat.

It's during the first song after the set break that Reed completely loses what's left of his mind.

He launches himself onto the rig at the back of the stage and starts climbing. Seeing him move without fear of anything has my heart racing. I know he's okay. I watched him climb the rig yesterday just to test it out.

He beams my way, and I know he's coming for me.

I don't even have the mind to tell him to stop. I'm too high on him. Too enamored by the surprise of what he'll do next. There's still anxiety in the pit of my gut, but for once, I don't feel the need to perform.

Because it's him, and he already knows the real me.

He pulls himself onto the railing of the platform and kisses me hard.

My heart has never been so full, and I've never felt so weightless.

If loving him is flying, I'll never stop.

"Are you wearing my shirt?" I ask against his lips.

"Yep," he replies. "Are you mad?"

"No," I say. "It's fucking hot."

He grins and pulls away, his fingers still lingering on mine as he begins singing.

I barely register the lyrics. His gaze doesn't move from mine. There's a tiny part of me that is fully aware of the thousands of people watching, but Reed… Reed is the only thing I see.

He's my home.

He kisses me one more time before heading down.

Reed jumps from the rig just as the lights dim, and I see him setting up. He points to the edge of the stage. James's pace quickens. He says something on his radio. Mads strums the line, and as the strobes begin to flicker, Reed runs.

A gasp leaves me that I can't stop. My hand clasps over my mouth as he launches from the stage and into the crowd. His feet land on the barrier somehow, and James grabs him before he topples over and into the crowd.

But Reed has a shit-eating grin on his face, and he doesn't miss a fucking beat.

By the time the song ends, he's standing on top of security's shoulders with his arms out wide, and the entire venue sings the lyrics back to him. He finishes the last line and punches the air as the lights dim and the crowd goes insane.

Reed jumps into the walk and James escorts him back onto the stage where the spotlight follows him while the rest of the band takes a breather.

"How you guys doing out there, LA?" Reed asks breathlessly into the mic.

The crowd roars.

Reed smirks crookedly and pushes his sweaty hair off his forehead. "I said *how are you fucking doing out there LA?!*"

The shouts are exponentially louder, and I can't swipe the stupid smile from my face.

"There you are. I thought you'd gone to sleep on us. I was ready to come out there again and punish you guys for that," he says, and people scream back at the notion, prompting him to laugh.

"Yeah, you'd like that, wouldn't you?" he asks before pressing a water bottle to his lips. He downs the entire thing and flings it out into the audience, winking at a couple of fans screaming down front.

"Alright, LA, do you mind if we get a little intimate? I feel like we've been fucking your faces hard for a while now. I like to change it up, get in a few long, slow strokes…"

Some girls down front scream, and he laughs, flipping his mic up and down once before heading back to the piano. He sits and strikes a few notes, making my ears perk at the melody.

Andi nudges my side and smiles as if she knows some secret that I don't.

"So, the last three years, we've spent most of our time on the road," Reed goes on. "Had a few months off here and there, but we never really stopped. And… it's fucking crazy to think that so many of you have been with us since the beginning, so thank you. Thank you so fucking much for supporting us and loving us through all the wild moments we've had… And for everyone here who might be new to the Young Decay cult, welcome to the fucking madness."

The crowd goes wild, and Reed changes up the melody to one of the songs from their first album.

Watching him play this has become my favorite part of their show. It's mesmerizing and comforting, and each time, it transports me back to the cabin. To where it's just us, and I'm sitting on that piano top watching his long, key-tattooed fingers stroke the board as easily as water rippling over sand.

And when he begins singing the song he was working on in Raleigh, I have to clench my teeth to keep my emotion in check. He's been humming it in bed the last two days, striking invisible keys on the counter when he's cooking. And each time he's hummed or belted out a random word, he's looked up at me through the strands of his shaggy black hair, his blue eyes dilated, and wore the same soft smile that he's wearing on his lips right now that causes my heart to swell and ache.

It's incomplete, but I don't care.

Because it's called Cross My Heart.

By the time the show is over, I've cried twice. Andi gestures to me to follow her down after they wrap up the last song and stay onstage to take photos and toss out a few guitar picks and drumsticks to the crowd.

Reed runs off of the stage and grabs his mom up, hugging her tight, making sure to hug the rest of his family before finally making his way toward me, and when he wraps his hands around my neck and brings me in for a kiss, my knees instantly weaken.

I don't know how to tell him how much he means to me—how much *all* of this has meant to me.

He chuckles against my mouth, apparently feeling me melt into him, and he wraps one arm around my waist. The way he looks at me when we part makes my heart skip.

"I think we have about twenty minutes until midnight," he says, holding my chin in his fingers. "I want to be buried inside you when the clock strikes twelve because that's how I intend to spend this entire fucking year." He nudges my nose with his, mouth quaking as he restrains himself from kissing me again. "Wait for me in my dressing room."

"Okay," is the only word I can manage.

He runs back onstage after giving my chin a flick. A hand touches my elbow when he disappears, and I look back to find James behind me. He jerks his head to the hall, prompting me to follow without a word.

It's another fifteen minutes before Reed finally makes it back.

I honestly expected him to take longer.

I almost laugh when he sticks his head inside the door, and upon seeing me sitting in lingerie on the counter, he curses under his breath and closes the door again.

"Yeah, I just need five minutes," I hear Reed saying outside the door. "Dude, I'm soaking wet—"

"Go fuck your girlfriend," I hear Zeb say.

I can already see Reed's grin as he opens the door a fraction. "I mean, if you insist," he says, and Zeb laughs.

"Meet you out back, man," he says to Reed.

Reed slides inside and shuts the door behind him this time. He's clicking his fingers, obvious adrenaline eating at his insides and begging to get out. I'm already throbbing at the wild look in his dark eyes. My bare feet hit the cold floor, and I feel my heart skip, eagerly waiting for whatever he's about to do to me.

"I only have five minutes," he says, taking off his wet shirt —*my* wet shirt.

"That seems excessive," I taunt. "What did you have in mind for the other four?"

He scoffs and advances. "I have a few ideas."

His hands are on my neck, pulling the roots of my hair as he roughly kisses me. Fuck, his mouth. His tongue. His hands. I don't think it will take more than one harsh thrust of his hardening dick to get me off right now. Not with the aggression threading from him and into me. Not with his bite, his lick, his grip.

My ass hits the counter as he backs us into it, head slamming into the mirror. He rips at my lacy underwear, his hand diving between my thighs, the other on my neck and shoving my throat back. I squirm beneath him, whimpering at the tease of his thumb on my throbbing clit.

And as two fingers slide inside me, I feel him pushing on me like he's trying to pick me up. I barely have to press my hands into the counter. Reed pushes me onto the counter. Breath catches in my restricted throat, and he yanks me forward to suck out what's left of the pocket of air I'm trying to take, simultaneously stroking my spot in a manner that already has me on the verge of tears.

His kiss breathes life back into me, grasp on my throat slackening. I throw my hands into his hair, and he sinks to one knee, mouth enclosing my clit, yet he doesn't let up on the quickness of his fingers sliding inside me.

I'm fucking weak.

Control has left my body.

I've never come so quickly before, yet when I do, I scream and jerk so much that I'm barely surprised at one of the mirrors cracking behind me. I'm still coming when

Reed grabs and pulls me out of the way of the shattering glass.

"Damn, babe," he says, grinning as he kisses me.

I laugh, drunk on him. "Maybe don't break any more mirrors?" I manage.

But Reed licks his tongue against mine, fingers dragging my release over my clit. "I still have three minutes. Something else is definitely breaking."

His lips are back on mine as he threads his hand beneath my jaw. I hardly get a chance to recover before hearing him unbuckling his pants. And when he pulls me off the counter and turns me around, I get a glimpse of us in the mirror.

He's smirking deviously around the side of my head, those piano keys on his fingers spread wide on my neck, my breast, and the sight of his stark, fully tatted arms against my pale skin makes me crawl with desire.

And there's something about the blown blue of his eyes right now that hypnotizes me entirely.

"All fucking mine," he growls in my ear.

His muscle contracts, hand squeezing my throat, and my jaw sags.

Fuck, that feels good.

The moment seems like an hour, but it's only a split-second of time that moves in slow motion between us. His spread fingers move to the nape of my neck, tangle in my hair, and as I feel his dick tickling between my thighs, he pushes me down.

My face smashes into the counter. He holds my hair and lifts my foot into the chair beside us. I'm stretched as he fills me, almost laughing at the insanity of how amazing he feels dragging me around this room.

Shit, is this what delirium feels like?

The sting of his wide slap on my ass ricochets through my entire body. I gasp and groan into it, shoulders relaxing and limping along with the rest of me, giving in to his thrill and guidance. One glance up at the raging lust in his eyes as he watches himself slide in and out of me makes my back arch. Each thrust buries me further into the cold counter. Drool slides from my lips as I try to hold on, to contain myself and ride wave after wave threatening to surface.

Reed whips me around and pulls me up. I throw my arms around his neck, my feet numb when he walks us backward and backward until I hit the couch on the other side. I fall onto it, hair splaying over my face. I can hardly see when I feel him crouching over me, his mouth on my throat, his dick finding my center.

I don't know how these long strokes of his do me in, but they do. They're drawn out, calculated, and numbing—like he's taken care to memorize exactly where my spot is and knows the precise angle that will make me cry with pleasure.

And I do.

God fucking dammit, I do.

His forehead meets mine, arm sliding under my thigh to hike it up to his ribs, and it's close like this that he moves with full intention of an end. My lips meet his, teeth grazing and biting his mouth as I try to hold out. I can feel him trembling with me, feel him straining just as much as I am. And when I can't take another second of denying this, I come with a scream of his name.

I hear him curse, feel him jerk, and he stills inside me to the hilt as he comes.

I close my eyes to fall completely into this moment as he finishes inside me, as he slackens and rests his chest against mine. And eventually, he kisses me softly, somehow threading the embrace in promises we don't even know we're making.

All I know is that I never want to let him go.

It's a few moments before our eyes open to one another, and when they do, my chest nearly collapses at the look in his gaze.

"I'm so fucking in love with you," he whispers in a trembling voice, nose nudging mine.

My heavy breath meets his as we rest a fraction apart. I feel my bottom lip quiver with his words, and I hardly hear myself when I whisper back, "I'm so fucking in love with you, too."

The clock on his phone goes off, making Reed smile against my lips. "Happy New Year, bird."

"Happy New Year, poser."

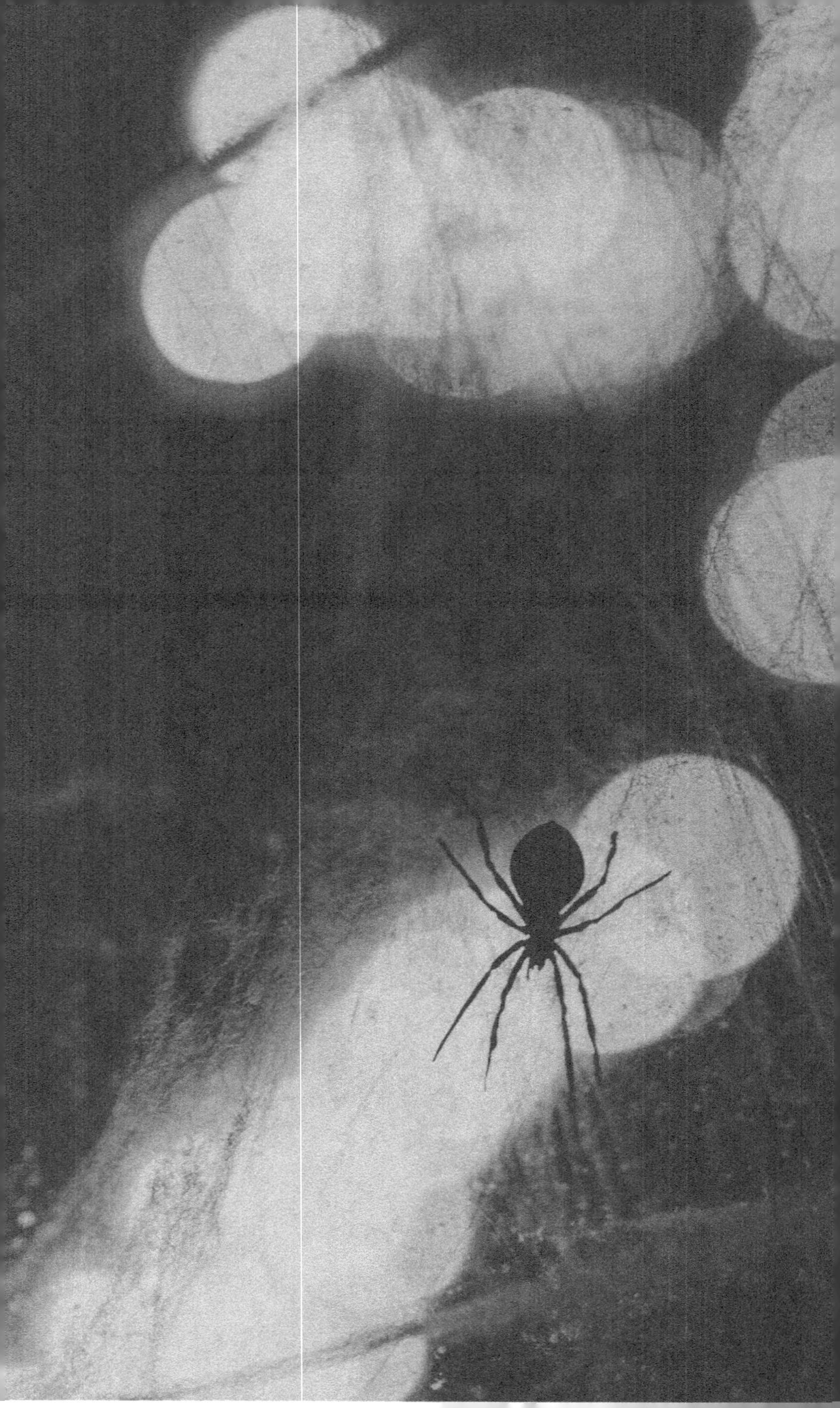

CHAPTER FORTY-SEVEN

"I HAVE to sign autographs out back," Reed says once we're dressed again.

"So, go," I tell him.

But Reed hesitates. "You'll be gone when I get back," he says.

I smile and wrap my hands around his face. "I will. But those fans are only here for one night. It's your last show for a while. I'll see you in three days."

"Or, you could skip meetings tomorrow and stay with me," he argues.

"You would like that, wouldn't you?" I taunt him.

"I would," he says. He leans in to kiss me, his lips lingering on mine even after our eyes open.

"Move in with me," he says, and my heart flutters.

"Here I thought you were moving in with me," I manage, though nerves are eating at my insides at the thought.

"Seriously, Wren," he says. "I mean it. I want you to move in with me. We're only about two hours from LA—"

"We?" I ask.

He smiles. "Mads and Andi live on the floor below," he

explains. "Above us we have a custom studio. We'll be working there so much next year, and with you traveling for work, I just thought… Anita could hang out with me."

"Oh, I see now. That's what this is about. You just want my dog," I taunt him.

"I thought that was obvious," he replies. "She'd have fun playing with Mads and Andi's dog, too."

I almost laugh. "You'd have to look after my plants," I say.

"I can do that. You have a chart."

"And deal with my doom boxes," I remind him.

He snickers. "Easy."

"I leave clothes everywhere. Most times, I don't do the dishes immediately. I leave clothes in the washer and forget about them, so I have to do them again," I say, because any normal person would tell me I'm crazy.

"None of these things are sending me running," he says. "When I say I want you, I mean all of you."

He's lost his fucking mind.

And yet, I want to move in immediately just to have him to come home to.

Reed leans forward to kiss me again as if he can see the wheels turning in my head. "Think about it," he says as his thumb swipes over my lips. "Text me when you land."

"I'll try to remember this time," I answer.

He scoffs. "I'll remember if you don't."

I'm still on cloud nine when I leave through the back door a few minutes later and get into Tara's SUV waiting for me. I catch Reed's eye as I get in, and he waves from the line of autographs he's signing.

"Where to?" Tara asks as I sigh back in the seat.

"Ah… I need to stop by Larry's to make sure Anita has everything," I tell her. "Coffee. Then to my apartment to grab my suitcase."

"Are you already packed?" Tara asks.

I meet her gaze in the rearview. "We're not discussing whether I'm packed or not. The point is that I know where everything is," I say, and Tara chuckles.

"To Larry's then," she says as she makes a right out of the venue.

By the time we make it to my apartment, it's already been two hours since leaving the concert. Tara parks the car out front, and as I slide out of the vehicle, my doorman, Tommy, greets me.

"Late night, Miss Kelly," he says, smiling when I hit the curb. "Were you out at the Young Decay concert?"

"I was," I reply. "It was a nice night."

"I thought that's where you might be. A couple of delivery men came by looking for you this afternoon. I told them that's more than likely where you were. They had bouquets of roses and gifts that someone had requested be left upstairs for you, so we let them in."

My high instantly bottoms out.

Two delivery men…

Oh, fuck.

Oh, fucking fuck *fuck*.

"What kind of gifts?" I ask, trying not to panic all at once.

"Floral arrangements. Big ones, too. I figured your boyfriend had ordered them as a surprise for you," he says.

It isn't too far-fetched that Reed might do something like that; however, Reed knew I would be gone for three days. If he was going to do this, he would have ordered them to be set up the day I'm set to return.

I'm frozen inside.

And I'm not the only one.

"What time did you say they came by?" Tara asks, unbuckling her seat belt.

"Ah… around six, I believe. Eddie let them upstairs to leave the roses," Tommy says.

"And where is Eddie now?" Tara asks.

"He was taking off right after. Assume he went home," Tommy says.

"Did you not see him leave?" Tara asks.

"We all take the back exit leaving." He frowns between us. "Something wrong?"

Oh my god.

This has to be a joke.

This cannot be fucking happening.

Tara gets out of the car at about the same time I find my feet.

"Everything is okay," she says as she escorts me to the door. "Thank you, Tommy. Keep an eye on the car for me."

Tommy frowns, but doesn't question us as we go inside.

Fuck.

Mother fuck—

"Hey—" Tara says once we're in the elevator. She snaps her finger in front of my face, forcing me to look at her. "You're going to let me go in first, you hear? Take this—" She hands me a taser. "Safety is off. All you do is click this trigger."

She takes her gun from its holster on her belt and presses it between both hands.

I can't even open my fucking mouth.

"Whatever happens, if they're still there, you *run*. I mean it, Wren," she says pointedly. "You run, and you call Reed's body-guard immediately."

I frown. "Why would I do that?"

"Because he's ex-FBI," she says.

Breath escapes me.

"Excuse me?"

Tara ignores my surprise. "There was never any need to pin

you with Reed except to get James closer to Damien," she goes on.

"What the hell are you talking about?" I ask, rage rising.

"James recognized Erik at Anne Tober's party. The next day, he called his buddies at the FBI to let them know he'd seen him, knew you were involved with something to do with them, and they decided to put him back on the case. His goal was getting the two of you close so that he could keep an eye on what was happening with Damien, possibly lure him into acting out or attempting to hurt Reed because of you."

"He knowingly put Reed in fucking danger?!" I nearly shout. "Does Reed know about this?"

"No," she says with a scoff. "It was better to leave both of you in the dark, let things play out naturally. And he was always watching Reed. He was never in real danger."

"Don't fucking tell me he was never in danger!" I snap.

Raging white lights nearly blind me as I try to put this all together.

The ruse was a fucking ruse?!

Oh, fuck, this is a nightmare.

The elevator doors open, the chime making me jump. Tara peeks out and glances up and down the hall before pointing her gun in front of her and stepping into the corridor. She tweaks her head toward my apartment for me to follow, and I do.

I'm already shaking.

Are they still here?!

Even with the fear of their being here, I'm still fucking reeling from Tara's claims.

It was all a fucking setup.

—My door is unlocked.

Tara meets my eyes and presses a finger to her lips. My teeth chatter, breaths short.

Please be gone.

She slowly twists the knob, and as it opens a fraction, it knocks into shattered green glass and soil, stopping it from opening fully.

There's a pause where Tara closes her eyes as if she's preparing herself for whatever might be on the other side. And in that second, sound numbs around me.

Tara kicks in the door.

Her gun points up in front of her. She speaks, though I don't hear what she says.

My apartment is in utter disarray.

Every plant I own is on the floor, tipped and ripped and broken. The vases and containers are in pieces everywhere. My couch and chair are turned over, cushions strewn and cut. Lamps cracked on the floor. Massive rose arrangements sit on my island counter. The only noise is the sound of my television playing whatever nature docu-series Reed and I had been watching before we left this morning.

And in the middle of the floor is the bleeding body of the day doorman, Eddie.

I gasp, hands clasping over my mouth.

Oh, fuck—

Movement catches my eye at the hall.

In a blink, I see the silencer pointing toward Tara, and I scream.

The bullet glances past her shoulder as she whirls on her feet. I drop to the floor, hands on my head. The muted gun goes off again. Tara falls to the ground and whips onto her back, gun pointed. She gets off her own shot as I scramble toward the open door.

"GO!" she shouts at me.

But she's bleeding.

"Wait—no—"

"Get out of here!" Tara yells again. She's backing up behind the overturned couch. I barely see the gunman, barely let a single thought run through my head as I panic and crawl to the door.

She's struggling through the pain of the two shots through her body—stomach and arm.

Footsteps stagger on the ground. I hear him curse. I know he's hit, but I'm not willing to look back to see how bad.

And just as he comes into view, as I crouch and ready myself to bolt out of the door, I see him limp around to the back of the couch where Tara is struggling for air.

One tap to her forehead is all it takes.

I scramble, unwilling to let the fact that one of my friends is now dead on the floor, because of me, make my feet stop moving. I have to go. I have to get to Reed—

A bullet grazes the wall past my ear as I bolt through the door.

Run.

Run.

Run.

My hands slam on the staircase door, and I sprint down. Each floor that I pass has my thighs burning. I pull my phone from my pocket, hands shaking as I look through it to find Reed's number.

Please be okay.

Please be okay.

I dial his number before I'm at the lobby.

Tara's fucking dead.

I can't feel my face anymore. Can't feel my teeth. My hands. My legs.

"Pick up, Reed," I say out loud as I pass the tenth floor. "Please, pick up."

Voicemail.

I want to scream.

I call again. Again. Again. I call until I nearly fall down the last flight of stairs, my feet so fucking heavy that I can barely pick them up. I can't see for the tears in my eyes. I don't know what breath is anymore. My lungs are tight and frozen. Nausea rises in my throat—

I push the door and run out into the parking garage behind the complex. It's too quiet. So quiet that all I hear is the rush of blood pounding on my eardrums.

With shaking hands, I tap James's name and press the phone to my ear.

Act cool.

No one is chasing you.

Shit, what if he took the elevator, and he's already down here?!

I walk calmly by the cameras, keeping my head down, waiting on James to pick up.

"Wren?"

"Oh thank fuck—James? Have you—do you know where Reed is? I can't find him. There were people at my apartment. Tara's dead—"

"Slow down, Miss Kelly," James says. "You said they were at your apartment? Are they still there?"

"I don't… I don't know."

"Where are you now?"

"I'm walking behind my building toward…" Shit, I don't know. I've never been on this side of the complex.

"I'm calling you a car," he says. "You're to go to the airport and get on your plane."

I stop dead in my tracks. "Excuse me?"

"The situation with Reed is being taken care of," he goes on. "It will look better if you aren't involved in this."

"Fuck what looks better, James," I snap. "Is Reed safe?!"

Silence staggers on the line. It's so blatant that I stop breathing altogether.

"James!"

Headlights flare behind me.

"James, tell me he's okay," I say, picking up my pace.

Another voice comes on the line that I don't recognize. "The situation is handled, Miss Kelly," the new man says. "Get on your plane. Someone will be in touch with the status tomorrow. Don't worry. We're doing what we can."

The status?!

Fuck this.

I hang up the phone, rage spreading through me at the noise of them treating this like it's some sort of transaction.

The headlights behind me are nearly on my ass. I cut short into the next alley, and when I do, I run.

Why the hell did I wear heels tonight?!

I make another turn and slow, pausing only at the brick wall to make sure the car keeps going. Hood over my head, I dial Reed's number again.

I don't care that I already know he's not going to answer.

Only two rings this time.

Mother fuck—

The next thought that enters me sinks my stomach. Even so, I need help. I need to find Reed. And assuming he's at that warehouse…

God, he's going to kill me.

I dial another number, more fear and shame weaving through me than even the thought of being picked up by some of Damien's goons.

Pick up. Pick up. Pick up.

Mads's number goes to voicemail.

Goddamn it.

I can't call Andi. I'm not about to tell her her brother might have just been kidnapped because his bodyguard is an FBI agent trying to catch the guy who killed my own fucking brother.

Oh god, I'm about to faint.

I dial the next best thing, heart in my throat.

Zeb answers on the third ring, the noise of the afterparty blaring in the background.

"Yeah?"

"Zeb? It's Wren. I'm sorry, I didn't… Mads gave me your number in case of an emergency, and I—it's an emergency—"

"Hey, whoa, slow down," he says. "What's up?"

"Is Reed with you?" I ask.

"Ah… no, not yet. I thought he'd skipped off with you. Why? Something wrong?"

"And Mads?" I ask. "Where is he?"

"He hung out for a little while but then left with Andi," he answers. "What's up? Is everything okay?"

I press my clammy hand to my forehead, heart slowly shredding. "No. No, no, it's not… I think Reed may have been kidnapped."

There's a beat of silence on the other end. I hear the music fading as if Zeb is walking somewhere quieter. And when there's nothing more than a steady hum of cars passing by, I hear him again.

"What are you talking about?" he says.

"I think he might have been taken by the guys that have been following him," I repeat. "Shit, this is my fault—"

"Where are you?" he interrupts me.

"I'm—"

Fucking hell, where am I?

"I'm behind my apartment. A few blocks over. I just started running. I don't know. I don't usually come this way."

"Send me your location."

But I can't turn my mind off.

I pivot and sway, searching for landmarks, street signs, anything—

"Hey, Wren, I need you to take a breath for me," Zeb says. "Tell me everything you see, okay? Walk me through where you are—hey, you haven't seen Reed, have you?" I hear him say offhandedly to someone.

"Um… I see…" I swallow the sticky lump in my throat and push half of a breath into my lungs, blinking back my tears. "Brick buildings. The park is three streets over. I can see the lamp. A post box…"

"You're doing great, Wren," Zeb says. I hear a woman's voice with him, though I can't tell what she's saying. "—can't find him. We're leaving. Get your shit. I'll tell you what I know in the car," he says to the woman. "Wren, you still there?" he asks me.

"I'm here," I manage.

"Okay, we're coming to get you. What else can you tell me about where you are?" he asks me.

"I don't…"

Headlights shine on the street over. I quickly back up against the wall and hold my breath.

Don't see me.

Don't see me.

I'm probably just paranoid. It's more than likely nothing.

However, as slow as they're driving, I'm not about to take any chances.

"Okay, Wren?" Zeb asks.

"I think they're looking for me," I breathe. "There's a car driving slow. I don't know… my security was shot—"

"Wren, I need you to send me a location pin," Zeb urgently cuts me off. "*Now.*"

I barely hear him as I dart behind a dumpster. A tear trickles down my cheek.

"Hey, I think I know where you are, Wren, but I need you to help me out here, okay? Text me a pin drop to your location," Zeb says.

The car passes.

"Wren."

I blink out of the daze and manage a, "Yeah," before finally finding the strength to peel my phone away from my ear and send him my location with trembling fingers.

"Did you get it?" I ask, my voice quivering.

"Ah… yeah. Yeah. Don't move." The noise of an engine humming to life sounds on his side. "We'll be there in fifteen. Are you okay?" he asks.

"No," I admit, my hand on my face. "No, I'm not. I don't… I need to find Reed—-"

"We'll find him. Stay low, okay?" Zeb says.

"Wait—don't hang up," I say, panicking. "You don't have to talk to me. Just don't hang up," I almost beg. "You can put me on mute if you need to, I just… don't leave me."

There's a beat of quiet on his end before I hear him say, "Okay."

I almost throw the phone to the ground in front of me as my ass hits cement. A sob chokes in my throat. I quickly hit the mute button so he can't hear me crying as relentlessly as I am.

Reed…

This is all my fault.

If he's hurt…

You destroy everything you touch.

I don't care what James says. If he's watching him or let him get taken on purpose or what's going on. Damien won't hesitate. No one will be fast enough to get to him.

Fuck. Where could he be?!

As I tear at the roots of my hair, I close my eyes and try to remember every turn from the day Damien's guy took me to the warehouse. The smells around me. The color of the building.

God, it feels fucking useless.

A red sports car pulls up to the curb fifteen minutes later.

"It's just us," Zeb says over the phone.

I slowly stand, careful to look around me as I make my way

down the alley. Zeb stares at me through his rolled down window, Bonnie peeking her head through the middle seats.

"Get in."

I frown at the sports car. "Whose car is this?" I ask.

"It's nice, right?" Bonnie says.

"That's what you two are talking about right now?" Zeb jerks his chin my way. "Get in the fucking car, Kelly."

I don't argue with him.

The tires squeal on the asphalt as we drive off.

"Where are we going?" Zeb asks.

Fuck.

"I don't…"

"You don't know?" he asks. "Wrack your fucking brain, Kelly. Tell me where my lead is."

"There was a warehouse that Damien took me to the other day," I say, pressing my hand to my forehead. "It was huge. One of—"

Zeb huffs and switches driving hands. "Was your phone on?" he asks.

"Yes," I answer. "I recorded everything."

He holds out his hand. "Give me your phone."

I do, and he opens up a few screens, one eye on the road as he zips in and out of traffic, and when he's found whatever he's looking for, he curses under his breath.

"What's up?" Bonnie asks.

"It's a half hour away." He hands me my phone back and glares sideways. "If something's happened to him—"

"It's fucking Damien," I snap. "We'll be lucky if Reed's in one piece."

"With his mouth, they might throw him back," Bonnie chimes in.

"They never threw me back," I reply.

A muscle tightens in Zeb's jaw beneath his black scruff, and he makes a right turn without looking at the oncoming traffic.

"Explain. Now," he says.

"I don't think it's important—"

"And I think one of my best friends has just been kidnapped because of some shady shit you're into. Bon and I deserve to know what the hell is going on. We have a half hour. *Talk.*"

CHAPTER FORTY-EIGHT

MY HEAD IS FUCKING THROBBING.

I don't know what happened. I was crouching onstage one minute, saying a silent goodbye, and a bag was thrown over my head the next. I don't remember struggling, fighting, or mouthing off.

Yet my hand feels like it's fucking broken, and the burning scratches on my neck and arms confuse me.

The taste of blood lingers on my tongue. There's a dirty cloth wrapped around my face and gagging my mouth. I can taste the salty stench of someone's sweat intermingling with the iron tang, and vomit rises in the back of my throat.

Fuck the zip ties around my wrists—that I can handle.

I need this gag *out*.

I can see a few figures through the woven fabric of the black bag over my head. I debate whether to make any noise, to let them know that whatever they did to knock me out is wearing off. I don't feel loopy. Maybe someone just took me out with the mic stand instead.

Could explain my throbbing head.

The bag is suddenly ripped off, some of my hair gets

snatched with it. I squirm at the sting, wincing at the blinding light that hits my eyes.

"Wakey, wakey, princess," someone says.

God, fuck off, I want to say.

"He is kinda cute," another guy says. "No wonder Kelly likes him."

I blink hard, trying to get rid of the black spots in my vision, and squint at my surroundings as they deliberately come into view. *What the hell.* I'm sitting in the middle of a huge open space. Ten guys surround me, four with large guns, the others with at least one small gun strapped to their waists.

I don't need to be a fucking detective to know exactly what's happened.

Shit.

Oh, shit—*Wren.*

My stomach bottoms out, heart skipping over itself. I peer around me, gaze darting from person to person, ears straining for any nuance of sound that might be her struggling.

Don't be here.

Please be safe.

But I don't see or hear her.

A relieved, heavy breath leaves me.

I fucking hope she's on that plane—far, far away from here. To hell with whatever is about to happen to me. As long as she's safe.

My attention staggers back to my surroundings, and I size these idiots up, one-by-one.

He thinks he's mafia, I can hear Wren saying.

The memory makes me laugh.

My amusement isn't shared. A hand strikes my face, the abrupt gesture stinging my skin. I flip my hair out of my eyes and mutter against the binding, glaring at the dumbass who hit me. I mouth off, continuing to make noise against the disgusting gag.

Come on, idiot.
Take it off of me.
Take the fucking bait.

My squirming sends my chair legs up. I yank and get it tilting, though not enough to fall. One guy jerks his chin when the one I'm staring at looks back at him, and finally, the latter removes the gag from my mouth.

"Oh, thank fuck," I breathe, spitting the taste onto the ground. "Sorry, I just needed to tell you about the massive booger hanging from your nose."

The handle of the gun comes down on my cheek.

Mother fuck—

I shake my head in an attempt to shake the pain away, but *dammit.*

That hurt like a bitch.

I stretch out my face, sniffing back my dripping sinuses.

"Shut the fuck up." The guy looks back at the one who jerked his chin at me. "Boss—"

"Man, you guys have really been watching too many movies," I interrupt, peering around the space. "Cliché abandoned warehouse. Bright light above me. Zip ties. It's all so *quaint.* I feel like the star of a movie. Thank you. Really. Film has always been a dream of mine."

"We should have cut out his tongue," one mutters.

"Then we wouldn't be able to hear him sing when we pick the nails off him later," another replies.

The sentence makes my nostrils flare, and I shut my mouth fast.

A smile creeps onto the lips of who I can only assume is Damien. His mid-length dark hair looks like each wave and lazy curl was gelled individually this morning so that it fell just right around his face. His beard is trimmed neatly around his smaller mouth and sharp nose, and he doesn't look much older than myself.

Impulsive and dangerous, I remember Wren calling him. *He thinks he's a god.*

I stare at Damien as he takes a step forward.

Match met, mother fucker.

"I assume she's told you who I am," Damien asks.

"Ah, yeah. Damien… something. I forgot your last name. Said you were some asshole trying to scare her. She left out the part about you being a shit dresser, though. Didn't anyone tell you three-piece suits went out in the 90s?" I ask. "Or maybe you just wanted to dress up for today—Does that make me *special?*"

"Jesus fucking Christ," another guy mutters. "What are we doing here, boss?"

Damien holds up a hand and zeroes in on me. "Tell me how many more flash drives she has."

The fuck.

"What?" I ask.

"Don't play dumb," Damien says. "You already look stupid enough."

"You forgot sexy," I retort.

How do I get these fucking zip ties off?

My feet aren't tied to anything, though my wrists are tied to the back of this wooden chair.

Maybe I am stupid.

Because the plan running through my mind right now is extremely questionable.

Damien takes his knife out and begins wiping it with a cloth as if he's showing it off. "The flash drives. Where are they?"

"I don't know anything about any flash drives," I argue.

"Bullshit. Your friend was the one that took the pictures and videos," Damien says.

"The fuck are you talking about?" I ask, completely bewildered. "I don't even know about any videos or pictures—and what do you mean my friend?"

"The one threatening us at Fashion Week," another says.

Ah, fucking hell, Mads.

The tip of Damien's knife thrusts beneath my chin. I can see him calculating as he stands over me.

I wish to hell I could get out of this chair. I'd put this dickhead to shame.

"Did she tell you what I did to her brother?" he asks.

My throat bobs at the mention, teeth clenching with the feel of the cool blade against my throat. "Vaguely," I say, recalling the story she told.

"I've had interest expressed in you already," he says. "Do you want to know what parts of you people are *most* interested in?"

"Probably my ears," I say. "Everyone tells me I have great ears."

The knife tip pierces my cheek. A growling groan of frustration leaves me, the noise an attempt to rid myself of the searing pain rippling from my face. I shiver and twitch, my eyes rolling upward to meet Damien's again.

"Must be my dick then," I go on.

The noise of a car revving up outside catches the air. The men look between each other, then peer to Damien for instructions.

My stomach is suddenly in knots. I know that rumbling engine, yet I fucking hope it isn't who I think it is.

Damien jerks his chin to his shoulder, glaring back at the dumbfounded idiots waiting for instruction. "Get out there, then!" he shouts. "Don't just fucking stand there!" He sighs heavily and wipes his face, fingers pressing into his eyes. "I'm surrounded by stupidity," he mumbles.

"Sounds like communication issues," I say. "Have you tried positive reinforcement?"

The handle of the knife comes down on my clavicle. *Goddammit.* An awkward pain moves down my arm. I want to shake it out. So much so that a quiet whimper leaves me from the agony of not being able to move.

A familiar scream echoes over the chilly air. My ears perk, stomach bottoming out, blood draining from my head and rushing into my feet.

White lights flash behind my eyes as rage piles in with shaking limbs and restless muscles.

If there's one fucking scratch on her, I'll lose my goddamn mind.

And as Wren's struggling figure comes into view, I nearly do.

Stay fucking cool, dude.

Don't charge forward.

Not yet.

She's…

"Get your slimy hands off of me," Wren snarls.

"Wren—get out of here! I'm fine. Go," I shout to her, but it only makes her squirm more.

"*Reed!*"

"Fuck," I hear Damien mumble. His head pivots left, gaze landing on a man who's holding a cloth to his shoulder like he's trying to stop bleeding from a wound.

"You took care of this?" Damien spat. "Is this what you call *taking care of her?!*"

"Wait. Boss, I—"

The man holds his hands up to try to explain; however, Damien already has his gun pointed.

He shoots without bothering to hear the man's side of the story.

"Oh shit," Bonnie says as the man drops dead.

The look on Zeb's face is almost amusing.

He's judging the hell out of this prick.

"Reed?! *Reed*—" Wren launches forward, nearly succeeding at trying to get out of the goon's grasp.

God, this fucking hurts.

"Hey, babe," I manage.

"Let him go," she snaps at Damien. "'Let him fucking go. *Now*. If you touch a single fucking hair on him, it's over."

Damien smirks, gaze raking over her in a way that makes me struggle against my bindings again. Like she's his property, a thing he gets to toy with and break.

Not anymore.

"Take your fucking eyes off her," I seethe.

"Cute," Damien says before turning all his attention to Wren. "I didn't realize you'd be joining us, Kelly," Damien says to her.

"Oh yeah? Is that because you expected my fucking carved-out heart instead?" Wren snaps.

"Head would have been sufficient enough," he replies. "Would have been less mouth to deal with getting information out of your boy toy."

"He doesn't know anything," she argues, struggling against the grasp on her arms.

Damien clenches his teeth, and he moves his gun to Zeb. "And what about these two? What do they know?"

"Whoa—easy, tiger," Bonnie says, hands up. "Start with a little foreplay, I mean…"

"Get your fucking gun out of my face," Zeb snaps.

"Do these two know where the flash drives are?" Damien asks.

"The hell are you talking about—"

"*You act like I go around involving everyone I know in your stupid fucking bullshit,*" Wren practically shouts. "You're not that fucking important, Damien. The only person who knows where the flash drives are is me. Let them go."

"Why don't I believe you?" Damien asks.

"Because your intelligence is questionable," Wren says.

The gun is back against my temple. I wince, almost expecting the barrel to be hot after its firing, though the cold metal sends a chill down my spine. I shift against its pressure, gaze moving back to Wren.

She's nearly foaming at the fucking mouth watching this guy.

"Did you come to bargain?" Damien asks in a taunting tone.

"I'm done bargaining with you," she bites out. "Your word doesn't mean shit anymore. Do you think I'm actually going to believe that you'll shoot him? He's worth ten times more to you alive."

Damien scoffs. "Look at you learning, Miss Kelly," he says. "Do you know what isn't much use to me?"

No one speaks.

"His tongue."

Oh hell no.

I immediately begin squirming.

Damien nods to the guy next to us. Hands grab my shoulders. A rope thrusts around my neck. I struggle, muscles fighting against the bindings. My chair is tipped back as a scream leaves me.

"*—hands off of him!*"

The overhead light stings my eyes. Someone tries to pry my mouth open, but I bite back, sending him howling as my teeth clamp on his finger.

"Reed—Damien, *stop!*"

Blood stains my tongue.

I can hardly comprehend the shouts and commotion going on nearby.

I'm kicking and writhing.

Spitting and biting.

Anything—*anything*—to stop them.

Not my tongue.

Not my fucking livelihood.

"Get off of me!" I hear myself scream.

"Stop!" Wren shouts. "No—I'll tell you. I'll tell you where they are—*just get your fucking hands off of him!*"

A knife gleams above me. I'm cracked across the face with the knife's handle. The blow debilitates me for a fraction long enough that clamps are thrust around the tip of my tongue. They pull, and I flounder, body quaking and trembling and—

"Damien, *please!*" Wren screams.

Another gun goes off.

My stomach flips, and a ringing silence billows through the space in the gunshot's wake.

Damien pulls off of me, glaring in the direction of the shot. "What—I told you shits not to—"

"Put my lead back on the fucking ground," I hear Zeb warn.

"*Now,*" Bonnie adds, her voice more daunting than I've ever heard it.

I manage to look up as the clamp slackens on my tongue. Zeb has two handguns pointed toward Damien, Bonnie a shotgun in her arms. Three more bodies lie on the ground— from shots, knives, or fists, I'm not sure.

And Wren is on her knees behind Zeb's leg, blood trickling down her gorgeous face.

I don't know what the fuck just happened.

The chair legs hit the floor, the pressure on my arms alleviates, though the rope around my throat remains.

Damien chuckles. "You're still outnumbered," he says.

"Captain Obvious over here," Zeb mutters. "I don't give a fuck. Let him go. He doesn't know anything."

"There are three drives," Wren blurts, getting to her feet.

His gaze moves to her. "Give them to me," Damien demands.

"I can't exactly pull them out of my ass, Damien," she snaps. "Let Reed go and give me a time frame. I'll get them to you."

"You'll get them to me, and then you're mine. Permanently," Damien says.

"She's lying," I almost yell. "I know where they are."

For a moment, time stands still.

Wren's chest caves. Our eyes meet.

A quiet snicker leaves Damien. "How fucking cute," he says. "The truth. Both of you. I'm getting tired of this."

"It's me. He's just trying to protect me," she says breathlessly.

"She's lying," I argue. "She told me where they are so they'd be safe in case you came back for her," I say, eyes never leaving hers.

Let me take this for you.

They won't kill me.

"It's okay, bird," I say.

Wren shakes her head, jaw clenching. "No," she says, starting forward.

Zeb grabs her arm.

"No, I can't… I'm not losing you, too," she begs, her voice quaking.

"Do you want to play a game, Miss Kelly?" Damien asks, head tilting.

Her attention draws away from me. "No."

"Too fucking bad," he replies. "I think I'll play a little rhyme you're familiar with, and whichever of you my gun lands on will be the first to die. You have until then to figure out if you want to tell me the truth. *Eenie*—"

Mother fucking hell.

Is this bastard playing eenie-meenie-miney-moe with our fucking lives?!

"—*Meenie*—"

His gun passes between us with every word. I look at Zeb as he swallows and sets his feet. I'm begging him to read my mind, to know what the hell I'm thinking in my head with this irrational plan.

Because it's all I fucking have.

And I'm *not* losing her.

"Wren, it's okay," I say, just to keep the charade. "I'll be fine. Let me tell them."

I tap Morse code with my heel—something Bon and I have been working on to help her communicate back to us onstage since she's behind us. Bonnie's gaze fixates on me, and I know she recognizes it.

My gaze shifts to Wren, and a breath leaves me as I finally look at her without panic.

Shit, she's fucking beautiful.

My plan is stupid. Insane. Probably won't work. But the only goal here is to get them out alive, no matter what it costs me.

"No," Wren says, voice cracking. "No, it isn't worth losing you over."

"It isn't worth losing you either," I argue.

"*—Miney. Moe,*" Damien goes on.

I wince as the gun lands against my temple, but I realize he isn't done.

"*Catch a tiger—*"

"We'll have to agree to disagree on this one," I say to Wren. "Let me do this. I don't want you to watch someone else go."

"And I can't go on without you," Wren manages.

A shadow moves by the warehouse door.

"*—toe. If he hollers—*"

Two shadows.

I try not to stare, except it's just past Wren's shoulder.

And I know exactly who it is.

I switch up my tapping, heart beginning to thump wildly in

my chest as Damien says the final four words. A steady breath leaves me. I set my feet.

"—meenie, miney—"

"I love you," I say to Wren.

"—*moe*." The gun presses against my head again, and I flinch away as Damien fixates upon Wren.

The shadows move forward, and as I see a glimmer of teal hair, I realize I'm right about who it is.

"Last chance, Kelly," Damien says to her.

Wren's glare is so cold, my blood stops.

"Fuck you, Damien," she seethes.

The words have barely left her lips when I throw my foot behind Damien's calf. He whips back, the gun goes off, and all fucking hell breaks loose.

Damien falls flat on his back. A man comes rushing up to help, but I launch myself forward, throwing my entire body into him. I catch on his back. My legs wrap around his waist, and he falls backward like I planned.

The wooden chair I'm attached to cracks and splinters. The brunt hit freezes me for a blink. The pieces of wood my wrists are attached to break off.

I swing one post toward the guy on top of me's throat as I hear Wren scream. I hardly notice the man taking his last breath, the jerk of his body atop mine as I shove him off and scramble to my feet. Damien is slowly standing up behind me. I see him grabbing for his gun again. He's not steady. He's flailing, yet still aiming for Wren. Panic fills me.

I can't lose her.

I *won't* fucking lose her.

Two guns go off just as I jump—

I know they say your life flashes before your eyes when you meet the reaper.

But that's not what happened to me.

I didn't see my life. I saw Death in a flash of lightning over me as I sat on the cold floor of a barely-lit, frigid room. Dried rose petals scattered along the tiled floor. Broken diamond-paned windows above a dingy sink. And when Death placed a rose-tattooed hand around my throat, a sharp, staggering breath filled my lungs. He slapped my cheek once, and deep scarlet eyes met mine as he uttered, "Get back to her," in a voice that shook my insides.

Burning, *searing* pain shoots through me.

I'm blinded by shock, by the noise of dozens more people suddenly rushing into the space.

My side is on fucking *fire*.

Oh, mother f—

"REED!"

No.

No. No. No.

No, this can't be fucking happening.

Reed crashes onto the ground at the same time as Damien's now lifeless body.

I rush to Reed, falling to my knees and hauling his chest into my lap. The gunshots are still echoing in my ears. The shouts of the federal agents suddenly deciding to rush into the scene are a hum that makes me want to lash out and slap each and every one of them for waiting this fucking long to interfere.

Never mind that.

Because Reed is bleeding.

"Reed—*Reed*—" I slap his face and hold him close as he groans and squirms. And when his eyes open to mine, I finally breathe. "Oh my god, Reed. Are you okay? Dizzy? Light-headed? Don't die on me—"

He huffs like he wants to laugh. "No, I think I'm okay," he says. "Everything hurts like a bitch, though."

Mads throws himself to the ground on the other side and lifts Reed's shirt, and upon seeing that the bullet just grazed his side, he sighs heavily and glares at his best friend.

"You're fucking mental," he says. "No one jumps in front of a goddamn bullet."

"You would have," Reed grunts.

Mads hesitates before answering, "Fuck off. I'm different."

"Yeah? Why? Because you think no one will fucking notice?" Reed spits the blood out of his mouth. "Fuck you. I did what I needed. I wasn't losing her," he says as he squeezes my hand. "And it fucking took you long enough," Reed says to him. "Zeb was over here about to go serial killer on these people."

"Maybe that's who he was in a past life," Mads says.

"It would explain a few things," Reed says.

I shouldn't snort, but it leaves me before I can stop it.

Mads looks like he might laugh, and just as I think he's going to snap back at Reed, he karate chops Reed in the stomach.

Reed nearly screams. "You mother *fucker*." He grabs his stomach and curls into me, agony blanketing his features.

"Yeah, you'll be fine," Mads says, clapping his shoulder. He looks at me, sorrow on his face. "I'm sorry you couldn't find me. My fucking phone died," he says apologetically. "Luckily, Bonnie has a big mouth," he adds, jerking his chin toward Andi who's standing nearby, a bloody baseball bat in her hands.

"You gave my sister a bat?" Reed asks.

Mads gives him an annoyed look. "She wouldn't fucking sit back and wait in the car, so I told her she could only help if she took a bat."

"Surprised you didn't handcuff her to the steering wheel."

"Fucking believe me. I tried," Mads mutters.

"I have another question for you," Reed says to him.

"I feel like you should have more than one," Mads says, eyeing him.

However, Reed chuckles, immediately clenching his wound when he does. "When the hell did Bon and Zeb become mob fighters?" he asks.

He isn't wrong.

Watching the pair of them take down some of Damien's goons and strip them of their guns nearly had me backing away from them.

"They've been going to shooting ranges and defense classes for months," Mads says, squinting at Reed. "You didn't know that?"

"What? No," Reed replies. "I've been on planes back and forth for months."

"Oh yeah, that's true," Mads says.

James comes up then, looking between us, and my entire body freezes as I meet his gaze.

I want to punch him in the throat for telling me to get on a damn plane and not come for Reed. I want to know why he didn't include any of us in this nonsense and put Reed in danger without his consent.

"Be right back," Mads says as he rises to his feet to talk to James.

"Is that the fucking FBI?" Reed asks me, finally looking around us.

"Something like that," I reply.

"Did you call them?" he asks. "Did you go to them with those flash drives or whatever Damien was talking about?"

"I didn't," I say. "I don't…" A heavy exhale leaves me, and Reed squeezes my hand.

"Are you okay?" I ask him.

Reed uses me to help sit up. "Can you ask me tomorrow?" he grunts. "I think I need the hospital."

A smile flickers at the corner of my lips when he's level

with me. I run my finger over the cuts on his face and neck, the bruises and blood on his jaw and lip.

"I thought he would have you in a truck shipping out to the highest bidder before I got here, or worse—under the knife ready to sell your parts."

Reed smirks crookedly. "Nah. If anything, he would have cut my tongue out. At least I would have had a back-up gig doing sign language at rock concerts."

A quiet chuckle leaves me. "You would smash that job."

"Fucking nail that job," he exclaims.

Our eyes meet, and he reaches up to my face with bloody fingers, lips landing softly upon mine. I practically melt into his grasp, into our little bubble of calm in a surrounding storm. And when we part, Reed presses his forehead to mine.

"I need to ask you something," he says softly.

"Anything," I breathe.

Someone clears their throat beside us.

We part to find James standing over us. He holds his hand out to Reed, and Reed takes it, holding his side as he gets to his feet.

"I should apologize for the forced charade," James says. "It was the only way we could get eyes on Damien."

"What?" Reed asks, clearly confused.

"You're going to have to do better explaining than that," I snap.

James nods. "An old friend of mine has been after him about ten years now. Back when I was an agent, Damien came on our radar as an up and coming guy just trying to get into black market trading. My buddy, Dell, and his team kept an eye on him just in case. Said he always thought Damien was reckless enough to do something stupid."

He clears his throat and glances my way. "They found out he was dabbling in organ and sex trafficking, though they could never get an agent on the inside. Damien was too unpre-dictable. He didn't have any kind of pattern to follow, and getting an agent inside without almost certainly condemning them seemed impossible. The team lost Damien after a few years, but when I recognized Erik at Anne Tober's party, I called Dell up and let him know. He said they'd found your brother's DNA and had been watching you for any indication that you were in contact with Damien, and Erik following you confirmed it. I knew we might have a way in, then. We just had to come up with a plan so that Reed would be within Damien's scope in the hopes he would act out irrationally at the thought of you telling him anything."

"Who out of my team knows about this?" I ask.

"Just Tara, who suggested getting the two of you together after the way Damien reacted to the pair of you leaving the Tober party," James says. "She heard Shannon and Amanda talking about getting you more publicity and was able to suggest the plan without raising too much suspicion."

"The fuck are you talking about?" Reed asks.

I glare at James, at the admission of the ruse. "Apparently, this dating thing we were coerced into was never about my need to appear *nice* to the public," I bite out. "Someone at the FBI decided to use us as bait."

"Well, that's a bit of a slant—"

"Oh really?" I roll my eyes. "Tell him what you said to me when I called you tonight," I snap. "Tell him how I was sobbing on the phone, trying to tell you my own security had just been shot, and you told me to get on a plane."

James's lips press firmly together. "We didn't want you to get hurt," he says. "We knew Damien would go after Reed thinking you had told him where the drives were since you were together again."

"How did *you* know about the drives?" I ask.

James's gaze shifts to Mads, who looks back at us and nods discreetly as if he knows what I just asked.

"Hang on," Reed says, pulling out of my arms. "You put me in deliberate danger but didn't tell me?" he asks James. "Forced me to date her just so you could get close to that creep? Knowing he might come after me or her?"

James took in his words for a beat. "Something like that," he says.

Reed turns into me. "Did you figure this out after we broke up? Did you come back to me to complete their plan?"

I balk. "Excuse me?" I snarl.

"Answer the question," he says. "Were you working for them?"

"I just fucking told you that I called James tonight to tell him you were in trouble— Do you think I faked being in love with you *just so you would get kidnapped?!*"

"It's well within the realm of possibilities," he answers.

He has to be joking.

My nostrils flare, breaths shortening. "Do you *really* think I don't love you?" I ask.

Reed considers me, his jaw tensing, and I almost break.

I scoff and turn myself in a circle, in complete disbelief that he's acting this way. "Jesus fucking hell, Reed," I hiss. "Do you need me to prove it somehow? Do you need me to post somewhere or make some dramatic gesture at one of your concerts to prove—*what are you doing?*"

What the—

I have to blink, have to force my legs rigid at what I find upon rounding on him again.

My face is reddening by the second, and I don't know what to do with my hands.

Because he's on one knee, and he's beaming at me with a ring between his fingers.

"What… what are you doing?" I manage, suddenly unable to breathe. "What are you… Why…Were you fucking with me?" I ask, heart dropping.

"Yeah, it was funny," he says with a shrug.

I gawk at him, unable to form words or a coherent thought, and Reed snickers softly when I can't speak.

"Probably not the most romantic thing to do after being kidnapped and beaten. Fucking shot, too…" A smile licks at his bruised lips. "But the best man I know once told me that when I found love that made me want to go to the ends of the fucking earth for, I needed to figure out a way to keep it—no matter what it might cost." His gaze flickers to Mads for the briefest second before it's back on me. "And I'll fucking do anything to hold onto you, Wren. So, apart from chaining you in a basement or branding my name on your heart, this…" He holds up the ring for me to see. "This might come close."

I swallow, the emotion swelling within me and causing my jaw to quake. "Reed… This… You don't think this is too soon?"

Reed reaches for my hand and kisses my knuckles, eyes remaining on mine. "Maybe… I know you think I'm crazy, and I don't care."

"I think you've lost your mind," I manage.

He chuckles under his breath, thumb swiping over my fingers.

"You barely know what it's like to live with me," I go on. "What if we're completely incompatible?"

"I know you," he says, beaming. "I think I'm the only person who knows you."

He is.

"Reed…"

"Tell me when you see your future, I'm not there," he says.

I pause, lump sticking in my throat.

He's there.

He's *everywhere*.

He's the only thing I care to see.

"Reed, this is wild," I breathe.

"Calm to your chaos, remember?" he says.

Tears burn behind my nose, a smile daring to flicker on my lips.

"Wren Kelly… Before I black out from pain and they cart me away on a stretcher, I need to know. Will you marry me?"

Our every encounter runs behind my eyes. Anne Tober's party. The kiss at the festival. Each event—each one breaking us more and more down to the people we've become today. The wedding. Breaking up. Being truly happy with him…

With *only* him.

"Yes," I breathe.

Reed hangs his head for a beat, his eyes closing as if he's somehow surprised. When he peers at me again, I notice the tears in his eyes. "Please help me up so I can kiss you," he whispers.

I laugh through my own emotions, help him to his feet, and as our lips meet, I know it was right. I know this is exactly where I'm supposed to be, who I'm supposed to be with.

Reed abruptly pulls away from me and points at Mads. "And *that's* how you're supposed to propose in public, bitch," he declares.

Mads's shoulders shake with his chuckle, and he flips Reed off. "Fuck you, man. My proposal was perfect for us. You just proposed, and now you have to go to the fucking hospital instead of taking her home."

Reed slides his hands on my cheeks and tilts my head back to look at him.

"I don't care," he says before kissing me once more.

I can hear the rest of the room going back to what they were doing, conversations beginning again, yet it's all a hum behind me. My only focus is him. The fact that he's alive and in my arms despite everything.

I swallow when we part, my heart somehow stumbling again as his forehead comes to a rest against mine, and I close my eyes.

"I told you I wasn't letting you go," he whispers.

"I never want you to."

EPILOGUE

REED

WREN'S dark eyes drag over me as she presses my knees up. I swallow beneath that tantalizing stare, breath catching as she palms my dick, her thumb swirling precum over the tip. Fuck, I haven't taken a proper breath since she walked out of the bathroom wearing black leather lingerie and holding a strap-less strap-on dildo.

A whimper leaves me as she passes the lube on my dick, holding the dildo in her other hand so that she's stroking them together. *Shit*. She's taunting me. Dragging out every second with a smirk on those ruby red lips.

I eye the toy in her hand when she lubes the small curved end that will go inside her, leaving a rather… *long*… dick for her to fuck me with.

I gulp and thank *fuck* we talked about doing this the night we decided on eloping so I could prep properly.

"For you," she says, handing me the remote that controls her end.

I kiss her knuckles when I take it. "I'll be gentle," I smirk.

Yet the coy smile that lifts into her eyes lets me know I may not be as lucky.

She leans forward and kisses me hard, still stroking my

dick against the strap-on as I cup her full breasts. Shit, these tits… this body… All her curves, dips, and creases… I love every fucking thing about her.

"You're so goddamn sexy like this, bird," I manage, my dick impossibly hard at the thought of what she's about to do to me.

She grins against my mouth before moving one of my hands from her tit to my dick, and she uses me to push more of the lube around the strap-on.

"Keep doing that," she tells me as she drips more on her fingers. She cups my balls, making me gasp, then tickles her finger between my cheeks, and when she slides that digit inside me, I groan.

"Fuck, Wren," I curse.

"Are you ready for me?" she rasps against my lips. "Do you want me to fuck this tight little hole, *husband?*"

I gulp as our eyes meet, gut hollowing out. "Yes," I manage.

She snickers. "Is my slut nervous?"

"I mean, maybe," I admit.

The most tantalizing laugh I've ever heard leaves her, prompting chills to rise on my arms.

She pushes a second finger inside me, and my dick twitches, orgasm rising to the point that my muscles tighten.

"If you keep taunting me like this, I'm going to come before you get inside me," I bite out.

Her tits press against my chest as she bends over me, teeth tugging on my earlobe after she licks the column of my throat. "Good boys come when they're told," she drawls.

Goddamn it.

Her voice is painstakingly sexy. Fuck, everything aches at the way I'm straining.

"Are you my good boy, poser?" she asks.

"Yes," I whimper, eyes shutting tight at the way she's massaging my prostate.

Her fingers strike my cheek—it's a sharp slap that widens my eyes and almost makes me come on the spot.

Once.

Twice.

"You want to put this inside me?" she asks, pressing the strap-on into my hands.

My cheek is still ringing when our eyes meet.

"Hell fucking yeah, I do." I eagerly take it from her hands and kiss her again, my free hand gliding between her thighs to her heated center. Shit, she's soaked. Fucking *dripping.*

"I think you're more excited than me," I tease, grinning against her lips.

"So fucking excited," she hisses. She groans and kisses me once more, and I slowly slide the curved end inside her, causing her to gasp softly at the way it bends to stroke not just her g-spot, but her clit.

"How does that feel?" I ask her.

She adjusts slightly, pressing her hand to the shaft and pushing it further into her. "Honestly, it feels like it's going to fall out," she says, and I laugh.

"Probably have to work out the kinks," I say.

"Maybe it'll be better when I'm inside you," she replies. "Are you ready for me?"

My gaze wanders over her entirely, taking in the whole of her sitting between my legs—the strappy leather lingerie, her cascading red hair over her shoulder, her tits, her stomach, the strap-on now between her thick thighs, glistening with lube.

I recline on the bed again, my back hitting the cool sheet, and she presses my knees up when I nod. And as she steadily eases inside me, all I can think is how fucking lucky I am to call her mine.

"Shit, Wren," I manage, sucking air through my teeth.

Her motions are slow and easy, each stroke a fraction deeper than the last.

"Are you okay?" she asks.

"Yeah," I force out.

I pick up the remote to her end as she closes her eyes, her palms bracing against my chest, and when I click it on, she jerks.

"Holy fuck," she breathes.

I cycle through a couple of settings, until finally her claws dig into my abs, and she sucks in a sharp breath.

"Oh, god, right there," she whimpers. "That one. Leave that one," she nearly begs.

A steady, slow vibration lingers between us, quickening at different intervals. She draws her bottom lip behind her teeth and pushes inside me again.

"Fuck, Wren," I curse.

She inhales a deep breath, eyes opening to mine, and she reaches for my dick.

"You like when I'm inside you?" she asks, stroking me.

I can feel that vibration against my balls, the sensation nearly ending me. "Fuck yeah," I say.

Glancing between us, I realize she's nearly all the way in. A look of triumph rests in her eyes. She drags her nails down my stomach before taking my cock in her hands again.

"That's it," she coos. She bends down, her lips brushing my ear. "Look at you. Taking all of your wife like a good little slut."

Fucking hell.

Chills erupt on my arms, and her pace quickens the slightest amount. It catches me off-guard, but one look at her face and I realize maybe the vibrations have her needing to reach her own end.

And her next plunge nearly makes me jump.

"Oh, shit—wait, *fuck*—slow down," I manage through a

laugh, squirming slightly beneath her. I have to fist the sheets, chest arching off the bed.

A quiet chuckle leaves her, and she leans over me as her pace slows again.

"Easy, bird," I say, taking her face in my hand. "I haven't done this in a long time."

She laughs. "One day, I'm going to fuck you like a ten-dollar-whore," she says.

I grin. "I fucking love you," I say.

Her lips press against mine, and as our bodies align, she fucks me in slow, languid strokes, drawing out the pleasure between us as if we have the rest of our lives to lay in this hotel together.

I grab her hands in mine and entwine our fingers together, then pull our arms up over our heads. A whine leaves her at that, the vibrations rising and rising. I'm on the verge of fucking tears from this pleasure, from the joining of our souls.

"Reed…"

"Please, bird," I beg as a tear stretches down my cheek. "Fucking hell, please. I need to come."

She licks my tear away and kisses me again. "Yeah?"

"Fuck, yes," I hiss.

"You want to come, poser?" she asks.

"Yes."

"Who's name will you scream when you come?"

"Yours. My wife. *Please*."

God fucking please.

"Wren—"

Wren curses under her breath. I can see it on her scrunched up face, hear it in her breathless voice. She's so fucking close.

"Shit, Reed… come with me," she finally says.

"Yeah?"

"Fuck—yes—*Reed!*"

"*Wren—*"

It's all I can stammer out before I come. *Hard*. Sticky strands of cum soak our chests as I release in wave after wave. Her nails are digging in my chest, body jerking, and I know she's coming too.

God, I love that look on her face.

"Off," she says, and my eyes narrow when she flinches. "Off—off—Reed, *turn it off!*"

"Oh shit." I scramble for the remote to the toy and quickly hit the off button, only relieving her because I know if I don't, she might fuck me sideways.

And I can hardly breathe.

A heavy groan leaves her when the vibrations stop, and she sits fully back, a smile licking her lips as she peers at me through her hair.

"I fucking forgot," I say, chuckling.

She scoffs. "I knew if you didn't, I'd pull out of you not-so-very-gently," she says.

"Well, thank fuck I stopped it," I say.

Wren blows a tuft of her hair out of her face and deliberately begins easing out of me. I hold my breath as she does, and when the fill finally leaves me, my head hits the pillow.

"Fucking hell, bird," I manage, suddenly empty. "Shit."

She reaches between us and takes the toy out of herself, then discards it onto the floor. "Fucking hell is right," she agrees. "That thing is powerful."

"Yeah, no kidding."

I push my hand behind my head and watch her wipe the cum from my stomach with a wet wash cloth that she'd prepared before we started this. Every drag of it across my abs has me flinching; however, the only thing I'm staring at is the ring on her finger.

Wren Kelly—

Ha. No. No, that's not right.

It's Wren fucking Matthews now.

My wife.

Her wedding band is composed of delicate diamonds that had once been parts of my grandmother's and her own mother's wedding rings, and now sits at the center of a reset piece with raw emeralds that I designed to present to her on our wedding day.

Shit, yesterday couldn't have been more perfect.

Wren couldn't decide on anything as far as decor, a date, or otherwise. It drove her wild. For six months after the proposal, she stared at wedding magazines and websites, even hung out with Andi and brainstormed ideas for what she wanted when she wasn't at work.

Though, nothing ever stuck.

The only thing she ever found was a dress—which is currently in a heap on the floor.

Two days ago, we were sitting on the couch after dinner when she told me how tired she was trying to force herself to put a wedding together when she wanted ten different things that didn't match. And as much as I told her she could take her time, the thought of it all was too much pressure.

"I don't know that I'll ever figure it out," she says, lying her head back on the couch. "Why is this so difficult?"

"Did you try listing all the things you didn't want?" I ask as I look up at her, my head in her lap.

"I did," she sighs. "It was concluded that I like nothing."

I chuckle. "I don't think that's true."

"I think it is." Another long breath leaves her. The sadness in her eyes makes my stomach twist. Fuck, I want to take that away from her.

"Why don't I just know?" she manages. "Andi said she knew exactly what she wanted the moment Mads asked her to marry him."

The sentences nearly nauseates me. "Are you having second thoughts?" I ask.

However, her staggering gaze upon me immediately lets me know it isn't that. "No," she breathes. "No. God, no, Reed. I think... I think it might be that nothing feels good enough."

I sit up, frowning as I turn into her. "What do you mean?"

"I mean... Nothing feels good enough to be marrying you," she admits. Her lashes lift, eyes meeting mine, and I hate that she feels this way. "I told you once that you deserve so much better than me, and I meant it. I want... I want to marry you more than anything, I just... I don't know that anything will ever feel like it's all that you should have. The party. The decor. Our friends and family and where they'll stay—and then there's the venue. The date—god, I don't know whether the best time is spring or fall or winter—"

"No summer?" I tease.

She gives me a deadpan stare, and I laugh.

"Definitely not summer, " she mutters. "And then," she goes on, her voice getting louder again, "There's the added expectations from publicity and fans and the spotlight on us. The pressure of making sure all of this is perfect makes me feel like I'm suffocating—"

"Bird, you know I just want you," I say, taking her hands.

Her chest caves with her exhale, the way she looks at our entwined fingers almost like she knew I would tell her that, yet she doesn't speak.

Fuck.

"I don't want to let anyone down," she finally says.

I swallow as I watch her, as I let her words and sadness sink in.

"Then let's do it tomorrow. Just us," I say, and her gaze drags to mine.

"What?" she asks.

I bring my knee up onto the couch so I can fully face her. "Let's go get married somewhere ridiculous tomorrow," I say. "Fuck the expectations and what everyone else thinks we should do. I know you." I squeeze her hands, noting the brightness rising in her pupils. "I don't want you to feel the pressure to perform or create a perfect day. Being with you is my perfect day."

"Reed, I don't know..."

"Let me take the pressure off," I say, bringing her knuckles to my lips.

A muscle feathers in her jaw as she takes in the suggestion. "Are you really serious?" she eventually asks.

Hope laces her words, and it almost makes me smile. "Yeah," I tell her. "We can plan a party for everyone else in a few months when the stress is off. We don't have to play perfect for anyone. And, it gives us a June date without getting you overly hot and sweaty if we do it at night."

She looks like she wants to laugh. "It sounds like you already have this planned out."

I scoff. "Vegas is decent at night right now."

Her brows raise. "You want to marry me in front of Elvis?"

"Hell yeah," I grin.

A quiet laugh escapes her this time, and she shakes her head. "Typical," she says, eyeing me.

I love that fucking sound.

My fingers squeeze around hers again. "I just want to marry you, bird," I tell her. "No pressure. No show. We can have this one, just us."

Wren throws her arms around my neck. I catch her around the waist and hug her tight, feeling the anxiety practically lift from her shoulders as I squeeze her into me.

"Thank you," she breathes in my ear.

The two words have me closing my eyes and letting loose a long breath.

Because I know when she says it, she means it.

"Just an FYI, I'm fully expecting you at DeathFest so I can introduce you to everyone onstage as my wife and say something about how that festival brought us together," I say.

She pulls back, a smile on her lips, and she chuckles softly. "I hate it, but that's better than having to worry whether or not the face I put on at our wedding is the right one," she replies.

I know the judgment she's worried about, and while I could tell *her all day that no one would care, I also know the anxiety might take away from her entire day.*

And I only want her to be happy.

Her gaze softens, and a lump rises in my throat at the sight of her genuine relief. "I love you."

I lean forward to kiss her again, feeling her exhale into me. "I love you," I breathe.

I never cared about where or when we got married.

Sure, a big celebration with everyone I've ever come in contact with might have been what people expected of me.

But Wren is my world, and fuck what everyone else expects of me—of *us*.

Holding her in my arms right now, in this cozy bed at a resort outside of the city, the desert sun rising outside the windowed wall … fuck, I know this decision was the right one.

We got married late yesterday afternoon at the Neon Museum in Las Vegas, and we didn't tell anyone. We *still* haven't told anyone. Yet the few preview pictures the photographer sent over already this morning had me in tears. Wren looked like a fucking pinup model in her satin mermaid-style wedding dress, the way it accentuated her hips and breasts and soft curves… And between all the neon lights and signs we took photos in front of, the Elvis impersonator, and absolute excess of stylized brilliance… it was fucking perfect.

Nothing could have been more perfect for us.

It's been nice being off the road and having time for our relationship to grow, especially with her living with me. My apartment had been a soulless, grey shell before she moved in —simply because being there by myself always reminded me how lonely I was.

Now, though…

We were able to salvage a few of her plants when we were allowed back into her place. Between dark paint job, the added brick and gold accents, the plants, the twinkle lights, blankets, dog beds, and more that we've curated into the space, it became our home.

Our home.

It took ages to get back into her apartment, or so it seemed. With the local police, and then the FBI, we had so many interviews and statements that for a few weeks, the days blurred.

Everything had been hidden from the press.

I still don't know how Shannon and the band's publicists managed to cap that one.

However, the only thing I cared about was that Wren was safe, and now, she would always be safe.

We burned the music box and the reminder of her brother inside. It had freaked me the fuck out when she eventually showed it to me. Even so, hearing her say that she was ready to let it go a few months after the entire ordeal had tightened my chest.

I think burning that jar allowed Wren to finally grieve her brother.

We'd driven out to the beach to do it, and after it was done, her sister, Sarah, met us.

It was her that Wren had sent the third flash drive to—with instructions to never open it, to put it somewhere safe that she would eventually forget about it, and do not, under any circumstance, contact her.

However, with Damien now dead, it was no longer a worry.

Their relationship continues to be strained, and after meeting her, I get it. Especially once Sarah found out everything that had happened with their brother. It had turned into an all-out shouting match on the beach, and I'd had to step between them and practically drag Wren away to keep her from doing something she might regret.

It killed me to hear her so upset on the way home. She'd trusted her sister, hoped that she might one day be able to be civil with her; though, all the conversation had done was push them further apart. And when Sarah had texted her a few days later as if they hadn't left each other screaming, speaking to Wren as if she were a child and telling her how stupid she was for trying to help Travis, and now getting engaged to a slutty rockstar who she'd never be able to trust, I'd very *politely* told her to fuck off and blocked her number.

Maybe that was harsh, but Wren had wanted to try, and all Sarah wanted to do was start controlling her again.

And absolutely, fuck that.

Wren tosses the dirty rag onto the ground and curls up atop me, and I wrap my arms around her as if I can somehow bring her closer. I love when she lets me hold her like this—entirely vulnerable and surrendered, walls and masks no where to be found.

My phone buzzes on the bedside table, and Wren groans.

"Turn it off," she says.

I chuckle. "Probably just Mads wondering where we skipped off to yesterday. We did lie about why we needed them to watch Anita."

She lifts her head and sets her chin on my chest. "Your husband can't go a day without you?" she asks jokingly.

"Nah, the world might end," I smile. I squeeze her hand and pick up my phone, not entirely to answer whoever it is texting me, but out of curiosity.

BEDLAM

Did you get the security brief from James?

It's Bonnie.

I immediately frown, causing Wren to do the same.

"What's wrong?"

"Ah…" I stare at the message and bring my arm up behind my head. "I'm not sure. It's Bon."

Wren shifts up on the bed so she can see the phone beside

me. "Security brief?" she says, and I know her stomach is knotting by the mild panic lacing her words.

"Probably nothing." I open up the messages and text Bonnie back, wary of the question. Bonnie and I's texts usually consist of talking shit to one another, rarely is it ever serious.

> Nah. Wren and I are out of town for the weekend.

What security brief?

> He's no longer our bodyguard. Going back into the FBI.

Did he say who the new guard is?

> Yeah.

Bonnie sends a photo of the guard—a woman with piercing, round hazel eyes, light brown skin, and black tightly-curled long hair pulled back from her face. She's stunning, the bland security photo doing her little justice, and yet her fierceness shines through that poignant gaze.

Another photo comes through, and this one looks like Bonnie pulled it from social media. It's a gym photo of the same woman, her hair in braids this time, as she deadlifts more weight than my own body mass.

"Holy shit," I exclaim.

"Oh my god," Wren says, sharing the same surprise. *"That's* your new guard?"

"Guess so," I reply.

She's terrifyingly hot.

> I know her.

I laugh out loud. "Typical," I say, and Wren shoves me.

Yeah?

Her name is Gemma. We went to high school together.

I haven't seen her in years.

History?

Not really. A few curious glances. Nothing else.

We were practically kids at the time.

I don't know that we ever shared an actual conversation.

Do you think it'll be a problem?

Three dots strum at the bottom of the screen for a moment. Her words have me pausing, have me considering how she's truly feeling right now at the thought of someone from her past being in charge of guarding her.

Wren makes a gagging noise. "High school secret lust, and now forbidden? I hate how cute that is."

I beam. "Do you know what else is really cute?" I flip out of my messages screen and over to the folder of the three pictures the venue photographer sent over hours after as a first look. The first I pull up is a picture of our first kiss in front of an orange and red neon sign taller than us. She's smiling against my lips as I bend her backward, her modeling instincts kicking in in front of that lens.

A muscle feathers in her jaw as if she's fighting a smile, but Bon texts again before I can show her any others.

BEDLAM

I doubt she even remembers me.

And I doubt anyone has ever forgotten you.

Maybe it'll be good to have someone you
already know and trust.

I hope so. James wants us in LA for a meeting
next week as a get-to-know her before the
festival in July.

Something else has to be up with her for her to be in this solemn of a mood.

Everything okay?

The texts started again.

My stomach drops. Shit.

"What is she talking about?" Wren asks.

I sigh. "Bon's had a stalker since before she joined the band," I say. "The person goes through phases of riding her ass. It was really bad when we were first signed to Death-Tower. And when we went on tour and the road started catching up to us, a groupie actually got hurt. Her stalker sent her the girl's fingernails with a note that said something like, 'the next time someone's fingers other than mine are in your pussy, I'll take their whole hand,' or something wild like that."

Wren stares at me. "What?" she finally says, blinking.

"Yeah," I say. "That stalker is one of the reasons Bon drove herself to the point of needing to go sober. None of us knew how bad it was until then."

"Does her stalker not creep on her now?" Wren asks. "Bonnie isn't exactly celibate."

"They've been quiet for a couple of years now," I say. "Can't imagine it was easy for them to keep track of Bon on the road. Maybe now that we're off, they've decided to come back."

A shadow darkens Wren's eyes, and I know the fear she's kept at bay for a while now is rising once more. I set my phone down, making a mental note to make sure to text Bonnie in a few minutes. Wren appears in a slight daze, and I reach my hand up to cup her face before pressing my lips to hers.

"He's gone," I swear.

"I know," she says, her forehead lying against mine.

My phone buzzes again. I hesitate to answer, but Wren pulls back and picks up the phone to read the next message.

> BEDLAM
>
> James says he's handing it over to Gemma
> and bringing her up to speed on everything.

"Does she need to stay at our place while we're gone?" Wren asks, and in that moment, I see her threading a kinship to Bon that I didn't know I'd ever see from her.

"Look at you being nice," I taunt.

Wren huffs amusedly. "Yeah. I guess. But I know how helpless it can make you feel."

I kiss her again. "I love you," I tell her, and Wren rolls her eyes, shoving me slightly.

"Ugh. Don't make a big deal out of it," she says. "I might retract the offer."

I chuckle and open up the text thread.

> Do you need a place to stay? Wren and I are
> out of town for a week or so. You can crash at
> our place.

> Yeah? What—did you two go get hitched in
> secret or something?

> Nothing gets past you.

> SHUT THE FUCK UP!

"Here we go," Wren smiles as she lays her head on my chest. "You might want to tell her to keep it quiet—at least until we tell Mads and Andi."

"On it."

We'll announce later. Don't tell anyone, okay?

Congrats, brother. You deserve it. I love
you two.

Thanks, Bon.

Mads has a spare key to our place if you want
to hide out for a while.

Okay, but is Anita there? I would like to go on
wiggle-butt walks with her.

I laugh.

Mads and Andi have her. Playing with Zero.

I love those dogs.

Okay. I could use the company. Thanks for
letting me crash.

No prob.

Are you nervous about seeing Gemma again?

"You're such a romantic," Wren says.
"And you fucking love it," I claim, kissing her nose.

BEDLAM

A little, yeah.

> Kind of feeling like I'm being stripped already
> since she'll be up to date with the stalker
> situation.
>
> I'm heading out to an AA meeting now. Those
> texts had me on edge.
>
> If you talk to Mads, let him know I'll be there
> tonight.
>
> If I text him, I'll spill secrets.
>
> > Okay, Bon. We'll see you when we get back.
>
> Have fun ;-)

I start to close out my phone; however, Wren pauses me.

"I want to see the other photos," she says, referring to the wedding photos.

"Oh really?"

She shoves me slightly, and I happily open the email again.

Her hands tighten around my arm, body curling into me, and I swear I see her beaming as much as she was yesterday as I show her the three photos.

"Was that just last night?" she asks softly.

I sigh, pausing at the portrait photo of me holding her, my forehead against her temple as she stares into the camera lens.

She was so fucking gorgeous that it hurt.

"Best night of my fucking life," I say, and she looks up at me.

"Best night of mine, too."

"Should we send one out to the fam? Open the floodgates?" I ask her.

Wren points to the full body one of us celebrating in front of the neon sign. "That one."

I pull up three chats—the group chat for my family, and the

band group chat, and finally, Larry, and I send the photo to all three.

"Here we go," I say with a sigh.

She takes the phone from my hand and tosses it off the bed. "Let's leave them hanging for a while," she says against my lips, and I grin at her.

"Anything you want, Mrs. Matthews."

I squeeze her into me and kiss her longingly again. And when our eyes meet after, when the chimes of the replying messages begin coming through, I swear I see the fucking universe in those emerald pools. Everything that I've ever wanted, everything that I will ever love… all of it, within her.

I used to wonder if I'd ever find this. If the hopeless romantic in me would go on wandering aimlessly from person to person in the hopes that someone decided to stick around one day. And I never fucking thought I would find love in what started as a publicity stunt.

Every day is both the easiest thing I've ever done, and somehow also the most challenging, and I fucking love it.

Because she's letting me love her the way she never thought she would deserve. She's feeling everything when she thought she would be numb for the rest of her life. And the way she loves me… She loves me with parts of herself that she isn't even aware of. I see it when she looks at me, feel it in her touch, her kiss, her words. I feel it in the fabric of our entwining souls.

I'll love her even after my last breath.

Cross my fucking heart.

THANK YOU for reading
CHAOS: *A Young Decay novel.*

If you loved this book, please consider leaving a review on
your favorite review site and/or social media platform. This
would really help me reach more readers.
I cannot tell you how much I appreciate this.

ACKNOWLEDGMENTS

I think this book started out as a fun rockstar novel that I didn't think would go as deep as MADNESS did. And I was fucking wrong.

CHAOS hit me in the face, slapped me around a little, and then said, "Let's fucking go," and I didn't argue. Writing Wren's character was so therapeutic for me, and the way that Reed saw her and loved her seemed to fill parts of me that I didn't realize were empty.

Wren's AuDHD experience draws from my own. Most of the things she struggles with are those that I struggle with. Most of her regulation strategies are my own strategies. And while I may not have a twin brother who tried to outsmart the mafia, I have dealt with the same invasive thoughts that plague her daily. I've often wondered what the hell I'm doing here, and if it would matter if I'm not. I grew up not understanding why I was different and feeling like I belonged in a fictional world because those were the spaces that seemed to understand me. I wanted to escape.

So, I became an author, created my own worlds to dissociate in, only to eventually find the space where I belong.

I've found my people—my favorite people—finally, in this journey. People who think the same way I do, who share the same experiences, and the way their brains work is similar to mine. And for anyone who grew up trying to find their place, that feeling of finally finding it is unreal. I still have bad days. I still need the music to calm my brain and ground myself. But I am so grateful to have found this little space.

And it took writing this book to truly realize that I had found it. It took meeting Wren to realize that I wasn't broken. Because she isn't broken, and Reed is never going to let her feel that way again.

Anyway, that's my rant for this book.

Let's do some thank you's.

THANK YOU to all of my readers who have been so patient with me over the last few years. You have no idea how much you all and your support means to me. And to all of my new readers, HI! Thank you for reading and supporting me and my stories!

To Nicole: seriously, I think we need more coffee dates to see what other characters we can come up with. Wren is definitely not the last!

To Alexis: thank you for always being down for the weird shit haha. Thank you for loving Wren first—and loving the way Reed sees her. And also, thank you for inspiring Reed's love for crop tops. I don't think he knows how to wear a full shirt anymore. Can't wait to do signings with you in 2025 and BEYOND!

To Kay: thank you for looking at this with daggers and slapping some realism back on it. I think Reed may have lost his golden retriever status without you (don't worry, he still wants to cuddle). And thank you for accepting all of my weirdness from the beginning. 2025 signings aren't going to know what to do with the two of us.

To Emily: thank you for all the work you've put into helping me over the years! My books would not be the same without you.

To Pru: I cannot thank you enough for squeezing me into your schedule and creating these amazing covers. The first time I see them in a book store, I'm going to scream (and it's going to happen).

To Angie: where would I be without you? You are so patient and understanding with everything I have going on, and just so supportive of my career. I could not be more grateful to have you in my life.

To Leah: thank you for helping me with my scatterbrain for this release! You knew exactly what I needed, and I appreciate you so much. I hope I get to see you more and more with all the signings coming up!

To my family and loved ones: I couldn't do this without you. I love you all so much. I'm grateful to have had such a great and supportive family growing up.

To my little dude: I love you, but I hope you never read these. Seriously, if you find it in the future, put it down.

To all of my author and reader friends and colleagues, and anyone who has been patient enough to answer my seemingly endless list of questions over the years: thank you for always being so kind and amazing, and for always pointing me in the right direction.

And finally, to music: I don't know who I would be without music, or if I would be here. Music inspires everything I do, who I am. And maybe that's why these books mean so much to me. It isn't just the rockstar element. I've tried to incorporate how music makes me feel, and I hope, as you've read this series, you feel it too.

Thank you again for reading.

BEDLAM is next.

ABOUT THE AUTHOR

Jack Whitney is a dark fantasy, paranormal, and rockstar romance author out of North Carolina, US.

You can usually find her playing in dark and strange worlds. Her characters are always in charge. She is fueled by coffee, whiskey, and shadow daydreams.

If you're reading her books, they probably came with a warning label.

Welcome to the Nightmare of Ravens.

Jack also feels very weird about writing bios because she's not sure what you want to know.

She is almost always stalking social media and procrastinating, so if you would like to find her to ask more questions, please feel free.

@Jack.Whitney.Writer (Instagram)
@JackWhitneyWriter (Tiktok)
Join the Nightmare (Patreon)
Stay up to date: Join the Newsletter on my website:
www.jackwhitneywriter.com

ALSO BY JACK WHITNEY

YOUNG DECAY ROCKSTAR SERIES

MADNESS
A Young Decay Novel (Maddox)
CHAOS
A Young Decay Novel (Reed)
BEDLAM
A Young Decay Novel (Bonnie)
Coming late 2024

SWEET GIRL DUET (EROS/PSYCHE)

Sweet Girl
Book One (Novella)
Finding You
Book Two (Novel)

NIGHTMARES DUOLOGY (PNR)

Ballad of Nightmares
Book one
Hymn of Shadows
Book Two
Coming Fall 2024

THE HONEST SCROLLS SERIES

DEAD MOONS RISING

BOOK ONE IN THE HONEST SCROLLS SERIES

FLAMES OF PROMISE

BOOK TWO IN THE HONEST SCROLLS SERIES

THE GATHERING

AN HONEST SCROLLS NOVELLA

BETRAYAL OF KINGS

BOOK THREE IN THE HONEST SCROLLS SERIES

COMING 2025

NOVELLAS

ANYONE AND YOU

AN AUTUMN EROTICA NOVELLA

BREAK THE GLASS

A HALLOWEEN EROTICA NOVELLA